WITNESS *to* TRIBULATION

LIZ FINNEGAN

Witness to Tribulation

Copyright © 2025 by Liz Finnegan

All rights reserved.

Red Penguin Books

Bellerose Village, New York

Library of Congress Control Number: 2025919342

ISBN

Print 978-1-63777-774-9 | 978-1-63777-775-6

Digital 978-1-63777-773-2

This story is fiction. However, nearly all the places mentioned in it exist. And many of the events woven into the story have been based on documented truth, although some of the names have been changed. The use of the Gettysburg College name and other business and family names is solely for literary effect, as well as historical accuracy, and without permission.

This book is dedicated to the three most important men in my life: my husband Robert, and our sons Bryan and Timothy. It was their love, support, patience, and inspiration that made it possible for me to fulfill a lifelong dream. There are many others who should be thanked as well for their encouragement and support, especially: Anthony Esposito, Dana Waite Esposito, Russ Sacco Janet Yudewitz, Sean Rafferty and the late John Lee.

Contents

Introduction

There's an old adage that states if we don't learn from our past mistakes, history will repeat itself. That happens in families, too. And it seems Emily Tomaso and her family have a lot to learn.

Emily is a bright, attractive woman in her twenties. She's had all the advantages of a sheltered, upper middle class life. Yet, she's had some serious disadvantages, too. Her father, Andrew, was killed when she was almost 12. His death plunged a relatively happy home into deep despair that shaped how Emily began to look at life.

The only salvation during those difficult times was her grandmother, Emilia Schmidt, who lived with the family from the time Emily was very young. Grams, as Emily called her, picked up the emotional slack of her disconnected mother, Mandy, whose demeanor seemed to get worse after Andrew's death. Although the relationship between Emily and her mother wasn't good, the relationship between Mandy and her mother, Emilia, seemed even worse. No one really questioned what the reason for that might be. What separated both mothers and daughters seemed destined to remain an unsolved mystery, too often dismissed as "bad circumstances."

However, Emily's circumstances had recently changed. After Emilia's passing, it was revealed that she'd bequeathed to her granddaughter the old family homestead in Gettysburg, Pennsylvania. Emily learned about the gift at nearly the same time a job offer had arrived. The teaching position she'd accepted was conveniently located in a town near her inherited house.

Emily had only been familiar with the town of Gettysburg and its role in the Civil War through the history classes she took, as well as from what she'd learned from Grams, who would often describe what it was like growing up there many decades after the war had ended. Her stories beguiled Emily enough to almost imagine it to be a magical place, with a lure that has kept both the curious as well as committed history buffs returning frequently. Grams would say visitors there sensed something they could not explain. While in Gettysburg, they all seemed to experience a mysterious conversion of the heart and soul, leading her to proclaim that the town was blessed.

Although Emily was excited about the move, she was also very frightened. It meant living alone, far from home, for the first time. Still, she was determined to get away from her mother, and stepfather, Zach, as well as the life there without her beloved Grams.

Emily would soon come to realize though that the move would be more than just a change of address. She was set to embark on a spiritual journey, one that would offer her a different perspective on life. After finding an ancestor's Civil War diary, her new home would serve as a guide along the way, as would the people she'd meet in Gettysburg, both the living and amazingly, those long departed as well. Within only one week's time, Emily—and seemingly those around her too—would begin to witness a personal change in the very place where mystical transformations are said to occur nearly every day.

A veil separating the past and the present, the living and the dead, will soon be lifted, and secrets revealed. Her new friends will help her to navigate between these new worlds. As she explores the town's history, she'll learn about her own history, and in doing so, will learn to overcome anger and fear, while growing a greater appreciation for her life. Emily will come to understand the true meaning of acceptance, forgiveness, but mostly, the eternal presence of family, and love.

Historical Background

Experiences in life often affect the way we see our world. If those experiences are traumatic, either physically or emotionally, we might never see the world in the same way again. This marring of the soul could take years to recover. Many of those that do recover retain scars, remnants of that painful memory.

To understand that statement, one must know the cause of those painful memories. In Emily's case, it began well over a century before she existed, during the Civil War battle at Gettysburg.

The American Civil War raged for four long years—from April 12, 1861, when the first shots were fired on Fort Sumter in South Carolina, until the fall of Richmond, Virginia, the Confederate capitol, at the beginning of April 1865. Confederate commander General Robert E. Lee surrendered on April 9 to his Union counterpart, General Ulysses S. Grant, at the Appomattox Courthouse in northern Virginia. It was a pivotal moment in our nation's history.

Nearly two years before that key meeting, a battle took place in Gettysburg, Pennsylvania that sealed the fate of this young country in three days, and in doing so it also changed the lives of Gettysburg's witnesses and the generations that followed.

In July 1863, life in the little southwestern Pennsylvania town of twenty-five hundred people was somewhat serene. Gettysburg had been located at the crossroads of several major highways linking other towns and was often a pitstop for those traveling between the northern and southern states. It contained a liberal arts college and Lutheran Seminary (both still exist), many houses of worship, and miles of fertile farmland, which would come to serve another purpose before long.

The many small businesses located downtown supplied the needs of the surrounding area. It was a meeting place, a place to come to worship, to be educated, and to shop. It was, in essence, as busy as a town of twenty-five hundred people could be at that time.

However, in mid-June 1863, as the Civil War was being fought in Virginia and further south, word began circulating in town that the Confederate Army was attempting a ride north. Some thought it was for food supplies, others thought they wanted clothing, perhaps shoes, all of which were becoming scarce in the war-torn south, deprived of the necessities that had been provided by northern industry.

Many residents took what was considered by some to be a horrible rumor as fact. They fled their homes to outlying, safer areas, taking with them whatever possessions they could. Then there were those who remained, defiantly protective of what they owned and prepared to take on whatever challenges would come. They could not have possibly anticipated the extent of those challenges.

The Confederate Army had defeated the Union Army in many battles up to that point and so were confident to travel across the Mason-Dixon Line[*]. Several regiments passed through other Pennsylvania towns before arriving in Gettysburg. Once there, they briefly occupied some empty buildings taking all of the food and

---

[*] The Mason Dixon Line was an imaginary line of demarcation running along Maryland, Delaware, Pennsylvania, and West Virginia (Virginia in 1863). At the time of the Civil War, it was known as a cultural boundary separating the northern and southern states.

clothing they could find. The terrified residents remained in their homes, uncertain of the future.

After a few days, the Southern Army moved on to other neighboring villages, and by June 30, the Yankees arrived. Once their own Union Army was entrenched in the town, the people thought the worst was over. It was only the beginning of what would be the end of the relatively peaceful world they once knew.

The battle officially began on July 1 with a barrage of cannon and gunfire that echoed off the surrounding green hills. The residents were trapped inside their homes, never certain if they would ever reemerge.

The soldiers fought in an area called McPherson's Woods, and on to a ridge near the Lutheran Seminary where the slaughter was so numerous, long trench graves were dug to accommodate the dead.

On the second day, the battle was fought in a peach orchard, then over to a wheat field where the blood flowed into a little stream and turned the water red. The previous night, the Union Army had retreated to higher ground and had fortified the hills they occupied: Culp's Hill and Cemetery Ridge. They also gained control of another strategic hill, Little Round Top.

Upon word from General Lee, the Confederates began attacking Union soldiers on Little Round Top from an area of lower elevation containing rocks and boulders named Devil's Den. The Rebels, exhausted by the previous day's battle, the 90-degree heat and oppressive humidity, struggled to climb up and around the huge mounds and began shooting their way up the hill.

The Union soldiers waited for the advancers behind tall pines and oaks, searching between the leaves and the bark, aiming at anything that moved. When they finally met, the battle was long and vicious. By the end of the day, the human toll was once again staggering.

On July 3, the Southern Army was considerably depleted of weapons and men. Each side waited for a sign of attack or retreat. When it didn't come, the Union commander at that time, General

George Meade—who had just fortified the Union line with several larger regiments— thought the worst was over.

General Lee, unaware of the Union fortification and unaccustomed to defeat, had another idea. He was weary from more than two long years of war with his fellow countrymen, so he planned one final attack that he hoped might destroy the Union Army and thus end the war.

It was three o'clock in the afternoon when a Confederate Division headed by General George Pickett crossed the open farmland toward the enemy line. The cannons and guns from both the Confederate and Union side of the field volleyed continuous rounds. The smoke and dust were so dense many soldiers could barely see through it; others could hardly breathe. Once the smoke cleared albeit briefly, the Yankees, crouched behind a low stone wall were shocked to see a line of Rebels over a mile long approaching quickly, without stopping to discharge their weapons.

Steadily, defiant, the Rebels advanced, unaffected by the approaching bullets. They jumped over dead comrades, barely disrupting their gait. Fueled by fear, fatigue and a show of unity, they quickened their step and released a high pitch scream in a final attempt to end it all. Up to that point they were considered defenders, fighting on home turf in the south. But there, far from home, they were the aggressors, with a bold display that shocked their enemy.

The Union soldiers, aghast at their arrogance, continued the volley of cannons and guns from their low stone fortress. When the Rebels reached the high-water mark*, the two armies fought face to face.

The battle escalated and eventually was sustained with the use of sabers, knives, stones, and even fists. By the end of the day, the Confederate Army at Gettysburg retreated and was diminished by

---

* A high water mark usually refers to the highest level reached by a body of water. But when reviewing the Battle of Gettysburg, it refers to the deepest penetration by the Confederate Army toward the Union line on the third day of the battle during Pickett's Charge.

more than half, having lost nearly six thousand men during Pickett's charge alone.

Ultimately, the Union Army of the Potomac held back the Confederate Army at the battle of Gettysburg. The price of their victory, as well as the Confederate defeat, was costly.

In all three days, Confederate losses including dead and injured numbered twenty-five thousand men. The Union toll was just as high. The carnage though was not exclusively human, for in addition to men, thousands of horses were killed. The end of the battle strapped the quiet town of twenty-five hundred people with nearly fifty thousand dead and wounded soldiers to attend. As a result, Gettysburg received the heartbreaking distinction of being the site of the bloodiest battle ever fought on American soil.

The screams of pain and anguish could be heard through the streets, echoing in churches, and streaming through the open doors of private homes, many of which were used as hospitals. Soon after the battle, rows of simple pine coffins were visible everywhere. However, the open carts of severed arms and legs passed unnoticed in time.

The intense summer heat quickly bloated the dead bodies and tore apart the flesh of those who remained unburied in the fields. Then, several days of torrential rain turned the dirt to mud, exposing even those soldiers who had already been buried. The stench of death and disease permeated the air, and the fly population significantly increased.

The people ran through the streets spending as little time as possible outdoors, fearful of the other uninvited dwellers that had invaded their town, vultures. They sat perched on treetops two by two, searching for their next meal, and there was plenty to be had. The citizens hadn't realized that the vultures were not to be feared. They in fact helped with a natural process in the disposal of the rotting human flesh that surrounded them. Still, it was a horrible sight to face. Those images of mortality were presented in a way they had never imagined.

In the weeks that followed, each shattered life that remained in town was assigned duties and became a provider of some sort. Some provided supplies, such as making bandages from clothing, others arranged for nourishment. They were appointed nurses, doctors, and undertakers.

The horror would not end for any of them for months. Even as President Abraham Lincoln dedicated the Soldier's National Cemetery in town with his immortal Gettysburg Address, the task of dealing with the remaining casualties had not yet been fully completed. That was November 19, more than four long months later.

The battle wrought destruction, devastation, and most of all, indignity toward human life.

All this would haunt the Gettysburg witnesses until their own dying day.

There are some people who say that the town has never recovered from that experience. Oddly, many seem to feel that the successive generations of those witnesses of the battle carry within them the scars from the pain and suffering their forefathers had endured. Stranger still, there are even those who claim that they are better for it.

Chapter One

Emily Tomaso lay in bed staring at the ceiling while a ticking clock competed with uninvited images replaying in her head. She really needed to get to sleep and awake refreshed for the long drive to her new home the next day. But her thoughts and that annoying clock refused to let her rest. Each passing moment highlighted the fear she couldn't shake of what lay ahead.

Deep down she knew she was childishly overreacting, but also realized that's what years of emotional dysfunction will do.

As she continued to toss and turn, Emily used the sheets to wipe away beads of perspiration on her forehead and neck due to the early summer heat wave. While thinking about living alone for the very first time, she wondered how she'd sleep the next night in a different bed in such a different place. She'd lived all her 24 years in the same house in East Springs, which was something she hated to admit, even to herself.

The move didn't sit well with her mother, Mandy, who repeatedly told her not to take such a drastic step so far from home, warning unsympathetically, "You won't last there a week." Although her comment mirrored her own feeling, she wasn't about to listen to what her mother had to say. Emily always assumed Mandy spoke from her own selfish needs.

Zach, her stepfather, felt differently. He seemed eager to help with the move. She wasn't surprised by his reaction, understanding he needed her to be out of the way. But Emily couldn't allow herself to think about him right then. Lately, thoughts of Zach had not been conducive to sleep.

Emily glanced again at the clock, sighed, and then reached over into the nightstand drawer and removed a sleeping pill, the last one in the vial. She didn't like taking them, but they were necessary in the weeks leading up to Grams' death; and even more so after she was gone. She promised herself to not renew the prescription as she swallowed the white tablet.

Falling back to bed to count the cracks in the plaster seemed like a better idea than counting sheep. One crack, which had the appearance of an arrow, pointed toward the painting of an angel on the wall across the room. The painting, which was given to her by her grandmother, was often used as a focal point to calm her after a difficult day. She focused on it again, and silently said a prayer asking for guidance, but most of all for sleep.

The taunting images in her mind soon began to fade; muscles relaxed, and a familiar feeling took over, sending her floating without a care. She looked over to the clock once more, Midnight, and then turned away before drifting off to sleep.

Chapter Two

The Journey Home

The clock's alarm jolted Emily out of a sound sleep as she fumbled in the dark to turn it off. She swung her legs over the side of the bed to sit up, yawned and noticed the time. *Five hours of sleep is better than none. At least the sleeping pill did the trick.*

She walked over to the window and looked out, wondering if that day would be as hot as the previous two. The northeastern section of the United States had been baking in 90-plus degree temperatures, making it feel more like mid-July instead of mid-June. She would have slept a lot better with air conditioning and so wondered why it wasn't yet turned on. There were other reasons why she couldn't sleep, but she didn't want to go there again. There was just too much work left to do. She lifted a heavy suitcase from the top shelf in her closet and resumed the packing she'd begun days before.

Mandy gently pushed the door to Emily's room open and watched as she packed the last of her clothes and pictures, remaining silent so her daughter would be unaware of her presence.

Alone in the dark, Mandy observed the person she wanted to touch, the child she longed to hold on to. Her eyes were swollen and red from a sleepless night, and her robe hung on her body uncharacteristically askew. Mandy Porter was always impeccably maintained, even before daybreak.

Emily noticed the dark figure standing in the hall as she walked over to turn on the light. "Oh, mother, it's you," she said, surprised. "What's wrong with your eyes?"

"Don't worry," Mandy replied, quickly turning away. "It's this hideous hot and humid weather. Kept me awake all last night. I should have listened to Zach and turned on the air conditioning."

Emily smirked and nodded in agreement while reaching to the top of her armoire to take down a framed photograph of herself with her Grams, Emilia. The picture had been taken at her high school graduation. She placed it into the luggage and then removed the painting of the Guardian Angel from the wall where it had hung since the day she was baptized.

"May I have this?" she asked, gazing down at the small canvas.

"Why not?" Mandy softly replied. "It belongs to you."

Emily carefully placed it on top of some shirts, zipped up the suitcase, and declared, "I'm all set."

"I notified Mrs. Angst last night," Mandy calmly said. "She's the caretaker for the property down there, and she's taken care of all the necessary arrangements for you. You know, telephone service, dishes, utensils, things like that."

"Thank you", Emily said. "But it is the 1990's. I don't need a landline. I have a cell phone."

Mandy ignored her comment. She suddenly seemed bemused, and added, "I didn't think you'd actually do this. I didn't think you had it in you." She hesitated, took a deep breath and after slowly exhaling, took on a more desperate tone, "Are you sure you want to go?"

"Why wouldn't I?" Emily responded.

"It's just so far away. You've never been so far away, alone."

"I'll adjust," Emily said, as she hastily removed the packed luggage from the bed.

"You could stay here with me and Zach," Mandy continued to implore.

"Oh mother, please, give me a break. I'm 24, not fourteen."

She brusquely threw some items that were on her dresser into a handbag before sharply turning, startling her mother so that Mandy hit her knee at the edge of the door's frame.

"We've been through this before. My mind is made up," Emily said. "I have a new home, job, car, money; what more could I ask for? It's all so perfect. You must realize that since Grams died, there's nothing left to keep me here. You're just upset because you can't have me under your control anymore."

"That's not true," Mandy shouted, rubbing her bruised knee. "I never controlled you. It was Emilia, your Grams who did that."

"Don't talk about her that way. She's dead," Emily snapped, and turned away, bracing herself with the bedpost, the closest thing to grab on to. She quickly regained her composure however, and added more calmly, "Mother, are you coming downstairs?"

"No," Mandy said abruptly, straightening her back and tightening her robe as she walked out of the room. "I have a headache. Anyway, I don't think it'll be too long before I see you again," she said in the condescending tone that seemed to define most of their conversations. "Like I said before, I'll give you a week by yourself down there. Alone."

"Don't count on it," Emily loudly retorted.

"Good luck," Mandy sarcastically added with a slight laugh.

Emily watched her mother's bitter retreat from the room. Despite her anger, she wanted to rush to her and tell her everything she felt Mandy should know. There was a sudden, intense need to be rid of the burden she'd been carrying for months. But she just couldn't bring herself to do it.

Later that morning as Emily backed the car out of the driveway, Zach waved to her from the front door. She saw him but did not wave back. However, she missed seeing the shadowy figure of her mother in her second story bedroom window using the lace curtain to wipe away tears.

As Emily slowly navigated the car through the residential streets of her neighborhood, she felt as though she was seeing them for the last time. She passed row upon row of attractive Tudor and colonial style homes, neatly trimmed by mature hedges and well-manicured lawns. She reached Sunset Park, just in time for the stoplight to turn red. Some of her most pleasant childhood memories were the times she spent there with her Grams. When Emily was little, the open acre of land provided a place where the two of them would go when they wanted to be alone. Time seemed to stand still in the park, and for an hour or so nearly every day she and Grams were truly happy.

The streets of East Springs grew less familiar as she drove further away from her house. She stopped at a gas station at the edge of town. "Fill it up," Emily said to the young attendant. "And please check the oil, too."

Despite her protests, Zach had taken care of the car only the day before, filling it with gas and making certain it was ready for her five-hour drive the next day. But she still needed to check it herself.

The attendant's face was familiar. Emily wondered briefly if they had attended the same high school. "Looks like it'll be another scorcher," the young man said, wiping his brow after lifting the hood of the car.

Emily nodded in agreement and then fixed her eyes on the war memorial that faced the train station nearby. The large, granite boulder had been strategically placed there by the brothers of a local man who was killed in the Vietnam War. It was the place they last saw him alive before he boarded a train to take him to his post. She stared at a man planting colorful impatiens around the rim of the stone.

Noticing the suitcases in the back of her car, the attendant asked, "Going on a trip?" breaking her concentration.

"Oh, uh Gettysburg," she said. "I've accepted a teaching position at a school near there and … ", she ended her sentence abruptly, wondering why she offered so much unsolicited information.

"Great," he said. Tipping his head over to the memorial, he added, "Guess you'll be seeing a lot of those down there."

It was a reality that hadn't occurred to her. Although she was well aware of Gettysburg's role in the Civil War, she never thought in terms of moving to a place so full of monuments, the constant reminders of the battle. It was certainly an odd oversight for a history teacher, she thought, even a new one.

"You're all good," the attendant noted with a laugh after closing the hood. "Didn't need any gas, either." Chagrined, Emily tipped him, and said under her breath as she drove away, "I knew that. Damn you, Zach."

There was something oddly comforting in the anonymity of the open highway as a new and exciting future awaited her in Pennsylvania. The day the acceptance letter arrived from the Hanover School District was the best she could remember in a very long time. The school position meant more to her than just a job. It meant freedom.

The wind blew through the open window, snapping Emily's long auburn locks across her face, as The Who's "I'm Free" blasted from the Classic Rock station on the car radio. She smiled blissfully, and said, "Thank you, Grams."

Emilia had taken very good care of her only grandchild. Upon her death, the large monetary gift, along with the deed to the family homestead in Gettysburg, enacted a change in life Emily never saw coming. And it came just in time, too. Life at home with her mother and Zach had become intolerable.

There were no more battles at home recently, though. That was in the past. The bitter, hurtful arguments she and her mother would have, which were often refereed by Zach and Grams, seemed to end just before Emilia's death. After that, there was just silence—impenetrable and disconcerting. And it was the silence that Emily found more disturbing than all the shouting and tears.

Mandy never seemed all that troubled by it. She thought it meant her relationship with her daughter was getting a little better. However, Zach felt it just as keenly as Emily did, and he wanted it to change.

Only days before Emily's departure, he'd offered his car to help her get some of the oversized shipping boxes to the UPS store. When she agreed, he began practicing his dialogue, hoping his well-chosen words might heal the wound between them. Just before they were set to leave, a neighbor intervened, offering to transport the boxes in his pickup truck instead. Emily swiftly took him up on his offer. She couldn't tell if Zach looked disappointed or relieved. But then the sinking feeling that had begun to settle deep in her gut was difficult for her to decipher, as well.

Her euphoria waned as memories from her past surfaced from time to time. But she just shrugged those feelings off. The past didn't matter to her anymore. It was over, history, not to be dwelled on or even remembered. Still, some memories always seemed to be at the edge of her mind. Though just as painful, she allowed them in and even struggled to keep those images clear.

Emily saw the exit sign for Pinecrest National Cemetery and signaled to get off the highway.

There was just one more memory she needed to revisit before putting it away, too.

The entrance to the cemetery was only a few yards from the winding access road. It had been years since she last visited there, and she needed to inquire in the office for the exact location of her father's grave. Grams had been buried only months before in East Springs, a few miles from home. Emily's father, Andrew Tomaso, a US Army veteran, and a hero police officer, had been buried in the National Cemetery with full military honors.

Andrew was known in the neighborhood affectionately as, "Officer Andy." It was not unusual to see him shooting basketball hoops with the local teens while warning them about the dangers of drugs and alcohol use. Mandy would say her husband carried his work a little too far, but she also knew that he wasn't the type to stop what he did best when the whistle blew. The truth was he loved his job, and everything else in his life, and that was just one of the many reasons his family had worshipped him.

Once summoned, the loving memories of him flowed so easily, wrapping around Emily like a warm blanket on a snowy day. The image of his smile, a broad, sweet, smile that narrowed his large, dark eyes and accentuated the dimples in his cheeks, also became clear. It was how she best remembered him; the last time she saw her father just before he left for work on the afternoon of that dreadful day twelve years before.

As she stood over her father's grave, Emily fought to keep the memories away, but they came anyway. She remembered the night the call came in, shaking her out of a sound sleep.

Mandy ran to answer the phone and then dropped the receiver as if touched by fire. Andrew had been shot during a drug-bust at a warehouse.

Grams practically got Mandy dressed, calming her, reassuring her everything would be all right, but she was shaking so badly she could hardly walk. Just as they were about to leave for the hospital, the doorbell rang. Two policemen stood somberly at the front door with Father Vinci from St. William's Church. Emily remembered hiding behind the large, wing chair in the living room, covering her ears to muffle her mother's anguish.

In the days to come, Grams took total control of the morbid rituals. She seemed to effortlessly handle all the arrangements, greeting the many mourners, and yet always took the time to ask, "Are you all right, Emily? Remember, Grams loves you." Mandy however remained silent, and stared blankly as their world around was falling apart.

There were many dark months ahead for Emily. Although her days passed quickly, the nights were endless. There were no siblings to share her pain. She was grateful that Grams lived there, too. Emilia would talk to her, comfort her, and help with schoolwork. Her mother was utterly useless, speaking only when spoken to, and then in short, unemotional sentences that seemed to say, "Don't bother me."

Emily was awakened almost every night by the chant-like weeping coming from behind Mandy's bedroom door. Grams would always come to her before going to bed, and say, "It takes time, dear. Mom will be alright. It'll just take some more time for her wound to heal."

A few months later, the day Emily came home from school with a failing grade on her report card, was the first time that Mandy had shown any emotion at all. "How dare you?!" she shouted. "Don't I have enough to be upset about? You're twelve years old now, you should be more responsible."

"Responsible?" Emily yelled back. "Why don't you be more responsible? I hurt too, you know. You don't care about me; you only care about yourself! Grams and Dad cared about me, now he's gone forever. Maybe you should have died instead."

Emily stopped abruptly, and covered her mouth, realizing what she'd just said. She remembered the year before when she quarreled with her father and threatened to run away from home. Instead of a sympathetic reaction, he threw her a coat and pushed her out the front door into the dark. Terrified, she screamed and ran back in. He called her bluff. "I wish you were dead," she yelled. How could she know that would indeed happen within the year? After saying nearly the same words to her surviving parent, she felt as though she'd just sealed her mother's fate.

"Emily!" Grams screamed in shock. But Mandy remained stoic, as if accepting the remark in silent agreement.

Although she never apologized for her outburst, Emily knew she didn't mean what she'd said. She was sure Grams understood that, never certain though if Mandy did.

Emily knelt to say a prayer and then reached over to touch the engraved date of death on her father's headstone. "He was so young," she whispered. In another section of the cemetery, she could see a military funeral underway. Near the flag-draped coffin was a Marine Color Guard preparing for a 21-gun salute. She sighed and hoped it was for a much older warrior.

Chapter Three

Mandy Porter stepped out of the shower in the Bay Hills Country Club's ladies lounge, toweled up and stood before the clouded mirror, using her hand to wipe away the mist. She stared at her reflection; the ravages of a sleepless night showed in shadows, aging her usually youthful face. *Pathetic.*

She quickly dressed hoping to escape the friendly ribbing about her horrible tennis match that morning, which she was certain would begin at Sunday brunch. Martha Nielson was finally able to overtake her on the court, ending the match with an astonishing win in straight sets. *Well, at least it took her three years to do that*, Mandy silently reminded herself.

But she wasn't really concerned about the ribbing. Mandy just didn't feel like talking about Emily and her big move, which had been the subject of conversation at the club in the preceding weeks. She wasn't up to doing that again, especially not that day.

Exiting the lounge with a tennis bag in one hand and her car keys in the other, Mandy hoped to inconspicuously slip out the side door closest to the parking lot when she heard a familiar voice call out.

"Mandy. There you are," Martha said. "You left the court so

quickly. I hope you're not upset about my big win," she added, with a sardonic smile. Her demeanor changed upon seeing Mandy's sad face. The sunglasses she wore outdoors had masked her appearance. "What's wrong?" Martha asked. "No, don't tell me. Today's the day, isn't it? Emily left?"

Mandy managed a feeble nod, straining to control the flow of tears that began filling her eyes. "I have to get home," she said.

"You'll do no such thing," Martha demanded. "You're joining me and Rich for brunch. What will you do at home anyway, wallow? Zach's still working long hours on that complicated case. He already told Rich he wouldn't be able to come today so that means you'd be home alone. You shouldn't do that. Please stay."

"Sure," Mandy said, managing a smile. She was too exhausted to face another match with her.

"I'll be out of the shower in a jiff. Rich is at a table near the big window. I'll see you there. Now, don't try sneaking out again," Martha warned.

"Okay, I won't," Mandy assured her.

Rich Nielson was seated with two other couples: Dan and Barbara Fergus and Stu and Shirley Larson, who had long been in her circle of friends at the club. The relationship she had with Stu however, was longer, reaching back to their childhood in West Springs where they were neighbors. She always thought of him as the brother she never had.

"Look who's here," Stu announced, and stood up to give Mandy a peck on the cheek while the others greeted her from their seats. "I hear you're solo again today," Stu said as he pulled out a chair for her to sit.

"Working again," Mandy said while exhaling.

Stu leaned over to her and whispered," Did Emily leave yet?"

"Yep," Mandy remarked, trying to sound blasé. "Today was the day."

"She'll do fine," he added. "You have to be proud of her going down there by herself. She's brave to do that, right? I mean, come on, that's something you'd never do," he added with a jab and a grin, before turning away to join in the conversation at the table.

Mandy stared out the window toward the green where golfers were just teeing up at the ninth hole. She wished then that she'd taken up golf. At least she'd still be outdoors, anonymous on the open course, instead of in that place making small talk when all she really wanted to do was scream. Stu hit a nerve with his last comment. It was true. She'd never have had the guts to do what her daughter was doing. It was a reality that both pleased and annoyed her.

Martha suddenly appeared at their table, looking refreshed, carrying photographs of her redecorated bedroom. Mandy shifted her gaze away from the window and on to the large, colorful photos showing every angle of the room. It was a pleasant diversion on such a somber day.

Chapter Four

The Gettysburg exit sign on the highway guided Emily to a curving, thoroughfare through miles of open fields with split-rail fences seemingly running down the center of each field. After several turns in the bucolic territory, one final turn brought her into a bustling downtown area.

Beautiful, old brick structures in the town of Gettysburg were interspersed with modern, stone, and wood-frame motels, restaurants, and other businesses that catered to tourists. She tried to imagine what the town looked like years ago, many years before the souvenir stores, wax museum, and the National Military Park. Spotting a gas station with a convenience store, she pulled into the parking lot and waited for an attendant.

Across the street from the gas station was the Soldiers National Cemetery, a resting place for many who had fought and died there. And, in the other direction, barely visible in the distance, she could make out the grand Gettysburg Hotel, one of the oldest hotels in the country, and a favorite for visiting dignitaries and American Presidents.

Emily noticed people popping into the many gift shops that lined both sides of the street. A young couple emerged from one store carrying a framed print that she recognized. It depicted the Civil War battle: Pickett's Charge, which had taken place less than a mile from where she sat. The painting shows Confederate General Lewis Armistead leading his troops to what he realizes could never be victory. In an attempt to encourage his troops, he spears his hat with a saber and holds it high while rushing to his demise. It was only then the irony of it all hit her: She came to Gettysburg to begin a new chapter to her life, in the place where so many others had come to act out the final episode of their own.

Her heart pounded in excitement as she drove toward her destination, closely following the map Zach had printed off the computer. When she saw a sign for Gettysburg College, where both Grams and her grandfather had been educated, she made a mental note to visit the campus soon. There appeared to be little structural change to the buildings since Grams' day there, but then, she only had one picture of the college, and of the town.

Emily turned a corner and didn't need to check the address to know the old family homestead. It was exactly the way it was described: a two-story tan and grey fieldstone colonial, with painted, raised-panel, wood shutters. The front of the building had a large bay window on the first floor, and on the lawn, a section of what was once a complete white picket fence. At one time the house was a one-family residence that was surrounded by fertile farmland. A huge barn behind the main building, which now could be used as a garage, was once a carpenter's workshop. Situated only a stone's throw from the town, with all of its schools, churches and shops, it's also just down the road from the place that raged in battle for three days. The first floor rooms have been rented to an insurance broker and an accountant. The large second story apartment, which had previously been rented to college students, was her new address. Before she went in, Emily read a plaque that was affixed to the stone near her front door noting the year the house was built: 1847.

The steep, narrow stairway was difficult to climb with two suitcases in tow. Emily began wondering if living in a one hundred and fifty-year-old house was a wise decision, even if she did own it. Once the door at the top of the staircase was opened, however, all doubts were quelled.

The rooms were large and airy, despite their low-beamed ceilings. Off-white stucco walls, unpainted wood molding, and bare heart-pine floors evoked a feeling of warmth. A gentle breeze flowed through the delicate lace curtains on the large, double-hung window facing the front of the building. It provided the necessary cooling on a hot summer day. She placed her suitcases down on the parlor floor before excitedly exploring the rest of the rooms.

The kitchen was small but functional. The bathroom, however, was oddly a bit larger than the kitchen, and had both a shower and a beautiful clawfoot tub. Two better than average sized bedrooms were in the center of the apartment just off the parlor. The larger of the two had a crawl space someone had converted into a closet, and the smaller one, though without a bed, had a lovely desk she thought would be perfect to work on lesson plans. Fresh linens were folded atop the bare mattress of the canopy bed in the larger room, left there presumably by the woman her mother had contacted to set the place up for her.

Pushing aside the sheer curtains on the bedroom window, she viewed the place she'd call home. From that part of her house, one of the main streets in the town was visible, obscured only by the beautiful sycamore trees within the boundary of her property. Church spires loomed high above the street in the distance, looking so much like a Currier and Ives print she had admired at a frame store back in East Springs. She turned away from the window and observed her new bedroom. The shaker-style maple furniture and abundant quilts reminded her so much of Gram's room back at home. She even smelled lavender; a scent Emilia always wore. Closing her eyes after taking it all in, she said, "Oh Grams, I miss you so."

Emily yawned while unpacking some clothing and sat at the edge of the bed, exhausted. Five hours of sleep before a five-hour drive wasn't enough. Putting the luggage aside, she began unfolding the linens in anticipation of a short nap. There was a knock at the parlor door as she tucked the rest of the sheets into place.

"Hello dear," said a very tall, thin, silver-haired woman who was standing in the doorway holding a cake.

"Hello," Emily cautiously replied.

The woman stared at her for a few seconds before offering; "I'm Mrs. Angst from down the road. Your mother called and asked that I look in on you, so I hope you don't mind that I let myself in. Is the place okay? I mean do you like it?" she asked, then continued rambling nervously. "I do hope the linens won't be too stiff. I just can't get out of the habit of using starch in the laundry. Did you have a good trip down?"

She moved and spoke so quickly, Emily could barely get a word in. Her five-foot-four frame felt dwarfed next to the towering woman, so she walked away from her before interrupting. "Mrs. Anst! Everything is wonderful. Thank you so much for all you've done. I really like the apartment."

"I'm so glad, dear. But my name isn't Anst. It's Angst, you know, like dread."

"Really?" Emily asked, looking perplexed.

"No, not really," the woman laughed. "It's only a name. I must go home now and call your mother to let her know you arrived safely. Here's my phone number and address. You can come over later and use my phone until yours is hooked up."

"This is 1997 and most people have cell phones. I have a cell phone and my mother knows it," Emily said, holding it up for her to see.

"Oh," Mrs. Angst said, surprised by the sarcasm.

"It's okay," Emily said apologetically. " I'll call her soon."

"That's good because your mother specifically told me you should call her," Mrs. Angst added. She didn't like to reiterate something she perceived was a sore point with Emily, but she needed to follow the mother's requests. She only recently began to speak with Mandy about caring for the property. She'd always dealt with Zach, and before that, Emilia so she didn't know how to react. *Best to just follow orders.*

"She has my cell phone number," Emily said, shaking her head as she glanced down as inconspicuous as possible to make certain her phone was turned off. She hated that her mother always treated her like a child and was embarrassed by the fact that Mandy had instructed this stranger to do the same.

"Is that cake for me?" Emily asked, changing the subject.

"Yes, angel food cake," Mrs. Angst replied, and began staring at Emily once again as though seized by a long, forgotten memory.

"Mrs. Angst," Emily said, breaking the woman's concentration.

"Oh, sorry dear," she said. "You just remind me of someone I used to know. And you look very different from when I last saw you. You've grown up," she said, and proceeded to put the cake on the kitchen table. "You're definitely not a baby anymore."

"May I ask you something?" Emily inquired as she followed the strange woman into the kitchen. "How do you know my family?"

"Your grandmother, Emilia, and I grew up here together. We were school chums and best of friends. Since she lived so far away, I helped her to manage the house when your great grandpa died. We hadn't seen each other in years, but we always stayed in close contact. I still can't believe she's gone," Mrs. Angst said, with a sigh. "Now, I'm in contact with Zach and more recently, Mandy. Didn't your mother ever mention how close Emilia and I were?"

Emily slowly shook her head.

Mrs. Angst paused, shrugged her shoulders, and continued speaking. "I'm glad you're here. I'd be happy to show you around the town if you'd like, maybe tomorrow."

Emily couldn't take her eyes off her. *Grams old school chum. That would make them around the same age, seventy-nine.* She so reminded her of her own grandmother, bright-eyed, energetic, the way Emilia looked before the cancer began eating away at her strength, swallowing her spirit.

Mrs. Angst pointed to several large boxes near a wall, and said, "These were delivered yesterday."

"Perfect," Emily said. "Now almost all of my things are here. I still need to get a new computer and maybe a TV."

The woman began nervously straightening needlepoint pillows on the overstuffed couch. "Horsehair," she said while punching the seats to even the stuffing. "The furniture has been in storage for the longest time. I'm happy they're all back in the right place."

"I sort of like this rocking chair," Emily said, walking toward an oversized, wing back, upholstered rocker covered in chintz. After moving one of the boxes near it away from the wall Emily raised her voice a few decibels. "A fireplace? I didn't even notice it when I came in," she remarked.

"Don't get so excited," Mrs. Angst warned. "That fireplace hasn't been lit in years. The opening for the chimney has been sealed off to allow a flue for the oil heater."

The woman saw the look of disappointment on Emily's face and wished she hadn't mentioned it. "Please don't be discouraged, dear," she said. She quickly added with excitement," You could still get the same effect of a real fire."

"What do you mean?" Emily asked.

She smiled gently and said, "You can put candles in it."

"Candles?" Emily questioned.

"Yes. Go to the Wick n' Wax Shoppe in town, and buy lots of candles, all different shapes and sizes, some are even scented. You just tell them that you're a local now, and that I sent you. When you want a fire, put them in the hearth, light them, and see what they'll do to the atmosphere of a room."

Emily smiled wryly and thanked Mrs. Angst for stopping by. But before she left, the old woman turned in the doorway, and said deliberately, "It will take you back years and years."

"What will?" Emily asked.

"The candles, dear," she softly replied, "the candles."

Mrs. Angst left the apartment, saying while descending the stairs, "I'll lock the outside door downstairs. You make sure to lock this one. You forgot to do it, and I was able to get in. Your mother wouldn't like that, and neither do I."

Emily rolled her eyes when she was out of sight, closed and bolted the inside door, grateful for her solitude once again. "Weird woman," she said.

Upon reentering her bedroom, Emily suddenly felt an intense chill, something she didn't expect in a place without air conditioning. She walked over to the window, opened the screen, and stuck her hand out into the hot, sultry air, swatting away some flies that had managed to get in. "Shoo," she said and quickly closed the screen.

She walked around the room, looking for the source of a draft, but couldn't find it or a logical explanation for the cold air. It felt good to her anyway, so she resumed making the bed, until she heard her inside apartment door open and close.

"Did you forget something, Mrs. Angst?" she said while walking back into the parlor. No one was there.

Standing in the middle of the room, Emily surveyed the space. Each chamber was completely visible from the center of the parlor where she was able to ascertain that nothing seemed disturbed. Still, she knew what she'd heard. Glancing once again at the door, she saw that it was bolted shut. *Could someone be here?*

Emily hastily grabbed the black, iron poker from the useless fireplace, and began cautiously searching the rooms, jumping back, with poker ready to swing, after opening every closet door. Nothing. Breathing a sigh of relief, she consoled herself by saying aloud, "Calm down, Emily. Alone in a strange, old house can make you hear things that aren't there."

When she returned to the bedroom, she noticed it was no longer cold. Placing her fears aside, she decided to take the nap she'd planned on earlier, and so set her alarm for four o'clock, giving herself exactly one hour to rest before stretching out atop the cool, cotton sheets.

The church bells synchronized with the college's clock tower bell, tolling three o'clock. The sound was hauntingly beautiful, and she shivered slightly despite the heat. Although the strange chill, and the sound of the door remained in her mind, they were no match for fatigue. After nervously sitting up, extending her neck to see the bolted door once more, she quickly reached down to the foot of the bed to grab the nearest quilt, and pulled it over her shoulders and head before dozing off.

Chapter Five

The town of Gettysburg was abuzz with a flurry of activity for a Sunday night. Emily was caught up in all the excitement. She passed a restaurant advertising Civil War cuisine, with a line of people out front just waiting to be seated. After briefly considering getting on the line to see what all the fuss was about, she decided instead to get a slice of pizza at an Italian place nearby with outdoor cafe tables.

It was entertaining to watch the tourists. There were adults sporting blue and gray military kepi hats, and children carrying either Union or Confederate flags, with replica toy muskets swung over their shoulders. "A historical Disneyland," she said under her breath in amazement. Feeling very much like the "local" Mrs. Angst referred to, she caught the eye of one of the restaurant's waiters. "Silly," she remarked while motioning her head toward the would-be Union general walking by.

The attractive waiter looked out toward the street before responding to her rather curtly, "Don't knock the tourists. They're our livelihood here."

Emily felt flush. Who was she kidding? A few hours in the town didn't give her the right to criticize tourists. She was just as foreign to the place as they were.

The waiter noticed her reaction and cracked a smile. He leaned over to her and said, playfully, "You wouldn't catch me dressed like that though."

They both laughed.

"Where are you from?" he asked as he brought her a cup of espresso.

"From a suburb of New York originally, but I've relocated here," Emily said. "Hey, how do you know I'm not native?"

He smiled, and said, "Because I am," as he cleared a table near her.

"I guess I'll have to get used to the small-town atmosphere," she remarked. "Where I come from, you barely knew your neighbors."

"That's sad," the waiter said. "What are you doing in Gettysburg?"

"I have a position at Hanover Junior High School this fall, teaching history," Emily replied. "I figured I'd need a couple of months to get acquainted with the area."

"What a coincidence," he said, stopping his work. "I'm also a history teacher, here at the college. This is only a part-time summer job. My uncle owns this place, and the college kids he usually hires to wait tables all go home in the summer, his busiest season. I give him a hand every once in a while. By the way, I'm Peter Sanders."

"Nice to meet you, Peter. 'Sanders?'" Emily said, looking surprised. "That doesn't sound very Italian."

"It's not," he said. "My mother's maiden name is Civelli though, and she swears that's the better half of the family."

Emily laughed, and said, "I'm half Italian, too. My name is Emily Tomaso, but my mother's maiden name is Schmidt."

"Something else in common," Peter said, broadening his smile.

She blushed. Grams always told her how pretty she was, but whenever she looked into a mirror all she saw was a plain, uninteresting face that was best kept buried in books. Emilia would sometimes pull off her glasses, grab her chin, point it toward the mirror and say, "Look how lovely you are. You have your great-grand-mothers incredibly large, green eyes. Why do you want to hide them?" Emily would smirk, stick out her tongue at her reflection, and put the glasses back on. "But Emily, they're only reading glasses," Emilia scolded.

Her long, wavy, dark auburn hair was usually pulled back tight and fastened at the nape of her neck. She wasn't built like her mother and grandmother, who were both tall, zaftig women. Emily's petite size four always drew her mother's criticism. "Whose daughter are you anyway?" she'd say. "I was never a size four."

Peter pulled up a chair and began talking about the restaurant, and the people he meets there, replenishing her coffee cup from time to time. Emily listened to him speak, trying to avoid staring into his light, blue eyes that seemed to glimmer in excitement as he spoke. His words flowed so easily, deliberately, making what he said all the more interesting. She imagined students queuing up to take his classes. She wondered why her college instructors didn't lecture that way. None of them looked like him, either. Slouched in the chair, he extended long, slender legs out beyond the table, his loosely clasped hands rested at his waist. Emily was surprised at how comfortable he seemed.

Peter continued to dominate their long conversation. He switched from speaking about the college, and the town's history, to listing the many events that would be occurring in Gettysburg within the upcoming weeks, occasionally pushing back his shoulder length, blond hair that reminded Emily of the surfers on the beaches of East Springs. His distracting good looks were enhanced by a sincere smile that was warm and wide.

"I'm bending your ear," Peter remarked, apologetically. "Hope I'm not boring you."

"Not at all," Emily said. "I'm actually learning quite a lot about my new hometown, so thanks."

"Glad to oblige," he said. "Have you relocated here with your family or anyone else?"

"Uh, no. I'm alone."

"Oh, alone," he said approvingly.

Emily glanced at her wristwatch. It was already nine o'clock. "I should be getting home now."

"Have another cup of espresso," he said. "Don't worry, the last two refills have been decaf."

"That's good," she said, looking relieved. "Thanks, but I really should go. I have a lot of unpacking to do."

"May I walk you home?"

"Um, that's okay," she stammered, caught off guard. "That's really not necessary."

"Maybe not in a New York suburb, but here chivalry still prevails," Peter said. "I'll just tell my uncle that I'm leaving now. It's the end of my shift anyway."

Peter disappeared behind a swinging door into a back room to change his shirt. He watched her through a window in the door as she got up to pay her bill at the register; her waif-like body moving with both uncertainty and grace. "God, she's beautiful," he said. He was overheard by his uncle who then looked to see who he was talking about. Smiling, he patted Peter on the shoulder.

Emily felt uneasy about Peter's offer to walk her home. She wasn't used to such a forward approach, especially from someone she'd just met. That never happened to her before. In fact, a friend once told her that most of the guys she met stayed clear of her, thinking she was a little standoffish. It was an opinion that rather pleased her at first into carrying it off as a badge of honor. After realizing that attitude left her dateless most weekends, she made attempts to be more outgoing, approachable. But any attempts to change that opinion seemed futile until she met Bill Ivers who rescued her from loneliness, at least for a while.

While placing the change into her purse, she was suddenly struck with the realization that in Gettysburg, her life was a clean slate: no prejudgments, no Bill, no Zach, and definitely no Mandy. As she caught a glimpse of Peter approaching, she quickly released her hair clip, pulled off her eyeglasses and shoved them both into her purse. "Where do you live?" Peter asked.

"7384 Hemsford Street," Emily replied.

"Ah, the older section of town. Are you renting?"

"Actually," she said, "I sort of own it. I mean; I do own it. The house was in my grandmother's family for many years, and then she left it to me."

"Isn't that Joel Levy and Mike Thurmon's business address?"

"If you mean the insurance broker and accountant, I live in the apartment upstairs."

"They're such a nice couple," he said.

Emily stopped walking. "A couple? What do you mean?" she asked. Peter looked dazed. She quickly added, "Don't bother," and nodded in understanding.

They passed a large group of people, who were led by a woman dressed in 19th century clothing and carrying a candle-lit lantern. "Who are they?" Emily asked.

"Ghost Tour," Peter replied, nonchalantly.

"Ghost Tour?"

"Yes." He playfully added with a forced quiver in his voice, "This town is very, very haunted."

"Are you kidding?" she asked, incredulous.

"No," Peter replied. "Every night there are several companies that provide tours to point out areas of supernatural sightings."

"What do you think?"

"I think it's a great way to see the town," he answered, candidly. "Well, seriously, I think there's certainly potential for some sort of metaphysical activity any place that experienced what Gettysburg did."

"Now you're giving me the creeps."

"Why? There's nothing to be afraid of here. It's really a very interesting place. See that bookstore over there?" Peter gestured over to an old, clapboard building. "It's one of the best anywhere, especially if you love reading about the war."

"What building is this, the Farnsworth House?" Emily pointed to a handsome, brick, Federal-style structure next to the bookstore. "Earlier, I saw people lined up to have dinner here. How old is it?"

"Pretty old," he said. "It was once the home of a very prominent Gettysburg family and was used as a Confederate stronghold in the days preceding the battle. Look at these musket holes," he said while showing her several gashes in the brick on the side of the house. "Sharpshooters were positioned in the garret, or attic, and exchanged gunfire with Union soldiers on the first day of the battle.

"Now it's a popular inn and restaurant. They have the best peanut soup north of Virginia," Peter added.

Emily closed her eyes as she ran her fingers over each of the holes in the brick, trying to imagine the day when the shots were fired. Suddenly, something that sounded like a whisper tickled her left ear. She opened her eyes, looked at Peter on her right, and asked, "Did you say something?"

"No," he replied.

Emily looked over her left shoulder. No one was there. She then spotted an iron hitching post near the street and walked over to it. "We had one of these at our house. Grams bought it at an antique store in town. She said it reminded her of home."

"Is she the person who was originally from here?"

Emily nodded while walking toward an alley in the restaurant's courtyard, acting as though she knew where she was going. That's when it happened again, the same soft whispering, only then it was clearer. "Excuse me?" she asked, swinging around to face Peter.

He raised his arms. "I didn't say anything."

"I could have sworn I heard you say, 'Remember'. But I guess ... I guess I'm mistaken," she said, lowering her voice as she looked around the empty alley, and up at a tall, oak tree as its leaves swayed in a passing breeze. "Ah. It's just the wind," she said.

As they walked on, Emily commented on how quaint all the shops and homes were on the main thoroughfare, especially those with an electric candle in each window. "What does it mean?" she asked.

"It's a sign of respect and remembrance. Sort of a memorial for all those who fought, died, or lived through that horrible time here during and after the battle," Peter explained. "They say if you were to put a candle in every window in this town, it still wouldn't be enough to acknowledge all of the suffering."

Emily briefly pondered his explanation and remarked, "Well, it looks charming anyway."

They approached a little stucco building with a large bow window, and she looked inside. It was the store Mrs. Angst had told her about earlier.

"They sell nice candles here," Peter said. "Would you like to go in?"

"Wick and Wax Shoppe," Emily read aloud the wood sign dangling from the side of the building. "No, not really," she said, and continued walking.

When they reached her front door, she held out her hand to Peter. "Thank you for walking me home. It's so nice to meet you."

He shook her hand. "Welcome to Gettysburg," he said. "Say, how would you like a tour of your new town tomorrow morning?"

Emily's eyes lit up. "I'd love it. As long as it's not the Ghost Tour," she added with a chuckle.

"Okay. "I'll pick you up at eleven."

Peter turned to leave, paused, and faced her again, adding softly, "It's very nice to meet you, too."

He watched her go into the old building, feeling momentarily frozen in place. A minute later, a light illuminated the second story window. There was something very familiar about the girl he'd just met. After several moments in thought, Peter turned and began jogging back to the restaurant to retrieve his car, wondering all the while why he felt so taken by her.

Emily didn't remember climbing the stairs to her apartment. What seemed like such a chore earlier in the day was completely facilitated by the light-headed feeling that lingered after spending a short time with Peter. He seemed like such a nice guy. Kind, interesting, and by far the handsomest man she'd ever met, far more attractive than her old boyfriend, Bill. What luck to meet someone like him the first night there. It all seemed so incredible, too incredible. She wondered if their meeting was more than just by chance. Somehow, she felt as though Peter was meant to be there for her. She'd experienced a similar feeling earlier in the day upon entering her new home for the very first time. Just as the house was waiting for her, perhaps Peter was waiting, too. "Absurd," she said, aloud, happy to hear her voice break the quiet. Emily was so excited; she hadn't noticed anything unusual and went straight to the bathroom to prepare for bed.

She slipped on a nightshirt, and went into the bedroom. Once again she picked up the clock and began setting it for the next day. Something was different though. Slowly, she turned her head toward the bed, gasped, and dropped the clock on the floor, which set off the high-pitched alarm. Emily backed out of the room until she was once again in the center of the parlor, shifting her eyes from left to right. She observed each corner of the room, quiet and still, but for the clock's deafening ring echoing in her ears. She began reviewing her day there while struggling to control her breathing in the hope it would ease her racing heart.

Emily retraced her steps after entering the apartment that afternoon, seeing everything as it currently appeared. She remembered being tired, and making up her bed even before Mrs. Angst came by. She recalled sleeping on the comfortable sheets, feeling the soft quilt against her skin. Why then were those same linens now completely removed, neatly folded, and once more placed at the foot of the bare mattress?

Emily wondered if Mrs. Angst would come into her apartment unannounced. And if she'd do that, why would she undo the bed? The sound of the door opening and closing after the woman had left, and the intense cold she felt in that room, reentered her thoughts as a sinking feeling settled into her stomach. She managed to calm herself though by believing it could all be a misunderstanding that she'd straightened out in the morning. There was little else for her to do.

After checking the lock on the door, she went into a suitcase, removed the photograph of herself and Emilia, as well as the gold-framed picture of the Guardian Angel, and placed them both on the fireplace mantel before blessing herself with the sign of the cross. She then ran in and out of the bedroom as quickly as she could, grabbing a pillow, quilt and the rosary beads that were on her nightstand, before sitting in the rocker near the hearth, prepared to spend the night. Before closing her eyes though, Emily once again reached for the iron poker, and placed it firmly across her lap.

Chapter Six

A Candle for the Sick...

A ray of morning sun flowed through the lace curtain, resting upon Emily's face. She squinted and stretched while getting up from the rocker and looked around. The fear that drove her from the bedroom the previous night had disappeared with the dark. As she entered the room to replace her pillow and quilt, she felt renewed in the warmth of the sunlight, broken only by the wood mullions on the pretty window near the bed. Any uneasiness that remained was quickly quelled knowing she'd slept undisturbed. She might have heard a pounding noise in her sleep earlier but wasn't sure. However, now there was no mistaking the sound of the doorbell, which began ringing impatiently as she put on her robe and darted down the steps.

"Telephone service," a stocky man announced, while holding a toolbox in one hand, and a telephone in the other. "Telephone," he repeated.

"Oh, I'm sorry. I didn't know you were coming today," Emily stammered. "I'll get done and out of here quickly," he replied.

Just as she got to the top of the stairs, the doorbell rang again. That time it was Mrs. Angst, looking annoyed.

"Your mother is very upset with you," she scolded. "She

expected a call from you yesterday. I told you to use my phone until yours was hooked up. Thank goodness I called her to tell her you arrived safely."

"I'm sorry," Emily said. "I forgot."

"It's all ready to go," the man said, pointing to the wall phone. "I'll let myself out."

"Thank you," Emily called out. She turned to Mrs. Angst, and said, "I'll call her now. But you know, I really don't need a landline."

"It was your mother who wanted it," Mrs. Angst said.

"Yes, of course she did," Emily scoffed.

She quickly, albeit reluctantly dialed her mother's number, and then proceeded to listen to a long lecture on how inconsiderate she'd been to not call or even recharge her cell phone the previous day. Emily had forgotten that she'd turned it off when Mrs. Angst stopped by.

"Why did you arrange a landline, mother?" Emily asked, abruptly. "I have a cell phone."

"It's for times like last night when your cell phone wasn't charged," Mandy replied in a tone all too familiar.

Emily felt her muscles tighten. Her mother had that effect. However, after realizing that her verbal abuse only had to be tolerated from a distance, she calmed down and changed their conversation. Emily began to speak about her trip, the town, her amazing apartment, and of course, Peter.

"Who is he?" Mandy demanded, sounding worried again. "How could you let a perfect stranger walk you home late at night? Don't you realize you have to be more cautious living alone?"

Emily smirked, and felt another retort coming on, but held her tongue. She ended the conversation with, "Alright. I'll be more careful."

Mrs. Angst handed her a cup of coffee. "How did you know I needed this?"

"I know how busy you must be with settling in and all, so I took the liberty of picking up some food staples for you, if you don't mind," Mrs. Angst said.

"Mind? I'm grateful." After one sip, Emily suddenly had an idea of how to learn something more about her mystery man. Mrs. Angst seemed like a good source to get the inside scoop on local denizens. She started by letting out a deep, affected sigh.

"What is it?" Mrs. Angst asked. "Is there something troubling you?"

"Well, in a way there is," Emily stealthily replied. "You see, my mother just brought something to my attention that I hadn't really thought about. Last night, I met a man at the Villa Verde restaurant. He was very kind and offered to walk me home. Now, we have a date today. My mother thinks I should be more cautious in a new environment. Maybe she's right. Anyway, I was wondering if you might know him."

"What's his name?" Mrs. Angst asked without looking up from making toast.

"Peter Sanders."

"Oh, you've met Peter?" she said, sounding surprised." I know him and his family very well. His grandmother and I play Bridge every Wednesday. He's a great guy, and smart, too. Teaches right here at the college. When I speak to your mother again, I'll tell her she shouldn't worry. And neither should you," she added, with a wink.

"Thanks. Anything else?" Emily timidly asked.

Mrs. Angst stopped what she was doing, but didn't answer. She seemed to be searching for a way to respond. After a few moments, she took the bread out of the toaster, and said, "Nope."

Emily's disappointment was brief as less pleasant thoughts reentered her mind. She tightly gripped her cup, and added, "By the way, there's something else that *is* troubling me. I had the strangest experience last night."

Mrs. Angst stopped buttering toast to look up.

Emily continued, "Yesterday, after you left, I was so tired from the long trip that I made up my bed for a short nap. That's when I noticed a change in the temperature. The air in the bedroom was so cold, and I couldn't figure out where the cold was coming from. As quick as it came though, it was gone. Then I thought I heard the inside door to the apartment open and close. When I checked it, the door was bolted shut.

"When I returned home last night, I found the bed undone; the linens neatly folded and placed at the foot of the bed just as you had done before my arrival. Do you have any idea who'd do something like that?"

"Why of course not," Mr. Angst replied. "Do you think there was an intruder?"

"No," Emily said. "Actually, I'm not sure what to think. Nothing else in the apartment has been disturbed, as far as I can tell. It almost seems like a practical joke. Does anyone else besides the two of us have a key to this place?"

"No," Mrs. Angst replied, emphatically. "And I don't play practical jokes."

"I know," Emily reassured her. "I wasn't implying it was you. It's just so odd."

"Well, did you take that nap?" Mrs. Angst asked.

Emily nodded.

"Maybe then it was your imagination," Mrs. Angst said. "Maybe you thought you made the bed, but really didn't, and slept on the bare mattress. You said you were very tired when you arrived. You could be mistaken."

Emily shook her head. "Not a chance. I don't have that vivid of an imagination."

"Don't worry," Mrs. Angst said. "It's perfectly safe in Gettysburg. Of course, you still need to take precautions, especially with so many tourists coming through town. But it's still very safe here."

"How can you be so sure?" Emily asked.

"Because nothing bad ever happens here anymore," she replied.

"Anymore?"

"All the bad that could possibly happen here, happened many years ago," Mrs. Angst said.

"You mean the Civil War battle?"

Mrs. Angst responded, "All of the battles, in war and life itself."

Emily briefly pondered her remarks before looking at her wristwatch. "Already ten o'clock," she said. "I don't mean to be rude, but my date is picking me up at eleven and I do have to get ready."

"Don't worry, dear," Mrs. Angst said, while getting up to leave. "I was young once. You get ready, and I'll just straighten up and let myself out. Here's my phone number and address again. Please call me if you need anything."

"Thank you," Emily said. She impulsively reached over to embrace the old woman, and for only a moment, thought she was holding on to her beloved, Grams.

Chapter Seven

Peter arrived promptly wearing a Union hat and waving a Confederate flag. "Ready?" he asked.

"Now who looks like a tourist," Emily said, laughing. "I'll be right back."

She ran up to the parlor to get her purse. It was then she noticed the breakfast table cleared and cleaned except for a box, which she hadn't time to investigate.

When Peter gave her a Confederate hat and a Union flag, Emily asked with a grin, "Any particular reason for the mix in loyalties?"

"No," Peter said. "Just remembering both armies who fought and died here." Emily cracked a smile though she thought his comment was strange. She wondered, *Why remember both armies? Didn't the South lose the war?*

As they walked out toward the street, a faint voice called from behind them. "Hello, Miss Tomaso."

Emily turned to see a small, frail man, about 50 years of age, bending down to water several potted geraniums in front of her house. She and Peter walked over to him.

"I'm Joel Levy," he said, and extended his hand. Emily shook it, and asked, "Are you the accountant?"

"No. I'm the friendly one," he giggled. "The accountant is in there," and pointed to the front window. "That's Mike Thurmon."

Through the window Emily could see a rather tall, attractive, younger looking man observing what was going on outside. As soon as he caught her eye, he turned away.

"Don't worry, he's just very shy," Joel apologized. "We're glad you're here. I did so love talking to your grandmother over the phone. I'm sorry we never got the chance to meet her. Mrs. Schmidt must have been an extraordinary woman."

"Yes, she was. Thank you. Nice to meet you," Emily said, and turned to leave. The accountant was looking at her again. She waved, but he didn't return her greeting; continuing to stare, almost scowl, she thought, before turning away once more. A shiver went down her spine.

"Maybe we can get together sometime for tea," Joel offered. "We'd love to..."

"We really must be going now, Mr. Levy," Emily interrupted. "See you again soon," she added while tugging on Peter's arm, leading him to the sidewalk.

When they were out of Joel's view, Peter turned to her and asked, "What happened?"

"What do you mean?"

"You cut him off just as he was trying to be hospitable. What's wrong?"

"Nothing," she replied, and continued walking.

"Is it because they're a gay couple?" he asked.

"Of course not," Emily snapped. Her eyes grew wide as she added, "We've just met, and yet you make these assumptions about me? What makes you think you know how I feel about that or anything else?"

"Touché," Peter remarked. "What is it then?" His voice was soft, and low with a sincerity that quickly diffused Emily's anger.

"Peter, can we just drop this? Please?"

Peter looked into her large eyes, larger then, but no longer in anger. He sensed sadness and fear buried deep in those dark, green oceans, a mystery he inexplicably wanted to dive into and solve.

"Sure," he said and reached down for her hand as they continued on their way.

Emily looked over her shoulder, toward her house, feeling her tenant's angry eyes upon her once again. She began wondering if Thurmon had a key to her apartment.

They walked past the Wick n' Wax Shoppe, and Emily stopped to look in through the window.

"We can go in now if you'd like," Peter said. "But I think they'll be open late tonight."

"No," she quickly assured him. "I don't need anything from there."

"Do you realize this is the second time we've passed this store in less than twenty-four hours, and you stopped to look in? With all the lovely shops lining the street here, this is the only one you seem to be interested in," Peter said.

Emily smiled, and said, "I guess I'm just intrigued by the name, Wick n' Wax. What a great name for a store that sells candles. Has it been here a long time?"

"The Wendel family started this business just before the war came here," Peter said. "The business flourished immediately after the battle though, selling the necessary products to provide light. The town needed much at that time, and illumination was just as important as all the other needs."

"What do you mean?"

"Well, many people in town had to work through the long, dark night caring for the wounded, and burying the dead. It didn't end quickly, either. Long into the month of November, and beyond, our people had to take care of those soldiers who remained, many sick and by then feeble."

"You said, 'our people.'"

"Sure," Peter noted. "We who call Gettysburg our home still feel a connection to all who live here, even those who came before us. They're our people, Emily, mine, and now yours, too."

"I like that," Emily said. "Isn't it a funny alliteration though: Wendel's Wick n' Wax? Say it three times fast, just like a tongue twister."

"Or a nursery rhyme," Peter said. He began to playfully recite: "Wick n' Wax, lantern and bell. A candle for the sick, a lamp for those well."

"Did you just make that up?"

"No," he shook his head. "That too has been around as long as the shop. I suspect it was used by Mr. Wendel to sell his goods." He added more seriously, "You know, a candle for the soldiers lying wounded, and sick in the hospitals. A lamp for those who cared for them." He reached down into his pocket, pulled out a set of keys, and a smile flashed across his face while pointing to a parked sports car, "Here we are."

"You own a Corvette?"

"Yes, as of two months ago. A classic, 1978, with a V8 engine. But it has a brand-new stereo disc player, four speakers, and as you can see, it's also a convertible."

"All that for such a little car?" she teased.

Peter looked annoyed. "I'll show you what this little car can do. But not yet. I want to acquaint you with my—I mean, *our*—town, first."

Driving in and out of the narrow streets, Peter pointed out different places of interest. "Here's the supermarket, and the pharmacy I use. They are convenient to get to, have plenty of parking, and stay open late. That's Dr. Brown's office over there; he's our family physician. I'll be happy to introduce you to him when you're ready."

Peter turned the corner and pulled into a small parking lot in front of a little store with a brown and white awning over the doorway. "This is one of my favorite places. Promise me you'll never tell my uncle, but after tasting the latte here, you won't want to drink it anywhere else."

"All right, I promise," Emily said.

They sipped mocha latte while watching several people work on an old steam engine at a train station that once welcomed President Abraham Lincoln. One of the men waved to them, and Peter responded with short blasts from his car horn. "That's my little brother," he said.

"Your brother?" Emily said, looking surprised. "Lucky you. I wish I had a brother."

"I have a brother and a sister," he said. " I'm the oldest."

"Do they both live here in town?"

"Yes. My sister and her husband own the store where I got these hats and flags."

"Oh," Emily said, fully realizing what Peter meant the night before when mentioning the town's livelihood.

"It must be great to have them so close," she added. "I'm an only child and always felt a void in my life. There were times I really needed someone, especially when my father died."

"I'm sorry."

"That's alright," she said. "It was a long time ago. Anyway, my best friend at the time, Ruthie Evans, had six brothers, and I was incredibly jealous of her."

"Six brothers?"

"Yes, and all older than she," Emily said. "But you know, by the time we reached high school they had all left home. Three went out of state to college, eventually staying there, and two went into the Army. The youngest, Stevie, was the restless one. He kept moving around from place to place looking for adventure, until he was killed in a hand-gliding accident.

"The day of his funeral, I sat next to Ruthie, put my arms around her, and realized she was just as alone in the world as me. At that moment, I felt so fortunate. You can't miss or grieve for a sibling that doesn't exist."

"What a pessimistic way to look at life," Peter remarked.

Emily quietly looked away.

He saw her reaction and regretted making the comment. Changing the subject, Peter said, "You know, we all spent some time away from this town.

"I studied at NYU for seven years and taught there for two semesters. I only moved back home in time to teach a few courses here during spring semester. I'll have a full schedule this fall though.

"My brother Will over there at the train museum, attended

Boston University, and dropped out after only one year. He's enrolled in the college here though starting this fall."

"What about your sister?" Emily asked.

"Lori went to a college down in D.C. where she met her husband, Bob. After graduation, they returned here to settle down, opened their store, and had a baby boy." Reaching into his glove compartment Peter pulled out a picture. "This is my nephew, Sean. He just turned two."

"He's cute," Emily said. "You know, I can understand the others coming back here, but how could you return to the farm, so to speak, after living all that time in New York City?"

"It's not what it seems," he said. "A big city like New York can become overwhelming, and besides..."

"You can't take the country out of the boy?" Emily interrupted.

Peter smiled, and said, "Something like that. The truth is, I wanted to get out of town, but then after a while, I felt the need to be home. There was this emotional force pulling me back here. Being away felt like an unfinished puzzle for me, or an open circle to my life. I'm not sure I completely understand the feeling, either. Maybe it's because of my studies that I realize how important this place is to me; how important it is to us all. Anyway, my whole family agrees, no matter how far away our lives take us, we'll eventually end up back here, home."

Emily exhaled, and said, "What a lovely sentiment. I only wish I could have that same feeling."

"Maybe Gettysburg will be your special place," Peter said.

"Maybe. My Grams always used to say this town was blessed. I didn't know what she meant then, but I'm beginning to understand it now."

"But you've only been here one day."

"Yes, and I've already met you," she said, surprised by her boldness.

Peter's tour of the town and the surrounding area included passing many farms and schools, a community hospital, and dozens of museums and shops. They drove by the college. "We'll save a tour of the campus for another day," he said.

He then drove to a nearby park. "Time for lunch," he said, while pulling into a parking space, and then proceeded to retrieve a picnic basket, and a blanket from the trunk of his car. He escorted Emily over to a grassy area where tourists were picnicking as well. He spread the blanket down on the grass and opened the basket, which was filled with artisan breads, cheeses and an assortment of cut up summer fruits.

Emily was astonished by it all, and thought, *This is too good to be true.*

During lunch, Peter spoke about his experience teaching in New York, and the syllabus he'd been working on for the new classes he'd teach in the fall. He gave Emily some tips on preparing her course outline as well.

They struck up a conversation with two families from Florida who had decided to take their kids on an educational summer vacation, visiting Civil War battle sites. Emily listened with admiration as Peter spoke to them about the battle, and the town, listing all the must-see places of interest there. The hour passed quickly.

They drove on through streets lined in elegant houses, with large open porches, and decorative wrought iron fences. Many of them were palatial Victorians, all trimmed with lush foliage. He slowed the car in front of a large, colonial. "That's where I grew up, my parent's house," Peter said.

"It's beautiful. Where do you live now?" Emily asked.

"Beyond that corner window, on the second floor," he pointed. "Guess I'm still growing up there," he added with a laugh. "But it's only temporary. I'm moving into an apartment on Baltimore Street at the end of next month. I'll show you." He turned the car around, and drove across town back onto Baltimore Street, and pointed to a brick building. "My apartment is on the first floor," he said.

"So, you'll be moving into the older section, too," Emily noted, with a grin.

He nodded, and sped up the road, turning several corners in the same, modest neighborhood with buildings nestled close to the sidewalk. An edifice protruded amidst the other structures, and he parked his car across the street from it.

"Why did we stop here?" Emily asked as Peter stared at the building.

"Are you a Catholic?" he asked.

She nodded.

"I guessed correctly then. So am I. I just wanted to show you this church, because it was used as a Civil War hospital."

"Weren't all, or at least most of the churches here in town used as Civil War hospitals?" she asked.

"Yes, but you belong here, right?"

Peter ignored Emily's curious look as he opened the car door for her. He truly had no idea why he'd brought her to the place he had avoided entering for so many years.

The stately white pillars of Our Lady of Souls R.C. Church seemed out of place beside the small, brick houses beside it. Since its construction predates the Civil War, a small bronze plaque appears near the entrance, acknowledging it as a Civil War Era building, like so many others Emily had seen that day, including the one on her own home.

Peter guided her through the oversized wood doors and to a pew where they sat down. He looked around as though refreshing his memory, until his gaze rested upon the large crucifix suspended above the altar.

Emily felt very much at home inside of the sanctuary, even though she hadn't been to church since her grandmother's funeral months before. She took in every detail of the building: the soaring ceiling, intricate, stained-glass windows, and carved woodwork that masked the history behind what was once there.

"It's hard to believe that a place this beautiful and serene was once used as a hospital," she said.

Peter added without disrupting his gaze, "Imagine all the final hour confessions these walls hold from the mouths of innocents who committed the ultimate sin. All those poor, sad, penitent souls."

Emily slipped her arm through his. He suddenly seemed different, almost somber. "Are you okay?" she asked.

"I'm fine," he said. "We'll have to get going now, though. My shift at the restaurant starts in about an hour."

They walked past a font, and Emily noticed a small stained, glass window near it by the side door. In delicate colors of blue, gray, green and white, it depicted a dove soaring above an open field, carrying an olive branch in its mouth. Below it was a plaque with the family name, Stone. "Stone," Emily said, in surprise. "That was Grams' maiden name. I just realized something:

"This is where my grandmother and great-grandparents worshiped. I guess all my ancestors were here."

Chapter Eight

Peter walked Emily to her door and apologized for having to go back to work. "My family really depends on me. I hope you understand."

"Of course," she said. "I had a great time. I think I really have a feel for this town now. Besides, I have a lot of unpacking to do. Would you like to see my apartment?"

"Maybe tomorrow," he said. "I'd still like to show you the rest of Gettysburg. You still haven't seen the best part. There's the campus, the whole battlefield, and of course, the National Cemetery." He delivered the itinerary with such childish excitement that she couldn't help but smile. "I'll pick you up at eleven," Peter said with a peck on her cheek.

As he turned to leave, Emily reached over and took his hand, but quickly let it go. Peter looked into her eyes; the green oceans seemed a little brighter. He placed his hands around her narrow waist and pulled her close to him. After holding her there for a few moments, he bent down and gently kissed her on the lips. "I'm glad you're here," he said.

"Me too," she replied.

Emily watched him drive off. She then noticed Mike Thurmon

staring at her from his office window. Once he realized she'd spotted him, he pulled down the shade.

"What's with him?" she said, under her breath, and ran up to her apartment. "Why would he be angry at me? We haven't even met." Emily bolted the door and quickly surveyed the space where everything appeared properly in place. Walking to the rocker, she peeked into each room as she went by, first the small room, and then the larger bedroom, briefly stopping to stare once again at the neatly folded bedding. The ring of the new telephone startled her.

"I'm just calling to see how your day went," Mandy said.

"Mother, we spoke only this morning. Anyway, it's been very nice, so far."

"Just nice?" Mandy asked.

"Okay Mom. What is it you want? I know you're calling me for a reason other than to just ask how my day was, so come out with it."

"Now don't be so touchy. I thought I'd just let you know that I spoke with Mrs. Angst today."

"Did she call you?" Emily nervously asked. She'd been concerned the woman might have contacted Mandy about the weird experience she'd shared with her that morning. Information like that could be very dangerous in the mind of Mandy Porter, and she didn't want to deal with its consequences.

"No," Mandy replied. "I called her."

Emily let out a sigh of relief as Mandy added, "I don't want you to think that I don't trust you. You just don't realize how much I worry."

She remained quiet as her mother continued speaking. "Well, I must share all I've learned about this young man who has befriended you, Doctor Peter Sanders."

"He's a PhD, not a heart surgeon," Emily threw in, mocking.

Mandy ignored her remark. "Like you, he also teaches history, but on a college level, of course. He comes from a very prominent family down there. His father is a judge in the county … "

" … and his uncle owns a pizzeria," Emily interrupted. She'd always thought of her mother as snobbish and so couldn't resist the chance to annoy her.

"Well, that must be the other side of the family," Mandy dismissed. "Not bad, Emily, a college professor. Anyway, I'm really happy you met him."

"Why? I hope you're not planning a wedding, are you?"

"Don't be silly," Mandy replied.

"You know, I really like being alone," Emily said, feeling confident. "Don't count on seeing me in East Springs anytime soon. I no longer need anyone else, like you, to care for me. I need to depend on myself."

Mandy was quiet as Emily thought about what she'd just said. She implied that her mother took care of her, but in reality, Grams was her caregiver during her early years, her role model as she matured. Her mother seemed more like a distant sister. However, she was feeling charitable that day and didn't bother to change the implication.

Resting the phone against her shoulder, Emily peaked out of her kitchen window and noticed her tenants leaving the office. As Emily watched them walk out toward their car, which was parked near hers by the barn, she saw the smaller man, Joel, lose his footing. He was protected from falling by Mike, who grabbed his elbow.

"How's Zach?" Emily asked.

"Oh, he's fine," Mandy said. "Yesterday, he was working so hard on that malpractice case, I hardly saw him. He said there'll be more late nights ahead."

"I guess you'll have to keep busy at the country club then," Emily noted.

"I went there to play tennis with Martha Nielson after you left and stayed on until long after brunch. Martha was showing off pictures of her bedroom she'd recently redecorated. She ordered furniture from North Carolina, beautiful 18th century cherry reproductions. I've been thinking about redoing our bedroom, if Zach agrees. What color do you think I should choose? I'm so tired of yellow."

"Grams liked yellow," Emily said.

Mandy ignored the comment. "I think maybe shades of rose. What do you think?"

Emily hastily agreed and made an excuse to end their conversation. "Call me tomorrow," Mandy said, before hanging up.

Emily rubbed her forehead, troubled by the loneliness she detected in Mandy's voice. It wasn't something she could help her with in any way, though. They just didn't have that type of relationship. *Zach's the one who should be there for her.* But then, that relationship changed. There were much happier times.

Emily remembered when Zachary Porter came into her mother's life. Mandy was a young widow, stuck at home with a widowed mother and teenage daughter. Not even the part-time job Mandy took at the designer boutique, nor the weekly girls' night out with friends, could quell her loneliness.

Zach was indeed Mandy's salvation. He was not as attractive as her first love, Andrew, but was very kind and understanding. An attorney with a flourishing practice in the neighboring town of West Springs, Mandy was quite impressed with his credentials. But it was he who seemed to fall head-over-heels in love with the tall, blue-eyed, redhead he'd met at a church social.

Emily remembered how nervous he seemed the night he proposed to Mandy. After dating several months, everyone knew they were getting serious. Zach cautiously entered their home, continually running his fingers through the short strands of his thinning brown hair.

He timidly handed Emilia a bouquet of white roses, her favorite. As her eyes lit up, she dropped her knitting, and said, winking at her daughter, "I always liked him, Mandy."

Zach gave Emily the most beautiful pen she'd ever seen. Covered in rose, gold and white cloisonné'. It had her initial engraved on the wide clip.

"I thought a freshman honor student could probably use a pen more than anything else," Zach said.

Emily could not conceal her approval. She reached over and

hugged him hard. As he exhaled in relief, she said, "Thank you Zach, for the pen and everything. Mom is very happy, and so am I." Looking over at Grams who could size up and access almost any situation or person, Emily saw that she was smiling in approval, too.

That night Zach gave Mandy a three-carat diamond engagement ring. From that moment on, Emily was certain their lives would fall neatly into place.

But as she watched the sun set behind the surrounding hills from her new home, Emily thought how strange that notion now seems. The man who had made everything right for years was now so totally wrong for them. She then realized that nothing in life is ever as it seems.

"Poor, naive Mandy," she said, surprised by the concern she was feeling for her mother.

Chapter Nine

The telephone rang that evening, and Emily reluctantly picked it up thinking Mandy was calling again. "Yes, Mother," she said, sarcastically. But there was no one on the other end; only the lonely sound of a dial tone. It rang several more times, each time with no response. Emily shivered, closing her arms around her body. "New phone. Must be a technical problem," she said, trying to suppress her fear.

Living alone for the first time was intimidating. That feeling was heightened by the strange events the day before. She thought once again about Mike Thurmon and the way he looked at her. She began to worry.

Could my mother be right? Maybe I'm not suited to live alone.

Emily's fear was like an illness, a terrible illness that kept her living in the status quo. She was so determined to never let it, or anything else, hold her back any longer. And yet, there in the quiet of the evening, as her confidence wore thin, she began to feel fear's debilitating grip on her once again in the one place she'd hope to find a cure.

On the kitchen table was the little box she assumed Mrs. Angst had left for her that morning. Wick n' Wax Shoppe, Gettysburg, Pa.

was written on top. Inside were three, tall pillar candles scented with lavender. Holding a candle to her nose, she smiled after inhaling the familiar, comforting scent. It was Grams' favorite scent.

Placing the candles on the fireplace mantel, between the picture of Grams and the Guardian Angel, Emily began reciting the rhyme she'd learned earlier from Peter: "Wick n' Wax, lantern and bell. A candle for the sick, a lamp for those well."

Chapter Ten

Peter cleaned and reset a table, before gesturing over to a couple waiting near the crowded restaurant's entrance. He pulled out a chair to seat the woman and then reached for the pencil tucked behind his right ear. As they mulled over the menu, he noticed his friend, Ralph O'Malley, walk in. "I'll give you a few moments to decide," he told the customers.

Peter walked over to Ralph, who was waiting to pick up an order, and shook his hand. "Do you have a minute?" he asked.

Ralph followed his friend into the back room. He was hot and sweaty after finishing a 25-mile ride on his bike, in preparation for an upcoming two-week jaunt in Hawaii with fellow cyclists.

"Which do you prefer, the classroom or the kitchen," Ralph joked while looking around the hectic space, as clanging pots, and shouting were heard in the background.

"I just have to help my aunt and uncle to get through the anniversary week," Peter said. "Then, I'm definitely quitting."

Ralph nodded in understanding. The town always swelled with tourists the weeks before and during the battle's anniversary.

After looking him over, Peter asked his friend, "How do you get through that workout after working all day?"

Ralph, who was in charge of the pathology lab at the local hospital, mockingly placed his hands on his hips with feet spread apart and grinned from ear to ear.

Peter laughed. The stance was one he'd become accustomed to seeing over the years throughout their lifelong friendship. "You're looking good, bro," he noted.

Ralph shrugged, and asked, "So, what's up?"

Peter stopped smiling and looked down at the floor. He took on an air of solemnity that Ralph hadn't seen in quite a while. It concerned him, and he asked, "Are you okay?"

"Absolutely," Peter remarked, his voice and demeanor lightened. "I wanted to tell you that I met this girl, this woman. She's beautiful, smart and thankfully just relocated to Gettysburg."

"God, you are a chick magnet. Another Pete Sanders babe?"

"No, it's not like that," Peter laughed. "I could see something happening."

"Oh yeah? That's terrific, Pete. I'm glad for you. Things seem to be working out pretty well since you moved back."

"I guess so. It's just, I don't know," Peter said. "There's something about her. We just met, but I was immediately drawn to her. I guess you could say she's the magnet. Different from all of the other women I've been with lately. She reminds me of someone else. You know who I mean."

Ralph paused for a moment, and added in a serious tone, "Come on now, that's long past."

"I know," Peter said. "I haven't thought about her in years. It's all very strange. I can't help it though. I don't know what to do."

"Look, maybe if it's a problem you shouldn't see this woman anymore," Ralph said.

"Emily," Peter said, softly.

"What?"

"Her name's Emily," he repeated. "Lives over on Hemsford. And, I don't want to stop seeing her, Ralph. Besides, I think she's fine. Yes, I'm sure of it," Peter said, more confidently. "I'm just over-reacting. Sorry to bother you with this. Say, when's your big trip?" he added, changing the subject.

"It's Saturday. How do you like the buzz cut I just got for it?" Ralph asked as he rubbed his hand across a nearly bald head.

"Don't need any extra hair to slow you down, right?" Peter remarked, smiling.

"I hope not. I'll see you when I get back, and maybe I can meet this Emily. Susan and I will have you both over for dinner."

Ralph returned to the counter to pick up his pizza, remaining deep in thought. As Peter walked by, he stopped him, and said, sounding concerned once again, "Just be careful, okay?" Peter nodded and returned to his table to take dinner orders.

Chapter Eleven

While preparing to spend her second night in Gettysburg, Emily ate a piece of Mrs. Angst's cake and relaxed on the comfortable rocking chair. She'd completed most of her unpacking earlier and so looked around impatiently to find something to do. She was sorry she hadn't shipped her television from home. But that really wasn't a favorite pastime. Her true love was reading.

She reached into a box, lifted out several of her books, and walked over to the large, mahogany cabinet resting against the long wall in the parlor. After opening the heavy wood doors, she stepped back. "What the," she said, and took two more steps back to get a better look at the treasure trove of dusty books, and magazines that were hidden there. Anxiously, she began to thumb through each one, stopping only intermittently to sneeze.

There were Better Homes and Gardens dating back to the early 1960's and some paperback romance novels. Old, leather-bound classics such as, "Moby Dick", and several volumes of Shakespeare's work reproduced in 1878, were tucked among loose pamphlets, and an encyclopedia collection. There was one small book that fell to the floor while she was searching, which she picked up and placed aside.

Emily reached up on tiptoe, and pulled down a thick textbook of some sort, and instantly, recipe cards that had been loosely placed there flew out in all directions. Laughing, she picked them up and imagined the reluctant cook who hid the cards with all good intentions of using them someday. While replacing the textbook, the small book fell to the floor again. She picked it up once more and carefully placed it on the shelf.

The magazines were so dated they were laughable, and she briefly thought about giving them away, or just throwing them out. But then, she found a LIFE magazine from1938, in which the center portion had been flagged with a piece of paper lace. Emily opened to the section that contained a photographic account of the 75th anniversary of the Gettysburg battle. President Franklin D. Roosevelt had just dedicated the Memorial Peace Light at a ceremony in the Military Park, which was attended by several Civil War veterans; most of them well into their nineties.

The old soldiers had wrinkled skin and haggard bodies, some without limbs. Her eyes scanned the pages and came to rest upon a picture of a Confederate soldier who was still wearing the uniform cloak of his youth, reaching over a wood fence to shake the hand of an old Yankee. She changed her mind about the magazines, dusted them off, and placed them back on the shelf leaving LIFE on top of all the others.

When the small book fell again, Emily picked it up for a closer look. The dark blue linen cover was attractively embellished with a gilded design. Inside, the pages were crisp and white, no yellowing or cracks, and the ink was clear and smooth. "Witness to Tribulation" was legibly hand-written on the inside page, and below it the word *Remember* all by itself, followed by a signature she couldn't decipher. Although the book appeared to be a diary, there were no individual dates on the pages. It was organized into sections or chapters, and each chapter always began with the word, Remember, and at the end, separated by one blank page. Emily placed the book down on a table near the rocker and began a three-hour mission of dusting and reorganizing the bookshelves, adding her own books to the spaces created by the reorganization.

After the exhausting work was done, she collapsed into the chair, and looked over to her bedroom thinking how nice it would be to sleep in a bed. She got as far as the doorway, looked once again at the bare mattress and folded linen and thought, *Who was in there? What is in there?* She returned to her place near the hearth.

A light rain was beginning to fall, brushing the leaves of a nearby tree against the window.

The swaying of the leaves, and the lace curtains sent shadows dancing across her dimly lit parlor and onto the pictures on her mantle. She watched the ballet, focusing once again on the photo with her grandmother and her angel painting, rocking herself slowly in rhythm to the gentle movement, overwhelmed by an incredible feeling of bliss. She thought about her new town, the teaching position she'd start in just a few months, and of course, Peter. "Grams," she said with a yawn, "I'm home" and fell asleep.

Chapter Twelve

While Lions Roar

The rhythmic pounding of a hammer awakened Emily at 6 a.m. It was the same sound she thought she'd heard the night before and had just cast off as a dream. As she looked out the window, she wondered who might be working so early in the morning. The first light of dawn was just beginning to brighten the sky, but a fog hung thick, and low, casting eerie images across the front lawn. A pungent floral smell filled the air, which was so still, she could hear her own breathing. It was then she noticed the pounding was gone and began to question whether she'd heard it at all.

After dressing, Emily waited to start breakfast, hoping Mrs. Angst would stop by. She wanted to thank her for the beautiful candles but was also looking forward to seeing her again. When she didn't come, Emily sat down to have a bowl of cereal alone. She put down her spoon when she heard a noise outside and got up to investigate.

Outside the front door, she found a bouquet of flowers wrapped in tissue paper with water sprayed on the petals to keep them moist. As she bent down to retrieve the flowers, swatting away some of the annoying flies that seemed to be taking up residence in the town, she looked around to find someone to thank. With no one in sight, she smiled thinking they must have been from Peter.

By nine o'clock, she decided to call Mrs. Angst anyway. "Good morning," Emily cheerfully announced. "Thank you for the lovely candles. I can't wait to use them."

"You're very welcome."

"By the way, did you also leave me flowers today near my outside door?" Emily asked. "No," Mrs. Angst replied. "They must be from your gentleman friend."

Emily was happy to confirm that.

"How do you like your new home, so far?" Mrs. Angst asked.

"You know, this will probably sound a little strange, but I almost feel as though I've been here before," Emily said. "I know I was here once but was too young to have any recollections from that visit. This feeling is different. I just think I was always meant to be here."

"That's not strange at all, dear," Mrs. Angst said. "Your grandmother grew up here. This town and that house were both a part of her, just as you are a part of her. So, in a way, you could say you have been here before."

"That sounds much too complex," Emily said. "I'd just like to think of it as a niche that has been waiting for me."

"Like predestination?" Mrs. Angst asked.

Emily chuckled thinking the woman was kidding, but her silence told her differently. The theory of predestination didn't sit well with her. She was finally able to make her own choices in life and wasn't about to yield to an ethereal force that logic could never explain. She added, more seriously, "I don't want to believe in predestination. I want to believe that we have control over our destiny. I'm comfortable knowing that I can choose my direction in life."

"Perhaps you are right," Mrs. Angst replied. "But maybe those choices are predetermined. Like, for instance, your niche, and the fact that you were able to get a teaching position not far away from your new home. What is that, coincidence?"

"I did make the choice to apply to an open position in Hanover, so it wasn't really a coincidence," Emily said.

"Okay," Mrs. Angst conceded. "I guess you're right."

Emily was left bewildered after their brief conversation, mulling over her circumstances with the house, the job, and how it all came about at just the right time. Nothing else in her life ever went that well. She thought once again about her chance meeting with Peter, and how she felt he was meant to be there for her. Perhaps that notion wasn't as absurd as she initially thought. Emily stood in the doorway separating the parlor from her bedroom, while entertaining the possibility that she wasn't alone in directing her future. Maybe there were other forces making those choices for her, too. But she still didn't think that was very logical, and for her, that meant not very likely either.

When Peter arrived, Emily insisted he come up to see her apartment.

"What a great place," he said. "Look at those ceiling beams. You don't see construction like that anymore. My parent's house isn't nearly as old as this. And then when it was updated in the 1960's, a lot of the classic details were stripped away."

She'd intentionally left the doors to her bookcase ajar, hoping he'd notice her assortment of books.

"This is incredible," he said, while rubbing his hand along the edge of the finely crafted cabinet. He then moved slowly around the apartment, looking into each room, until stopping at her bedroom door. He pointed to the unmade bed, and asked, "Laundry Day, already?"

Emily paused, and said, "It's a long story. Coffee?" she asked, holding up the pot. She wanted to tell him about what happened that first night there, and why the bed wasn't made, but still had some doubt he'd believe her. She could hardly believe it herself.

"How has it been being back with your parents?" Emily inquired, changing the conversation.

"It's been an adjustment after living alone for so long. I'm a little embarrassed to admit that arrangement being 28, but the truth is, it's just so darn convenient. I don't think I've had to cook or do my own laundry more than just a few times since moving back."

"I bet it's cheap, too," Emily said.

"You got that right," he laughed. "Actually, I'm saving up to buy a house. It's not that easy on an associate professor's salary, but I'll get there."

"Any place in particular?"

"No," he replied. "Just as long as it's here in town. I love having the option of walking to work."

Emily knew another reason. Their time spent together the day before was somewhat revealing. He'd admitted a deep, emotional connection to the town, and she thought she might be feeling it, as well.

Peter walked over to the fireplace and lifted the photograph. "Is this your grandmother?" he asked.

Emily nodded.

"Pretty painting," he remarked, pointing. "Is this your Guardian Angel?" he chuckled.

"In a way, yes," Emily said, smiling. "It was a gift from Grams."

"Oh, by the way, thank you for the gift of flowers," she said, while gesturing to a vase containing daisies and pink peonies.

Peter looked over to the blooms and shook his head. "I'd like to take credit for that, but the truth is they're not from me."

She looked confused.

"Now I'm getting jealous," he said, as he put his arms around her. "Maybe they're from your friend, Mrs. Angst."

Emily nodded, knowing however that it wasn't so.

"Are you ready for another day of Gettysburg, and the college?" Peter said, rattling the car keys.

"I've been looking forward to it," she said, glancing once more at the flowers before departing.

Chapter Thirteen

Peter turned his car into the campus' parking lot and began lecturing on its history. "Gettysburg College was founded in 1832 and had originally been named Pennsylvania College. The name was changed in 1921," he said.

Emily marveled at the old buildings. She commented on how the more recently built structures on campus seem to architecturally usher the college into another century.

He pulled into a parking space labeled, "Reserved", right next to a large, white building with a cupola at its peak. "This is my building, Old Dorm," he proudly announced. "It's an administration building now, but there are some classrooms here. Come, I'll show you my office."

They ascended the stairs and opened the heavy wood and glass doors. Once inside the building, Emily felt a chill as she looked around the attractive hallway with carved wood moldings, doors, and soaring ceilings.

"It must cost a fortune to cool this place," she said, rubbing her arms.

"You've got to be kidding," Peter said, as they stepped into the elevator. "We're lucky to at least get heat in the winter. Now, that costs a fortune. It would be prohibitive to fully air condition this building, or any of the other buildings on campus, except for the new library."

Yet, she felt the unmistakable chill, even on the second floor as they proceeded down a long hall that was lined with classrooms. The rooms were small with somewhat dated furniture. It was only vaguely reminiscent of the classrooms at her much younger alma mater.

"Here's my office," Peter said, as he opened the door to a room only slightly larger than a walk-in closet. It was dominated by an oversized desk, upon which loose papers were haphazardly strewn amidst open notebooks, textbooks, and an unwashed coffee mug. On the floor were piles of books standing like trophies around the perimeter of the small space. "Believe it or not, I know where everything is," he said.

From his window Emily could see clear across the attractive campus and caught a glimpse of an open tract of land.

"Do you like the view?" he asked.

"It's beautiful," she replied. "Is that the battlefield over there?"

"Just part of it. I'll take you to where you can get a much better look."

They climbed a steep and winding staircase that led to the top of the building. Standing inside of the cupola, they had a radial view of the town on one side, and the battlefield on the other. The structure provided little shelter from the hot sun. Beads of sweat were forming at Peter's temples and on his top lip. But Emily felt cold, very cold.

As Peter pointed out areas of interest, she had the strangest feeling of being watched. Emily looked over her shoulder, expecting to greet someone. They were alone.

"Do you see the library?" he pointed to a contemporary building to their left. "When the ground was dug up for construction, some human remains were discovered."

"What did the workers do?" Emily asked, aghast.

"They stopped working," Peter said. "Many of them refused to continue until the ground was blessed."

"What a horrible and unlikely thing to find, especially here at a college," Emily said.

"It's not unlikely," he said. "This building was used as one of the many hospitals during and after the battle. There were so many amputations done here that some accounts note the limbs were stored for the longest time in piles outside first floor windows. No, I'm not surprised they found that here. But then, almost every part of this town is consecrated ground.

"You know, it's been said this campus is also haunted," Peter added. "There are many stories about strange, inexplicable incidents occurring in this building, even up here, right where we're standing."

Emily backed away from him. "I hope you're not just saying that to frighten me, because I'm not afraid," she said, determined to believe her own words.

"Of course you're not. You shouldn't be. But it's supposedly true, even though I've never experienced anything like that. I'm sorry to say."

Emily was astounded by his comment. *Why would he be sorry about that?* She was definitely experiencing something there, and wished it wasn't happening at all. She was frightened, and didn't understand why. Her heart began pounding wildly as she looked around the empty space; filled with something she couldn't identify. She began feeling nauseous, and the room began to spin as the walls closed in.

Peter thought she looked pale and put his arm around her shoulder. She felt cold to his touch. "Are you alright? Oh no! I have frightened you," he said, apologetically.

"Yes. I mean no," she replied. "It's just very close here. I need some air."

They left promptly and began descending the staircase. She was happy to be on her way out of that unwelcoming place. Halfway down though, Peter said, "I forgot to close the door at the top. You continue, and I'll be right behind you."

"It is closed," she said.

"Are you sure?"

Emily nodded and remained silent while listening to his self-criticism on being so forgetful. But she knew it wasn't he who had closed the door. She guessed he hadn't heard it close by itself after they descended the first few steps.

As they walked over to his car he asked, "Better now?" She smiled and looked relieved.

"I'll be right back. I just need to lock my office." He turned and walked back to the building as if nothing was unusual.

She watched him disappear into Old Dorm and wondered how he could go there every day.

How was he able to work in a place she found so cold and frightening? What was there, she wondered, that made her feel so unwelcome? The windows that her own loving grandparents might have peered out of during a history class, now seemed to stare at her, almost command her to leave.

Looking out across the green, she saw the library and thought about all the poor souls buried beneath it. She looked back at Peter's building, the hospital building as it was known back then, and imagined the piles of severed arms and legs, once connected to young, healthy bodies, piled up outside the windows.

"Is there anything I can do for you?" Peter asked, while starting up the car. Emily exhaled deeply, and said, "I'm fine now. I just needed fresh air."

He shifted the car in reverse, glancing at Emily before backing out of the parking space. She was still staring at the building. *What haunts you, Emily Tomaso? What is it that haunts you?*

Chapter Fourteen

The campus disappeared in the distance as Peter turned off the highway and onto a path that led to a section of the battlefield that was surrounded by tall grass. At a narrowing, trees were beginning to appear on both sides of this road, lined up like sentries standing guard at the gates of their domain. The road began to climb and twist around a huge boulder, and the forest grew dense. Enveloped by the tall trees and thicket, the light from the sun was partially obscured giving the area the appearance of early twilight. Around each turn a monolithic stone monument appeared, placed inconspicuously amidst the brush. Each of these monuments was inscribed with an insignia of a military regiment, and the names of the soldiers who had fought and or died on that very spot.

"I'll park the car a little further up, so we can get out and walk around," he said.

People were everywhere, walking between trees, climbing rocks, and standing on a ledge that gave an almost aerial view of the battlefield. The hill they were on, Little Round Top, was the site of a skirmish on the second day of the three-day battle.

"Up there is where the 20th Maine, among others, defended this hill on July 2," Peter said, pointing to a site of higher elevation near the road.

They walked up the hill hand in hand and she tried to imagine what it must have been like for the soldiers as they were shooting in between the trees at the approaching enemy. Some of the bullets hit wood, some flesh and bone, not knowing the final result until an anguished cry answered doubts.

Emily looked up, awestruck at the towers surrounding her, and asked, "I wonder if these trees hold any feelings from the barrage of bullets they accepted that day? They too were victims of the war."

Peter stopped walking and looked shocked by the odd question. He did however understand it and felt somewhat surprised and amused at having done so. "I suppose they didn't feel too bad," he said. "Many continued to thrive despite the bullets, while men died. You know, even though not as dense then, as it is now, the forest was considered both a curse and a blessing."

"How so?" Emily asked.

"Although the trees got in the way of targets, they probably saved many soldiers who found shelter behind them."

Along a path that led a little further up the hill, was a clearing where a small, granite stone stood all by itself, with one name inscribed on it, Andrew Jameson.

"This looks like a headstone. I guess some soldiers are buried here?" she asked.

"All of the dead were cleared from the battlefield in the weeks and months afterward," Peter said. "This stone has a very special meaning.

"Apparently there were two brothers from New York who were in the battle, Terry and Andrew Jameson. The only problem was, one of them, having lived in Alabama with his new wife preceding the war, wound up fighting for the Confederacy, in the 47th Alabama that was stationed down there. The other brother was stationed to the right of the 20th Maine, with the 44th New York. Well, they never expected to be in battle together, no less come face to face on this hill.

"Terry, a Union man, was in front of the line, shooting to save his life, when he caught a glimpse of a Rebel emerging from behind a tree. He aimed at him, and then the Rebel looked up. Instinctively, he called out, 'Andrew', in surprise and fear. Startled, his brother looked over, giving another Union soldier a perfect aim. The moment their eyes met; Andrew was shot dead."

"Oh my God, how horrible," Emily cried out.

Peter nodded. "Terry realized he was responsible for his brother's death. He threw down his rifle and risked his own life by dragging himself over to where his dead brother lay. There he sat for the remainder of the skirmish, cradling him in his arms, oblivious to the bullets that flew wildly around him.

"Many years later, in his old age, he convinced authorities to allow him to place that headstone here. It was roughly the spot where he last saw his brother alive."

"Last saw him alive," she whispered, while recalling the old man planting flowers around the war memorial back in East Springs. Emily reached down and touched the top of the stone lightly and silently said a prayer. As Peter led her away, she turned back to look at the site once more, and said, "My father's name was Andrew."

They continued quietly exploring the area, when a gust of wind soughed through the trees. To Emily, it sounded like a whisper or a cry. She shivered as she looked at Peter who seemed totally unaffected. A little further up in a clearing, she stopped walking, turned to him and said, "Do you feel something?"

"Like what?" he asked.

"I don't know. It feels strange; almost like a gentle vibration going through my body right in this very spot. But not here," she said, as she moved two steps to the left. "Why don't you try it," she added.

Peter moved into the spot in question. "I don't feel anything," he said.

Emily moved back into position. "It's definitely here. Feels almost magnetic."

Peter moved into her spot again, closed his eyes, concentrating on trying to feel what Emily was experiencing. After several attempts, he ruefully shook his head.

The wind picked up, disturbing the stillness in the woods. As they stood amidst the tall oaks and pines infused with the many souls of those who'd lost their lives among them, so many years before, Emily began to feel intrusive. "I think we should get going," she said, and led him back to the car.

Crossing the road, they stopped and waited for a double-decker bus to pass. The bus was filled with tourists who were taking a two-hour, tape-recorded tour of the battlefield. Emily thought about how lucky she was to have Peter as a personal guide.

He was so knowledgeable, and passionate about history, a passion she could understand and appreciate. In that way, Peter reminded her of Bill, her former boyfriend. But Bill Ivers had forgotten all his passion, his dreams, or so it seemed.

Bill shared Emily's interest in American history, and after graduation stayed on with her full-time in college to complete their graduate degree in Education. They both wanted to get the degrees out of the way before looking for employment. Once they were settled with jobs, they could find an apartment, move in together, and begin a new life. Both desperately needed a new life, away from tensions that grew increasingly more disturbing at each of their homes.

Bill and Emily were the only two graduates who didn't have a teaching position by the end of that first summer after finishing school. Some of their classmates had to move out of state for jobs, and that wasn't something they were willing to do, at least not yet. Both were offered the opportunity to sign up with a government program for eighteen months, after which they'd be guaranteed a teaching position almost anywhere. But that wasn't something they were willing to do, either.

Emilia was sick, and though her condition at first was not considered terminal, she didn't want Emily to leave her. Bill stopped looking for a teaching position and took a job with his father's big construction company, something he swore he'd never do, and then got used to the good money he was making. That bothered Emily. For months she questioned how he could find happiness in anything other than what he'd worked so hard to achieve.

"Why are you wasting your time working with your father?" Emily scolded. "You and your father don't even get along. What happened to your dream of being such a great teacher? Have you lost all your ideals?"

"I haven't lost any of my ideals," Bill said. "I'm finally doing what I want to do. I know it's not what I went to school for, and lord knows it's certainly something I couldn't ever imagine myself doing before, but the truth is, I like working with my dad."

"What about our plans, Bill? Our apartment? Our new life?"

"I need to do this now. I need to be with my father. I'm no longer interested in running away from that."

"I don't believe you," Emily said, abruptly.

"Stop it," Bill yelled. "Damn. Why do I have to go through this every time I come here?"

"You know why, Bill. You know why," she said, and sat down, turning away from him.

Bill's voice softened as he said, "Emily, I know we've talked about how we didn't get along with our parents, but there's something I never told you that's very embarrassing to me. When I was a boy, I used to tell the kids on my baseball team that my father was dead, because for me, that would be his only legitimate excuse to miss all my games. I grew up hardly seeing him. All he could tell me was how hard it was getting ahead in life. That's why he worked so much overtime, to build a successful business for me, and my future. He didn't want me to ever have to depend on anyone else, or to be disappointed. But I was already disappointed. I couldn't see myself doing what he did. I didn't want to be anything like him. I always thought he was just trying to control me; trying to fit me into the same mold he'd arranged for himself. That terrified me. I had to prove I was better than him. But then, I realized something, I wasn't.

"I'm not saying I'll never consider a teaching position, but for right now, this is what I want. And the added benefit is I finally have a great relationship with my father. I think that's all I ever really wanted."

Emily shook her head. "You're just selling yourself short," she said. "Bill, you've fallen right into the mold you were always afraid of."

"Believe what you want about me," he said. "What about you? Is this what you planned to do with your education?"

Emily had taken time off from job-hunting to care for her sick grandmother, but Bill saw it quite differently. "Look who's talking," he admonished with a glower in his dark, brown eyes.

"What a mean-spirited thing to say," Emily chided. "You know how sick Grams is, and how close I am to her. I need to be here. She needs me and wants me here. How could you hurt me that way?"

"Are you sure that's the only reason? She doesn't seem to be so bad."

"So bad? Bill, the doctor doesn't think she has very much time left. Have some pity!"

"I'm sorry about that, but your mother told me she offered to get someone in to help care for her, and you refused. You want this sacrifice. Anyway, I think you're just hiding behind the sick room door if you ask me," he added.

"I'm not asking you," Emily said, raising her voice. "Oh, so you've already discussed this with Mandy? When did you and my mother start discussing my life, behind my back? You don't understand the suffering that's going on here. Just get out, Bill," she screamed. "And remember one thing: It's my choice."

Before he walked away, he turned to her and said, "I made a choice, too. Now I'd like you to also remember one thing, if you're even capable of it. Sometimes our lives don't end up the way we expected. Our circumstances often cause us to do things we don't initially understand, and it leads us away from the truth. Fear does the same. I'll give you some advice," he said. "You have to face what you're most fearful of in order to understand it, even if it hurts."

"I'll give you advice: Save your lectures for a classroom," she said, and dismissed him with the wave of her hand.

"I'm done. Have a good life," he said before walking away.

Emily spent several quiet moments in thought controlling her disappointment, and anger. He'd never spoken to her like that before. Suddenly, she called out with tears in her eyes, "Bill, don't leave me." But he was already gone.

For weeks she waited for the call from Bill that never came. She couldn't bring herself to call him, either. She was haunted by their argument, her last contact with the man she thought she loved. As she brushed her grandmother's hair, and rubbed her back, she prayed the pain would disappear for them both.

She and Bill were linked by a life filled with a certain degree of vulnerability, and discontent, at least until then. The past few months he seemed confident, secure, happy. So, she wondered, what was wrong with her?

Though it was very early, Emily briefly pondered what might ultimately separate her from Peter, should their relationship continue to progress. She wondered what had she learned from her split with Bill? *I don't want to screw this up, too.*

A small bridge appeared on the battlefield, stretching over a stream that was dried up. Emily and Peter crossed it and parked in an area nearby that was surrounded by huge boulders. It was where the Confederate Army had launched the attack on Little Round Top.

"Devil's Den?" Emily asked.

"Unmistakable, isn't it?" Peter said.

They climbed the uneven boulders, sometimes struggling with the steps that were intended for use. Peter helped her to maneuver over the rocks. "This is definitely sneaker territory," he said, as he reached over and grabbed her arm, protecting her from a fall. When they got to the top of the largest boulder, they surveyed the ground below.

"How exciting," she said. "All those years of reading about it, hearing the stories Grams used to tell me about this place, like having races up these rocks when she was a little girl. Now, I'm finally here. Why didn't I come sooner? Do you come here a lot?" she asked.

"Not often. Sometimes, if I feel troubled, I like to come here to think. It's so quiet and peaceful. A lot of the tourists stay away because of the steep climb, so there's plenty of privacy."

"Does it help?"

"Sure," Peter said. "My problems aren't always solved, but I certainly leave with a new perspective on them."

"Oh, and what's that?"

"*Nothing* is so important in life to waste valuable time worrying about," he said. "You make your choices and hope for the best. That's all anyone can do."

Emily noticed to their right what appeared to be a commemorative plaque with a picture attached to it. "Whose picture is that?" she asked, too tired to get up to read the inscription beneath it.

"That's a picture of a dead Confederate soldier; probably a Texan that a photographer found a few days after the battle was done. When the other soldiers and volunteers removed the bodies, for some reason, they didn't know he was here, hidden somewhat by the rocks. The photographer propped the dead soldier up near those stones, took this picture, and then reported it.

"Four months later, he returned to this very spot. Presuming of course all the dead were accounted for, he was shocked to find the remains of this boy, still forgotten. At that point, no one could ever find out who he was, or even what regiment he belonged to, so this area was made a memorial to him."

"Dear lord," she said. "There are so many horrific stories here. In a way, all that killing, when looking at it from this perspective, it all seems so senseless. I mean the war was necessary to end the scourge of slavery. I understand that. But there were so many deaths."

Looking across the field to the hill they had just been on, Emily added, "This is probably where Terry's brother Andrew was before he made it up Little Round Top. I wonder, since he was originally from an abolitionist state, did he fully understand he was fighting for the preservation of an immoral society? Did he even have a choice? Had he known his brother was up there, would he have been so anxious to attack? And, if Terry knew his brother would be approaching, wouldn't he have tried to warn him long before, regardless of their opposing views on the reasons for the war? How many others were in similar situations and never realized it? "

"That's true," Peter said. "But keep in mind most of the Confederate soldiers had little to do with slavery. Only about 10 percent of them owned slaves. No doubt many more supported that institution though. When the war broke out, since they lived in the South, which is where most of the battles took place, many felt pressured to protect their home. I imagine that's how Andrew felt, but we can never know for sure."

"Anyway, what's the difference whether the soldiers here were related? "Emily said. "In essence, they were all brothers, right?"

Peter gently touched Emily's face. *What a sweet and naive observation, and yet so true.* He put his arm around her, and said, "Nowhere is the futility of war more evident than on a battlefield."

"I'm sorry," she said, sounding forlorn. "I guess I'm getting too emotional."

"This place does that," he said, suddenly swathed in a sadness that touched her heart. Emily felt an urge to kiss away all the sorrow on his handsome face, whatever that trouble was, and hold him tight. She kissed his hand instead.

Peter was surprised by the endearing gesture that he so wanted to return. He leaned in to kiss her but then stopped. He stood up, and said, "How about a bottle of water? I have some on ice in the trunk. Wait here. I'll be right back."

Emily watched him master the rocky descent, wondering why he aborted the kiss, at least that's what she thought would happen. Perhaps she misunderstood.

Leaning back on her hands, she closed her eyes, and pointed her chin up to the sky to catch a warm breeze as it brushed across her face. After a few moments though, the atmosphere changed, and the familiar uneasiness accompanied by an enveloping cold crept in once again.

She sensed she was no longer alone. Emily held her breath and slowly looked over her left shoulder. She was pleasantly surprised to see a Civil War reenactor, in full Confederate regalia, leaning on his rifle, watching her.

"Hi," she said, feeling thankful someone was actually there. "I love the outfit. Is there an encampment near here?" she asked, squinting in the sun for a better look.

The soldier stared at her for several moments before tipping his hat. "Ma'am," he said, and turned to walk down the steep hill until he disappeared behind a boulder.

Peter appeared around the same turn on the hill, and said, "Here you go," while giving her a water bottle.

"Thanks," she said, and took a long drink. "By the way, did you see that re-enactor?"

"No."

"Come on, you had to see him. He probably walked right past you by that big rock."

"I didn't see anyone. What did he look like?" he asked.

"He was dressed in a Confederate officer's uniform. Acted very much the part, too. He just tipped his hat and called me 'Ma'am' or something. Boy, they really get into character, don't they," she said.

"Yes, they do," Peter said, looking around excitedly.

"I saw him, too," said a man who was standing off to their right. Emily hadn't noticed he was there. "I was reading this memorial, and I saw him," he added.

"Oh, good," Emily said, smiling. "See Peter, I wasn't imagining it."

"I wasn't suggesting that you were," he retorted.

"It's still strange though," the man said, in earnest, noticeably upset as he stared down at the memorial's photograph. "I watched him walk away, and he just seemed to disappear, down there," he pointed to an area low on the path. "I think it was a ghost. Maybe even his ghost," he said pointing to the picture before him.

Peter saw the concerned look on both of their faces, and said, "Listen, there are many re-enactors up here all summer long. They know this area like the back of their hand, so it might look like he disappeared, when he just found another path behind the rocks that leads to his camp."

"I've toured the whole battlefield, and I didn't notice any encampments," the man said.

"Well then, he's most likely with the park service. Many of the historians dress up in character while giving tours of the battlefield." Once Peter saw they were relieved by his explanation, he added, "I'm certain it's a park ranger you both saw."

Satisfied, the man thanked him and walked away.

Peter wasn't satisfied though. He looked around the park anxiously scanning the area to find the dressed historian who would confirm his account of what had occurred. No such person was in sight.

They sat quietly for a while, dangling their feet off a ledge. Another breeze blew across the field, that time filling the air with the sweet smell of honeysuckle, and they inhaled deeply while gazing pensively on the rocky terrain below.

Chapter Fifteen

While Peter and Emily headed back to his car, he glanced up at the changed, overcast sky, and said, "The morning weather report mentioned the possibility of a severe thunderstorm hitting the area. I guess they were right. We'd better hurry and get in a few more sites before the lions start roaring."

Emily stopped in her tracks. "What did you say?" she asked, looking astonished.

"We'll probably have a storm this afternoon."

"No, not that. I mean the other thing you said."

He put his head down, and tried to figure out what she wanted, then looked up and smiled. "Oh, you mean the lions roaring?"

"My Grams, and even my mother would say that to me whenever there was a storm. I'd never heard anyone else use that analogy, until now."

"I know," Peter said. "It's a local expression."

"I didn't realize that," Emily remarked. "It's funny, Grams told me so much about this place but never mentioned where that expression came from. Do you know what it means?"

"No, not really. It's just kid stuff," he replied.

"She used it all the time," Emily said. "I use it, too and let me tell you, I've gotten quite a few strange looks from people as a result of it."

"I know what you mean," Peter said. "It's something only our people understand."

Emily hadn't realized that the lions began roaring long before Grams became the most important person in the world to her. It was the sudden death of Emilia's husband Allen, after a heart attack, which brought her to live with her daughter, Mandy, and son-in-law, Andrew. Emily was only two years old.

Emilia initially resisted that arrangement, wanting to maintain her independence, but her house in West Springs was so empty without Allen, and she could no longer bear the loneliness. Her plan was to stay with them for only four months while her house was up for sale. After it was sold, she would return to her family home in Gettysburg.

It certainly had been a long time since her last trip down there, almost a lifetime. She had planned many visits but always changed her mind about going at the last minute. Allen used to tease her by saying she was fearful of returning there, because then she'd never want to leave. "Silly man," she'd say, but wondered if he was right.

New York's suburb wasn't exactly in Emilia's plan, although she'd often dreamed of something different for her future. After college, she was expected to teach at the elementary school she once attended, marry a local boy, and settle down in the family house with her parents, just as her mother had done. There was a certain order in that sleepy little town, an arranged fate. But love so often changes fate, and so it did for Emilia.

Allen Schmidt was not exactly the type of person she was looking for in a lifetime mate either. Having grown up near New York City, he seemed so wild and worldly, or at least compared to her, a product of a demure upbringing. He was very energetic, upbeat and amusing in an almost salesman sort of way. Emilia was sold on him from their first meeting, and knew they'd be together forever.

Sarah, Emilia's mother, was completely heartbroken when they announced they would marry, and leave town immediately after graduation from Gettysburg College in May, 1942. With war raging overseas, Allen had to take the government-sponsored position he was offered at the defense plant in New York before someone else did. A pre existing heart condition kept him from active service.

"You can't leave," Sarah pleaded with her daughter. "You have to stay here, and raise your children in this house, just as I did, my mother did, and your great-grandmother before her. This home, this town, is your legacy."

"I'm sick of hearing about my legacy," Emilia snapped. "The only legacy I have is *you* directing my life. When are you going to let go? Isn't 22 years enough?" Emilia's face softened, as she added, "Anyway, I'll probably be back."

Sarah shook her head.

There was no time for an elaborate wedding. Sarah had to alter her own wedding dress for Emilia and quickly put together a celebration of some sort for that day. Her reluctance to the event was never noticeable as she dialed the phone numbers in lieu of engraved invitations, and baked all the different types of cookies, instead of the fancy tiered cake. There was just no time for the frivolities she once thought she'd plan for her only child's wedding. Despite her true feelings, only Emilia knew the extent of her struggle.

"It's only for a few years," Emilia said. "After the war, and when Allen gets some experience, we'll be back to settle here. Maybe he'll find a job in Philadelphia. That isn't too far from Gettysburg."

Sarah said nothing and continued with her baking. Diligently, she measured the flour, and while lovingly kneading the dough, she choked back the tears that so easily flowed when she was alone. She was careful about not showing her daughter those feelings. But Emilia knew.

Twenty-five people attended the wedding at Our Lady of Souls,

R.C. Church. Allen's family wasn't there. They planned a celebration for when the couple arrived in New York.

After the small reception, when it was time for the newlyweds to leave, Emilia walked over to her parents to say good-bye. Sarah turned away. John sobbed as he hugged and kissed his daughter. Emilia reached over, touched her mother's shoulder, and said, "I'll be back soon. Please, I beg you, be happy for me."

Sarah turned to her, and gently placed a kiss on her cheek, a soft kiss, as she had done so many times before. She brushed the hair away from Emilia's forehead, looked directly into her daughter's eyes, and said, "You will never return." She then walked away.

Emilia stood frozen with John's arms wrapped tightly around her, unable to detach her gaze from her mother's solemn retreat into the house. It was a scene that would often be replayed in her mind for many years to come.

That September, Allen was called to act as a consultant for the U.S. Army on defense munitions. They spent the next year traveling from city to city across the United States, wherever there were Army bases and soldiers to instruct on the use of war equipment. He asked Emilia if she'd like to return to Gettysburg and stay with her parents until their lives were more settled, but she refused. She wanted to be with him. "I like living like a gypsy," she said. It was such a different way of life for her, and she was enjoying the novelty of it all.

In California, she received a telegram, which was delivered almost two weeks late. With all the moving around they were doing, and for security reasons, the Army had trouble locating them. The message was that her mother had passed away quietly in her sleep. Emilia was devastated. She sobbed as Allen called John to explain why they received the telegram too late to attend the funeral. He advised them that he was all right, and there was no need for them to return home at that time.

"Oh Dad," Emilia cried, "I should have called her more often."

"Now don't go blaming yourself," John said. "Mother knew you loved her."

Sarah had resisted seeing a doctor for a persistent cough, even though she hadn't felt well for quite a while. Probably her heart or her lungs everyone said, but no one knew for sure. The only certainty about her illness was that her condition seemed to deteriorate after her daughter left home.

Emilia slid into a depression that lasted for many months. Allen was desperate for her to be happy again but felt totally helpless. "How are you feeling," he'd ask his wife for lack of anything else to say.

"I'm not sure what I'm feeling," she replied. "But whatever it is, I want it to go away. Make everything just go away," she'd cry on Allen's shoulder late at night, when her feelings so often got in the way of her sleep.

After a couple of years passed, Emilia's nights gradually became more restful. The war was over, and she and Allen moved into a new house in West Springs. Her days were filled with decorating the house and sometimes socializing with new neighbors. When John Stone came to stay with them for a few months, he spoke of plans to split the Gettysburg house up into two sections, taking an apartment upstairs, and renting the downstairs to provide extra income.

"Is that okay with you? I mean, did you want me to keep it the way it is?" John asked his daughter.

"I think your idea is great, Dad. I don't have any plans of ever moving back there." Her childhood home no longer held the same memories. Whenever her mind would allow her to pleasantly remember the place, it would always end with her mother's back in the doorway.

"Before construction is started, I promise to send you some of your mother's things," John said. "I think she would've wanted you to have them."

"Sure, whatever you say," Emilia coldly responded.

"Are you certain about the house?" he questioned, once again.

"I'm very certain. I've never been more certain of anything," she said, reassuringly.

The years drifted by uneventfully, until 1956. By then, Allen had a very successful real-estate business. After two miscarriages, followed by years of infertility, Emilia was finally expecting their first child. But in her sixth month of pregnancy, she developed Preeclampsia and had to be admitted to a hospital to be closely watched. Day after day, Emilia sat staring at the four walls of her private room. Her solitude uncovered buried thoughts and feelings from which she could no longer escape.

Allen would visit with her before and after work. He'd bring her magazines, books and funny cards from the people in his office. But Emilia rarely smiled. She was cordial to the friends and neighbors who occasionally stopped by with flowers, glancing frequently at her wristwatch as they filled her in on local gossip. She wasn't interested in the flowers, cards or gossip. She didn't want those people there at all. Sometimes, she didn't care to see Allen, either. And, as her due date approached, she began to also feel she no longer wanted the baby she laid so still to protect from harm. What Emilia wanted was the only thing she couldn't have. There, in her fear and loneliness, she wanted the only person who could protect and comfort her at that trying time in her life. She wanted the person who turned her back on her. She wanted her mother.

John Stone passed away that year, the day after Christmas. He'd been ill for a few months, so his passing was not a shock. Still, Emilia took it hard. Since her condition would not allow her to go to the funeral, Allen went alone to take care of all the necessary arrangements. Emilia was grateful her circumstances, once again, kept her from the dreaded task of burying a parent.

When Allen returned several days later, he found his wife in labor, two weeks before her due date. Mandy was born ten minutes before the clock struck the New Year. As the doctor handed Emilia her new daughter, he asked, "What's her name?"

Allen looked at his wife, and said, "It's Sarah, of course."

"No!" Emilia adamantly replied. "I want to name her Amanda, after my grandmother. I'll call her Mandy."

"But why?" Allen asked, in shock.

"Because Grams was always there for me," she answered.

The next morning, an unusual winter storm developed, mixing snow with electricity. The thunder rattled the window in her room, causing baby Mandy to respond with a scream. Emilia carefully placed the baby down on the bed beside her, turned away and whispered, "Don't be frightened little one. It's only the lions roaring."

A deluge of water descended on Peter and Emily as they drove to the Peach Orchard section of the battlefield. After pulling over to the side of the road, they jumped out of the car and tried to manually lift the heavy folded roof of the convertible, hysterically laughing at every fumble. Once that was done, they got back into the Corvette, and Peter turned on the heater. "I never thought I'd have to use this in the middle of June," he said.

Emily pushed the wet hair away from her face and used a tissue to wipe the excess raindrops that glistened atop her delicate, light skin. Peter was mesmerized as he watched her glide the tissue around her face, neck and chest. When she leaned over to wipe his cheek, he grasped her hand, gently kissed it and drew her shoulders closer to him. He kissed her mouth, and she succumbed by wrapping her arms around him. Locked in an embrace, their wet bodies were so close; they each could not tell whose heartbeat they were feeling.

Emily felt a rush of excitement with his kiss that she'd never felt with Bill. Peter felt her body press against his, and knew she needed to be kissed almost as much as he needed to kiss her. He was rapt in passion when suddenly a face flashed across his mind, the same face that had once haunted his most intimate moments. Alessa. He opened his eyes, and quickly pulled away from the embrace, catching his breath.

Emily was left bewildered. Peter saw her puzzled look and needed to console her. He took a deep breath and leaned into her again, pressing his lips hard against hers when a bolt of lightning hit a tree near the road. They separated in shock just in time to see the smoke escaping from its bark.

"Now, that's a kiss," he said, causing her to blush. His light-hearted remark masked the feelings that lingered long after the disturbing image had reappeared.

They sat for nearly a half-hour watching the light show over the hills and fields surrounding them. "It's so exciting, isn't it?" he remarked after another bolt flashed across the sky.

"I don't know," she said. "I still can't get past the danger to relax and enjoy its beauty."

"Don't be afraid," Peter said, pulling her close again. "I'll protect you."

Emily did feel very safe with him. She offered, "When I was little, I used to sit up to all hours of the night nervously anticipating a storm if one was approaching. I guess even as a child, I felt it would be better to be awake, and prepared for it, rather than jolted out of bed from a sound sleep, caught totally off guard. Grams would come into my room and say, 'It's only the lions. They can't hurt you. They can only hurt themselves.' 'But Grams,' I'd say, 'I don't want them to get hurt either.' She'd smile and say that the choice was up to them whether that happened, and there wasn't much we could do about it. I stayed awake long after the storm passed, and prayed the lions would be all right. What did you think, Peter?" she asked.

His eyes were wide in amazement at her colorful description of a saying he'd taken for granted over the years. "Well," he said. "I just thought there were lions roaring."

"That's it?"

He sheepishly nodded, feeling somehow that his childhood was cheated.

The rain was still pounding the pavement hard when he drove her home. "I'm sorry we didn't get to see very much today," he said.

"There'll be plenty of time to see the rest. I'm not going anywhere," she replied.

"I'm glad for that. We can do this at the same time tomorrow. And it's also my night off, so I can take you out on the town, if that's okay with you."

"I can't wait," she said, and kissed him goodbye. "Don't bother escorting me to the door, it's raining too hard."

Peter watched her run toward the apartment entrance on the side of the building, using her purse as a shield against the rain. He waited there until she was safe inside before driving away.

Chapter Sixteen

"Hello, dear girl," Mandy greeted her daughter with a lilting tone, after Emily ran to answer the phone. The daily check-in from her mother was beginning to annoy her. *Dear girl? Who was she talking to?*

"How was your day today?" Mandy asked.

"It was wonderful. Peter took me to the college Grams and Grandpa went to. In a way, I'm sorry I didn't listen to Grams and attend Gettysburg College. How old was I when you and Dad brought me down here?"

"I think you were either two or three years old," Mandy said. "I'm not sure, but I know it was before you started nursery school."

"Why didn't we come down more often?"

"Oh, I don't know," Mandy replied. "I guess there really wasn't any reason to go, and nothing there interested me."

Emily rolled her eyes. It always amazed her how superficial her mother could be. Her comment about nothing interesting in Gettysburg was so incomprehensible, even for her, because her own mother grew up there. Emilia had been so knowledgeable about the history of the town and often spoke to her about it with such enthusiasm. Emily wondered why that enthusiasm didn't rub off on Mandy. *Nothing of interest here? What's wrong with her?*

"Well, what about Grams," Emily asked. "Why didn't she come back here, at least to visit?"

Mandy hesitated before responding. "My father said something about bad feelings but never explained it any further. Besides, you probably know more about that than I do."

"What do you mean?" Emily asked.

"She always found time to have those intimate discussions with you about her life in that place. She never had much time for me."

There was a definite brusqueness in Mandy's comment. Emily picked up on it and was surprised. She knew their relationship was not the best in later years, but it never dawned on her that Grams hadn't spent the same quality of conversation with Mandy when she was a child.

"Well mother, maybe she sensed your lack of interest. How long were we down here?"

"Just one day. We had to straighten out some business with the house, so we were only there for a few hours. Mrs. Angst has been wonderful all these years, helping Emilia to manage the place. She's been paid so little for all she does."

"Well after all, she and Grams were very good childhood friends," Emily said.

"Really?" Mandy remarked. "I didn't know that."

Oh no! More privileged information. Emily changed the subject by asking, "What's new with you?"

"Well, I have some exciting news. Zach finally has some time off. We're going to the Larsons' house over at the beach. We'll be there for a few days, so I won't be able to call you as often. Will you be alright?"

"I'll be fine," she replied. "I'm so happy you and Zach can get away. I think you both really need time together."

"What do you mean?" Mandy asked.

"I mean, with all the long hours he's been putting in on that new case, it'll be nice to have some time together. That's all."

Emily was cautious. She knew things about Zach her mother

didn't. Serious things, upsetting things, and she didn't know how to handle all that she knew.

"How's Peter?" Mandy asked, in a playful tone.

"He's great. Handsome, smart, sensitive."

"Now, don't get too carried away with him," Mandy warned.

"Carried away? What are you talking about?"

"Do I have to spell it out for you?" Mandy said, lowering her voice. "I think you know what I'm talking about. Just be careful with what you give away."

Emily strained to keep from laughing into the phone. She and Mandy never had those intimate mother-daughter talks, so sex wasn't a subject either of them felt comfortable in discussing. Her mother just assumed, perhaps hoped, she hadn't yet given anything away, even at her age. Mandy never realized Emily had lost her virginity to Bill, years before. In her eyes, she was still untouched, and pure, at least by her standards.

"Don't worry," Emily said. "I'm always a lady." A good response she thought, at least one Mandy would be able to handle.

The doorbell rang, and Emily rushed down the steps hoping it was Peter. To her surprise, she found her tenant, Joel Levy, standing in the light rain, holding a plate of cookies.

"Hello Miss Tomaso," he said, in an almost breathy whisper. "I'm starting to get a cold, so please forgive me, but I just wanted you to have these."

"Thank you," she said as she took the cookies. "Did you bake them?"

"No," he responded, "Mike did."

Even in their brief meeting, she had Joel pegged as the more domestic one. He was quite effeminate compared to the rugged, masculine, good-looking Mike. She naturally thought Joel would be the baker in the family, a sexist thought, even for a gay couple.

"They look delicious, Mr. Levy. Thanks again."

"You're welcome," he replied "Please call me Joel. Mike and I would like to invite you to lunch tomorrow at Noon."

"Tomorrow, that's Wednesday, isn't it?" she stumbled. Emily had absolutely no desire of ever sharing a social relationship with these two men, however brief, even if they shared the same building. Joel seemed to be a very sweet, and good-natured individual, but Mike frightened her. She could tell he didn't like her. She didn't like him, either. She needed an excuse, and she needed one fast. "I have plans tomorrow but thank you anyway."

"Then Thursday," Joel insisted.

"We'll see. I'll let you know tomorrow."

After he left, Emily began to think of a good excuse for Thursday, mumbling under her breath, "God, he's persistent."

She took a chocolate chip cookie, and walked over to the window to see the two of them leave. Six o'clock on the dot, they proceeded to walk out toward their car. Mike took a hold of Joel's arm. It wasn't an affectionate hold, she thought, more like a protective one. Emily then wondered if Joel was ill. She was sorry she hadn't invited him in from the rain. Mike glanced up at her after Joel said something to him, but that time, it was Emily who looked away, feeling ashamed. Her thoughts then drifted to a place she didn't want to revisit, and she was sad once again.

Zach had been a surrogate father to Emily ever since he married her mother. Kind and understanding, he had many of her father's attributes. The harmony he created in a house filled with discord a couple of years after Andrew's murder, was more than just welcome. It was a blessing.

He was a compassionate referee during the many arguments with Mandy. After each ordeal, Zach provided a warm shoulder upon which Emily could rest her head, consoled by his soft voice.

There were many lunch meetings with Zach over the years where she'd fill him in on all her classes, teachers and new friends. And for him, it was a time to share interesting stories about the people he'd met, too. They were always first to queue at the local theater to see the newest action movie. Then, after the movie, they'd spend time discussing the plot and characters over fast food.

Wise and sensitive, Zach was always available to give her advice. In fact, it was a need for his advice that completely altered their relationship.

Grams had provided the money for Emily to purchase a new car to replace the ten-year-old Volvo, which got her safely back and forth to college. She'd been leaning towards another Volvo but needed his opinion. Emily knew he was in his office, because when she arrived there, she could hear his voice in conversation.

Zach's secretary, Louise, was out to lunch, so she waited briefly for him to end the discussion with the person to whom he was speaking before knocking on the door. As she got closer to his office, she could hear a low moan, and the sound of lips touching and separating. She turned to leave, thinking her mother might have been with him, but another voice broke the passion. After noticing that the door to his office was slightly ajar, Emily hesitated for a moment, took a deep breath, and gently pushed it open. There lying prone on the couch, was her beloved stepfather, naked, in an embrace with another man.

Emily grabbed her stomach and ran toward the office bathroom. Her head was spinning as she knelt over the toilet and threw up her lunch.

"Emily darling," Zach called after her. "My poor girl." He gave her a wet paper towel for her head as he tucked his shirt into his pants.

"I'm not your girl!" she snapped, as she ran out of the office, pushing past the tall, handsome stranger who had taken the place of her mother. Weeks later, she would come to know the stranger as her stepfather's colleague, Carl Manera.

Chapter Seventeen

The rain fell harder, pounding against Emily's parlor window as she looked out on a sky growing forebodingly dark. The apartment lights began to flicker and dim. A howling wind wrestled the branches of a nearby tree until one limb snapped off in defeat. The wooden shutters that rested loosely against the house rattled so—she was sure they'd come undone. She then heard the outside storm door opening and closing, as if blown by the wind. She thought she'd locked the door after Joel left but had some doubt.

When Emily got up to investigate, she heard what sounded like the rustling and shaking of wet clothes. There was then the distinct sound of heavy feet ascending the stairs. She ran to the inside door, once satisfied it was bolted shut, placed her ear against it to listen. The footsteps seemed to move slowly, as if laden by a weight of some sort, there was a muffled sound of heavy breathing and a sloshing sound of water dripping. When the noises finally reached the top step, they stopped. She stood motionless for what seemed a long time hoping to out-silence her unwanted guest and hear what he or she would do next. No other sounds were heard.

Emily rushed over to the telephone and put her hand on the

receiver. *I need to call someone. Whom should I call?* Phone numbers from home began twirling in her head. She took several deep breaths to calm herself down. It worked. She then assessed her next move. After gathering some courage, she grabbed the iron poker and walked back to the door, briefly listened once more to the silence, held her breath, and slowly opened it. The stairway was empty, no intruder, not even an indication that rain-drenched feet had just climbed there. Running down to inspect both outside doors, she found they too were locked shut just as she had suspected.

When the telephone rang, she was relieved to hear Peter's voice. "I just wanted to warn you that the weather service says the storm will be getting worse, and we may lose power. Are you prepared for a black-out?" he asked.

Emily was happy he seemed concerned. "Yes. I have matches and candles, so I'll be alright," she replied, surprised by her bravery.

"I probably won't get there tonight, but I'll call you first thing in the morning. Are you sure you'll be okay?" he asked again.

"I'll be fine," she said. "Thanks for the warning."

"Now, don't stay up too late worrying about the lions," he teased.

Emily giggled and kissed the mouthpiece before hanging up. She intentionally did not tell Peter what just happened. All that day, especially at the college, she acted so strange, and was convinced, should she bring up this new, odd experience, he would surely think her mad. She was beginning to question her own sanity. Still, there was a need to tell someone. She opened the desk drawer and took out the paper with Mrs. Angst's phone number on it.

Emily began explaining to the woman what had just happened. "Has anyone ever thought that this place was haunted?" her voice cracked.

"No," Mrs. Angst assured her. "There's never been any complaint like that. Besides, why are you frightened in a place you should find so much comfort? That house belonged to your grandmother, and all your mothers and fathers before her. If there is a ghost, it's bound to be the spirit of one of your ancestors."

"But there's no such thing as ghosts, " Emily stated. She quickly added, less assuredly, "Is there?"

"Would that be so terrible?" Mrs. Angst replied.

"Yes, I mean, I don't know," Emily answered, feeling more uneasy, and sorry she brought up the subject.

Mrs. Angst picked up on her fear, and said, "So much of what haunts us has nothing to do with the dead. It's the living we're haunted by, like our own relationships and transgressions."

Emily listened to the lecture-like response from the wise woman who was so much like Grams. Mrs. Angst ended the conversation with, "Be brave child, and look inside yourself for the answers you seek."

"But I'm not even sure of the questions," Emily said.

"Hearing with your ears and seeing with your eyes are not enough. You must listen with your heart and *feel* with your soul."

She only understood half of what Mrs. Angst said but was consoled and more relaxed by the time their conversation had ended.

Emily sat by the window for the next hour, and watched the angry sky grow darker in the storm and approaching night. Looking at her wristwatch, she saw it was almost nine o'clock just before another bolt of lightning cracked the apple tree across the street in two. The lights went out a few minutes later.

She fumbled in the dark to light the lavender scented candles, and settled into the rocker, hoping the night would pass quickly. Just after sitting down though, she jumped up fearing the candles would burn the pictures near them on the mantel. Looking around for a safer spot, she remembered Mrs. Angst's suggestion and placed them inside of the hearth.

The light from the candles reflected off the brick and cast a lovely glow around the room. Feeling quite content, she rocked slowly and listened to the "lions roaring" outside her window, for the storm was not letting up.

She placed a flashlight and her booklight beside her on the

rocker and while still seated glanced over to the case holding the books and magazines. *I need to read something really distracting,* she thought. That's when the room became cold and she once again felt no longer alone.

Again she heard footsteps, that time right behind her inside the apartment. Emily was frozen in place as a lightheaded feeling took over. Her heart began to race and her rapid breathing grew more shallow as the feeling of a ghostly presence grew more profound. When she felt what she thought was an icy hand on her shoulder she couldn't stand the fear any longer. She jumped up from her seat, swung around, frantically flashing the light around the room with one hand while the other hand braced the table near the rocker to steady her shaking body. She was alone and the cold air was suddenly gone.

What's happening to me? Am I imagining all this? She stood for a few moments to regain some composure, glancing in every corner of the dark space. *There's nobody here. It must be my imagination. It's got to be that.* It was then she noticed on the table under her hand was the book she'd placed aside the night before. She sat back down and picked it up. *What is this?* "Witness to Tribulation," she read aloud, and opened to the first handwritten page.

Remember ... May the Lord have mercy on my soul, and that of my precious family. As I write this, the men in gray have entered our homes and taken some of our food. Many of our neighbors have fled the impending peril that has been predicted these past two weeks, but we have chosen to stay. Alas my poor Jonas, by virtue of his trade, has been summoned to assist in what will be necessary in the days to come.

Emily stopped reading and turned back to the first page to read the title again," Witness to Tribulation", and closed the book. Inspecting the cover, she noticed a worn area near the bottom marked, *1863.*

Oh my. This is about the Civil War! Though she could hardly believe her eyes, she read on, so focused, she forgot about the storm, and all else that had occurred up to that point.

I have taken the opportunity to keep the oven lit a little longer each day to bake extra loaves of bread. My dear brother, Stephen Klee, who resides with us, has closed his haberdashery in town and hid what clothing he could from the certain pilferage that will occur. My daughters Amanda and Sarah, now aged four and five years, have stayed close by my side, sensing the danger that lurks around every corner.

I've kept the curtains drawn all through the day and night to protect my own from the peering eyes of strangers. The children have asked to go out to play, but I have persisted in keeping them somewhat amused indoors with the cloth dolls I sew long into the night as they sleep. Sarah though has developed a cough these past two days, and I fear her condition will worsen without access to a doctor.

For days now, the soldiers have come, some on horse-back, most of them on foot, and marched past our home in continuous succession. I have watched them through the small opening between the curtain panels. Placing our Bible to my chest, I ask the Lord and his Mother to help me find compassion for these intruders. They come from Virginia, North Carolina, and Georgia, my fellow countrymen turned enemy. These same faces but a few short years ago might have passed through town on a journey to a city north and were offered a refreshing drink at our well. Perhaps we shared a mid-day meal. Now we must close them out, parched from the sun, starved, some with bare feet, blistered and bruised.

My dear friend, Abigail Wells, visits us late each night, bringing news from the center of town. There her husband, Dr. Wells has kept vigil at a hospital that has been arranged in Pennsylvania College to wait for what is to come. She returns there each night with many loaves of my bread to help sustain our neighbors who have also remained. I will ask Abigail this night to bring medicine for Sarah when she returns tomorrow. I pray that she will be well...E.W.

Emily stumbled to the kitchen in the dark for a glass of water. She clutched the book tightly while quenching her thirst and looked around the room.

She inspected the book and found it had the same handwriting and initials, E.W. Going back to the inside cover to the signature, she carefully studied the sharp curves, and flattened letters until she was able to make it out. Emilia Wahler: Grams' namesake. Her namesake.

She took the flashlight along as she began going through all the drawers, and closets in the apartment, trying to find pictures or other documents that might have belonged to her great-great-great-grandmother. She wanted to see an image of the woman who left the descriptive account of a story she's known about most of her life. She wondered if Grams ever saw this diary. Perhaps that's where she got all the stories she used to tell. While looking for papers in the crawl space of the dreaded bedroom, she wondered maybe then she knew who her ghost was, if indeed she had one. But nothing was found.

Upon returning to the parlor, Emily noticed that the storm had ended. No longer afraid to be there alone, she opened the book, and read the first writing over again, soon realizing however, she could no longer read. She finally fell asleep, barely noticing the sound of the rhythmic hammer, which had begun once again outside her window.

Chapter Eighteen

A Time for Remembrance

Emily was awake by dawn. She could hear the same hammer tirelessly pounding away, but she did not get up to investigate. She knew it would end shortly after sunrise, fading away almost as unnoticeably as it began.

Peter called later, as promised. "That was some storm," he said. "How did you make out?"

"Thank goodness I had some candles in the house, real good ones. They barely burned halfway," Emily said. "What happened at the restaurant?"

"We actually did great business," he said, laughing. "People who were stuck there just kept ordering food."

"Peter, can we skip the tour today?"

"Sure," he said. "What's up?"

"I just want to get some shopping done. We'll see each other tonight, right?"

"Yes, we will. There's this terrific restaurant in town, the Dobbins House. You'll love the ambiance there. May I pick you up at seven o'clock?"

"It sounds really nice. I'll see you then," she said.

Emily almost told him about the diary but wasn't sure she

wanted to share it with anyone just yet. She walked back to the rocker and opened the book. The second writing began just as the first, with the word, "Remember," and at the end, the initials, E.W. She began to read,

Remember...May the Lord have mercy on the souls of this family...

She stopped. The bright light of day and the noise from the saws cutting up a tree that fell in the storm were too distracting. "Well, it's been here this long," she said. "I'm sure it will keep until tonight." She looked around the apartment for an appropriate hiding place to store the treasured heirloom and finally chose to put it under the mattress of her unmade bed.

Emily tripped over another bouquet of flowers as she walked to her car. The bouquet was very similar to the one she'd received the previous day, except the new one had a red ribbon attached to it. Again, she looked around, but no one was there.

She got behind the wheel of her car, anxious to begin her quest. Not a quest for groceries, as she had alluded to Peter, her mission that day was to find information on a part of her family, long forgotten. The diary she found ignited an intense desire to know more about the person who wrote it. Her first stop was the Gettysburg Public Library, which she thought would be the most likely place to obtain information on local families.

She spoke at length to the librarian, who referred her to several books by local authors. After thumbing through them to no avail, she spotted a young man sitting at a desk in what appeared to be the Head Librarian's office.

"May I help you?" he asked.

"Maybe, but I'm not sure."

"Well, what is it you want?" he added, impatiently.

A closer look at the man showed he was not as young as she

initially thought. He seemed more middle aged, with thinning hair and a deep wrinkle between his eyes hidden somewhat by large, black, horn-rimmed glasses.

"Well, I need to look up some local families," she said.

"Why come here?" he questioned, curtly. "Why not check the local directory?"

"No," Emily said, and smiled. "I don't think you understand. I'm looking for information on my family, but they haven't lived here for a very long time. Do you have a newspaper archive?"

"Of course we do. Just follow me."

He led her down a long hallway, passing conference tables and occupied computer terminals, to another desk that had a large book on top. "Just sign here," he said. "There are only two other people ahead of you waiting to use the viewers. What month and year are you interested in anyway?" he asked.

Emily swallowed hard. "Let's just say any month, 1863."

He stopped organizing papers, pushed his eyeglasses low on his nose, looked over them directly at her, and took a deep breath. "I'm not sure we have that information," he said. "No, I don't think we do. Why didn't you do that research before visiting Gettysburg?" he asked. Before she could reply, he lowered his voice to almost a whisper, and added, "You know, I'm very sorry to have to say this, but I'm getting a little sick of you tourists who come here all year long looking for a connection to this place."

Emily stood with her mouth open, not certain what words would come out. She wanted to tell this pompous, self-righteous individual that she was not just a tourist. She was a homeowner, soon to be taxpayer, with a lineage there that may even surpass his. Instead, she chose a soapbox lecture by noting, "Oh really? So you're sick of us, are you?

"I must let you in on this little secret: Just because you reside here doesn't mean you have exclusive rights. That battlefield held the blood of people from many corners of this country; so, don't act as if you're holding a special ticket. Maybe we are so moved by what we see here that we feel a connection to this place, however contrived it may seem to *you*. But every American already has a connection to it. We don't need anyone to tell us that, and we certainly don't need your approval. Furthermore, don't knock the tourists. They're the ones who provide most of the livelihood here."

She smiled to herself as she walked away. Her spontaneous courage and wit surprised her, even though she borrowed a few lines from Peter. Passing a table where several high school students were seated, she noticed they were applauding her. One of the girls in the group caught her eye.

"Don't worry," the girl said. "He just moved here a few years ago. He's not like us," she motioned to the rest in her group. "We like tourists." She added, "Do you know the name?"

"Excuse me?" Emily asked.

"Your family name. Do you know it?" the girl asked again.

"Why sure," Emily replied.

"Then I know where you can get that information: the cemetery. Ask someone in the office there and they'll even map out where you should look. It's really cool. You should go."

"Yes, of course," she responded. "Thank you."

Emily drove by the brick arch in front of the town's oldest cemetery, which backed up against the Soldier's National Cemetery. That's where her information might be held, but she decided to put it off for another day so she could get in some shopping before heading home to get ready for her date.

Driving through the streets, she passed houses and other buildings that were now familiar to her thanks to Peter. Everything and everyone seemed so much friendlier with him by her side.

But she knew he was just one part of her life there so far, and she couldn't always depend on him to adjust. She had to learn to rely on herself. *I'm doing pretty well.*

Turning into the narrow driveway of her home, she noticed Joel Levy sitting inside his office near the front window. Emily accelerated slightly hoping he hadn't seen her as she turned the car around the back of the building. But he greeted her anyway by her apartment door.

"I knew that was you," he said, and gave her a big smile.

"Hello Joel," she returned the smile.

"What a night we had," he said.

"Yes," she replied. "Plenty of lions around."

Joel furrowed his brow. It was then she realized he was not native to Gettysburg. "I was referring to the thunder," she explained.

"Oh, yes. It was terrible. Mike and I were wondering if you would join us for lunch tomorrow."

"Sure," she said, for lack of a good excuse. And then quickly added, "May I bring a friend?"

"Your friend is also welcome," Joel said. "Come to the office at noon. I'm so happy we'll have a chance to get to know one another."

As Joel walked away, he muffled a cough, and Emily thought he didn't look very well.

The flowers found at her doorstep that morning matched those received the previous day, though the newest bouquet was slightly wilted after sitting all afternoon in a hot car. She immediately placed them in a vase that held the other blooms and wondered who left them. She knew they weren't from Mrs. Angst, nor were they from Peter, a realization that saddened her a little. She thought briefly of Joel Levy but quickly dismissed that notion. He'd just seen her with wilted flowers in hand and would have said something about it if they were from him. *Who could it be?*

Chapter Nineteen

Emily opened the doors to her closet and began searching for an outfit to wear that night. She was plenty prepared for casual dates with sneakers and jeans, but an elegant restaurant required something else. She pulled out a little blue slip-dress purchased in a moment of weakness. The price tag and manufacturer's tickets were still attached.

She removed her robe and stood in front of the long, narrow mirror that hung on the back of the bathroom door. Emily recalled the times, early in their relationship, when she and Bill made love late at night in his family's basement. She always insisted on having the lights turned off.

Bill always thought it was to protect them from getting caught. But she was just self-conscious about him seeing her naked. Now, as she studied every curve of her slender body, she thought, *I'm not so bad.* She slid the silk dress over her head.

Peter arrived at seven o'clock, looking very handsome in a gray suit, white shirt, and red paisley tie. His thick blond hair was pulled back tight, secured with a rubber band.

He followed her up to the apartment, sprinting up the steep staircase with one hand behind his back. When he reached the top step, he presented her with a bouquet of white roses, with baby's-breath tucked in between the stems.

"Thank you. They're so beautiful," she said.

"So are you," Peter said, staring at her scant dress. Glancing over to the kitchen table, he noticed the mystery wildflowers overflowing in the vase. "Oh, I see you already have some."

"I can't imagine who's been leaving them at my doorstep every morning, "Emily said. "It happened again today."

"A secret admirer?" he asked.

"Perhaps," Emily smiled. "Or maybe just the welcome wagon," she added, consoling him with a kiss. She walked over to the table, removed the wildflowers, and replaced them with his bouquet. "My Grams used to love white roses."

"So beautiful, fragrant, and pure," he recited. "And yet, they're so fragile."

Emily had a sudden desire to tell him about the diary. She excused herself and walked into the bedroom to get it. But once she felt the stiff binding, secure under her mattress, she changed her mind.

The wood sign dangling from a post in the restaurant's parking lot noted that the stone structure was built in 1776 and is listed on the National Register of Historic Places. Peter explained, "Gettysburg operated several Underground Railroad Stations that provided safe shelter for runaway slaves on their journey North. One of them was located here inside this building. It's now a museum."

They walked over to peek into the pocket-sized rooms that were used for this purpose. Peter said, "Those poor people—sometimes as many as twenty-plus—had to spend several days here crowded together before they could be safely moved."

Emily tried to imagine how terrifying it must have been to be locked into that small space for days. She shook her head and solemnly remarked, "Bondage, even in freedom."

As they were escorted to their table, Emily imagined corseted women in large hoop skirts brushing past the mahogany and burl furniture. She wondered if Emilia Wahler had ever been there?

The low lighting darkened the rooms, giving the appearance of being lit solely by candles. Each room was decorated with antiques and arranged to maintain the home's original chambers. They were directed into the bedroom chamber upstairs and to a linen-draped table. The table was situated under a canopy, which was once part of a bed. It was so much like the one she avoided being under at her home. She stared up at the familiar covering. "Do you like it?" Peter asked.

"Yes, of course. This is wonderful. Thank you for inviting me here," she said.

Peter saw the light from the candle reflect in her eyes. It sent flickers of color dancing in her emerald-green pools, like waves gently rippling on a pond. He reached over, took her hand in his, and for the first time in a long time, he was totally speechless.

A waiter approached and handed him a wine list. "Red or white?" Peter asked her.

"Either is fine."

"Then let's go with a Pinot Noir. It's versatile for whatever we order."

She nodded, and the waiter took away the wine list, and replaced it with menus. "What's your pleasure?" Peter asked, looking over the menu.

"You seem to know what you're doing, so why not order for me," she replied.

"All right then, let's start with shrimp cocktail and Caesar salad. The Seaford Isabella is very good here, and so is the prime rib. Which do you prefer?"

"I guess prime rib," she said.

"We think alike," Peter said, smiling. Emily thought he might have blushed.

The waiter returned with their wine, uncorked the bottle, and gave Peter the cork to smell.

After pouring a small amount into his glass, Peter swirled it, tasted it, and nodded in approval for the waiter to continue filling the glasses. Emily was impressed. *He's been here before.*

The wine was smooth, and only slightly bitter, still holding on to the taste of the earth. She could feel the heat from the fluid going down her throat, entering every blood vessel, relaxing the muscles in her neck and shoulders.

"So, have you adjusted to your new home yet?" Peter asked.

"I'm getting there. It's just so different from East Springs."

"What was it like for you there?" he inquired.

Emily thought he meant her family life. "My life there is a long story. I don't think we'll have enough time to cover it all tonight. Let's just say, I'm free of that entrapment."

Peter realized she misunderstood but seized the opportunity to delve deeper into the history of the girl with whom he'd become infatuated. "Entrapment?" he repeated as he filled her wine glass to the top.

"I couldn't stay there anymore," she said. "At least not after Grams died. There really wasn't much left for me."

"But, what about your mother?" he asked. "She's alone now, isn't she? You mentioned that your father died."

"Well, she's remarried," she said, lowering her head. "Anyway, my mother and I don't get along. We have very different views on life."

"Like what?"

"For instance, she'd feel right at home in a place like this," she said, waving her hand around the room. "However, she wouldn't take into consideration the history that abounds here, such as the furniture, the pewter, the antique plates on display in that cabinet. And look at these wide floorboards. You know they were probably made from trees that were once in the surrounding area. Things are only important to her if they're expensive and look nice," she concluded.

"Well, you too can superficially appreciate this place, can't you? They are after all, as you say, only things," he noted.

Emily took another sip of wine and didn't respond.

"Tell me what your father was like," Peter continued to interrogate.

"Andrew Tomaso was a great man who truly felt as though his mission in life was to protect people. He was an undercover narcotics officer. He used to say; 'Now listen Emily, there's a war going on all around us.' He spoke about a war of crime and injustice where drug pushers and their kingpins jeopardized innocent lives. He thought that every arrest he made saved his family and friends from one more threat to their lives." After taking a large gulp of wine, she added, "Unfortunately, he didn't include his own in that hypothesis. He was killed in the line of duty."

"How old were you?" he asked.

"Almost twelve."

"I can't imagine being so young and losing a parent."

"It was the abruptness of it that was even more devastating. No warning, no chance to say goodbye or tell him that I love him one more time. At least with Grams, I was prepared."

"You and your grandmother were very close, weren't you?"

"Close?" Emily said, tightening her grip on the glass. "That was before Dad died. After him, she was everything to me."

She released the glass, took a deep breath, and began twisting her college ring around her finger. "I think I'm being a little too hard on my mother, though. She did for me what she could do. The rest she knew would be taken care of by Grams."

"And your stepfather?" Peter asked.

Emily ignored his question, instead reached over to a bread-basket on the table. "I think I need to eat something to soak up this wine," she said, and began buttering one of the warm baguettes on her plate.

Peter joined her and was momentarily quiet, only then feeling as though he was prying.

After a few quiet moments, she broke the silence. "So, Peter, enough about me. How long have the Civelli and Sanders families lived here?"

"The Civellis are the more recent arrival at the turn of the twentieth century." He added laughing, "I guess even back then they realized a college town needed a pizzeria.

"But the Sanders family goes back almost as far as Mr. Gettys himself. They were farmers. In fact, my cousin still lives in the original Sanders homestead about a mile from here and runs a dairy on the property."

"I guess the Sanders family certainly did see their share of the Civil War then," Emily noted.

"Yes, they did. A few of my ancestors served with the Fourth Corps in the Army of the Potomac, but they missed this battle. My grandfather had a uniform that belonged to one of them. After he passed away, my grandmother donated it to the park service. She's held on to a few letters that were written home during other campaigns in the South.

"And then some members of the Sanders family assisted in the Underground Railroad. Not this station, another one that was just a few miles from here. I'm very proud of that."

"You should be," Emily said. "Sounds like your family provided plenty of information for your doctorate thesis. Did you write about the battle?"

"No," Peter said. "I researched and wrote about the growth of unions in the Industrialized North."

"Really?" Emily remarked. "I'm surprised."

"My head was in a different place in New York," Peter responded, pensively. He added, "Anyway, there's more to history than just the battle of Gettysburg or the Civil War." He paused for a moment before a smile flashed across his face. "But I have to admit, I'm enjoying reading about the battle and the war again. In fact, I'm preparing to include new information in several lectures next semester for a course I'm teaching about Gettysburg battle strategies and other mid-war engagements. "

"I'd be interested in hearing about it."

"Sure," Peter casually replied. "So now, tell me how far back does your family go here in town? You said your grandmother's name was Stone, and then Schmidt. Was your grandfather from here, too?"

"No. My grandfather was from New York. He met Grams here while they attended Gettysburg College."

"No kidding," he said, widening his grin.

"Yes Peter," she smiled. "They might have sat in your classroom. But you know that was the last time she was here. Three days after graduation they married, and promptly left town so my grandfather could accept a job offer.

"In spite of all the enthusiastic stories, and the discussions we'd have about the town's history and all, she never came back. It didn't really dawn on me how strange that was until I arrived here. My mother said something about bad feelings, but I doubt she knows the real reason. I don't think anyone ever did. It's almost as if she couldn't return."

"Maybe this town was her entrapment," Peter said.

Emily ignored his comment and said, "She died this past March, right before my twenty-fourth birthday. I wanted her to be buried here with the rest of her family in the cemetery on the other side of town. I felt she belonged here. But my mother insisted she should be buried in New York with my grandfather."

"That's understandable," Peter said.

"I guess so. Well, all that's in the past, and now I'm here with you in this beautiful place," she said, smiling while holding out her glass for a refill.

"It's good to see you smile again. Now, let's get back to your family tree," he said, filling her glass. "Who came before the Stone family?"

"Well, before the Stones, the family name was Jacobs." She held the wine glass to her lips, and added, "Before that, the family name was Wahler. Have you ever heard that name mentioned before?"

He shook his head. She continued speaking, "I really do want to learn more about them. I know that my great-great-great-grandmother Emilia Wahler's maiden name was Klee. Her brother Stephen owned a clothing store in town, and they were one of the families who remained in Gettysburg during the battle."

"My goodness," he said. "Did your Grams tell you all this?"

"Yes," Emily said, hoping he didn't pick up on her lie. Emilia was very explicit in describing what life growing up there was like, and the town's history, but avoided any information that dealt specifically with her own family, other than mentioning their ancestors' names.

"I went to the Public Library and met this nasty librarian. Anyway, they don't keep records that old there," Emily noted

"Forget the library," Peter said. "I'll take you to our historical society headquarters. They retain information on local families. I'm sure they have plenty available on yours."

"That's great," she said, excited. "Where's it located?"

"That's the best part. It's on campus, downstairs in my building, Old Dorm."

He said this as she was taking a drink of wine, causing her to nervously begin to cough. *That horrible place.* Realizing she wouldn't be able to go back there alone, she asked him, "Will you help me tomorrow?"

"Actually, I can't," he said. "I'll be in Philadelphia at a seminar all day. Maybe the day after that?"

Upon realizing he would also miss the luncheon with her tenants, she sighed. "Don't look so sad," Peter said. "You can't get rid of me that easily."

Near the end of their dinner, Emily noticed she was on her fourth glass of wine. "Peter," she said, "I'm drinking too much."

"Well, I have to drive," he responded.

"But I feel like such a lush."

"No. Not you, dear Emily," he softly assured her.

Chapter Twenty

The night was still young by the time Peter and Emily left the restaurant. As they strolled to his car hand in hand, she said, "It's so nice out. Let's go for a drive."

Peter smiled, and said while opening the car door, "You took the words right out of my mouth. I know a perfect spot."

After lowering the top of the convertible, he proceeded to drive very fast down the straight, narrow street enveloped in blackness, and then onto an endless highway that stretched for miles passing farms and open tracts of land. The full moon shone brightly, outlining a silhouette of the hills surrounding them.

"What are you doing?" Emily shouted out above the sound of the raging motor.

"I'm keeping my promise," Peter said, with a playful nod. "Just showing you what my 'little car', as you called it, can do. Yeeeaaagh," he yelled, playfully.

"Yeeeaagh," Emily echoed, and tilted her head back against the rushing air, and released her hair clip. The wind blew through her long locks sending a moonlit veil of bronze and gold brushing past Peter's face. She didn't ask him where he was taking her; she trusted him and didn't care why. The past few days were the first time in a long time she felt carefree, and more than that, she was beginning to feel good about her life.

There was a fork up ahead in the road where large blue and gold-colored signs were beginning to appear near the shoulder. Peter slowed the car to almost a stop and pointed to one reading Hanover, Next Exit. "This is where you'll be coming to work in September," he said. "It's not so far. It only took us fifteen minutes."

"That's with *you* driving," she said, and laughed. "I think it'll take me almost twice as long." He exited the highway, and drove through a residential neighborhood where newer, ranch-style houses alternated with old, wooden farmhouse-type dwellings. The town almost mirrored Gettysburg in character, but was smaller, and a lot quieter.

At a stop sign, a group of teenagers crossed in front of their car. Emily looked into their faces and wondered if she would be seeing any of them in her school come fall.

"Here it is," Peter said as he pulled into a parking lot. "Hanover Junior/ Senior High School."

He casually draped his arm around her shoulders as they sat on the school's steps. "What were your junior high school days like? I bet you broke a lot of hearts," he said.

"Not quite. It was pretty boring."

"No boyfriends?" he asked, incredulous.

"Oh, I had a boyfriend in college, but not in junior or senior high. I guess you could say I was a late bloomer. A lot of my friends had boyfriends back then though. They'd go to all the football games and parties, and I'd just think they were acting silly. What's the importance of it all? I was the smartest girl in school, and they'd all come to me before midterms and finals to help them study. Now, that was more important than anything, so why didn't they realize that when they were out partying?"

"Because they were teenagers," Peter said, chuckling. He asked, more seriously, "Did you turn your back on them?"

"Of course not. That's how I kept friends."

"That's pretty sad."

"Why would you say that?' Emily asked.

"Because they were only friends with you when it was convenient for them."

She pondered Peter's comment, before adding, "Deep down I always knew it wasn't their fault. They were only acting their age. I was the one who was different. Never allowed to date or join in with them, at least until I started sneaking out. But I didn't do that very often either.

"My mother filled my head with all these bizarre situations she thought could happen when teenagers had too much freedom. She had successfully managed to convince me of the dangers that lurked beyond the protection of home. Grams would try to tell her that teenagers need a little bit of freedom, but she wouldn't listen. She'd say that I was her daughter, and she'd have to raise me as she saw fit, and that would be the end of the discussion. But it was Grams who really raised me, you know. Mandy would just jump in occasionally and flex her muscles."

"You missed an important part of your childhood," he said. "Still, I guess you must assume some responsibility for that, too. I mean, most kids wouldn't tolerate such a strict lifestyle. I can understand your anger toward your mother, though."

"Anger? I hated her! I hated the way she acted after Dad died, like everything else in her life died with him. For the longest time she barely noticed I was there. The shock of my father's death left her not quite right, if you know what I mean."

"Yes," he said. "I see how that could happen under those circumstances. So, in a way then, it wasn't her fault, either."

Peter touched a nerve, igniting feelings Emily had never felt before, and she was suddenly lost for words.

"We're all victims of circumstances at some point in our lives," Peter said. "I was also considered a high achiever in school. All the hard work was focused on reaching my ultimate goal, which was to attend Harvard University. I was intrigued by the school's history, Boston, the famous alumni. My parents thought I'd attend college here, but when I was accepted there, they supported me.

"I studied day and night. And even though I didn't miss as much as you did, sacrifices were made. When I finally arrived at Harvard,

I thought my life was complete. Then, I had to leave after barely finishing one semester. I was crushed, thinking I'd never be happy anywhere else, but I survived."

"You didn't mention you attended Harvard," she said. "Why did you leave?"

"I … I just had to," he said.

There was an uncomfortable feeling about the conversation that Emily sensed should go no further. She put her arms around him and said, "I'm sorry that happened to you. You know, you're so right. We all manage to survive, yet sometimes it's hard."

Tears filled her eyes as she continued, "Why is it always the innocent victims of circumstances, the bystanders so to speak, who are the ones that suffer the most? They're the people who are forced to live through the consequences of other people's choices. It just isn't fair."

The gravity in Emily's voice stirred concern. Peter suddenly stood up from where he was seated beside her, bent down to gently cradle her face in his hands, and said defiantly, "But we did survive, Emily. We'll continue to survive or else, what's the alternative? You must accept what you can't change, and try to change the things that you can, whatever the circumstances."

His abruptness startled her. She became quiet, only then realizing he was talking about more than just leaving Harvard.

Peter recoiled upon seeing her reaction to his comments. A moment later he flashed his toothy grin, and said, "So, what happened to the boyfriend?"

"It's a long story," Emily said, and smiled. "What about you? Any girlfriends in your past?" she asked, teasing.

"There were girlfriends," he said, and nodded.

"What happened to them?"

Peter took a deep breath, and said, "Long story."

The drive back to Gettysburg was slower and more sedate. She sat on the console between the bucket seats and rested her head on his shoulder. The lightheaded feeling experienced with the wine was wearing off, and she was getting very sleepy.

"You're not going to fall asleep on me, are you?" Peter asked, nudging her with his shoulder.

"Why? Where are we going?" she responded with a yawn.

"I told you," he said. "I know a great spot. This is the perfect night to go there."

"I thought you meant the school," Emily said, sitting up more awake.

Peter slowly shook his head.

They exited the highway and were once again on the narrow road in Gettysburg that runs through the center of town. He then turned onto one of the side roads that put them on track with the entrance to the National Military Park.

"Where are we going?" Emily nervously asked, after looking at her wristwatch. "We can't go in there. It's well after eleven o'clock. The park is closed."

"There are no gates to close us out. Besides I know most of the park rangers, they never bother me. Relax," Peter assured her. "You'll love it here."

The strange road curved around and began to climb until it became once again familiar. She recognized the area they traveled to the previous day, "Little Round Top?" she asked.

He nodded.

Leaning back in her seat she stared out toward their destination. Emily strained her eyes in the darkness trying to see something, but could only make out the outline of tall, straight trunks of trees on both sides of the road. They were close and uniform, as bars in a cell, crossing over one another above forming a tunnel-like appearance that she could only liken to being swallowed by a beast.

"Peter. It's so late. Please take me home."

"Trust me," he said, and made a sharp turn where signs were posted warning visitors to stay away. He inched the car a little further, parked on a rock plateau, and pointed to the scene beyond the front windshield. "Take a look at that," he said. The car was situated on a ledge considered one of the highest natural points in the park where the view was breathtaking.

As she looked out on the moon-lit terrain carved out of history, she said, "Oh my. Isn't that something?"

They sat quietly for a few moments looking out in awe. And then she asked, feeling more comfortable, "Is this a favorite parking spot for local teens?"

He smiled and moved closer to her. "Maybe not just teenagers," he said. After gently tilting her head, Peter pressed his lips to her forehead and encircled her face with caresses until finding her mouth. The yearning he'd felt since the start of their evening was unbridled in one long kiss, with only short interruptions to breath. The air was warm and wet. As he kissed her neck he tasted the salt from her sweat mixed with perfume.

She ran her hand through his hair and released the band that held his locks. Her fingers moved stealthily through the long wavy strands, and around his shoulders, chest and further down his body, tracing every inch of his handsome features. They remained in a passionate embrace, blocking out the passion of a different sort that surrounded them.

A gust of wind blew against the car, chilling the air. The night had become overcast, blocking some of the light from the moon. Emily could feel the dampness in the air tickling her nose and cheeks as a soft mist sprayed from a water bottle. The mist formed pockets of fog close to the ground, resembling shadows in search of their creator, until the quiet once again proved more disturbing than comforting.

"What's that?" she asked, sitting straight up looking around. Peter joined her by looking in different directions.

"I thought I heard something. Are you sure this place is safe? I mean we're so isolated here, so far away from everything."

"We're safe," Peter said. "But I'll get out and check."

As he walked around the car, Emily concentrated on keeping him within her view. Another gust of wind passed, and she yelled, "I heard it again."

Peter bent down to pick up a small tree branch that had broken off in the wind. "Here's the culprit," he said, as he handed it to her.

She exhaled in relief, feeling her face blush again. "I'm sorry," she said. "I guess I'm not as comfortable here as you. It's just kind of spooky in a way, knowing all the terrible things that happened in these woods. The darkness makes it seem that much worse."

"The darkness closes the gap in time," he said. "That's what's so frightening to you. During the day, the historic markers; the memorials, and of course the many tourists, provide the distance from the past that can be reassuring in a place like this. But in the silence of the dark, all things seem as they were. Except for our car, all that remains visible to us is the same as it was back then. Don't you see, that's the beauty of it," he said, sounding excited. "That's why I like to come here. But, if you're that uncomfortable, we'll leave."

"No, no," she said, feeling a little ashamed. "You're so right. It is lovely here. I can certainly get used to it, at least with you nearby. You'll never find me up here alone after dark though.

"I bet it did look the same way back then. That's the high-water mark down there," she pointed to a clump of trees barely visible in the distance. "That was the end of Pickett's Charge, which nearly obliterated the Southern Army."

"That's right," he said. Peter hesitated for a moment, before cautiously adding, "You know, local legend has it that on a night like this so close to the anniversary of the battle, you can actually see small lights down on the fields that some believe to be the ghosts of soldiers wandering in search of their comrades."

Emily's eyes grew wide as she said, "I don't believe in such things." She quickly added, "Did you ever see the lights?"

"Once, at least I thought I did," he said. "I wasn't sure if they were there or were only there because I wanted them to be. Sometimes our desire to see or hear something is so strong; we tend to unconsciously create it."

"You wanted them to be there? Are you serious?" she chided. "In that way we're different, Peter. I'm satisfied just reading about history and visiting historic sites. What you're saying is you'd like to somehow witness that horrible time in history. The truth is vicious battles were fought and lost here. The human toll during those three days was incomprehensible. That certainly isn't something I'd ever want to witness."

"Nor would I," he said, in defense. "What I'm doing is remembering. You're afraid, because you refuse to remember."

"What are you talking about? I remember. I remember every time I read about the war."

"Those are merely words in a book. Please don't tell me you're going to be that type of a history teacher," he reprimanded. "You have to *feel* history in order to fully understand and appreciate it. Here you can feel it. Once you feel it, you're no longer frightened or feel unwelcome."

Emily looked confused. Peter's description of what he felt in the park was a little unnerving.

She definitely sensed something there that night, and even the day before, but the only feeling she could identify for certain bordered on fear. And yes, she did feel unwelcome. Still, she pressed on trying to understand him. "Unwelcome? What do you mean?"

"Let me explain," Peter continued. "People from all over the world come here year after year, some with the curiosity one might take to an amusement park. But they leave with a different feeling about it, at least most of them do. Amidst all the monuments, a different memorial is formed in their mind for all the sacrifices that took place here. And with that, they discover a new understanding and respect for their own lives and the lives of others. Isn't that the real history lesson? Shouldn't history teach us to face our own mortality by what we've learned from the past, and thus live our lives in a better way for future generations?

"I truly believe that people need this sort of wake-up call in life every once in a while. They realize it, too. I bet that's why we get so many returnees. The world would certainly be a better place if more people followed that course. It's only when you complete that process of understanding that you can truly say you remember. And that's when you're no longer afraid of the past or feel unwelcome around it. It's not just about what happened here either, Emily. We can apply that principle anywhere that's witnessed tribulation of this caliber, or just the other disturbing events in our lives."

"Now I'm really confused," she said.

"Tell me that you can face everything in your present situation, or remember events from your past without fear, and I'd have to say you're not being completely honest with yourself," Peter said.

Emily was offended by his comment. *Perhaps I shared too much of my personal life with him tonight.* "What about you, Peter?" she snapped. "Can you face your life or your past without fear? What happened to you at Harvard?"

Another branch broke off the same tree, and she jumped in her seat. "I'd better get you home," he responded curtly, as he started up the car.

The short drive back home was quiet. Emily felt in some way she'd hurt his feelings but couldn't figure out how. She knew how intense his feelings were for his town. It was the same intensity of feeling she saw in Gram's eyes whenever she spoke of it. Yet, she still had trouble understanding.

"Peter," she asked, as he opened the car door. "Would you like to come upstairs for a while?"

"Thank you, but I can't," he said. "I have a busy day ahead of me. I'll need to be well rested for the seminar."

The walk to her front door was also quiet, and she began to wonder if his excuse to get home was a rejection. "I had a wonderful time," she said. "The restaurant was lovely. I enjoyed the trip to the school, and even to the park."

He looked at her questionably.

She frowned, and added, "I just hope I didn't offend you in any way."

"Offend me? How could you do that?"

"I guess I'm having trouble completely understanding Gettysburg. I'm sorry."

"I know. But you will understand," he assured her. "Don't worry, you will."

He held her tightly for a few moments before kissing her goodnight.

Peter walked back to his car slowly, hesitantly, turning back several times, waiting to see Emily's light go on in the apartment. When he saw that it did, he got into his car, started the engine, and lingered. He looked back at the illuminated window. Seeing her shadow, as it moved across the room, he was besieged by only one thought: *I will help you to understand, Emily.* He thumped the steering wheel with his fist before driving away.

Emily reached her window in time to see Peter's car pulling out from the curb, his blond hair blowing in the breeze as he drove away. She blew him a kiss, as though it were a final farewell, and felt the familiar emptiness taking its usual place beside her.

They had been so revealing to each other that night. Peter had shown a part of himself he'd probably only saved for chosen people. Emily was glad to have been chosen but also realized she hadn't responded the way he'd expected. She could tell how disappointed he was by that, and now she wished it could all be changed.

His reactions reminded her so much of Grams. She wondered why she couldn't react to him the same way she reacted to her?

Emily understood her Grams very well, even as a little kid. The nightly bedtime stories were always so special. She could almost hear her announcing what story she planned to read.

"No Grams. I want to hear a story about when you were little, like me. They're my favorite."

"Sure!" Emilia would respond with a smile and sit at the edge of her bed. She began, "It was Memorial Day, and the town was very exciting. Everywhere else in our country people put out one type of American flag, but in my town, we display two different types of flags."

"Why Grams, why two different flags?" she asked.

"Because at one time our country had two different flags. That was during the Civil War, many, many years ago. Soldiers from both flags died there, so it wouldn't be right not to display them.

"Anyway, everyone in town would line the main street to watch the big parade. All the neighborhood kids were allowed to sit on the curb so they could get the best view. We saw many different types of soldiers dressed in colorful uniforms, some on horseback, too. Then, there were local groups like the fire department, the historical society, and the park rangers who would march down the street next. They'd throw little hard candies wrapped in red, white and blue paper to all the children. We had so much fun collecting it.

"After the last group walked by, the people from town, starting with the kids, would file in behind the parade, and follow everyone to the Soldiers National Cemetery. At the cemetery, there would be a special dedication."

"What's a dedication?" Emily asked.

"It's a special way to remember," Emilia said.

"What did you remember?"

"We would remember all the terrible things that happened there during the war and pray it would never happen again."

"Nice bedtime story," Mandy said, glaring at her mother, after she stopped in the doorway while passing her child's room. "What ever happened to stories like Cinderella?" she smirked.

Emilia turned to Emily, and said, mocking, "Mom wants me to read you Cinderella. Would you like to hear Cinderella?" she asked, with a knowing grin.

Emily wrinkled her nose and said, "That's for babies."

"Well, then," Emilia said, smiling, "I guess I'll just continue with *my* story."

Emily looked back at her mother who was sullen in defeat. She beseechingly held out her arms to her, and said, "Come Mommy."

Mandy's face lightened; she took two steps into the room and stopped. She thought Emilia looked uncomfortable, so she turned and walked away.

Emily's eyes dropped, even though she was used to being disappointed by her mother. She turned to Grams, looking curiously while she waited for her to continue. But Emilia remained quiet, sadly looking at the empty doorway where her daughter had just been. After a few moments, her lips parted in a smile, and she said, "Remembrance is very important, Emily. If we don't forget our mistakes of the past, we probably won't make them again in the future. Do you understand?" she asked, looking more serious.

Emily nodded slowly, while noticing tears forming in Gram's eyes, and asked, "Are you sad, Grams?"

"No dear," she responded, wiping her eyes. "Never with you. Now where was I? Oh yes, after the dedication, everyone in town would go over to John Doyle's farm. His daughter, Gertie, and I were best friends. Each family would bring food, drink, and dessert for a huge picnic there. After eating, there would be banjo music, dancing and games.

"When it got dark, we would watch a fireworks display while listening to music, which Mr. Doyle played on the Victrola he set up in his parlor window. My father used to have to carry me home every year until I was nine years old. I'd wake up in bed the next morning, not knowing how I got there."

"That's a nice story, Grams," Emily said, while yawning. "Gettysburg sounds like such a great place."

"Yes, it is," Emilia said, with a sigh. "It's truly blessed. I only wish you could see it," and kissed her grandchild goodnight.

Chapter Twenty-One

Emily tied her robe, while running to the kitchen to answer the whistling kettle. She dropped a Chamomile tea bag into a mug, hoping it would help her sleep. *I should have refilled that damn sleeping pill prescription.* After retrieving the diary in the bedroom, she returned to the rocking chair near the hearth.

She clicked on a small floor lamp and then lit the candles in the hearth. There was something truly special about the candles. She enjoyed the ambiance they created the previous night.

While lighting the pillars, she could smell the lavender scent they emitted with the burst of each flame. It was then she recalled the disturbing events of the stormy night before. After confirming she was alone, she glanced cautiously towards the door. Upon seeing the dead bolt turned shut and latch in place, she continued to read on,

Remember ... May the Lord have mercy on the souls of this family. Today we are told it is safe to go out. Our own Union soldiers have arrived in town and are attending their needs before the great battle is set to begin. We are told

some have their doubts as to the probability of this battle, while others are fixed on its certainty.

The children are happy to return to the fresh air, though it is laden with heat and dampness.

This is the hottest summer I can recall, yet it is not yet July.

My dear Sarah is still plagued by this terrible cough and seems somewhat weak and tired compared to Amanda. The medicine Abigail brought should have done her well, but it has had little effect of cure. She is in my prayers to the Blessed Mother every day.

I pray all day, but my prayers go beyond that of my own family. I pray while preparing food for our soldiers, as many of them share a meal with us. I pray while sewing the spare burlap to make blankets. I pray while cutting apart my beloved mother's chemise—God rest her soul— into long strips to be used as bandages. I pray these blankets will cover no sick and these bandages will find no wounds to dress. Mostly, I pray my dear husband's added work will all be in vain.

Today, we were honored to share bread with General Reynolds. He is one of our own, born and raised in Lancaster. He has reminded Jonas of his parent's purchase of two of his chairs. He is so certain of the fine craftsmanship that he has asked to spend the night on the three set alongside one another by our back window. We are happy to oblige.

The General spoke about the battles he fought in the South and how he would often assist the slaves that his Corps would come upon during their journey. These fearful souls with broken bodies were so desperate to escape a terrible fate. He said each encounter sealed his faith in the need for this war, and he would gladly give his life up to that cause. He was very happy to hear that Gettysburg was doing *their part by secretly operating several stations in and around town where these runaways are sheltered until being moved to another safer place up north. We are all grateful for that as well. Our nearness to the border of a slave state has made those efforts more difficult, though.*

There are three of his aides, all Lieutenants, who are with us this night. They are all Pennsylvania men, God fearing, and respectful. My brother, Stephen, has recalled the one named James from a recent trip to Philadelphia to buy material for his store. He and James seem to be so well acquainted, as if they have known one another much longer. All through dinner and thereafter, they have remained close, sharing words no one else could hear. The two other officers occasionally would listen in to their words, only to be stopped by the General himself. I hope Stephen has not been engaged in any military corroboration, though it may be for the good of our country. I fear for his safety...E.W.

Emily sat at the edge of the chair. The tea was supposed to make her sleepy, but she was very much awake. She wanted to share the diary with Peter, now more than ever. After having read an excerpt from her ancestor's personal account of the war, which put one of the more famous Union Generals, John Reynolds, at her own house, her head was spinning in excitement. She picked up the phone to call him, but realized it was so late, and regretfully replaced the receiver.

Before she sat down though, she heard the rhythmic hammer pounding the phantom nails somewhere outside of her window. It began low and gentle, as one might sound fixing a stray nail from a fence, slowly increasing in intensity as if by an angry hand. Her curiosity gave her the courage to follow the sound to every open window in her apartment. It seemed to be the loudest outside her kitchen window, which faced the barn. The structure was dark and quiet, except for the ghostly sound piercing the night.

"Could I possibly be the only one who hears this?" she said. Emily closed all the windows despite the heat, hoping to muffle the noise, but it had little to no effect.

The third writing began as the previous two:

Remember...Dear Lord, please have mercy. Sarah is no better this day, and we have no means of reaching Dr. Wells. Abigail has not come to us this night, as it would be too dangerous for her to do so.

I have heard the roar of the cannons since early morn. The dreaded battle long predicted, has begun. Now, many of our people are hurt. I fear for my children who I have placed into our damp cellar to keep them safe, but this act will no doubt worsen my dear Sarah's condition.

Our General, now friend, who was here only this morning, has been reported shot in the neck. His wound is said to be most certainly mortal. I am glad Mr. Georg's bed is his place to rest, as I do not feel I can bear witness to his death. Stephen has rushed to the Georg home, bringing my handiwork of bandages, and blankets for our wounded friend. He has returned with the news that his Lieutenant friend, and all the others who were here, are safe. This seemed to give him great relief amidst the tribulation all around us.

As the sun begins to set, the soldiers pass our home supporting wounded comrades with their own bodies, dragging the more severely wounded on the ground with blankets. Many have tears in their eyes as they look back to the fields where they left those who are no longer in need. I pray for those souls, and the souls that will be taken tomorrow, for I fear the worst is yet to come...E.W.

Feeling both tired and awake, there was energy within that Emily could not ignore. She hastily turned the page of the diary for yet another glimpse into the life of the witness she longed to know. Again, the word Remember, its redundancy more poignant, bracing her for the words that followed:

Remember...Dear Jesus, pray for our souls and the souls that have departed the earth this day.

It is quiet now as I sit beside Sarah, the fever burning her small body within, as the summer heat burns outside my own. There are no words to describe what I am presently feeling, as I watch her gentle spirit slowly slipping away. The cool water I have placed on a cloth atop her head does little for the extreme discomfort she is experiencing. Her words are short, and sometimes senseless, yet I listen to each sound in hope I might hear a sign she is better.

The horrors seen and heard this day proved too burdensome for all. My Amanda screamed in fear from the cellar at the sound of the raging guns and cannons echoing off the hills surrounding us. Unrelenting they fired; their smoke blocked the light from the sun. Sarah could hear it I am certain, as she raised her brow after each explosion. Feeling lost for words that might give her comfort at this time, I asked the Mother of God for guidance. I then leaned close to her ear and whispered, 'It is only the lions roaring, dear Sarah. Do not fear them, for they are far away in the jungles and cannot bring you harm.' The skin near her brow became smooth, and the corners of her mouth turned up in a smile, and I knew the fear had left her. Amanda was later told the same and she too seemed more comforted.

Emily paused briefly, realizing where the saying, "lions roaring" may have originated and choked back a tear, which had snuck into her nervous laugh. She read on:

Stephen has returned to our home at midday with word of our dear General's death. James has accompanied him back to our home, his eyes swollen with grief. I thought it strange that he should leave his post at a time of such confusion, but he explained he had come to collect something for our fallen leader from my husband.

As we walked to the barn to see Jonas, we could hear him working as persistently as ever, and I looked forward to seeing what he had created that day. However, once the workshop doors were parted, the sight I beheld brought me to my knees. The beautiful chairs and chests once covering its walls and floor are now replaced with an infinite amount of plain, unfinished pine boxes. They are roughly hewn without grace or thought, and a form to suggest haste and indifference. I looked into my dear husband's eyes, once happy and proud of his work, now red and drawn, hiding a silent prayer for reprieve. I understood Jonas' commitment to producing what is necessary for our nation at this time, yet I was not prepared for the enormity of it.

Stephen and James somberly removed a coffin suitable for the General and carried it away to the Georg home.

As this terrible day drew to a close, I saw Stephen return with the young Lieutenant. What is the Lieutenant's business here, I wonder, now that the task he was sent here for earlier is done? What matter of espionage is Stephen involved in, and what secrets are now being shared at my home? I pray for our protection...E.W.

Emily turned the page.

Remember...Blessed Mother, please hear my prayers. This night I retire to bed, but I cannot sleep. Fear has consumed me, and I cannot rest. The air is damp and very still outdoors, the quiet foreboding, as the calm before a storm. I want to believe that the fighting here is over, but I know that may not be so. There is movement in the trees and dense smoke from the campfires, confirming the dangerous presence that remains near my home.

Oh, I wish I could take my children, and leave this dreaded place, but the danger that now exists is far worse than even one day ago. But then I would leave my husband, as his work must keep him here at this time. I cannot bear the thought of being without him, so I will stay until the time is right for us all to leave.

My brother's bed is empty, and I know not where he might be. Earlier, he told me he would help Jonas with his work, but Jonas is working alone in the barn. I questioned Stephen about his possible engagement with the Army, and he has denied all involvement. I have warned him to take great care in not committing himself to any activity that may disgrace our country. He has stated that he would no more disgrace our country, any more than he would disgrace his family. I must believe his words are true. Yet, as I look out into the blackness of the night, I remain in question of his position amidst this storm of uncertainty. For there are lions still in these woods, and I fear the hunt has only begun. And I, and my own, must remain within this house—as rabbits in a snare—waiting, waiting for what may be our end, as well.

Please, Heavenly Mother, watch over Stephen, and help me to watch over my family, for the storm is still upon us, and the lions have yet to capture their prey...E.W.

Emily closed the book. She could hear the pounding outside still but was too tired to care about it anymore. She wanted to continue with the reading, trying to fight back the sleep that had weighed down her eyelids. Finally, she succumbed, clutching the diary as tightly as her tired arms would allow before falling asleep at one o'clock.

Peter awoke and sat up in bed. He could hear his brother coming into the house after a night out with friends. He turned on the light, looked at his wristwatch on the nightstand and saw it was one o'clock. It was good to know Will was safe back at home.

For Peter, home had always been a place of refuge from distress. He remembered a time when he was tucked in there while feeling intense sadness and the pity it garnered from others that seemed to define his life after he returned from Harvard. He hadn't thought about that time in a long while, until he met Emily.

He began mulling over fragments of their conversation that night. From what he could glean, Emily no doubt had a troubled homelife. So did his old girlfriend, Alessa. Peter's mind then began wandering back to that previous time, a decade ago, but he wouldn't allow it to go any further.

"Emily is not Alessa," he said assuredly out loud. He closed the light and laid back down to sleep.

Chapter Twenty-Two

The Solitary Fruit

"Mrs. Angst," Emily called the one friend in town she knew would be available to see her that day. "Please come by, I need to speak with you."

"What is it, dear?" the woman asked, sensing the urgency in her voice.

"I can't discuss it over the phone. I have something to show you."

"Well, I have a doctor's appointment later this morning. May I come over now?"

"Yes," she said. "That would be great."

Emily embraced Mrs. Angst as soon as she came through the door. She complimented her floral print, cotton dress.

"Now, what's all this about?" Mrs. Angst asked.

"I don't know where to begin. I already told you about what happened to me the day before yesterday. I also told you about my first night here, and the incident with the bed. Well, I was dusting and rearranging the bookcase over there, and found this," she said, while handing her the diary.

"Witness to Tribulation," Mrs. Angst read aloud, and smiled. "So, you've found it."

"You know about this book?"

"Of course. Just about everyone who experienced those three terrible days during the war, and life here in town immediately after it left some written account of their ordeal, similar to this."

Emily frowned. "Gee, I was beginning to feel special."

"You are special. The fact that you still have this is special. Most of the other witness accounts were sold to newspapers and magazines after the war was over. Many were lost forever, including my own family's account, which has been missing for years. I suspect my parents might have sold it when they needed money. I'm sure many others ended up on the auction block, too."

"You know," Emily said, "I can't help but feel there was a special reason for me to find this, although I can't figure out what that reason might be. Just the way it kept falling off the shelf that night was almost like it was calling out to be found. Does that sound strange?"

"No," Mrs. Angst replied. She then added, nonchalantly, "Maybe your ghost planted it."

"Ghost?" Emily said, raising her voice.

"Oh, I don't mean to suggest that you have one. But yesterday you implied that you thought this place was haunted. I can't say that I agree with you, but I now see there have been some very odd, unexplainable things that have happened to you here. Has there been anything else unusual?"

Emily poured a cup of coffee, straining to keep her hand steady. "I thought I heard and felt something in this room the night of the storm. And then there's the pounding," she replied, cautiously.

"Pounding?"

"Yes. It's as if there's this invisible carpenter outside my window fixing boards."

"Or making something?" Mrs. Angst quickly interrupted.

"No," Emily said. "It's too redundant. There doesn't seem to be anything creative about it. It always begins sometime after midnight and ends after the sun comes up. It's getting a little unnerving," she whispered while looking out toward the barn.

"Don't be afraid, dear. There's nothing here that can hurt you. You're home."

Emily swallowed hard and said, "I know Gettysburg is said to be very haunted, at least that's what I've been told."

Mrs. Angst laughed. "I guess you've seen all the ghost hoopla, and tours going on around town. Some people figured out how to cash in on what we've taken for granted all these years. It's alright though. It's just another way for them to share our history with others."

"I do not believe in ghosts," Emily said. "I'm a realist. I must see, hear and touch something to believe it exists."

Mrs. Angst looked around the large, open room. Her eyes rested upon the picture of the Guardian Angel leaning on the wall above the mantel. "What a lovely painting," she said.

"Thank you," Emily replied, welcoming the change of subject. "It was a gift from Grams, so I couldn't bear to part with it when I moved."

"Are you as devout a Catholic as Emilia?" she asked, picking up the rosary beads on the table near the rocker.

"I guess so," Emily said. "More so when I'm afraid," she added with a nervous laugh.

"I'm Lutheran," Mrs. Angst said. "My father was a Catholic, but we were raised in my mother's faith. Pop used to kid mother and say, 'Catholicism will one day find its way back into the Doyle family.'

"My brother's son, John, married a Catholic girl. Guess what? His children are being raised in his wife's faith. I can almost see Pop in heaven shaking a finger at my mother, and saying, 'See Nora, I told you so.'"

They both laughed.

"I have no children of my own. Now, with my husband, brother, and sister-in-law gone, John is all I have left. He's like a son to me. I often accompany them to their church for Sunday service. It's very nice. There's even a prayer I recognize from my church; it begins; 'I believe in God the Father, the Almighty, Creator of Heaven and Earth.'"

"That's the Apostles Creed," Emily noted.

"I think the next line is, 'I believe in all that is seen and unseen,'" Mrs. Angst said as she placed her arm around Emily. "Do you believe in all that is seen and unseen, dear? Do you have faith?"

Before Emily could answer, though, Mrs. Angst glanced down at her wristwatch, and said, "Look at the time. I must leave or I'll be late for my appointment."

Emily followed her as she walked toward the door, "Please come back tonight. I'd like for you to hear some of what's written in the diary."

"I'm not sure I can," Mrs. Angst replied. "But I'll call if I'm coming."

She stopped in front of Emily's bedroom and stared at the folded linen atop the bare mattress. Turning back to her, she said, "This is your home now, and you are welcome here. You belong here. Please, do not forget that."

After kissing Emily on the cheek, she added, "By the way, don't call me Mrs. Angst anymore, we're practically family. My name is Gertrude, but you can call me, Gertie, if you'd like. Emilia always did."

While growing up, Gertie and Emilia had been inseparable. Their playground was often on the former battlefield, where the girls laughed and skipped, oblivious to the monuments nearby. They hopped over the remnants of streamers, and flowers that were left from the ceremonies that often took place there. The large, granite edifices, the cannons, the personal histories of fallen leaders engraved in stone, were as much a part of their lives growing up in Gettysburg, as the college, churches, and other historic buildings that made up their little town. Even the National Cemetery was a place for them to explore.

One of Emilia and Gertie's favorite things to do was sneak a basket lunch into the cemetery.

There they would sit near a pergola and watch all the tourists. To them, history was alive. And they had great respect for what was there. That respect was nurtured by the stories they were told on those endless nights, before the invention of television. The stories were from the people who either experienced what had happened there, firsthand, or had heard about it from others.

Emilia's mother, Sarah, would always ask them about their day.

"We were down near the spring collecting treasures," Emilia said. "We pretended the rocks were precious jewels, and the spring was their mine. I collected diamonds and emeralds. Gertie got sapphires as blue as the sky, and rubies as red as blood. Then we took them to a trader who gave us thousands of dollars."

"Oh, and what are you going to do with all of that money?" Sarah asked, playing along.

"Gertie and I are going to New York City to book passage on the Queen Mary, and go everywhere it sails, searching for jewels that could never be found here."

"I don't want to go around the world, Emilia. I want to stay right here," Gertie said.

"Don't be silly, Gertie," Emilia retorted. "What kind of excitement can you find here? It's always the same thing. Now, if we get to China, think of all the wonders that await us there."

Sarah would listen to their conversation. It was usually the same, and it always disturbed her. She was bothered by Emilia's rants for excitement, beyond the borders of their comfortable environment. Though only eleven years old, she knew her little girl was a free spirit who would be difficult to keep home.

Sarah and her daughter were the most recent survivors of a long line of women who lived and eventually died in that house. She didn't want the chain broken with Emilia's quest for adventure. Besides that, she had incredible difficulty dealing with the possibility of ever letting go of her only child.

"Gertie's right," Sarah would always say. "There's as much excitement here as you need. Besides, the world is a cruel place, sometimes. Here you will always be protected."

Gertie asked Emilia why her mother always seemed so upset about the game.

"It's not the game she's upset by, Gertie," Emilia solemnly responded with wisdom beyond her years. "It's not the game."

Chapter Twenty-Three

Emily stood in front of her tenant's door and hesitated before gently knocking. Clutching the wildflower bouquet, which she found once again that morning near her apartment door, she thought of all the other things she'd rather be doing instead. The church bells tolled Noon as a flock of birds flew overhead in the clear, blue sky. She sighed deeply.

After several minutes, she was about to knock again when Joel opened the heavy, oak door. "Welcome," he said, with outstretched arms. "Have you been standing there for a long time? You know, this is a business, you could have just walked right in."

Emily managed a feeble smile.

The office area was large, and open, lacking partitions, which usually separate multiple service businesses. It was beautifully decorated in an opulent, early Victorian style, appropriate for the historic time period of the building.

Heavy burgundy and blue drapery had golden fringe tassels dangling from each side of the perfectly constructed festoons above the large front window. The matching mahogany desks that faced each other in the center of the room were ornately carved with such intricate detail, she knew they must be antique. There were several shield-back chairs scattered about, all covered in a pattern that blended well with the drapery, and the paint color below the chair-rail. Many oil paintings were hung on the walls, giving the room a museum-like appearance. She stepped gingerly over the silk Persian rug, staring at each piece of furniture as one admires works of art.

"You did say you sold insurance, didn't you?" she asked, while looking up at a brass and crystal chandelier.

"Yes," Joel replied. Noticing her reaction, he added, "Mike and I are also avid antique collectors. In fact, that's how we ended up settling here. We were on a 'collection outing,' as we call it, when we saw the rental sign in the window. We fell in love with this town, and the people in it."

Looking around in awe, she said, "It's very beautiful. Where are you from, originally?"

"Thank you for the compliment," he replied. "We're both originally from Baltimore, Maryland."

"Baltimore?" she responded in surprise. "How do you adjust to such a small town like this, from a city like that? I mean, it's not as if you have roots here."

Joel was about to speak, when a bellowing voice emerged from the other room. "Because we like it," Mike boldly stated, causing her to flinch.

Mike carried in a silver tray filled with hot canapés. As he approached, she noticed his wavy brown hair was brushed back in a way that accentuated his deep-set, steel gray eyes. He extended his arm and said, "The shrimp puffs are the best." She took one.

"Mike worked as a chef at La Cote D'Or restaurant in Baltimore while finishing his MBA at UB Towson. That's where we met," Joel said, glancing lovingly at his partner. "He makes the best Quiche Lorraine I've ever tasted, but you'll judge for yourself later. Where's your friend?" he asked.

"He had a previous engagement," she said. "He couldn't make it."

"Too bad," Joel said. "Maybe next time. Should I take these?" he asked, pointing to the flowers.

"Yes, of course," she replied, forgetting she still held them.

"Look, Mike. Aren't they lovely?"

Mike didn't respond as he took the flowers into a back room, reemerging with them arranged in a tall, porcelain vase.

"Do you also live here in town?" Emily asked, as Joel set a round table for lunch.

"Yes, on the other side of the college campus. You know, we really wanted to rent your apartment upstairs, but we were told it was taken. That would have been perfect for us. Sometimes we work so late into the night that even just going across town seems like such a distance."

"How long have you been here?" she asked.

"Almost two years," Joel replied.

"Who was the apartment rented to back then?"

"Why, no one." Joel said.

"Then, why were you told it was taken?" she asked, looking confused.

"Because Mrs. Angst said it was being saved for Mrs. Schmidt's granddaughter. That's you, right?"

"What about the college students?" Emily asked, still bewildered.

"The apartment has been unoccupied all the while we've been here," Joel said. "You know, I'd love for you to see our home someday. Maybe you can come to dinner with your friend."

"Sure." Emily said, as her eyes scanned the room. She focused on a painting that was illuminated on a wall near a doorway and pointed to it. "I love the still life."

The painting consisted of a large bowl filled with shiny apples of different sizes, some overflowing onto the table upon which it sat. All the apples were red, except for one whose color was not decipherable.

"I love it, too," Joel said, gently caressing the gilded frame with his fingers. "My daughter painted it. She gave it to me last year on Father's Day."

"Your daughter?" Emily asked in a surprised tone.

"Sherry. She's the apple of my eye," he said, and winked. "A senior at Berkley, studying art, of course. The painting was based on an old parable called, 'The Solitary Fruit.' Ever hear of it?"

Emily shook her head. Joel began to explain, "The story is about a man who sends his young son into his apple orchard to pick the fruit to be sold at market that day. When the boy returned, he had a bushel full of apples, all red, except for one that was this odd color, somewhere between green and brown.

"'What's this?' the father asked. "'I didn't plant any like this. It's either not yet ripe, or it's already spoiled, so we'll leave this one aside.'"

"The boy, having been color-blind since birth, couldn't figure out what all the fuss was about since he didn't notice any difference. But, his father insisted, and so while the rest of the apples were sent to be sold, this solitary fruit was left at home.

"Every day, the boy and his father checked to see if the apple had changed color. But after several days, it hadn't.

"'Look', said the boy, 'you say this fruit has not changed in color, yet it's not rotten. But, if we leave it alone, it will definitely waste'. With that, he took the apple, and bit into it. 'This fruit is no different than the others', the boy said. 'The sweet flavor is exactly the same.' He then offered his father a taste.

"'Ah, yes,' the man said, with a revelatory smile. 'It would take a color-blind child to improve an older man's vision.'"

Joel stared a little longer at the painting and began to cough. Almost immediately, his coughing grew deeper, more intense, clutching his throat, he began gasping for air. Emily swung around to get help, but Mike was already there with a glass of water. Joel was able to drink some, and disappeared into a back room, still coughing uncontrollably.

Emily looked at Mike with concern, "What's wrong with him?" she asked.

"Whom are you worried about?" Mike asked, smiling wryly, "Joel or you?"

Emily grimaced. Mike was rude and inconsiderate. She needed to get away from him, and even thought about leaving when she heard Joel call out, his voice low and strained. Joel was different. He had an endearing quality, a softness that was familiar to her. She put down her purse and went into the adjoining room to find him sitting at the edge of a settee, his head bent down in an attempt to control his labored breathing.

"Are you all right, Joel?" she asked. "Should we call for help?" He raised his arm and shook his head. Mike sat down beside him.

"Just relax, Joel, you'll be fine," Mike said, and lovingly placed his arm around his shoulder, drawing him close. Joel rested his head against his partner's chest and began to regain some composure.

"He sometimes gets these anxiety attacks," Mike explained.

Emily was shocked he'd offered her an explanation. The fact that he even addressed her without a tone of criticism, amazed her even more.

Joel raised his head and looked into Mike's eyes. "I'm okay now," he said.

Even though Joel seemed so weak and tired, both he and Mike insisted on resuming the luncheon. The meal was slightly rushed; however, Mike's culinary skill was evident.

"This really is the best quiche I've ever tasted," Emily said.

"Thank you," Mike responded without looking away from his partner.

Joel seemed a little better but barely touched the food on his plate. Both he and Emily tried to make small talk in an attempt to lighten the somber feeling that lingered after what had just occurred.

Mike, however, didn't say a word. He offered nothing to their conversation, except an occasional nod in agreement to whatever Joel happened to be saying. Emily noticed how he concentrated on his ailing partner, observing, and assessing his every move.

"So, how do you like it here so far?" Joel asked.

"I love it," Emily replied. "Everyone is so friendly, though most of the people you see are just passing through."

"I know what you mean. We felt the same way when we first arrived. But after just a short while, you get to know the locals. It's really a special place."

"What do you mean?" she asked

"Everyone belongs here," he replied. "And not just the locals, or the college kids, everyone. I think that's why people here tend to be so tolerant of tourists, at least more so here, than in other vacation places, and as a result they're even more understanding and accepting of the people they live among."

By the time her visit was over, Emily felt more relaxed in their company. It was already two o'clock, and she couldn't get over how quickly the time had passed. As Joel escorted her to the door, Mike removed the "Closed" sign hanging in the front window.

Recalling something he said, Emily stopped walking, turned to Joel, and asked, "You said you sometimes work late into the night. How late have you been here?"

"Sometimes during tax season, I stay to help Mike until one or two o'clock in the morning."

Her eyes widened. "Has anything unusual ever happened here? Have you noticed any odd noises?" she persisted.

"Noises? What sort of noises?" Joel asked, as he looked at Mike.

"A pounding noise," Emily said. "Like a handyman who works his hammer all through the night. Or maybe footsteps?"

"Do you hear that?" Mike asked, surprising her again.

"I think so," she cautiously replied. "Have you?"

They both shook their heads, and Joel added lightly, "Well, if there were any of those noises, we were probably too tired to notice."

Emily thanked them both for lunch and inquired once again to Joel how he was feeling. He assured her he was okay. As she turned to leave, Joel reached over, put his arms around her, and kissed her on the cheek. She instinctively held him close, rubbing his back for a few moments, before departing.

When she reached her apartment door, she turned to see Joel carry a watering can over to an outside faucet. He bent over awkwardly while filling it and struggled to lift the laden can over to the large, half wine-barrels resplendent with red geraniums. He coughed again while watering the flowers. As she watched the gentle creature lovingly caring for the plants adorning her home, she thought, *He's a very nice man, someone's father*. She began to think about her own father and Zach, which caused a twinge deep in her gut. She didn't want to remember them nor her mother, not when she was trying so hard to forget.

Chapter Twenty-Four

The sound of a passing car sent Mandy rushing over to the window just in time to see a neighbor's SUV heading up the road. Zach was late, and they were due at the Nielson house for dinner in less than an hour. *He'll be home in time,* she reassured herself.

She went to the living room mirror to check her make-up, passing the luggage that was on the floor still packed for their overnight trip to the beach that day, which did not take place.

Zach's colleague, Carl, called right before they were leaving, and told him that the important meeting they'd been waiting for was finally going to happen.

"I'll make it up to you," Zach said, repentant, as he held Mandy close.

Mandy was becoming accustomed to all the disappointments; the missed parties, dinners and lonely days, while he worked for months on that big case. The lonely nights though, disturbed her even more. She and Zach had not made love in the longest time. She missed his gentle touch, and the feelings that made her life seem tolerable. Those intimate moments, when she was able to give and receive so much happiness, was the only time that truly gave meaning to her life.

Andrew had been the only other person who was able to make her feel that way.

She glanced at her wristwatch, exhaled deeply, and began pacing around the house to get her mind off the time, hoping Zach was already on his way. She climbed the stairs to the second floor of the house, checking the angles of the custom-framed prints on the stairwell wall.

While passing her mother's room, she decided to open the door, something that hadn't been done very often since her death. Staring at the bed, Mandy shivered while remembering the difficult months before Emilia's passing, when she couldn't get beyond the door frame. That strange reaction to her mother's illness didn't surprise her though. Emilia always managed to shut her out of her life in some way or another. Mandy slammed the door.

The room next to Emilia belonged to Emily. It was her mother's idea for them to have adjacent rooms. Mandy opened Emily's door, looked into the empty space and sighed, realizing she barely knew she was gone. *Emily probably feels the same way about me.*

When the floor clock in the dining room tolled seven, Mandy began to worry. She reached for the telephone to call Zach, first at the office, and when he didn't answer, she tried his cell phone. When he didn't answer on that phone either, she got upset. *He would have called if he was going to be so late. Something must be wrong.*

Grabbing her keys, she darted out the door toward her car and headed to his office. When she got there, she could see the conference room lit up, and his Jaguar parked in the reserved space. She felt relieved. Carl's sports car was parked there, too.

Mandy opened the door to Zach's suite of offices and went in. The reception area, and the conference room were both empty. She looked around the silent space, bewildered, after noticing Zach's briefcase on the floor, resting against one of the blue leather chairs. Slowly, she walked down the hall to his personal office, uncertain of what she'd find. She pushed open the door and gazed in horror into the room. Feeling as though the blood had suddenly been drained from her body, she fell back, knocking over a plant on her way down to the floor.

Chapter Twenty-Five

The day retreated into an artist's palate. As the bright orange ball of fire disappeared behind the surrounding hills, the rays of light reflected off clouds, which sent purple and peach colored hues swirling through the blue and white sky, reminiscent of a Renaissance painting.

Emily saw that it was eight o'clock, and she had not yet heard from Peter. It had been too long to go without a phone call from him, so she began to worry. She sensed unspoken tension between them at the end of their date the night before. She glanced at her watch and back to the Michelangelo sky for several more minutes and picked up her silent cell phone. It was turned on and charged.

She had misplaced Peter's cell phone number and didn't have the number to his home.

Emily wanted to call the Villa Verde Restaurant to see if he was there. Once, she even dialed the number but hung up as soon as the connection was made. It was after a second attempt to call there that she heard her front door opening. *Oh no!* She braced herself.

Once again, there was the sound of footsteps ascending the staircase. Slowly, reluctantly it moved, whatever it was, as if each step was a burden or chore never wishing to complete. There was the sound of dripping water, even though it wasn't raining and the sound of heavy breathing. Emily could feel the tension building in her chest and called out, "Who are you?" with such emotion, that the sound of her voice confirmed the fear within. Then, the footsteps stopped.

She walked to the locked inside door and listened but heard nothing more. That time there was no courage left to open the door and investigate, so she ran to the telephone, and quickly dialed the restaurant once again.

"Villa Verde," a soft-spoken woman answered.

"May I please speak to Peter Sanders, one of your waiters?" Emily asked, trying to tame her raging fear.

"I'm sorry, he has the night off," the woman said.

There was a long pause, perhaps too long, before the woman asked, "Are you Peter's friend, Emily?"

Startled, she replied, "Yes, you know of me?"

"Of course. I'm his Aunt Patricia. I've heard lots of nice things about you. Uncle John and I would love to meet you someday."

"I'd love to meet you, too," she answered. "Do you know where I might reach him now?"

"Probably at home," Patricia said. "He called in after returning home around seven-thirty, feeling tired from his trip. Why don't you call him there."

After writing down his phone number, Emily thanked Patricia for the conversation after which she felt completely different, more relaxed and in control.

She walked around her apartment for a while trying to decide if she should call him at home. His aunt said he was tired so she thought maybe it would be best to just let him sleep and call him in the morning. She picked up her mug, set the kettle on the stove for tea, put down the tea bag, turned off the stove, and continued her aimless pacing once again, nervously glancing at the bolted door to her apartment. Finally, she dialed his cell phone.

"Hello," a weary voice answered.

"It's me, Emily."

"What took you so long? My aunt called me over fifteen minutes ago and told me you'd be calling."

"I just wanted to get a cup of tea," she said, staring down into her empty mug. "How was your seminar?"

"Pretty good," he said through a yawn. "How was your day? Did you miss me?"

"Yes," she said and held her breath.

"I'm glad," he answered. "I missed you, too."

Only then did she exhale, and asked, "Would you like to come over tonight?"

"I'd love to, but I'm really beat. I didn't get a lot of sleep last night. I guess I was anxious about the seminar. Listen, I have work to catch up on in my office tomorrow. Why don't you come with me, and we'll finish our tour of the town later."

Emily shivered at the thought of entering his building again.

"Why not finish your work there, and then meet me over here," she offered. "After all, there isn't much for me to do there. I might get in your way."

"Actually, it's more like I'll be too distracted with you nearby. I have an idea: While I'm working, you can do some research on your family tree in our historical society library downstairs. I'll be happy to introduce you to our director; he's very knowledgeable about local history. I'm sure he'll be able to assist you. Meet me on the steps of Old Dorm at our usual time, eleven o'clock. I'll wait for you there."

Feeling more confident, Emily slowly opened the door to her stairway. Once reassured no one was there, she laid down on the antique sofa opposite the fireplace, which was bright with flickering candles. There were bumps and indentations in the upholstery, not yielding to her body. The dampness in the air mixing with its old threads gave off a musty smell, so she returned to her comfortable rocker near the hearth and began brushing her long hair.

Earlier, she'd retrieved Emilia Wahler's book from where it was left under the bare mattress in the bedroom. She put down her hairbrush and picked it up. The pages released a very distinct fragrance as soon as it was opened. Emily wondered which of her three perfumes she was wearing when she'd last handled the book, but didn't remember any of them smelling quite that way.

Flipping through the scented pages, she sensed a comfort, a feeling of warmth, a fearless energy neither ghostly footsteps nor hammer could shatter. The little book provided a different focus to her life.

Remember...My Jesus, pray for us. I feel the trembling of the earth still, though the last of the cannon fire ceased hours ago. The sky is dark and sulfurous; its yellow haze burns my eyes. I can bear the smell no longer.

This day of fighting proved fiercer than the previous two. It is said many of our countrymen have littered the fields with their bloated and mangled bodies. I have no doubt that is true. The deafening screams of guns and cannons raged on as to herald judgment for the world. Dear God, forgive us our trespasses, and bring us the peace and tranquility we once knew.

Our neighbor, Mrs. McClellan, who had just given birth, must tend to her sister Jennie's lifeless body, which now lies in her cellar, a victim of a stray Rebel bullet. Just one week ago her home was filled with such joy that comes with the birth of a child. Now, her home is filled with the despair that comes when a life has ended. I will pray for her, and her departed sister. Mostly, I will pray for her little innocent one whose anniversary of birth each year will be marked by so many painful memories.

Sarah sleeps comfortably now, though she does not respond to my words and her fever persists. I trust she has been somewhat spared from all of this, as I am certain she is in a different place.

Amanda clings to my side in such fear; she's not spoken a

word all day. The thought of lions roaring gave her little comfort during those tyrannous hours.

Thankfully, Jonas and Stephen have been at home all this day remaining in prayer. Though they are silent, their eyes are full of preoccupation.

In the distance, I can see our soldiers returning from the fields of battle. They pass our home bruised, bleeding, bandaged. Many a uniform is torn and tattered, red stains covering the blue. They draw their bodies forward, with spirits left somewhere behind, like so many weary knights, uncertain of valor...E.W.

Emily turned the page and continued to read on. So much of what troubled her in her own life disappeared on the pages filled with her ancestor's words.

Remember...Dear Lord, give me the courage to complete this task. I have been appointed nurse, and my home has been made a hospital for fallen soldiers.

This night, as I lay beside my sick child, the officers banged on my door. I summoned Jonas, still busy in his work- shop trying desperately to complete enough coffins to meet the present needs of our town. This, the third day of the battle, is endless, yet I gather all my strength as he gathers his, to maintain my calm in light of what I have just faced. Surely, the same awaits me in the coming days.

The floors of our home are now covered with more men than they can possibly hold, each man seemingly wounded beyond repair. I step over their crumpled bodies, trying to avoid inflicting any further discomfort. These, our protectors, have valiantly fought to save our homeland and ensure that all our country's citizens are free from the evil of enslave-

ment. I must cast away all thoughts of personal comfort, and do what is expected of me, what is most certainly just.

The long summer light gives way to darkness very quickly. I lit the hearth, and used all my candles, even the special ones, to provide the necessary illumination.

Lord, so much blood, so much misery. I placed Amanda upstairs with Sarah for the cellar must also be used to shelter the wounded. I pray their agonizing screams will not disturb my dear children.

The Army Surgeon, Dr. Harlow, called me over to the kitchen table, which was pulled close to the light of the hearth, and asked for my assistance in a matter. He was so soft spoken and courteous, as one might ask to prepare water for a bit of tea. On the table lay a soldier writhing in pain from his injury. The doctor implored me to hold a lamp very close to him, which I did, and he began to cut away at the young soldier's pant leg. He then reached down into a bag and removed what looked to be a saw of some sort, and to my horror, proceeded to cut off this man's leg. I gasped as the soldier's body jolted, no doubt feeling the pain through the Chloroform.

Upon hearing my scream, the surgeon stopped and looked up at me. His sullen eyes spoke what no words could say.

I then backed away from the table, tears blocking my sight, and felt a soft object below the heel of my right shoe. I lifted my skirt to see what it was. Lying beside where I stood was a boy appearing no older than sixteen years of age, whose hand I'd just managed to step upon. I quickly moved my foot away, and bent down to apologize, as he was looking up at me in an odd way. It was then I realized he was gone. He'd neither felt the heel of my shoe, nor the pain caused by the bullet, which had ripped through his chest. Those lifeless eyes were frozen in such anguish and fear that could only come from sudden death. I know they will haunt me the rest of my days.

All through the night a continuous flow of Jonas' pine boxes entered our home and departed shortly thereafter, taking with them the fruit of many an unsuspecting parent. My God, Heavenly Father, what was all of this killing for? Only three days before, as we discussed with General Reynolds, the purpose of this war seemed very clear. Now, with all this before me, I ponder, at what cost is the life of someone's child? Husband? Father? I've not known war before and pray I shall not know it ever again.

The next to be removed from our home was the young boy whose hand I'd stood upon. As they lifted his lifeless body into the coffin, I slipped my rosary beads into his swollen hand and said a prayer. It was only then I noticed his cotton nightshirt and realized him to be a Rebel. This solitary fruit, a lonely Johnny amidst all these New Yorkers – as if that really mattered.

I spent several long hours into the night aiding as well as I could my unexpected guests.

Presently, the Army surgeon has sent me to rest. He has complimented my devoted duty to the cause of our Nation, but said I will need all my strength tomorrow. As I write this, the first light of dawn has streamed through my window, and I realize tomorrow is already here. It is the Fourth of July...E.W.

Going back two pages of the little book, Emily began reading certain lines over and over, ... "tears blocking my sight,...those lifeless eyes,...lonely Johnny,...this solitary fruit..." She recalled the old parable Joel had recited to her, and her tears began to flow, dropping down, forming little pools on those precious pages. Quickly, she wiped away her tears, hoping the water would not destroy the ink. It didn't.

Closing the book, she noticed the invisible hammer begin pounding once again outside. It was ten o'clock, too early for the specter's visit, as though eternity had a time frame. It no longer was disturbing. After reading a heartfelt rendition of her ancestor's living nightmare, she was too emotionally moved to be scared. She just wanted to sleep and escape what she was feeling.

Chapter Twenty-Six

Another Casualty of War

Emily awoke the next morning and went directly to her kitchen window to listen. There were no hammers at work. *Thank God. I must have slept through it.*

A little later, the ringing telephone rushed her out of the shower, causing her to answer with a breathless, "Hello."

"Good morning, Emily," a husky voice on the other end announced.

"Mom?" she questioned. "Is that you?" The lilting tone only two days before was gone.

"Yes, of course. Who did you expect?"

"I'm not sure," Emily said. "It just doesn't sound like you. Are you alright?"

Mandy ignored her daughter's question, instead began her own questioning. "Have you been out with that Sanders man again?"

"Yes. As a matter of fact, I'm meeting him this morning."

"That's nice," Mandy sighed.

"I can tell something is wrong," Emily said. "What is it you're not telling me? Did you go to the beach with the Larsons? What happened there? Is Zach alright?"

"My, my." Mandy began to answer mockingly. "What question

should I answer first? Let's see, no to the first question, nothing to the second, and I guess so."

"Stop," Emily yelled. "Stop acting like a child."

"How dare you speak to me like that," Mandy snapped. "I'm still your mother, and I want respect. You know what respect is, don't you, Emily? It's the way you treated your grandmother. Well, I demand the same!"

Emily thought, *So, she wants to pick a fight before morning coffee. Well bring it on.*

"Oh, now you're sounding more like yourself," Emily chided. "Are you trying to equate our relationship to that of me and Grams? I don't think so. We could never have what Grams and I had. It's too late for that."

There was sniffling in the earpiece, and Emily thought her mother might have been crying, but she was too angry to question her about it. Mandy had always acted only a little more than aloof toward her for years, so why was she now demanding the same respect as Grams? Still, there was an element of respect toward her, but it could only be compared to that of an older sister, or maybe one of her father's cousins she used to call Aunt. Gaining some emotional control, Emily said, "I don't want to fight with you. I'd like to think that we're beyond that now. Can we talk about this later? I'm running a little late."

After a pause, Mandy replied, "Sure, whatever you want. Have a nice day."

The sad reserve in Mandy's closing prompted Emily to implore, "Wait Mom. Please don't hang up yet. I need to know what's going on with you. Don't tell me it's nothing, because I know that isn't true."

"It's...it's not your concern," she answered hesitantly.

"I won't hang up until you tell me."

"It's Zach," Mandy replied. "We're not getting along. No, I take that back. We do get along. That's why this whole situation seems so unreal. I just learned something, and I'm having a tough time handling it."

Emily swallowed hard. "What have you just learned?"

"Well, he's having an affair," Mandy replied. "There, I've said it."

Emily remained quiet as Mandy continued to explain. "He was late for a dinner party we were invited to last night. He's been late before, but this time he was so late, I began to worry. Zach isn't like that," she said, and began crying. "He always calls if he's going to be very late. He's so considerate.

"I went to his office. His car was parked outside, and I could see that the light was on. I let myself in. And then, and then I...I found them together."

Emily gripped the phone, straining back her own tears. "Who was it?" she inquired.

There was a pause, and Mandy replied, sounding in more control of her emotions, "His secretary."

"His secretary? You mean Louise Arnold? But she's my age."

There was another pause, and Mandy replied with a simple, "Yes."

"I can't believe that," Emily said, bewildered. "Are you sure about this?"

"She wasn't really a good friend of yours, right?"

"No, not at all," Emily answered. She began thinking: *Zach must be out of his mind. He must be going through some sort of mid-life crisis. I'll take care of Louise.* "What a bitch!" she said, loudly into the phone. "How dare she do that to us. I'm calling Louise right now."

"No!" Mandy screamed, "Don't call her. Don't call anyone."

"Why?" Emily asked. "We've known her so many years, for God's sake. Guess who recommended her for that job?"

"No," Mandy persisted. "Please, don't call." Her sobs were deep and hollow; the same endless wail of emotion after Andrew's death, until finally, she whispered, "It's not Louise."

"Who is it then?"

"Don't worry, it's no one you know. I'm sorry I had to tell you this, but I didn't have anyone else to talk to. I know how hard it must be for you to hear this. Zach has been a good father to you. I have to go now," she quickly added, lowering her voice. "His car just pulled into the driveway."

At that very moment, Emily realized her mother knew what she knew about Zach. The lover was not Louise, or any other woman for that matter. Zach was having a romantic affair with his colleague, Carl. She realized something else, too. Mandy intentionally didn't tell her who it was to save her the added shock of learning about her beloved stepfather's homosexual affair, and by doing so, acted more like a mother to her then than at any other time in her life.

"Don't hang up, Mom," Emily said, fretfully. She didn't want to let on that she knew about Carl but searched for some way to help her mother out. "Don't say anything. Just listen to what I have to say. There's nothing you can do to prevent something like this from happening.

"However, you must make a choice whether to stay with him and then follow through with your decision. You can always come down here and spend some time with me until things are settled in your mind. But, if you choose to stay, you must ask him to also make a choice and be prepared for his decision. Do you understand?"

Emily listened intently for a response from the woman for whom she'd had such ambivalent feelings most of her life. Suddenly, she was hit with feelings of sadness, pity, remorse, and somewhere deep down, pushing its way out of the depths of her soul, she felt love.

"Do you understand me, Mom?" she repeated.

Mandy replied, calmly, "Yes. I understand. Thank you. Will you call me later?"

"Of course I will."

"Do you promise?" Mandy childishly asked. When there was no immediate response, Mandy asked again in a more desperate tone, "Do you promise? Please say you will."

"Yes, I promise."

Emily stood frozen in place with the phone still wedged tightly in her fist. She stared blankly as water dripped from her wet hair and the saturated towel, which had been hastily wrapped around her body. There were no thoughts now, no description of what she was feeling. Her life at that moment seemed suspended, dangling, and she needed to anchor herself to Grams.

Though Emilia was no longer there to comfort her, just the memory of that love and support provided the comfort she needed at that very moment. But it was Mandy who needed Grams, even more so than she did. Emily wondered if her mother knew that. Mandy and Emilia always seemed so distant emotionally, exactly like her own relationship with Mandy. She wondered, *How did it happen that way between us, and between the two of them? Why doesn't Mandy know Grams' love and support, even if she now has to reflect on it to get it?*

Emily might have realized the answer to those questions if she knew what it was like for Mandy growing up with Emilia as her mother. The answer might have even been buried in a trunk.

One day, Mandy dug deep into the wooden trunk, tucked under one of the eaves of her parent's attic, trying hard not to make any noise. She knew the trunk was there for years but was told by her mother to never touch it.

"But why can't I open it, Mom?" she asked Emilia. "Because I said so," was her only response.

Every Christmas that Mandy helped her father get down the ornaments, she would catch a glimpse of it out of the corner of her eye, the longing to open it growing stronger each time she passed with the twinkle lights and colorful glass balls. The fact that it was off limits intrigued her even more.

The wide wooden slats were dark and dusty, and the metal clamps on the top and sides were old and rusted. When no one was looking, she'd walk over to it and give a little shove, hoping it might give her an indication of what was inside. It wouldn't budge.

"What are you doing?" Allen asked when he caught her snooping near it one year. "What's in it, Daddy?" she asked, her eyes filled with excitement and wonder.

He laughed and said, "Don't worry; there are no jewels in there. Just a lot of things from your mother's family."

"But why can't I open it, and look inside?"

"That's something you'll have to discuss with her."

"What's the point?" Mandy said. "Every time I ask her about it, she just tells me to forget it, and that it's none of my concern."

Allen put his arm around his little girl and gave her a big hug. "I guess she has her reasons, sweetheart. You know, sometimes there are memories attached to things that we just can't share with anyone else. Understand?"

Mandy nodded even though she really didn't.

One day a few years later, while her father was at work and her mother was out shopping for the afternoon, she seized her opportunity. The floorboards creaked as she tiptoed across the open space. After plugging in a lamp on the paint-stained chair nearby, she pulled the trunk out from its protected alcove, took a deep breath and opened it. It was an act, which seemed at best anticlimactic, at least initially.

Inside, she found an incomplete set of silver spoons and knives, some chipped blue and white colored plates and pieces of an unfinished quilt. Digging deeper though, she found yards of white ribbon, yellowed with age attached to a little prayer book. Inside the fragile pages of the book were the dried-up remains of flowers to be lovingly preserved. Underneath some brown material was a lace wedding dress. She carefully draped it on the floor and continued looking into the trunk.

Except for some loose threads and odd pieces of material, it looked empty. She was disappointed there was nothing else, and was about to start replacing the objects, when she noticed that the inside depth of the trunk did not match the appearance outside. She reached in, found a latch, and after lifting it up, found another compartment.

Inside were photographs, so many photographs. Mandy couldn't believe her eyes. She removed one of the pictures, a wedding picture, and saw that the bride and groom were her own parents. She gasped as she looked over to the dress, realizing it was her mother's wedding gown. Mandy wondered why she was told there were no pictures of her parent's wedding, or any other family pictures. And why have these pictures been kept hidden?

Some of the photos appeared very old, with long skirted women in upswept hairdos, and men with bow ties and straw hats. There were some pictures encased in small metal folders with ornate carvings within the metal. The one she liked best were of two little girls, seemingly close in age and appearance. The bottom of the folder was engraved *Amanda and Sarah, 1862.*

Near the children's picture was a portrait of a young woman, her hair, pulled back tightly at the forehead, fell loosely over her shoulders and onto her lace dress. Though the collar was different, it looked very similar to the dress lying beside her on the floor. The slight looking woman had a wreath of flowers in her hair, and dangle earrings matching the strand of pearls close to her neck.

Mandy stared for the longest time into the woman's eyes. She couldn't tell from the black and white photo if they were blue like her own, but large, and hauntingly beautiful. Her stare was almost trance-like, and despite the upturned corners of her mouth in a smile, she seemed very sad. She shivered slightly, and she quickly put the picture down.

The other pictures were of a town with old brick buildings, and a pretty stone house with a white picket fence around it. The house was so different from her parents' shingled split-level, typical of early 1950's architecture.

There were school papers, her mother's Gettysburg College diploma, and other loose papers, receipts of some sort, strewn about. However, Mandy was no longer interested in them or anything else she found in the trunk. The only thing that held her curiosity was the wedding portrait she was continually drawn to of the mysterious woman with the beautiful face, and eyes that touched a place deep within her. She held the picture close without breaking her concentration, as if anticipating it to speak. There were no words, yet it spoke to her just the same. It called out to that void in her memory, begging for remembrance of people and stories she had yet to know.

Her trance was broken by the sound of her mother's car door slamming shut. She unplugged the lamp and hastily replaced everything she'd taken out to its appropriate spot in the trunk. Just after moving it back under the eaves though, she saw that the portrait was left out. Too late to replace it, she took it down to her bedroom and tucked it under her mattress.

Mandy had forgotten all about the picture, until a week later, when her mother called her into the living room with such formality, she knew in some way there was trouble. It had been a stormy, mid-summer afternoon, and the crash of each thunderbolt made her flinch. "Lots of lions around," Mandy said, kidding.

But Emilia wasn't amused. Instead, she stoically sat on the massive, upholstered wing chair, her shoulders straight against its back, with her arms folded across her chest. Her hands gripped the inside of her elbows tightly, and her breathing was deep. She instructed Mandy to sit on the small wooden side chair across the room from her and glared at her child in such a way, Mandy's heart began to race.

She began to question Mandy about her experience of being left alone the week before.

Emilia's tone was low and even, and each word seemed carefully chosen. Mandy began to relax, when suddenly, her mother reached down under her chair and pulled out the portrait that had been hidden, and asked, "I found this under your mattress when I was changing your linens today. Do you mind explaining to me how it got there?"

Mandy couldn't understand what all the fuss was about, and impishly replied, "I'll tell you, if you tell me who it is."

Emilia slowly rose from her chair and began walking toward her. "You had no right to go into that trunk, especially after I told you not to," she tersely lectured.

"Who is she, mother?" Mandy interrogated. She was not easily intimidated by Emilia. Her mother had always been somewhat cold to her emotionally, increasingly more so as she approached the rebellious adolescent years, and so she learned to expect a certain stern attitude. She repeated, "Who is she? Why do you keep all those pictures and things hidden like that?

"What happened to you in Gettysburg anyway? Did you kill someone?" she laughed.

"I didn't kill anyone," Emilia snapped.

"Then, what is it? What is it you're ashamed of?"

Emilia suddenly extended her hand and slapped her hard across the face and said, "Don't ever speak to me that way again."

Mandy was in pain, physical pain and emotional pain, but still, she refused to cry. Neither of her parents had ever hit her before, and she knew she'd never forgive her mother for even this one incident.

"Who is she, mother?" she asked again, more defiant.

Emilia stared down at the hand that did the unthinkable, and as she slowly walked out of the room she said, emotionlessly, "Your grandmother," with the picture dangling loosely from the unforgiven hand.

Mandy ran after her and demanded, "You must promise me you'll tell me all about the people in those pictures, the house, the town, and my grandmother. I have a right to know. I want to learn about everything you've kept hidden from me. You must promise me mother. You owe me that!"

Emilia quickly swung her body around, and Mandy instinctively put up her hands to protect her face. Lowering her head, Emilia walked out of the room replying softly, "Someday Mandy, someday."

"Do you promise?" Mandy insisted as a bolt of lightning lit up the room.

There was a brief silence before a response. "Yes, I promise," Emilia said, as the roar of the lions muffled her reply.

Mandy never did have the discussion Emilia had promised. After many years of questioning and sometimes pleading for that information and the secrecy surrounding it, she finally gave up. Whatever she learned about her mother's family and hometown of Gettysburg was always second hand. Nothing more was ever mentioned about it between them, and Mandy never again asked.

Chapter Twenty-Seven

Peter was waiting for Emily as promised on the steps of Old Dorm, that beautiful, foreboding place she'd tried to avoid. When he wrapped his arms around her, all her fear was forgotten.

"You're late," he admonished with a smile.

"I decided to walk here. And, I had a phone call," she casually dismissed.

"Well, let's get started so we can have the rest of the day to play," Peter said. "I'll take you to Mr. Gelsen's office. He's our local genealogist."

The cavernous hallway leading to the office of the historical society evoked a similar reaction as her first encounter in the building. Almost immediately upon entering the dark, dank, exquisite structure, she felt the deadly chill. But this time she was prepared for it. She brought a sweater.

Gerald Gelsen was a surprisingly young-looking octogenarian, with an unquenchable thirst for information about people who came before him in his historically significant town. He could still be considered a rather attractive man despite his eighty-four years, a fact he was happy to impart by describing all the female suitors who were "after him" at the local Senior Citizen Center. The veracity of this declaration was evident by the many different baked goods in fancy packaging laid out proudly on his desk.

He offered Emily a butter cookie, and said with a twinkle in his clear, blue eyes, "It's from my favorite girl."

Emily thanked him, and after biting into it said, "I can see why she's your favorite."

He nodded while laughing, tossing his long silver locks in front of his face. Pushing them back with his hand, he asked, "Now, what can I do for you? Peter mentioned that you moved into the old Stone house."

"Yes. I just inherited it from my grandmother."

"Emilia Stone was a very fine young lady. I had my eye on her once," he said smiling.

"You knew my grandmother?"

"Sure. I knew everybody. I still know just about everybody in town. Look, when did you arrive?" he asked.

"Sunday."

"See, not even here a week, and I already know you." Emily laughed.

"Who else in my family did you know?"

"Well, I knew your great-grandfather, John Stone, a terrific football coach, and Sarah, your great grandma. Boy, she was a real looker in her day." He whistled, looked at Emily, and added, "In fact, you could be her double."

Emily placed her hands over her face. She had absolutely no idea what her great-grandmother looked like. Other than a casual comment from Grams about her having the same color and shape of eyes, she knew nothing. There never seemed to be any family pictures around at home, and so she felt somewhat ashamed she had to learn of that resemblance from a perfect stranger.

"Don't tell me no one has ever mentioned that before," he said, incredulously.

Emily blushed and shrugged her shoulders. "I was wondering if I could get some family information that goes back a little further."

"You mean Jacobs?" he offered.

"No," Emily said. "I want to learn more about the Wahlers."

Mr. Gelsen pondered the name a few moments, then jumped up from his desk with the energy of a man twenty years his junior and walked over to a bookshelf. He mumbled softly to himself while pulling out a large, loose-leaf binder. "That name, that name. I know it well," he said.

She silently watched the youthful, old man run his finger down several pages in the book, until he yelled, "Ah ha!"

He walked over to a drawer, pulled out a roll of microfilm, and placed it into the viewer near his desk. "Have a seat here," he said, excitedly. "I think I have something that might interest you."

The Gettysburg Tribune was coming into focus as Mr. Gelsen adjusted the accuracy of the lens, and he said, "This piece was written in November, 1863. It's entitled, "Another Casualty of War."

"What's the story about?" Emily asked.

"Well, it's not really a story. It's an obituary for one of your ancestors, Jonas Wahler."

The name had become familiar to her by the nightly diary readings, yet she had at best only a glimmer of interest for this man whose sole function seemed to be making comfortable chairs or coffins, whatever the needs were for the community at the time. She began to read the typical Victorian eloquence,

"An above all gentlemen. He was a gallant soldier among the Civilian Corps. God fearing, God loving..."

Emily quickly skimmed the article to read his list of survivors and stopped. She read them again. There was something wrong. The only survivors listed were his wife, Emilia, and daughter, Amanda. *Where are Sarah and Stephen?* She returned to the beginning of the page, and read, "Mr. Wahler was considered one of the most outstanding of all men in this community, especially over the course of our tyrannous months. He might have left when fear began to plague our town at the inception of summer, hence save all those close to him from the devastation they had to face. Instead, he chose to stay, anticipating the imminent needs of his neighbors and fellow countrymen. Indeed, it would have been far more difficult without his contribution.

"He did pay dearly for his selflessness. The cost was the life of his child, brother-in-law, and ultimately his own. Our prayers are now with his widow, Emilia Klee Wahler, and his daughter, Amanda, as the dark shadows continue to fall around them.

"It has been said by some that he had become full of the devil in the madness that took over him after months of producing his ugly ware, often working through the night with neither food nor sleep. But we who knew Jonas all those years, the gentle carpenter of Gettysburg, we knew that could not be so. There was really no evidence of that. However, there was evidence all around us of the true evil. For it was the devil, who although did not consume Jonas, nevertheless drove him to that unthinkable place in his life. It was the demon that stole away his little girl when his devious work prevented her condition from being properly attended. It was he who sent poor Stephen Klee, Jonas' brother-in-law, to the edge of the hilltop with a gun near the place that bears his evil name. He is the one who has caused Jonas' good wife the pain of all her losses. Sadly, it could only be the un-Godly one himself who has brought our town to the un-Godly place where it is now.

"Later this day, President Abraham Lincoln will parade through town accompanied by dignitaries and orators from all over our Nation. With pomp and ceremony, they will dedicate a National Cemetery for all the other victims of the devil's deed. But we, the people of Gettysburg, will silently bury in our own cemetery our dear servant, the chair maker, the coffin maker, Jonas Wahler, another casualty of this terrible war."

Emily exhaled and felt a tightening in her chest; the feeling was one of overwhelming sadness and despair. The realization of her forefather, yet another one of her fathers, cheated out of life, by the circumstances of life, seemed too much an added burden for that day.

"What's wrong?" Mr. Gelsen asked. "You suddenly look a little pale."

Emily stared at the screen for several more seconds before

asking, "According to this article, Jonas Wahler was considered by some to be insane when he died, but it doesn't say how he died. Was there anything else written about my family?"

Mr. Gelsen lowered his head and stuck out his bottom lip. "Unfortunately, there is," he replied. "When you mentioned that name, I remembered these newspaper articles I'd become fascinated with years ago. Of course, your family wasn't the only one to have suffered as such. All families living here at the time of the battle had their own horror stories to tell. But I thought this story was somewhat incredible."

"What do you mean?" Emily asked.

"Well, I do have to hunt a little longer to find all of the microfilm containing that information if you want to read it, but as I said, I know the story very well and can fill you in a little until we can get to that."

Emily nodded for him to continue.

Mr. Gelsen began, "Jonas Wahler was one of the finest furniture craftsmen around at the time. When word of an ensuing battle circulated through town, he was set to leave but stayed on at the request of several of his neighbors. You see, they had some foresight as to what the needs of the community would be by the recorded accounts of other battles, which had occurred up to that point.

"Jonas, along with several other men, was asked to stay on in town to create simple pine coffins for the many soldiers they anticipated would die, should indeed that battle take place. In return, they were promised compensation from the United States government for their service.

"Jonas was a very quiet, well-liked individual in Gettysburg. Although it was speculated his initial reaction to this request was to leave town anyway, after careful thought he decided to remain and serve his country in the capacity in which he was able.

"The need for coffins far exceeded what they anticipated. Materials were replenished regularly, but help was not. There were only five other individuals in the town making them. They however lacked the commitment of Jonas; hence he felt more pressured to complete his work.

"He was said to be a big man, a strong man, with the proper constitution to handle almost any difficult situation. However, several long weeks after the battle was done, his attitude and appearance had significantly changed. He became more quiet than usual. He had lost a lot of weight, sometimes barely eating one meal a day. He was weary from lack of sleep, often working through the night, his tireless hammer heard by many pounding away until dawn..."

Emily gripped the arms of the chair. "Did you say he worked through the night?" she asked, interrupting Mr. Gelsen.

"Yes. Many seemed to think that the death of his little girl was what really sent him over the edge. She'd been ill for several days prior to the beginning of the battle, probably pneumonia.

"When the fighting was over, so much attention was drawn away from her and put on the wounded soldiers, she was not properly attended. Who is to say she wouldn't have died anyway, but the war certainly didn't help. It was speculated that Jonas felt a certain degree of guilt having stayed on in town, instead of taking his family away to a safer place before the onset of that catastrophe.

"The poor man had to build his own child a coffin. Then, with his wife in such despair, he took it up to her room and placed her tiny body into it by himself. He carried her down through the torrential rains that fell that July, over to the cemetery, where he buried her alone.

"For weeks, his wails echoed in the still, summer nights. As he pounded the nails into the wood, he called out the name of the child he'd forsaken, but I can't remember it right now."

"It's Sarah," Emily whispered.

"Maybe," Mr. Gelsen said. "But whatever it was, it was the only word he uttered for months before he took his last breath. He died from madness, pneumonia or both, while working on the very coffin they buried him in. Ah, Emily my dear, the world is full of irony, isn't it?"

He sighed as he got up from his seat, not hearing Emily whisper the child's name once again, "Sarah."

An elderly woman entered the office carrying a plastic storage container and called over to Mr. Gelsen. "Oh, excuse me," he said smiling. "My lunch is here."

Emily watched the silver-haired woman set Mr. Gelsen's lunch atop his desk. He bent down and kissed her on the cheek, causing her to giggle like a schoolgirl. Emily smiled but found it hard to be jovial considering what she'd just heard. Family remembrances again proved too painful, so she solemnly stood up to leave.

That's when a more intense chill surrounded her. The same icy fingers that she'd experienced there several days before were on her skin, pinching the hairs all over her body until she felt as though they were all standing on end. The cold was accompanied by an overwhelming feeling of sadness that quickly escalated to terror and despair. She grabbed her sweater and put it on, buttoning it all the way, rubbing her arms to create heat.

Mr. Gelsen, having just said good-bye to his lady friend, noticed what was happening, and walked over to her looking sincerely concerned. "Are you feeling ill?" he asked.

"No, I'm fine." Emily said, shivering.

"I don't think so," he said, shaking his head. "I'd better call Peter."

"I'm fine, really. Please believe me. I want you to continue to tell me more about the Wahlers. What happened to Emilia's brother, Stephen?"

The old man looked into her eyes with some uncertainty. He then exhaled, and said, "Well, if you insist. But I will only continue if you allow me to make you a cup of hot tea."

She smiled and nodded.

When he returned with her tea, she appeared calmer to him. He began, "Stephen Klee was a very handsome young man. A successful businessman, he was considered a good match for any of the young ladies here in town. Although he lived with his sister and her family, it was only believed to be temporary until he was ready to take a wife. It was thought Mary Mullin would most likely be the future Mrs. Klee. He'd been courting her for several months.

"Mary and her family were among those to join the exodus out of Gettysburg in the weeks before the battle. Then, given the conditions in town afterward, they stayed away. When Mary and her family returned over two months later, she found the man she'd hoped to marry being charged with murder."

"Murder? Whom did he murder?"

"No one," Mr. Gelsen said. "It was a very sad, miserable story, born out of the misery that existed here after the end of the battle. Emily, the people could no longer take the burden they were given. Gettysburg was left with fifty thousand dead and wounded to deal with. There were so little resources. Life was more than unbearable, not only for the poor innocent civilians, but also the remaining Union Soldiers who stayed on in town to help deal with what the armies had left behind. People started turning against each other, sometimes fighting over the littlest, insignificant things. Temperament was weak, and anger grew stronger every day. Can you imagine what life must have been like living here at that time: the disease, the stench of death, the inhumanity of it all?"

"No," she said, shaking her head. "It must have been completely devastating."

He nodded and continued. "There was a soldier friend of Stephen Klee who had stayed behind to bury the dead. Because of this friendship, many nights, Stephen would bring supplies from the town to the camp where this soldier and others were stationed. During one of these visits, a bitter argument broke out between the two friends, ending with Stephen taking the man's gun and shooting him dead with it."

"That's impossible. Stephen wouldn't do that," Emily said, definitively. Mr. Gelsen looked at her oddly.

She turned away, feeling a little embarrassed by the strange remark. The diary only gave her a small indication of the friendship the two had shared, yet somehow, she felt in her heart that something like that could never have happened between them.

"Well, you might be right," Mr. Gelsen said. " Stephen was arrested, and detained for a few days pending an investigation. You see, several eyewitnesses there testified that Stephen was not the murderer. But, since it was the night of a new moon, the darkness made it impossible to say for certain who pulled the trigger."

"What did Stephen say?" she asked.

"Well, that's the strangest part of all. Stephen claimed it was one of the other soldiers, another lieutenant serving in the same regiment as the murdered officer. Of course, the accused officer denied the allegation, and he had several other soldiers who were there that night to back him up. So, no charges were formally served. Stephen was let go, and the murderer and motive remained a mystery."

Remembering the concerns Emilia Wahler had written about, she asked, "Was it espionage? Perhaps Stephen was involved in some sort of treasonous activity?"

"Perhaps," Mr. Gelsen responded. "But, as I said, it's still a mystery."

"What happened to Stephen?"

"He was so wrought with despair over death: first of his young niece; then the loss of his friend, that he lost the will to go on. But there were other reasons. Even though he could not be formally charged, the Army still felt he was in some way responsible for the young lieutenant's demise. In that belief, they set up an element of doubt of his innocence among all the people in town. Although he was never really treated as an outcast, Stephen felt he no longer belonged.

"One day that September, near the end of the summer of his twenty-fourth year, he walked over to the Devil's Den and climbed to the top of the highest mound. There, among the jagged stones and shattered pieces of dreams, he placed a pistol to his chest and fired."

Emily stared in shock.

Mr. Gelsen put his arm around her shoulder. He said, compassionately, "Don't be too upset, they're all in a better place now. Aren't you glad you came to see me?" he teased. "I bet you didn't realize what a famous family you had."

"More like infamous," she said, taking off her sweater, feeling warmer.

"That doesn't matter," he said. "What really matters is that now you can say you know about them, and in that way, you can remember them."

Emily furrowed her brow as he walked away and was about to question him again when Peter walked into the room. She noticed he looked a little concerned after Mr. Gelsen said something to him. When he saw her though, his face lit up in a smile.

"Are you ready?" Peter asked, still smiling.

Seeing him erased all questions from her mind, and she happily got up from her seat to take his hand.

"She has an illustrious background here," Mr. Gelsen called out to him.

"Thank you for your wealth of information," Emily said. "It's absolutely amazing what you can recall."

"True. I'm glad something still works," he said with a devious grin, and winked.

Emily laughed as she departed the office carrying her sweater, not realizing she no longer felt cold.

Chapter Twenty-Eight

All through lunch Emily had a hard time concentrating on Peter's summary of his seminar.

She was too preoccupied with the people from her past, which at that moment included Jonas, Stephen and another Emilia. She was sad for Stephen Klee and Jonas Wahler; both men were physically strong, yet emotionally weak, and undeniably victims of life's harshest circumstances.

She tried to imagine the pain Jonas must have experienced with the loss of his child, his town, and people. And the guilt he must have experienced for not taking his family away to a safer place. She realized that if she did indeed have a ghost, it was most likely the spirit of the "gentle carpenter," doomed to pound the phantom nails outside of her window every night and into the morning. Emily felt guilty at having been annoyed by the noise.

It may well have been Jonas' unearthly feet that climbed her steps, and into her parlor, too. His ghost might have been the one who undid the bed her first night there, and perhaps even planted his wife's diary so it would be conspicuous. All those thoughts were swirling around her head as Peter described the guest speakers he'd met and the many workshops he'd attended in Philadelphia.

He noticed Emily staring out the window and paused. "Are you listening to me?" he asked, looking skeptical.

"What? Oh, yes," Emily said, snapping to attention. "You said you saw one of your former professors from NYU, Professor Johnson. Isn't that what you said?" she asked, hoping he didn't notice she was daydreaming.

"Yes," Peter said, still doubting she'd been listening. He continued on, "Well, as I was saying, there's this new book ... ," his words trailed off as Emily's concentration was diverted once again.

She began thinking about Stephen Klee, robbing himself of his future at her age, an age when he should have been enjoying life. And she thought of Sarah, robbed of life, even before she'd any idea what to expect from it. Then there was Emilia, all alone, picking up the pieces of debris that were left to her life. She also couldn't get little Amanda out of her mind, for she was the most innocent victim of all.

As Peter continued to speak of the reunion he'd had with old friends, Emily thought about the reunion she'd had with her ancestors that day. Their sorrowful stories, though distanced by time, had still managed to settle deep within her. Somehow, although she had no idea how it could be possible, she was beginning to feel their pain.

Chapter Twenty-Nine

The sun peaked out between two clouds after they had finished lunch, and Peter said, "I think it'll be a better day than we expected. Let's go for a walk."

Emily smiled, grateful for the distraction from her thoughts. They departed the local diner hand in hand, bumping into the many tourists that seemed to be flooding the sidewalk.

Emily asked, "Is it my imagination, or are there more people than usual in town today?"

"Your observation is correct," Peter said. "The weekend always brings more tourists here in the summer, and besides, we're only about a week away from the anniversary of the battle. In a few days, you'll start to see the different reenactment groups, both Union and Confederate. They come in from all parts of the country. Some even come from as far away as Canada and Europe."

"You're kidding!"

"No, this is a big deal," Peter continued to explain. "Though the reenactors are busy all year long visiting different battle sites, this is the one they look forward to the most, at least that's what I've heard. Gettysburg is really a Mecca for all Civil War enthusiasts. This is where the course of the war changed."

They proceeded up the long, cement walkway at the entrance to the Soldier's National Cemetery, which is flanked by heavy, black, wrought iron gates. At a slight incline, stands a statue depicting several Union soldiers attending a wounded Confederate soldier. People stopped there to read the inscription, a prayer for all those lost in eternity, buried beyond the gates.

They entered the lush green field that was spotted with a plethora of tiny, stone markers surrounding a large, memorial statue. Many of the markers were nameless, but inscribed with just a State and Regiment number, or a simple, lonely, "Unknown."

Her heart grew heavy as she looked down and around at the uniform markers, row upon row, all in semi-circle design, no beginning and no end to the small granite reminders of what had happened there long ago. "So many of them," she said, softly.

"And these are just some of the Union soldiers," Peter said.

Beyond the iron fence near where they stood was another burial ground nestled close to the National Cemetery, and Peter pointed to it. "That's where my ancestors are buried, and probably yours, too. We should go in there next," he said.

"Wait," Emily said, tugging on his arm. She sat on a park bench nearby looking weary and forlorn. "I don't want to go in there," she added, staring down, childishly kicking the gravel beneath her shoes.

Peter could no longer contain his frustration. "What's going on with you?" he sternly demanded, causing her to slump down further in her seat. "You've been acting strange, first at the college, and then in the park the other night, and now here. Mr. Gelsen told me you looked ill today. He was concerned, and frankly, so am I. What is it?"

She ignored his question, remaining deep in thought caught somewhere between bewilderment and desperation.

Peter exhaled deeply, and said, "I look at you sometimes, and all I can see is fear. What are you afraid of? Please Emily, I want to help you. Let me inside," he added, softly.

"I don't think anyone can help me," she said. "I came here for a different focus to my life. I was in a sense running away from my problems, my fear, but it just followed me here. I guess it'll follow me wherever I go."

"Get a hold of your fear and try to conquer it," Peter said.

"I'm not sure I'm capable of conquering anything."

"Then let me help you," he said. "I care too much to let you go on feeling this way."

"How can you help me? We barely know each other," Emily said in a strained voice that seemed to be struggling to contain her emotions. "If you knew me better, you'd know that I have no one left. And these cemeteries are a constant reminder of all the losses," she added, causing Peter to lean in closer to her as though fearful of missing even one of her words.

"My father's been gone for years. After him, the most important person in my life was Grams, and now she's gone. Every relationship I've ever had ultimately left me alone, even my friends."

"Don't you have any close friends?" he asked, astonished.

"My friends have drifted; we're still in contact, but not so much anymore. Last year a lot of my time was spent caring for Grams so I didn't have time for them, and they didn't really have time for me either. Most of them are married now or getting married. That might have been me too, except it didn't happen. And I'm glad. My boyfriend Bill abruptly broke off our two-year relationship after just one argument. He left me to face my grandmother's death alone. Why didn't he care enough to be there for me?"

"I would've been there for you," Peter quickly answered.

Emily was surprised by his deliberate reaction. "How do you know, Peter?" she asked.

"I just know that I'd want to be there during that trying time, to comfort you," he stammered a reply. He wasn't entirely sure why he felt that way, either.

"Ah comfort. I wonder what that feels like," she said. "You know, besides Grams, my stepfather Zach was the person I was closest to until a few months ago. Now, he won't be around much longer."

"Is he ill?" Peter asked.

"No," Emily said, her voice low and once again strained. "I just think that he'll be leaving very soon. It's not something I can talk about right now."

"Aren't you forgetting someone here? What about your mother?"

"I think I've given you some idea of our relationship," she smirked. "We've never been able to comfort each other, not even when Grams died. And that was the worst time in my life, even worse than losing my father. I had Grams back then and she made it a little easier.

"I never really felt good about my life. Starting over in Gettysburg was supposed to help me to feel differently, to feel better about it, and about my past. I went to the historical society today to find some positive, reassuring information about my family that was here. But do you know what I found out? I discovered that my great-great-great-grandfather died insane, and just before that, another ancestor who had been accused of *murder* committed suicide. In fact, he shot himself near the very rocks we sat on the other day. It seems their lives turned out just as miserable as mine. Maybe misery is inherited."

"I'm sorry," he said. "Perhaps I shouldn't have taken you there."

"No, don't get me wrong, it's good to know all this. But it doesn't give me the comfort I sought. Neither does this cemetery. Look, the government put it here as consolation for all those terrible military losses during the war, right? What about all the other losses because of that war? Like the civilians—my family, probably your family, too —who were left to pick up the pieces of their broken lives? Their cemetery is over there, but I don't see a government memorial to them."

"You actually think there should be a government memorial for Gettysburg's citizens? What good would that do?" Peter asked. "How would that make your situation today any better?"

"I'm sorry," she said. "I'm just upset. I guess I sound a little frag-mented, and believe me, that's how I feel right now. It's not your fault."

"It's all right," Peter smiled, feeling relieved that her tone had lightened. "In a way, you sound just like our forefathers," he explained. "They realized the necessity for this national cemetery, but they also felt somewhat angry, and forgotten by their leaders. There was such indifference toward our government that when the cemetery was finally dedicated four months after the battle, an invitation was extended to President Lincoln almost as an afterthought. Famous orators and scholars were contacted first.

"On November 19th, the day of the ceremony, Lincoln, though the tallest man there, was given the smallest horse to ride on in the parade. People snickered at the absurd sight, his long, thin legs practically dragging on the ground. When he gave his two-minute speech, it was only after Edward Everett completed his, which was two hours long. Imagine, the President of Harvard University taking precedence over the President of the United States.

"One could say that by his treatment here, and certainly, ultimately his assassination almost a year and a half later, Lincoln was also a casualty of that war. But you know, there are political and civilian casualties in every war, you can't get around it. Just as we discussed Wednesday night, there will always be victims of circumstances that are beyond their control."

Peter continued to lecture from the park bench. "Listen Emily, there are raw deals handed out in life every day: accidents, disease, disabilities, losses, and even a lifetime rife with dysfunctional relationships. No one is immune to it. The suffering, because of this anguish, will affect how the world is perceived. Yet, we go on because we've learned how to draw courage and knowledge from that tribulation. Hopefully, that experience will help us to make better choices in how we live our lives. But we have to learn to accept and respect other people and their choices, too. It's only when that's done that you free yourself and others from being victims. Hey, it sounds like a long shot, but maybe if we could all figure out how to live that way, there won't ever be another war, right?"

"I guess so," Emily said, smiling. "I feel like one of your students. I can tell you're a really good history teacher, Peter. I guess we're all victims of our own personal wars."

"We just have to try to understand what it is we're fighting," he added.

After a few quiet moments, she offered, "I guess what I'm fighting is loneliness. So many bad things have happened to me that left me feeling alone. I'm afraid of what might yet happen, even though somehow, I manage to generate a lot of my problems. I don't know why that's so."

"Yes, you do," Peter whispered into her ear with a kiss. "Emily, delve a little deeper into your problems, your fears, your loneliness, and try to change that relationship with yourself. And, while you're at it, try to change all your other relationships, as well."

"I know I have to change how I deal with my mother; that's for sure. She hasn't had very good luck, either. But she's also generated some of her problems. In that way we're similar. I've been thinking that she really needs me now." Emily paused, and added, "I'm thinking that maybe, I need her, too. Does that sound a little nutty after all I've told you about her?"

Peter smiled and shook his head.

"I'm glad at least you seem to have it all together," she said.

"I wouldn't exactly say that," Peter responded softly, while draping his arm around her shoulder.

Chapter Thirty

Emily felt closer to Peter that day, more so than at any other time they'd spent together. His sensitivity touched a part of her that connected them. He seemed to understand her life and her feelings better than anyone else had before, even Bill. But she also realized that by the end of their relationship, Bill had figured her out, too. She just didn't know it at that time. Still, it was different with Peter. In the short time she knew him; their relationship seemed to have evolved into something that was based way beyond that of simple friendship. Emily was beginning to believe their connection went as deep as the soul.

She spent the next hour telling him about the diary she found, and how familiar she was with the various people she'd garnered more in-depth information about from Mr. Gelsen. Peter listened intently as they drove on the very streets that held all the memories she was describing, which had been written in her ancestor's hand.

"That's incredible," was all he could muster to say. "I know," she said.

"But there's more."

He parked in front of her house and listened to her describe the bizarre, paranormal events she'd encountered since arriving in the town, rubbing his forehead as if trying to relieve the pressure of what he was taking in all at once. Peter knew there was something going on with her and was very happy she'd finally shared it all with him. He had noticed vulnerability in her at their first meeting that reminded him of Alessa. That frightened him, especially as his emotional attachment to Emily grew. But he soon realized Emily was different, stronger in will and for that, he was very relieved.

Emily invited him up to her apartment to read Emilia Walher's book. As they approached the front door, she slowed her stride and fixed her eyes on the "Closed" sign in Joel and Mike's office window.

"That's strange," she said. "Joel and Mike aren't in. It's way past their lunch hour, and too early for them to close. Now that I think of it, they were closed when I left home to meet you this morning."

"Maybe they had other plans today," Peter said.

Emily peeked through the window into a quiet office. Looking beyond the gold tassels dangling from the drapes, she saw papers neatly stacked on the desks, and the darkened computer screens. Her eyes rested once again on Joel's daughter's painting.

"I think something's wrong," she said. "Yesterday, Joel was ill during lunch. Do you know where they live?"

"No, not exactly," he replied. "But I'll call my friend from your apartment and ask him. He's a client of theirs."

Emily carried the diary over to Peter as he placed a call to Ralph O'Malley.

"I left a message for him to call me here. Is this the diary?" he asked, while gently caressing the cover with his fingers.

She nodded.

After reading the first few lines he fell back onto the sofa. "You know, I've seen a few witness accounts, but never one this descriptive, and in such great shape. I wonder if anyone in my family kept a diary. May I continue to read on?" he asked.

"Of course." Emily said, "Just as long as you only read the sections I've read. The rest I want us to read together."

He nodded and continued to read as Emily lit the candles in the hearth.

Peter was engrossed in the diary when Emily called her mother, as promised. Mandy answered on the first ring. The huskiness in her voice was still evident. "How are you, Mom?"

Mandy didn't respond to her question. She began to say, "I took your advice and spoke to Zach."

"Well, what happened," Emily anxiously asked.

"I did everything you said I should do. I told him that I was trying to understand what had happened and that I was not going to blame anyone. Then, when he admitted he still loved me, I told him that I still loved him too and would be willing to work this out. But I said he had to make a choice, and he had to make it now. He told me that was okay, for he didn't need any extra time. He'd decided long before I approached him."

"What was his choice?"

"He didn't choose me," Mandy said, her voice trembling once again. "He told me that he'd had a discussion with you about this several months ago and so had a lot of time to think about it. He said he was just about to approach me with his decision when I walked in on the two of them."

"I'm sorry mother," Emily said, her voice cracking. "I didn't know how to tell you about it. I was hoping I wouldn't have to tell you. I thought, no I prayed, that he'd stay."

"That's all right, Emily," Mandy said. She paused, and added deliberately, "I forgive you. Look, I'm still in such shock over this. I may have to take you up on your offer to come down for a visit. I really need to get away from here."

"Don't worry," Emily said, wiping her tears. "I'll call Mrs. Angst and ask her where I can get a cot for the spare room."

"Thanks. I'll call you either tonight or tomorrow morning to let you know what I've decided. God, and I thought saying goodbye to a dead husband was difficult," Mandy added, coldly.

Emily hung up the phone and began thinking about the day she faced her stepfather after discovering his secret.

"I was expecting you," Zach said, as he closed the door to his study. "What can I say? I'm so ashamed you had to see that."

"That's not important now," Emily said. "What matters now is what are you going to do about it?"

"I don't know. Carl and I go back many years, long before I met your mother. The love we shared, I thought would never end. When he went away, I felt as though I could never love anyone else, until I met Mandy. With her I felt alive again.

"After I met you and your grandmother, I knew we all belonged together. I was happy, you know. I'm still happy.

"But, when Carl came back, I became confused. I love my family," he said while removing his wire-rimmed eyeglasses to wipe away tears. "You must believe me. I love you and Mandy very much. I'm sick over what's happening to Emilia. I feel the pain she's going through, no less than you, and your mother. My God, she's been like a mother to me, too."

Emily rushed to her stepfather, threw her arms around him and cried. "I love you, Zach. But I feel so hurt."

"I know, and I'm so terribly sorry. I don't know what to do to fix that."

Emily's face lit up and she said, "I have an idea. No one needs to know about this. You must let go of Carl for our sake. Tell him it's over, and no one will be the wiser. I promise to never say anything to anyone."

Emily waited for a response. When she didn't get it, she released her embrace and stepped away from Zach.

"I can't do that," Zach said, lowering his voice.

"But you said you still loved us."

"I do still love you."

"Then do this for me, for us," she continued to beseech.

"I can't. I'm too much in love with Carl to let him go now. Yet, I'm not ready to let go of Mandy, either."

"What?" Emily said, anger replacing her tears. "How could you be so selfish and cruel? You must make a choice and make it now."

"Please," Zach sobbed, and pleaded. "Don't force me to choose. I can't do that now. I won't do that."

Emily's eyes were fixed on his, hers frozen as ice while he

continued to plead. "Please don't tell Mandy yet. I want to be the one to tell her, but only when I'm ready."

As she turned to walk away, he called out, "Remember, I can't help being what I am, any more than you can help being what you are. So please, don't hate me for it."

"Sure Zach," she smirked, coldly. "I'll remember," before slamming the door.

"Now what's wrong?" Peter asked upon seeing her solemn face when she reentered the room.

"My mother will be coming for a visit, an unscheduled visit," she said. "There's just one more tidbit about my family that I haven't mentioned yet."

Emily began to explain all the details of her bisexual, adulterous stepfather, and her lost and lonesome mother. "Well, Mr. Gelson did tell you I had an illustrious background," she remarked. "I think he meant to say, notorious."

Lost for words, Peter brought her a glass of milk to where she was seated on the floor in front of the fireplace. "I couldn't find anything stronger," he said, smiling, and sat down beside her.

"You've had a rough day," he continued to console, rubbing her shoulders. "I've had a few of them myself. I can remember a time when I felt as though I was the only one in the world going through the unbearable misery I was experiencing."

She looked up at him curiously, and asked, "When was that?"

"It was a long time ago. It really doesn't matter now."

Emily sat pensively for a few moments before asking, "Did it have anything to do with you leaving Harvard?"

When he didn't respond, she knew that it did. "What happened to you there that caused such unbearable misery?"

"It's not important," he brusquely answered, appearing angry. "I said it was a long time ago and no longer matters."

"Why won't you share it with me?"

Peter took a deep breath and said, "I don't like talking about it. I still have a hard time, even now, so many years later. It's best to not go there."

She took his hand and gently brought it to her lips. "But it's important to remember, right?" His anger diffused, he then drew his knees up close to his chin and closed his eyes.

"I want to help you, too," she said, softly. "Peter, let me inside of you. Please."

He pressed his hands together in meditation, touching the tips of his fingers to his mouth.

After a few quiet moments, he turned to her and began explaining.

"I met Alessa Gellanos during our first week at Harvard. She was a beautiful woman, just a girl, actually. She'd been a brilliant student in high school, the Valedictorian of her graduating class at a Catholic girl's school in northern New Jersey.

"That semester, I felt somewhat burdened with my Liberal Arts studies. But Alessa, she seemed to breeze through all her tough science classes. The daughter of immigrants, she was the first in her family to attend college. The thought of one day having a doctor in the family must have seemed like a dream to her parents, owners of a small bakery.

"We dated for the few months we attended school there and fell in love. At least I thought I loved her. During that time, we shared our ambitions for the future, our bodies, but little else.

"There was something in those dark eyes of hers. There was darkness beyond the color, a mystery I could never understand until it was too late. And even then, still no answers.

"Initially, when we met, you reminded me of her. They say the eyes are the windows to a person's soul, Emily, well I do agree with that. You had the same haunted look as Alessa. Fortunately, that's where the similarity ends."

"What happened to Alessa?" she asked.

"She never seemed to make very many friends," he continued. "She was always so busy studying. She made time for me, though. But she was so private that I never really got to know much about her life before we met. Never bothered to find out, either. Occasionally though, she'd make unsolicited comments about her parents. She called her mother an 'obedient wimp'. I never questioned what that meant. Alessa said she really hated her father though and called him 'the aggressive brute'. I'd chuckle at the thought of a tough disciplinarian. Eventually, I realized his aggression was probably a lot more than what I initially imagined. I should have picked up on those clues, but I didn't. Why didn't I ask? If I loved her I should have asked, right? I might have been able to save her.

"It seemed as if life was just beginning for her there at college. Yet, the only time she socialized was with me, and when I took her to different dorm parties or outings with my friends. One night, I took her on a date that ultimately got us thrown out of school.

"I shouldn't have brought her to that party. Recreational drugs were all over campus: pot, cocaine. So many students were using them, including me, I'm sorry to say. But, not Alessa. She wouldn't have any of it. Still, we were there, and so were the drugs. Several of the students at the party ended up in the hospital. When the ambulance arrived, so did the police. Everyone there was arrested, including us. We both spent the night in jail. I can still see the shock and hurt in her eyes when she realized what was happening. I let her down.

"The college officials said everyone at that dorm party would be held responsible, whether they were using drugs or not. They had to set an example for other students that this type of behavior wouldn't be tolerated on campus. We were all expelled. I was sick! A simple, two-paragraph letter from the Dean erased all my dreams. My parents got the letter the next day.

"Alessa's parents received the same letter. However, they were not as understanding as mine. Her father told her she would never be allowed to attend college if he had to pay for it. She had to go home and work in the bakery until she was able to pay for it herself, and then she'd only be permitted to attend a commuter school near home. He no longer trusted her to be away. She was crushed. All her pleading to school officials, and to her parents, fell on deaf ears.

"The night before we were to leave campus, Alessa called me.

She was crying, saying she needed to talk to someone, a friend. She said she couldn't bear the pain of having to face her family, especially her father, and go back to the very place she'd studied so hard to get away from. She begged me to see her. I had my own feelings to deal with, so I told her I couldn't see her, or even speak to her right then. Emily, if only I realized what was going on, I wouldn't have put her off like that."

He bit his trembling lip as his eyes filled with tears and Emily put her arms around him. "What happened, Peter?" she asked.

He paused, took yet another deep breath, and continued. "When her parents came to pick her up the next day, she didn't answer the locked door to her room. Her roommate had gone home for the weekend. So, they asked several of the other students on the floor if they'd seen her. When they realized something was wrong, one of the girls called me. I got there the same time as the police. My God, there was blood all over the place. She'd slit her wrists," he said, crushing the dreaded words in a sob.

"How horrible!" Emily cried out. "What a terrible thing for you to see."

"It's something I'll never forget. I can still hear her parents' screams. I did quite a bit of wailing myself, curling up on the floor in a corner of the room. Some of her classmates rushed over to comfort me. I couldn't be comforted, though. She was gone.

"When all the questioning was done, and they removed her body, her father looked over at me accusingly. He was a large, burly man, and as he approached, he clenched his fists, swung his arms up to hit me and screamed, 'You killed her.' But he was restrained by a policeman.

"I was so enraged! How could he say that? It wasn't my fault she killed herself! It had nothing to do with our friendship, the party, or getting thrown out of school. I wanted to tell them that *they* were the reason for her death. They were the reason she couldn't go back home. There was a mystery to her home life I'll never really know, something that haunted her way beyond anything I could figure out in the short time I knew her. I think she was finally going to explain all of that to me when she called. If only I had realized that and gave her the chance to release some of that pain.

"I pushed past the policeman, walked over to her parents, and was about to tell them all this. And then, I looked into her mother's eyes. They were hollow and dark, just like her daughter's, and so all I was able to say was, 'I'm sorry.'"

Peter's knees were drawn up tighter in a ball as he rocked slowly, saying, "I'm guilty of bringing her to that party, for being a jerk, and not meeting with her that night, but it's not my fault that she took her life. It's not my fault." He bent his head down and cried.

"Of course it's not your fault, "Emily said. She stroked his hair as he rested his head on her shoulder. "How could you know that would happen? As terrible as it was, ultimately, Alessa was the only person responsible for the choice she made, right?"

Peter nodded and then wiped the tears with the back of his arm. "Wow," he remarked, sounding relieved. He continued to explain.

"After that, I lost nearly a year of my own life consumed with sadness and especially guilt, spending a lot of time in my bedroom reading. In a small town, everyone pretty much knows your business so I didn't want to face the pitiful reaction that seemed to follow me around. But my family and friends were a great comfort to me during that time, especially my friend Ralph. I had some counseling, too. After a while, I just wanted to run away, somewhere, anywhere. Ralph eventually convinced me to get on with my studies, so I moved to New York and registered at NYU. I didn't come back home to Gettysburg for over two years, and then only for holidays. I didn't want to be reminded of anything connected with my life during or after Harvard. I wouldn't allow myself to be reminded of her. I wasn't going to allow *her* to kill me, too."

"What made you decide to come home?" Emily asked. "You said you had a job teaching in New York."

"My family wanted me to move back. Deep down, I needed to come back, too. When I was offered a position at the college here, I had no excuse to stay away. That horrible time was more or less history to me and to everyone else here in town, or so I thought.

And then, I met you. Did I tell you how happy I am to have met you?" he said, as he took her in his arms.

Emily kissed the top of his head, happy this time to be the one to give comfort. Peter had been so supportive of her the past week there. He'd touched her intellectually, emotionally and spiritually, and did it all despite the pain he too had been carrying for so many years.

Peter held on to Emily tight, happy she now knew his secrets as well as he knew hers. Their lives had crossed at a time when they both needed compassion and guidance. Now he felt closer to her than ever.

They lay down beside each other on the cool, hard floor, kissing away all the tears they each cried that day. With passion ignited, they quickly shed their clothing, as though they were shrouds covering their lives, and then in the rapture of enlightenment, their one soul was one body.

Chapter Thirty-One

Friday afternoon was ending as Emily and Peter stretched out on the floor holding on to one another, each not wanting to let go. They clasped their hands, fingers intertwined, basking silently in their newly discovered intimacy.

She reached up to caress his long hair, wrapping a curl around her finger. "Beautiful locks," she said. "Did you always wear it this long?"

He nodded. "Haven't cut it in quite a long time. At least I spared you the beard. Shaved it off a couple of weeks ago when the weather changed. It's too hot."

"Thank you for that," she said, smiling, gently stroking his smooth face.

Peter glanced at his wristwatch and sat up quickly. "I can't believe it's this late," he remarked, and began putting on his pants.

Emily sat up and grabbed her shirt. "Are you late for work?"

"Not yet, but I will be in about ten minutes." He turned to Emily, and said with concern in his voice, "I hate to run off like this. Please, don't misunderstand."

She smiled and gave him a big hug. "We know each other much better than that."

"I promise to call as soon as I get off work. But I have to warn you, it's Friday night, which means that won't be before midnight."

"Don't bother," Emily said. "Hopefully, I'll be fast asleep before then. I'm exhausted. But I'll expect a call bright and early tomorrow morning," she added, wryly.

"Don't worry. You'll hear from me."

Peter had been gone only half an hour when his friend called.

"This is Ralph O'Malley. I'm returning Peter Sanders' phone call."

"He's at work now," Emily said. "Actually, he was calling you as a favor to me. I'm the one who wants Joel Levy's phone number, and address."

"Oh, hello Emily," he said, in a more familiar tone of voice. "I've heard a lot about you, from Peter."

"Really?" Emily said, playfully.

Ralph's voice took on a more serious tone. "Are you a friend or client of Joel?" he asked.

"Actually, I'm his landlord. I got a little concerned when I noticed they didn't open the office today."

"Joel had a relapse, and I understand it doesn't look good for him," he said.

"Relapse?" she questioned.

"Yes." he repeated. "It doesn't look good."

"What sort of a relapse?"

Ralph hesitated, and said, "It's uh...I'd rather not say."

She hastily took down the phone number and address. Just before hanging up, Ralph said, "I'm leaving for a vacation early tomorrow. If you do go there tonight, please give my regards, and tell Mike I'll call when I get back."

"I will," she said, and thanked him for the information.

Joel and Mike's brick Cape Cod-style house stood majestically upon a slight hill and was surrounded by some of the most beautiful gardens Emily had ever seen at a private home. Near a flagstone walkway, leading to the back of the house, was a wood gazebo highlighted by a bed of wildflowers at the foundation. They were identical to those in the bouquets she found near her door the previous few days. It was then she realized she hadn't received any flowers that day and understood why.

Mike answered the door after she rang the bell a few times. He was dressed in tee shirt and jeans; his hair was uncombed. He seemed shocked to see her, but didn't question her presence as he invited her in.

"How are things?" she asked. Mike's eyes seemed very swollen and red. He didn't answer immediately, and she offered, "I was concerned when I didn't see the two of you at work today. Then, remembering what happened yesterday at lunch, I got very worried. Where's Joel?"

"He's not well, Emily," he said." "He's in the bedroom."

The solemn procession to the bedroom at the rear of the house revealed several rooms, including a living room and dining room, which were as beautifully decorated as their office. Mike stopped in the doorway of a simply furnished chamber, where there were many flowers filling crystal and porcelain vases in every corner of the small space. Upon seeing her reaction, he said, "Joel likes flowers." He held out his hand for her to enter the room.

Joel lay on a twin bed of plain, white cotton sheets. The delicate, lively creature only the day before was unconscious and still, except for the labored breaths that shook his chest with every gasp of air.

"Oh Joel," Emily cried, and touched his motionless hand. It was warm, still holding on to the sliver of life, which seemed all that was left in him. "What's happened?" she asked, grasping his hand with both of hers. "Except for the anxiety episode yesterday, which he got over, he seemed okay."

Mike turned to her with tears in his eyes, and said, "Joel hasn't been okay for many years. I've been with him almost five years now, and this is what we always knew would be ahead for us." When she seemed confused by his words, he remarked, "At one time they called it the 'virus of the century'. Isn't that a wonderful name for it? So monumental, extraordinary! Well, that it is."

She quickly let go of Joel's hand, backed away from the bed, and stood in the doorway of the room, looking sheepishly at Mike.

"It's okay," he said. "Most people have the same reaction." After taking a deep breath, he sat down at the foot of the bed. "You know, Joel once told me, the only prejudice he thought he'd ever have to face was from just being gay. But he never really knew what prejudice was, until he got labeled with this."

Emily swallowed hard. "I thought they've made many advances in AIDS research and treatments," she said.

"Yes, and no," Mike noted.

After a few moments Emily said, "My grandmother died this past March. I know how hard it is to lose someone you love."

"I still can't believe he's leaving me. I don't know why I'm so shocked. I've been expecting this for some time now. His condition has been rapidly deteriorating over the past few weeks. He returned to work only on Monday, looking pretty good, I thought. But then he came crashing down all at once yesterday. It happened just like the doctors said it would."

Emily handed Mike a tissue as he brushed past her while leaving the room. His brusque nature was transformed by grief. The sad circumstances he faced were not unlike her experience.

"How long has he been like this?" she asked, still watching him from the doorway.

"About twelve hours," Mike said. "I've already called his brother and daughter, both live in California. They should be here by tomorrow morning."

"My Grams looked the same way," she said, with a shiver. "There was that horrible breathing, followed by a period of silence when you think it has ended, only to have it begin all over again. And then you watch, perched at the edge of the inevitable, praying for a miracle you know won't happen."

Mike leaned over to whisper in her ear, "No matter how differently we live, we basically all die the same way."

His remark raised concern and she asked him, "And you, Mike? Are you okay?"

"You mean am I sick, too? No. At least not yet," he said, lowering his head.

As she was leaving, Emily asked Mike to call her if she could help in any way. Just before walking out the front door she turned to him, and said, "I don't know what to say. I'm just so very sorry."

He nodded, and said, "So am I, Emily. So am I."

Chapter Thirty-Two

Emily returned home with the last of that day's light barely illuminating the way to her door.

In the distance, she could hear thunder, and wondered if that meant another storm was approaching, a possibility that no longer bothered her. She was tired, but not sleepy, feeling somewhat emotionally drained from her visit.

Mrs. Angst called just as Emily crumpled salted crackers into a cup of instant soup. "I hear you're expecting a visitor already," she announced.

"Have you spoken to my mother lately?" Emily anxiously asked.

"Yes," Mrs. Angst said. "She's arriving at four-thirty tomorrow afternoon at the Harrisburg Airport. She asked me to tell you to not bother picking her up. She'll just get a taxi from there. If the flight is on time, you should probably expect her at six o'clock. Can I get you anything?" she asked.

"Yes, thank you," Emily said. "I'll need a cot or something for her to sleep on when she arrives."

"Why?" Mrs. Angst said. "She could use your bed. You haven't slept in it lately. Have you?"

After a long pause, Emily answered meekly, "Yeah, she could do that." She quickly added, "Please keep everything I've told you about the apartment between us, yes?"

"Don't worry about me," Mrs. Angst said. "That's between the two of you."

As Emily lit the candles in the fireplace, she noticed the diary on the floor. She picked up the little book and took her place by the hearth. Listening to the storm in the distance, she thought of the wonderful and terrible stories Emilia Wahler had given her about the Civil War and all the other wars her ancestors had to endure. So much, she thought, is different now, and yet so much is still the same.

She thought about Peter's old girlfriend, Alessa, and the trouble she must have been trying to escape at home. Surely, it was far worse than anything she'd ever experienced. And all those years Peter had been fighting a debilitating guilt, wondering what might have been had he acted differently.

Glancing over to the trash pail holding the wilted wildflowers, she thought of Joel, who was fighting a horrible war, too. Though the disease was incurable, it was only one of the battles he'd had to face in his life with Mike.

Then, there was Zach and Mandy, both united and divided by love, probably the most devastating war of all. She remembered all the casualties in life's wars and smiled to herself when she realized she was no longer disturbed at remembering them. Suddenly, her circumstances seemed to be very different, and she was beginning to feel less like a victim.

Emily began thinking about her mother. She was concerned about Mandy's visit but not upset. She laughed to herself at how odd that seemed. *I couldn't wait to get away from her last week. Now I'm actually looking forward to seeing her.* Her mother seemed very changed during their last two conversations. Although she wished the subject matter could have been different, it had opened a line of communication and confidence she'd never had with her before, and that made her feel good. She hoped there wouldn't be any of the typical confrontations that would occur when the two of them got together.

There, she was finally beginning to experience the peace in her life she'd always wanted. *I hope Mandy finds peace here, also. Oh, if only Grams could be here too, then maybe we could've found a way to be the daughters to her that we should have always been.*

That thought was never possible when her Grams was alive. All three of them seemed blind to their destructive behavior. However, in the end, Emilia's vision became perfectly clear. That was many months ago, the last time the three of them were together.

Emily had a daily routine to care for her sick grandmother. Every morning, she'd open the nightstand near Emilia's bed and take out a plastic basin and some liquid soap. After squirting a bit of the soap into the pan, she'd walk over to the doorway and call out to her mother to come fill the basin with water. Emily then gathered some clean linen and towels and lined up the talc powder and mineral oil on the dresser.

Emilia Schmidt lay very still in her bed, weakened by two years of an illness that was bringing her life to a painful end. Though too weak to move, she was able to follow her grandchild with her eyes, watching her carefully orchestrated ritual of providing for her basic needs. She smiled to herself thinking *I taught her well. Everything organized, and at easy reach, with little wasted time in the process. Poor Mandy, she can't seem to fill a basin of water in less than ten minutes.*

Turning her head to one side, Emilia noticed what appeared to be white lines floating in the air. She blinked to clear her vision, but they remained. It took a few seconds before she realized they were beams of the morning light streaming through the semi-closed blinds on the window.

Counting the perfectly formed twelve beams, floating ghost-like through the room, she thought of all the finite things in life observed when one is confined to bed. She could almost think her position advantageous, if only there wasn't so much pain.

She saw Mandy standing in the doorway of her room while Emily handed her the bath basin.

They move like robots, completing tasks together without emotion, and some-

times even without words, she thought. *They pass in the hall of our home like two ships in the night, never stopping to notice if the other was sinking.* They were both sinking, these two daughters of hers, and it was too late for her to do anything about it.

When Mandy returned with the basin, Emily tested the temperature of the water while swishing it around with her hand. She gave her mother an annoyed look. "How many times do I have to tell you to mix the soap and water?" she said, tersely.

Mandy remained in the doorway, a point she had not been able to get beyond in weeks, and said, "I keep forgetting." She added, "I don't know why you're doing this. I told you we could get a live-in nurse, hospice, someone. Why do you insist on doing this, especially so near the end?"

"Shh!" Emily walked toward her mother and pushed her into the hallway. "Don't talk like that in front of Grams. She knows she's dying. You don't have to keep reminding her by blurting out your insensitive comments."

Mandy narrowed her eyes and said, "Fine. But you're a young woman, too young to be strapped with this responsibility. Why are you doing this?" she asked again.

Emily stared into her mother's cold, hateful eyes, a wasteland where emotion blindly enters to be lost forever, and said, "Because I want to."

Lost for words, Mandy stormed back to the kitchen. She slammed the latest issue of Town & Country down on the table and began flipping through the pages.

"What's wrong?" Zach asked.

"I can't seem to do anything right."

"What do you mean? I think you do everything right," he said as he bent down to kiss the top of her head.

She shrugged, and said, "I'm always somewhere I'm not supposed to be, and never where I should be."

"Is it Emily who's troubling you?"

"Yes," she said softly. "It's always Emily. She and Emilia remain a team to the very end. There's never been any room for me."

She closed the magazine and threw it on the floor. "What will happen to Emily after Emilia is gone? Who will she turn to then? I bet it won't be me," she blurted, her eyes filled with rage. "That woman took care of that a long time ago when she took control of my child."

Zach interrupted, "Don't say that. She's dying. Anyway, you know you created that situation when you allowed your mother to move in with you. You made the wrong choice."

Mandy swung around with tears in her eyes, and said, "That was a plan for me to get close to her. But Emily took my place. Now, my daughter treats me like I'm responsible for this disease her grandmother has."

Zach put his arms around his wife. "Who are you angry with, Emily or Emilia?"

Mandy dabbed her wet eyes with his handkerchief and said, "Is there a difference?"

Zach walked into the sick room and asked Emily to have a word with him in the hallway. She reluctantly interrupted the bath, only after placing a blanket over Emilia's bare shoulder.

"What is it?" she asked, looking away.

"Don't be so hard on your mother. She loves you very much."

"Is that what you called me out here for? Her mother is sick, and all my mother cares about is herself."

"That's not true."

"Then why doesn't she come in here to help?"

"She gets upset, sick to her stomach to see someone so ill," Zach noted.

"That's a poor excuse."

"Remember Emily, your mother is not responsible for your grandmother's illness. Doing all this, and rejecting the idea of hired help, is like flaunting what she's incapable of in her face. You're not being fair to Mandy."

Emily turned slowly to face him, and said, grinning slyly, "Fair? I'm not being fair to Mandy? I think it's very odd that you should say that. Don't you?"

Zach stiffened his back and walked away.

"I'll be working late tonight," he said in a voice barely above a whisper as he passed his wife.

"Again?" Mandy asked.

"Yes," he replied, without looking at her. "Don't wait up for me."

She sighed as she watched him walk out the back door, feeling once again defenseless and all alone.

Mandy climbed the stairs to the second floor, opened the door to her mother's bedroom, and poked her head through the doorway. "Can I get you anything?" she asked sheepishly.

"How about some assistance," Emily asked, while tucking in the clean bottom sheet. She smiled to herself knowing Mandy wouldn't be able to get past the door frame.

Mandy took two steps in and began to feel the room spin. She clasped her hand over her mouth, ran into the bathroom, and slammed the door with such force the pictures on Emilia's bedroom wall shook.

"What happened?" Emilia asked, breathless. "A hurricane?"

"Yeah," Emily sarcastically laughed. "Hurricane Amanda."

"Poor Mandy," Emilia said.

Emily looked at her grandmother in disbelief. "Poor Mandy?"

"Don't be so hard on your mother. She doesn't know any better."

"Oh, she knows," Emily said, nodding. "I hate her."

Emilia lifted her head and tugged on Emily's arm with strength she hadn't had in weeks, and said, "No! Please don't hate her." She fell back to the bed and caught her breath. "Don't blame her for the way she is."

"But Grams, I hate the way she treats you, even now."

"She's not responsible for the way she is. Just like the rest of us, she doesn't know any better."

"What do you mean?"

The old woman put her hand over her heart before she spoke. "She's just a victim, a victim of bad circumstances. I realize now, it's my fault. It's all my fault."

"No Grams! Don't blame yourself for the way she is. I'm a victim of circumstances, too."

"Yes, that's true," Emilia said. "And I'm sorry for that. But there were other things."

"What other things?"

There was a pause, and Emilia said, "It doesn't matter now."

"I don't think you're correct anyway," Emily continued. "People can choose to change their lives and make it better for everyone concerned." She stopped speaking, lowered her head, and added, "that is, except for you, of course. You poor darling, you didn't deserve this terrible disease," and wiped a tear on her sleeve so Emilia wouldn't see her crying.

"My disease is my cure," Emilia said. "You see, sometimes we don't realize that choice until it's too late. It's too late for me, my dear. It's not too late for you and your mother."

"Don't say that. We'll still pray for a miracle, it could happen. Please, don't give up," Emily said.

Emilia held Emily's hand tight. "Listen to me child: hate and anger breed guilt and regret. Those feelings are far worse than any disease. It will take a miracle to cure that! Please, while you and Mandy are still young and healthy, listen to me."

She began gasping for air. Emily grabbed the oxygen mask on the side of the bed and hastily placed it over Emilia's face. "Please Grams, don't give up. Please, pray."

Emilia shook her head, and said, "If I pray for anything now, it's that you remember what I just said."

Mandy walked over to the doorway and stopped at her place within the frame. "Is everything okay?" she asked.

"No," Emily snapped. "How could anything be okay?"

After Mandy walked away, Emilia raised her hand and looked into her granddaughter's eyes.

"What?" Emily asked as she leaned closer and gently lifted the oxygen mask. "What did you say, Grams?"

"Remember," Emilia said before closing her eyes, and fell asleep.

Three days later, Fr. Vinci went into the sick room to give Emilia the Holy Sacrament. She had been drifting in and out of consciousness for two days, so everyone knew the end was near. Zach and Emily stood on either side of the priest and watched him touch the sacred oil to the forehead of the crumpled body that had once been a tall, very attractive woman.

Mandy stood in the doorway, gripping the frame, and bit her lower lip. After the prayers were completed, Emily and Zach followed Fr. Vinci to the front door.

Mandy remained in her position, staring into the face of the mother she barely recognized, and never really knew. As the old woman gasped for air, with periods of silence in-between, Mandy wondered if there was any life left in her to hear what she needed to say, what she should have said long before. She took a deep breath, stepped past the imaginary restraint that kept her from entering the room in weeks and slowly walked to the bedside.

Gently, she touched her mother's hand and instinctively wrapped her fingers around hers. Though they felt cold, there was a sense of warmth that was comforting, a feeling she hadn't experienced in a very long time, and Mandy began to cry.

Quickly regaining her composure, she called, "Mom?" There was no response from Emilia, but Mandy continued. "Mom, I'm not sure you can hear me, but I need you to know something. I realize I've not been the best daughter to you. Ha! That's an understatement, isn't it? Well, at least I gave you Emily. All those years growing up, I wanted so much to be a part of your life, but you shut me out. I felt hurt and rejected. I still feel that way. I could never figure out what I did wrong.

"I thought when I had Emily, and you moved in with us, things would change, and she'd bring us close. Instead, she just widened the abyss that already existed. Now, I look at the two of you and I'm jealous. I wanted her to look at me the way she looked at you. More than that, I wanted you to look at me the way you looked at her. Oh mother, I know you loved me. But that wasn't enough! You should have told me what was wrong. And, I guess I should have persisted in asking. There's no excuse for unspoken words between mother and daughter. Didn't you know that? We're both intelligent women so why didn't we know that?

"Remember the day I found Grandma Sarah's picture in the attic along with all the other pictures of Gettysburg? You promised me we would talk about her and everything that was important to you there. You promised me you would share that part of your life with me, but you never did. I felt I wasn't privileged to know about it, and I was too proud to ask anymore. But you know you gave Emily that privilege without her even asking. You shared things with her that should have been meant for me first. Why?

"Anyway, all of this is in the past. At this point, nothing can alter what has already come between us. But now, while there's still a chance you might hear me, there's something I need to say to you, because I don't want anything else to be unspoken. That's why I must tell you that I love you. I've always loved you despite the way I acted. Mother, I forgive you, and I hope if you hear any of this, you'll find it in your heart to forgive me. Mom? Did you hear me?"

Mandy looked at her mother for a sign, an acknowledgement of what was just said. She stood there quietly and watched but saw nothing. It was then she realized she'd spoken too late.

As she walked away though, she thought she heard something coming from the direction of her mother's bed. In a faint whisper, it almost sounded like, "I'm sorry." But she knew it couldn't possibly be, for when she returned to the bedside, Emilia was dead.

A family friend did the reading of Emilia's Will, exactly one week after she was buried.

Coincidentally, it was Emily's twenty-fourth birthday.

The attorney, Stu Larson, had an intimidating loud, raspy voice, but a kind face, which looked very uncomfortable reading the last Will and Testament of a woman he'd known personally most of his life.

Zach and Mandy sat facing Stu on the leather client chairs opposite his desk. Emily sat alone on the sofa, which was placed on a sidewall of the sparsely furnished room. Stu cleared his voice several times before beginning.

"I, Emilia Schmidt, being of sound mind, if not body..." He stopped and smiled. "She always did have a sense of humor."

Zach and Mandy smiled, but Emily remained stoic, staring down at tightly clasped hands resting on her lap.

Stu continued, "...do solemnly declare this to be my final request. I bequeath all my belongings to my daughter, Amanda Porter, and my granddaughter, Emily Tomaso.

"To my daughter Mandy; I leave my platinum watch (an anniversary gift from her father) and my gold chain and Crucifix. I leave her the total sum of several accounts at the National Bank in town, totaling approximately $390,000.00, and all my furniture left in her house. In addition, she is to be left the large, antique wooden chest, and all its contents that is presently located in the attic of her home. I hope it will bring her some comfort."

Mandy lowered her head and took a deep breath. No one could tell she was straining to control the emotions that were causing her heart to skip beats.

Emily stared at her mother through a pool of tears that had welled in her eyes. She wondered how she could remain so calm, so empty of feeling for the woman who'd given her life and now had given her everything she had in life.

Stu continued, "To my granddaughter Emily, I leave my platinum and diamond wedding band. I hope someday it will bring her as much happiness as it brought to me. In addition, I leave her the remaining sum of my checkbook at the aforementioned bank. After the cost of my funeral is deducted, the balance should be approximately $48,000.00.

"Since she has no debt, as I have paid for her college education and the cost of her car, I feel this would be an adequate amount of money for a young woman to begin her life. I am indebted to my darling granddaughter for her love, support, and commitment to me this past year, so I am also leaving her the means to begin a new life."

Emily looked up from her clasped hands and stared into the attorney's face. He paused to take a drink of water, shifting a look of uncertainty from Emily to Mandy, and back to Emily again. He continued, "I leave Emily Tomaso the Deed to my childhood home, located at 7384 Hemsford Street, Gettysburg, Pennsylvania."

"What?" Mandy said, slightly rising from her seat.

"It's what Emilia wanted," Stu nervously added. "I questioned her about it, but she insisted that Emily take total control of the house down there. She even had me change the name on the Deed."

Emily sat silent, too shocked to say anything.

"That's preposterous," Mandy said. "What does Emily know about running a house, especially one over 300 miles away? Besides, Zach handled all the correspondence with the caretaker ever since my mother's illness prevented her from doing so. How could she do this to me?" she said, turning to her husband for support.

Zach turned to look at Emily who was still staring at the document the lawyer held tight in his hands, and said, "Listen Mandy, Emilia wanted it that way. What would you have done if she left the house to you? Be honest."

"I suppose, eventually, I would have sold it," she said. 'After all, it's so far away. I don't know why my mother held on to it all this time. She never even wanted to visit there."

"See," Zach said. "She knew you'd sell it, and she didn't want her old family home sold."

"What will Emily do with it?" Mandy said, turning to her daughter who remained speechless on the couch.

Emily quickly recovered though, looked accusingly at her mother, and said, brusquely, "I don't know. However, I'm sure I'd never be so inconsiderate to sell Grams precious memories."

"How dare you speak to me that way," Mandy yelled, apoplectically. "Who do you think you're talking to..." She stopped herself. The argument was hauntingly familiar, and she needed to end it.

"By the way," Zach added, trying to calm his wife. "I had our accountant look over the figures a few weeks ago when I thought the house might become yours. He said it wouldn't be worthwhile to have the house anyway. It's best if you don't own it."

Mandy appeared more relaxed, nodding her head in agreement.

She was not relaxed, though. There was a knot in her stomach, and tightness in her throat that made it difficult for her to swallow.

After the signatures were done, Emily quickly grabbed her raincoat and headed toward the door. It was raining hard with bolts of lightning brightening the gray sky.

Mandy, Zach and Stu began discussing an upcoming tennis tournament at their country club, so they didn't notice her leaving. Mandy turned and saw Emily just as she was walking out the door, and said, forcing a smile, "Be careful driving. Lots of lions out there."

Emily turned away and slammed the door.

"She'll be okay," Zach said, and put his arm around his wife. Mandy sat down and placed her face in her hands.

"Are you that upset that Emilia didn't leave you the house?" he asked.

"I don't care about that house. I never did. I only care about my daughter. She finally did it," Mandy rambled. "Finally did it."

"Did what?" Zach asked. "Who, did what?"

"My mother. Even after death she's found a way to keep me and Emily apart."

"Don't be silly!" Zach said. "You have nothing to worry about. Emily won't be leaving home anytime soon. Even with her inheritance, without a job, she's in no position to relocate.

"Why would she go all the way to Gettysburg anyway? There's nothing for her down there." Mandy relaxed when she realized that was true.

"You'll see, now with her grandmother gone, Emily will need you more than ever," Zach said. "She'll learn to depend on you for the emotional support Emilia always gave her. I'm sure the two of you will become close."

The next day, Emily received notification from the Hanover School District in Hanover, Pennsylvania. It was regarding a position to which she had applied only two months before, along with a few other school districts scattered around the northeast. After several telephone interviews, she was offered a job in the junior high school, located only a short commute from her inherited house.

Chapter Thirty-Three

Though the night was hot, and remained damp, a breeze blew through the window, after gently whistling its way past the leaves of a nearby tree. Emily enjoyed the calming sound as she situated herself on the rocker, prepared to read the diary once more.

Remember... Jesus pray for us all. Today the Rebel Army has been seen retreating down the Pike, heading toward their homeland. I am grateful it is finally over. Despite their intrusion, I pity the weary souls in their long journey with the weather as it is now.

The rain began to fall as I arose this morning, with the wind sweeping waves of puddles into my home. The soldiers are lying in pools of water now tinted with their own blood. I do not see this situation changing soon.

My child, Sarah, remains very ill. I have tried to attend to her as well as I attend to the many others here, but there are just too many of them. When I leave my post for more than a few moments, Dr. Harlow calls out my name in such despair, I must leave my child to attend to his needs. I cannot blame him. I understand his demands are not born out of selfishness for his predicament, but rather complete desperation over the incredible burden that both armies have left for him. Still, I will insist on attending to Sarah, also.

I have seen Abigail this day. She has brought us word of the terror and despair at the other hospitals. Since all the churches in town are now being used in this manner, she has stated foolishly that she is concerned there will be no services anywhere for the Sabbath tomorrow.

I've not seen Jonas since yesterday, as he continues his work as I continue mine. The meal I sent him was returned untouched, and I fear he will succumb to illness himself unless he takes the proper rest and nourishment.

Stephen has returned with information from the fields where the armies battled. He had offered his assistance to our Union Army in the burial of the many fallen soldiers who remain there, and now he has come home to rest, bringing with him disturbing news. He wept as he recalled the unsightly vision of torn flesh and limbs, some laying several feet away from the torso to which they belonged. He spoke of the futile attempts to bury these divided bodies, only to find those they had buried uncovered amidst the dirt, which has now been transformed to mud by the rain. What inhumanity, such degradation.

Mr. Lorhner, my neighbor's seventy-five-year-old father, did manage to bring some degree of levity to this day. It was reported to me only several minutes ago by his daughter, that upon seeing a Rebel soldier, probably a deserter, walking slowly toward his barn this morning, he immediately put himself into action. He loaded up his Brown Bess and followed behind him as quietly as he could. When close enough to realize the man was unarmed, he hollered, "Halt." The old man then escorted the willing prisoner over to where he knew he'd find a Union officer to accept his captured foe. The proud Mr. Lorhner was commended for his bravery despite the terrible weather conditions, and his state of dress. It was only then he realized he'd exercised his courage wearing only his nightshirt, no shoes, and no pants.

I pray that tomorrow will find the conditions of my child and the others improved. I pray the conditions all around us are as well. Perhaps too, Mr. Lorhner will commit another act of heroism, for now we need what little smiles we can get...E.W.

Emily smiled as she turned the page for another reading of the incredible story she was privileged to know.

Remember... Lord, hear our prayers. Three days have passed since I have documented the trials to which I am witness. I do not see any improvement in what is happening here. The soldiers remain in my home in agony, as well as my little Sarah, whose life I have placed completely into the hands of our Heavenly Father. She is beyond asleep, but still with us currently.

My dear Jonas has remained in his workshop all day and night. However, I believe this devotion to his labor has nothing to do with the need for what he is producing, but rather a desire to avoid witnessing what is occurring in his home, especially to his own child. He has not visited with her in two days, though he understands she may not be with us much longer. The pain of that realization is too much for me to bear. I shudder as I write those very words, yet I know in *my heart they are written in truth.*

I have sent Amanda to stay with my neighbor, Mrs. Johnson. There, she will be protected from having to face what is happening here. Since Mrs. Johnson's house is too small to be used as a hospital, it is free of the misery that presently exists in my own.

Dr. Harlow has been very determined to stay awake and care for the injured in our home, and at several of the other homes nearby, which are also being used as hospitals. But I will insist he must rest, for we must avoid the possibility of him taking ill. He is a brave and honorable man.

I will enter my observations as often as I am able, but my time to do so grows shorter with each day, as I have so many in need of my time ... E.W.

A gust of wind rustled the papers on the open bookcase, causing some to fall off the shelf, and Emily rushed to pick them up. When the wind died down, she noticed the pounding hammer begin outside the rear window once again. She walked back to the kitchen, looked out at the active workshop she'd just read about, and smiled, remembering who had come back for a visit.

Remember...Dear God, have you forgotten us? To all who find this writing, please realize the pain of this witness! The most unbearable situation for a mother occurred last week.

Sarah was taken to Heaven. I know she is in a better place, but that knowledge does little to comfort me now. I miss her so very much.

It has been more than two weeks since my last entry. The weather had temporarily cleared, but now the rain has returned, falling almost as intensely as my tears. Poor Jonas had been given the ugly task of taking her to the place near our departed family. Alone in the cemetery amidst the torren-

tial rains that fell that day; he hastily said a prayer over where she now rests. I, being too wrought with emotion, could not accompany him there. I am committed to go however when this new bout of inclement weather passes.

Jonas returned to me early that evening after his miserable deed was done. His feet climbed our stairs with such burden, I could hear the despair with his every step. When I held out my arms to him though, he seemed to look past me, as if I was not there. He then turned away and silently departed.

His temperament remains unaltered since that dreadful day of Sarah's passing. He needs my comfort now, I am certain, almost as much as I need his. Why then does he turn away from me? I will speak to Dr. Harlow tomorrow, for I fear my dear Jonas may now need his help...E.W.

The mystery of the heavy footsteps in the stairway was finally solved. Emily exhaled slowly and closed the diary. She was thinking about poor Jonas Wahler, facing the pain no parent should ever have to face. She imagined him carrying Sarah to the cemetery and burying her alone with no one near for support. She thought about how he looked beyond his wife, before turning away from her, and Emilia's reaction to him doing so. For Emily now knew what, at that time, Emilia did not. Jonas' behavior was only the start of the further despair that was yet to come. It was only the beginning to what would be the end of the gentle carpenter of Gettysburg.

Emily walked over to the window closest to the barn, where the pounding noise seemed to be the loudest. She opened it all the way, bent her body over the sill, and called out to her ghost. "I know who you are now. You are one of my forefathers, Jonas Wahler, and I now know your pain. I remember you, Jonas. My God, I will always remember you."

Chapter Thirty-Four

Candles in the Hearth

Gertrude Angst walked by the many tourists brushing past one another on the crowded sidewalk near her home. She effortlessly pulled the two-wheel, metal shopper's cart behind her, stopping briefly to allow some disappointed new arrivals out of the driveway of a motel, which had its No-Vacancy sign lit up. She passed the Civil War reenactors popping in and out of a store selling the clothing and accouterments of a different time. Then, she nodded toward a man, all dressed up as a Union General, standing outside the store with his wife. Mrs. Angst gently pulled the cart around the General's wife, careful not to disturb her fine linen skirt ballooning out above a wide plastic hoop. Finally, she stopped in front of the Wick n' Wax Shoppe and waved to the woman inside.

The intoxicating smell of scented candles in the store recalled many happy memories. Each time she entered, it seemed as though she smelled another scent she hadn't noticed in years, igniting a particular memory of her life long ago. That day, she was filled with the familiar smell of lavender, and she immediately reached for the pillar candles scented with it.

"You must really love these candles, Gertie," the chubby, red-cheeked proprietor said. "I only sold you three like these a few days ago."

"Oh, they're not for me," Mrs. Angst, corrected. "I'm buying them for a lovely, young lady who has just come home. I promised my very dear friend I'd take good care of her granddaughter when she arrived here."

While the saleswoman rang up the merchandise and wrapped them in a box, Mrs. Angst looked around the store and smiled. Everything appeared to her then, as it did in her youth. The open rafters above dangled dried herbs and flowers from the garden located at the rear of the building, wicker baskets held smaller candles, and the wooden shelves supported different styles of glass oil lamps. Though reproductions, she thought about the time when they were original, and had stood upon many tables in the town.

Looking around brought back memories of when she and Emilia worked there during those golden summers toward the end of their high school years. In between serving customers, they'd whisper to each other about boyfriends and fellow classmates, sharing secrets they'd take with them through life.

She remembered asking her best friend, "Don't you just love it here, Emilia? I wish we could always work together in this place."

"No Gertie," Emilia said, in a critical tone. "There's more to the world than just the Wick n' Wax Shoppe, and even Gettysburg. I know you're happy living here, and I certainly don't fault you for that. My mother has always been happy staying here, too. But I want to experience something else, something more than just what my mother experienced. I know eventually, I'll want to go away."

"You'll go away and forget all about the town, and me," Gertie sighed.

"Silly goose!" Emilia teased. "I could never forget you or anyone else here. I know wherever I am, the smell of perfume candles will always take me back to our town, this place, and you."

Mrs. Angst then waved to the storeowner as she left, but before placing the candles into the cart, she held the box to her nose and inhaled deeply. "Ah, Emilia," she said, with a smile. "It's so good to remember you again."

Chapter Thirty-Five

Emily had just hung up the telephone when Mrs. Angst reached her door. She answered with such a solemn look, the old woman began to worry. "What's wrong? Has anything happened to your mother?" she asked.

"No, my mother is fine, I guess. It's Joel Levy. He just died."

"Oh, poor Joel," Mrs. Angst said. "I hope the end wasn't painful."

"He was already comatose when I saw him last night," Emily said.

"I knew the end was getting near when I last saw him," Mrs. Angst said. "Mike will have to find the strength to go on without him."

Emily silently helped her to unload the metal cart, which was full of extra sheets and pillows in preparation for Mandy's arrival. She broke the quiet when she saw the box of candles. "Are these for me?" she asked, her eyes lit up in a smile.

"Of course," Mrs. Angst said. "You sounded so pleased when I last gave them to you that I wanted to replenish your supply."

"Thank you so much. These candles are truly special," Emily

said, placing them beside the others. "What a wonderful feeling they give to the room when lit in the hearth, just like a real fire."

"I told you so," Mrs. Angst said. "You know, fires summon the soul. It doesn't matter if it's coming from a single candle, or a stack of seasoned wood. It calls out to a part of ourselves we've lost contact with long ago. It stirs our imagination, our desires, but mostly it invites us to remember."

Emily looked her in the eye and nodded, realizing then she understood her complex and somewhat ethereal explanations of life. She was pleased to admit she actually knew what she was talking about.

"There's so much for me to remember, Mrs. Angst," she said. "I've learned more about myself in less than one week here than I did all my life in East Springs. It's as if this town has brought me to a better understanding. I'm almost beginning to feel at peace."

"I know," she replied. "Most people here are at peace."

"Why is that?"

"Our town—our people—are continually faced with reminders of their heritage."

"Do you mean the Military Park?" Emily asked.

"Yes. But there are other reminders. Once, all who lived here knew great pain and suffering. That suffering left scars that can never be forgotten. You see Emily; most of us who are the descendants of the people who lived here during the Civil War battle have more than just a physical connection to our ancestors. Somehow, we also carry within us their emotional scars that were left from that experience.

"Since you are also descended from our people, those scars are within you, too. Having grown up somewhere else, you've just lost the connection to them, until now. Those scars help us to confront fear, injustice, conflict, and remind us of how bad life could be again. Most of the everyday problems we face today pale in comparison."

"Carry emotional scars? How is that possible?" Emily asked, looking once again very confused.

"It's hard to explain," Mrs. Angst said. She paused for just a moment before placing her fingers at both temples in deep thought, then turned to Emily and asked, "Have you noticed the many flies our town seems to have at this time of year? Even in the center of the shopping district, miles from farms and livestock, there are the incredible hoard of annoying flies that we are forced to live among every summer. Have you noticed?"

"I did notice them. They seem to be everywhere."

"Be patient, it's only for a few more weeks. They'll be gone before the summer ends," Mrs. Angst said. "The flies are the good generative stock of the very many who were born because of death, disease, the inhumanity that had occurred. They reappear every summer around this time, reminding us of what was once here. Just like the vultures that people sometimes see perched on the treetops of the Devil's Den. They return every year, somehow holding on to an instinctual memory of what brought their ancestors to us in the first place. We hold memories too; the poignant reminders of what people are capable of doing to each other."

"Ah, I see," Emily interrupted. "The people who live here tend to be more accepting of one another because their ancestors once witnessed the horrendous result of human conflict. I think what you're saying is living here fosters harmony, respect, and reject being, dare I say, angst?" she added, wryly.

"Now you've got it," Mrs. Angst laughed.

"That's unbelievable," Emily remarked. "I mean, it does seem pretty far-fetched. But I guess that's why Grams used to say this town was blessed. Why didn't she ever come back here?"

"Emilia left town after marrying your granddad, right after they graduated from the college."

"I know, but she never came back. She stayed away from the very place she considered blessed. I just can't understand that."

"People react differently to feelings they can't comprehend," Mrs. Angst said. "Some look into what causes them to react a certain way, finding answers to their own questions. There are others who find that act too painful because it forces them to remember things they'd rather forget. Your Grams, Emilia, was one of those people.

"When she left, Sarah, your great grandma, was heartbroken. She had the same emotional attachment to this town as all the others who came before her. She couldn't understand why Emilia would want to leave. It was a different time back then Emily, people stayed put. There was a lesser desire to find adventure and excitement. Emilia was different. She was a strong-willed spirit, that's for sure.

"Sarah never wanted to hold her back but felt compelled to do so. When Emilia left, it was the end of a multi-generational link to this very house. It was like breaking up a family chain, once a link is removed, the others just fall apart. But, she had more selfish reasons. There were four miscarriages after Emilia was born, and one stillborn son. Her daughter was all she had, so naturally there was this need to hold on to her for as long as possible. Emilia always felt her mother was trying to control her, hold her back.

"Now, I'm not saying that Emilia didn't love your granddad. I always knew there was an immediate, mutual attraction. Allen was so funny, sweet—a really terrific guy. But, for Emilia, the attraction went beyond his affability or sense of humor. She knew after graduation he'd return to New York, and she was determined to go with him. He was her ticket to the life she'd always wished for beyond the limits of Adams County, and there was nothing Sarah could do to stop it.

"May I please have a glass of water?"

Emily nodded, and as she walked to the kitchen to get her something to drink, Mrs. Angst walked over to the fireplace and lit all the candles in the hearth. She drank the water, sat down on the couch opposite the hearth, and stared into the flames. Raising her eyebrows slightly, she continued.

"It was so pathetic, you know. Just listening to her, I could hear the sadness, the pain in her voice. I could just tell it was something she'd probably never get over," Mrs. Angst said.

"You mean, Sarah?" Emily asked.

"No. I was talking about Emilia."

"Grams? What sort of pain was she in? She had her way after all and ended up living the life she chose."

Mrs. Angst looked away from the candles, and said, "Yes, she did, but there were consequences to her choice. Because Emilia left rather abruptly unfinished business with Sarah remained. She knew she'd hurt and disappointed her mother, but instead of coming home to visit, calling more frequently, or even writing letters, she stayed away. They might have been able to work out the bad feelings before it was too late. But Emilia was just too weak to face the person by whom she'd always felt somewhat imprisoned. Then, even in freedom, she felt locked in a different sort of restraint: guilt.

"Sarah had forgiven her, but Emilia didn't realize that because she never took the time to allow her mother to explain. Then, before it could be made better, Sarah passed away. When your great grandma died, a part of your grandmother died, too. Sarah succumbed to a disease that attacked her lungs, but Emilia was strapped with a disease in her soul."

"I can't imagine my Grams feeling so much guilt. She always seemed to be so together, so strong. I thought she could handle almost anything." Turning to Mrs. Angst, she said, "You make her sound like a coward."

"We are all cowards at times, Emily," Mrs. Angst, ruefully remarked. "In spite of our strength, our faith, sometimes we just don't have the emotional fortitude needed in this world, often a cruel world. We all fall victim to that at some point.

"I loved Emilia. She was, and will always be, the one friend whose memory I'll take with me through what remains of my life. But I began to hate what she was doing to her life, especially after Mandy was born."

"What do you mean?" Emily asked. "How does my mother fit into this?"

"Do you think Emilia and Mandy had a good mother-daughter relationship?" Mrs. Angst asked, with an insightful grin.

"No," Emily timidly responded. "I don't know why they didn't."

"Well, I do. You see, after Sarah died, Emilia was deeply depressed for a very long time. If only she'd been given professional help. They didn't do that too freely back then.

"Anyway, Allen wanted to be a father. Emilia had several pregnancies over the years that ended in miscarriage. Despite that though, she seemed to be feeling better emotionally, until she became pregnant with your mother. Having already decided that motherhood wasn't in the cards, she was terribly upset when she found out that she was expecting again, and that she'd carry full term. However, she consoled herself by thinking she was carrying a boy. Do you know why she preferred to have a son?" she asked, as Emily shook her head. "Because she knew that every time she'd look at a daughter, she would be reminded of the one person in the world she couldn't get away from, herself. Isn't that strange? Most women would be delighted to give birth to a daughter. For Emilia, that concept was devastating."

"But we had such a good relationship," Emily said.

"They say time heals wounds," Mrs. Angst continued. "Still, by the time you were born, the wound she had created with Mandy was deep. They'd distanced themselves so far apart that it would have taken too much effort to change it. But with you, Emilia saw a chance to make everything better. She was going to be the mother to you she never could be to Mandy. She was going to love the fruit of her child in a way she could never love her own. In doing that though, she distanced you from your mother. Am I right?"

"Yes," Emily whispered. "I hated my mother almost as much as she hated Grams. I hated her for hating Grams, and I hated myself for hating her. But Mandy never tried to change it. We constantly locked horns leaving Grams, my father and later Zach to be the mediator. Why didn't she try to make things better between us?"

"Like I said, sometimes we do things we don't understand. But I can't speak for your mother," Mrs. Angst said. "Maybe the two of you will be able to work that out when she gets here. You must speak to one another and express your feelings. It may not solve anything; however, it's still a start. But I'll tell you this, if it's going to be solved anywhere, it will be solved in Gettysburg. Here, your ancestors, who can never forget, will help you to remember."

"Are you referring to ghosts?" Emily asked, staring out toward Jonas's barn. "I mean, like the spirits of our ancestors guiding us?"

"The spiritual guidance is here," Mrs. Angst said, while pointing to Emily's heart.

"My friend Peter told me that my fears were rooted in my inability to face them and remember. I thought he was crazy," Emily said. "What does remembrance have to do with anything? But now I understand what he meant. I only wish Grams understood."

"She did in the end," Mrs. Angst said. "That's why she left you this house. She knew she was ill years before anyone else in the family did. She knew, and I knew. It was then she confided in me of her desire to give you this house, and that's when she stopped renting it to students. She saw it as a way to correct her mistakes in life."

"Mistakes are not always correctable, though," Emily said, with a sigh.

"True. But you're here, and now by a strange coincidence, less than one week after your arrival, Mandy will be here, too. Maybe you can put your anger aside for a while and try to remember where those feelings came from. Look at the time," she said, glancing at her wristwatch. "I really must be going now."

"Mrs. Angst, Gertie, please come back tonight after my mother arrives. Peter will be bringing over pizza and wine from the restaurant. Later, we're going to read Emilia Wahler's book together. Will you come?"

"Thank you for the invitation, but I don't think so. I must get to bed early, or I'll be overtired, and end up staying awake all night. I'll see Mandy tomorrow."

As the old woman walked to the door, Emily hastily reached over to the table, picked up the diary, and held it out for her to see.

"What do you think this means?" she asked, looking desperate for an answer. "All these stories about the Wahlers, and Stephen Klee; why was it so important to remember them, when the key to what's wrong in my life occurred generations after this was written?

"I think I'm haunted by Jonas Wahler's ghost every night. I hear sounds as if he's still working in the barn. I've heard his footsteps on the staircase and once I even felt his presence in this parlor. I still don't know whom or what undid my bed that first night here. Why?" she implored.

"I told you Emily, the people of Gettysburg can never forget. You are the legacy that will allow their suffering to have meant something. Through you, they will never be forgotten nor will anything else that has happened here."

"Then you do believe I am haunted? It's been neither my imagination nor fear ruling me here? You believe I have a ghost?" she asked, vehemently.

"It's not important what I believe, only what you believe," Mrs. Angst replied. "If that belief helps you to work out your inability to cope with certain aspects of your life, then that's all that really matters. Just as long as you understand there's nothing here to fear. This is your home now—you, and for however long she decides to stay, Mandy, too."

Mrs. Angst continued walking toward the door and suddenly stopped. "Do you know where the saying, 'lions roaring' came from?" she asked.

"Yes," Emily said, "I read it in the diary. I believe it was Emilia Wahler who coined that phrase to help her children through the noise of the guns and cannons during the war."

She smiled and nodded. "I'm not sure *she* was the one who originally coined it. However, that was certainly a phrase born out of the incredible noise of the three-day battle. Almost everyone in town still uses it now to refer to the noise of a thunderstorm. But you know that analogy was not entirely correct. Lions kill for protection or survival, but they never intentionally set out to destroy their own."

After she left, a memory flashed across Emily's mind that seemed to give credence to the last thing Mrs. Angst said. She remembered back when she was 10, she took a broken bicycle out after being warned by her parents to stay away from it. The dislodged metal spoke of the wheel impaled itself in her calf after she fell off the bike while attempting to turn the wheel.

"Oh my God!" Mandy yelled. "Someone get help. Call an ambulance."

"Wait," Andrew said. "I think I can get it out."

Emily recalled how her father remained calm while gently manipulating the dagger-rod that had torn apart her leg, blocking out the deafening screams of his daughter. The spoke slipped out quickly but left a deep wound.

At the hospital, Emily remembered the doctor telling her family that she'd need at least fifteen to twenty stitches in her leg. She had asked for both her mother and grandmother, but the doctor said only one of them would be allowed in during the procedure."

Mandy cried, "I have to be with her."

"Nonsense," Emilia yelled. Emily could hear the argument from behind the bed curtains. "Look at what a wreck you are," Emilia said to Mandy. "You'll only upset her more if she sees you this way. I'll go in."

Before Mandy could respond, Emilia turned to her son-in-law and said, "Andrew, get her out of here. Take her to the coffee shop in the lobby and buy her a cup of herbal tea to calm her nerves. I'll take good care of Emily."

Emilia pushed aside the bed curtains and rushed to her grandchild. She was restrained on a stretcher with the open wound exposed in preparation for the surgical procedure. Gently, Emilia brushed aside her hair and kissed her face creased with pain. Emily remembered opening her eyes and asking in a whimper, "Where's Mommy?"

"She's having a cup of tea with your father," Emilia said.

"But I want my mother!" she sobbed louder.

"I know, my dear," Emilia said, with a smile. "That's why I'm here."

"Oh my God!," Emily exclaimed, wide eyed, after revisiting that memory.

She looked over to the photograph with her grandmother where it stood next to the angel painting, and stared at the images for a few moments. She then walked to the fireplace, picked up the photograph and angrily turned it down on the mantle.

"My poor mother," she sighed.

Chapter Thirty-Six

Emily set out to do some shopping that afternoon before her mother's arrival. She stopped in the walkway after noticing a man near her tenant's door.

"They're not in today," she said. "May I help you?"

"I know. I just came to leave a message on the answering machine and hang up this sign," the man said pointing to it. "I'm Joel's brother, Ben," he added, and held out his hand to shake hers.

She shook his hand, and said, "I'm Emily Tomaso, his landlord. I'm so sorry for your loss. Joel was a very nice man."

He nodded and took off his sunglasses. Emily noticed the family resemblance; however, Ben appeared to be a few years older than Joel.

"Thank you," he replied. "Have you known my brother for a long time?"

"No. I just moved here. A few days ago, I had an opportunity to spend some time with Joel and Mike. I'm glad I was able to get to know him, even if it was only for a few hours."

"Joel was certainly a great guy, smart, kind, considerate. I knew him all my life, but that wasn't enough."

Emily nodded, adding, "He left me flowers from his garden

every morning after I arrived here and never looked to get credit for his thoughtful deed. Even after I brought them as a gift to the luncheon he'd invited me to, he never said a word about it."

"That was Joel," Ben said, smiling. "You know, I was proud of him. I was proud to say he was my brother," he said as he replaced his sunglasses to conceal his emotions.

"Is there anything I can do for his family, or Mike?" she asked.

"Mike is also his family," he corrected. "Actually, you can do something. Joel loved the geraniums over there in the wine barrels. Since we'll be mourning for the next week at their home, would you mind watering the flowers?"

"I'll be happy to do it."

Ben smiled, and bit his lower, quivering lip as he said, "The people in this town are really lovely." He raised his hand in a silent wave and walked away.

Emily turned to leave and noticed the white poster edged in black, hanging in the front window of the office:

To All Our Dear Friends in Gettysburg,

Joel Levy passed away peacefully in his sleep in the early morning hours of June 23rd. His service will be at 1 o'clock Sunday, June 24th at Evergreen Cemetery.

Many thanks for your loyalty and support through all the difficult months. Joel felt very blessed being here among you, the wonderful people of our adopted town.

Sincerely,

Mike Thurman and the Levy family

Chapter Thirty-Seven

Mandy checked her seat belt after the sign was turned on inside the airplane's cabin. The captain announced that the inclement weather on the ground could make the takeoff a little bumpy. She laughed to herself at how appropriate those words sounded.

She felt the airplane slightly shudder while tipping upward, and as it climbed above the clouds, her shoulders gently pressed against the back of her seat. Once leveled off, Mandy looked out the window into a clear blue sky, beautiful and calm, with a bright sun shining warm rays of light onto her face. Down below the wings of the plane were the dark clouds, which had caused the turbulent path. But it was so peaceful up above all that disturbance, a peace she longed to bask in indefinitely away from all that existed below.

The trip she was taking could never be considered pleasurable, considering what she was running away from at home. However, what she was running away *to* concerned her more. Even though Emily had invited her to visit, she felt it was done out of pity, and perhaps guilt for the months of deception that had been occurring right under her nose. She wasn't angry despite the fact Emily knew about Zach's affair and had never attempted to tell her about it. She knew her daughter was not responsible for her actions. It wasn't her fault the two of them never had an open line of communication. Mandy took full responsibility for that.

Emilia, however, was Emily's support and confidant, and there was no doubt in her mind that had her mother still been alive, Emily would have shared what she knew with her. In fact, she wondered if she'd known anyway, since Emily realized Zach's secret before her grandmother's death. But she dismissed that possibility because several months before the end, Emilia was so uncomfortable and weak, she was certain Emily would have spared her details that might have caused her even more pain.

Emily was the light of Mandy's eye. A difficult delivery by Cesarean section, her birth was a relief after having endured months of bed rest due to Preeclampsia, a condition her own mother experienced as well while carrying her. The baby's light peachy toned skin reflected her own Irish and German heritage, and the dark auburn hair was a result of her husband's Mediterranean influence. But her eyes, which were so large, and the most unusual deep green color, were not initially determinable. Andrew Tomaso's eyes were brown, and both she and her parents' color were blue, so beyond some ribbing from innocent Tomaso family harassment, the baby's eyes remained a mystery. However, Mandy knew she'd seen those eyes before and was certain of ownership to its gene.

To Mandy, Emily's birth represented a time of hope for a new relationship with family, particularly with her mother. She and Emilia were always so out of touch emotionally, she'd hoped the baby they both adored would somehow bring them closer. She'd even been the one who suggested the more updated version of her mother's name for the child. But any action Mandy took to bring them closer was always done in vain. What separated mother and daughter went beyond anything Mandy could ascertain.

"May I get you something to drink?" a flight attendant asked.

"Yes," Mandy nodded, "a double Scotch and soda, please." She reached into her purse, pulled out a ten-dollar bill, and handed it to him. While waiting for her change, she thumbed through some old pictures, which were barely visible through the smudged and scratched plastic cover of the wallet: Emily's high school graduation portrait, her baby picture, and a picture of Zach taken before their wedding. Behind that was another, much older photo tucked in between some other papers. Mandy pulled it out and sighed.

"Here you are ma'am," the young man smiled, as he handed her the cocktail and change.

Mandy touched the glass to her lips and hesitated before taking a long drink. She looked down once again at the old picture in her hand, and grimaced. It had been taken on her first day of school, the year she started the seventh grade. She and three of her best friends were posing together at the bus stop, dressed in new clothes and shoes. All seemed to be wearing the brown or tan penny-loafer style shoe that had been the fashion, except for her. Emilia always insisted she wear the practical, and comfortable black, leather tie shoes, which were by all accounts, ugly.

"Mom," Mandy insisted. "No one but me has to wear these nasty things."

"Then I guess you'll be the only one with comfortable feet," Emilia responded.

Mandy only saved the photo as proof of a battered childhood. Sometimes, she'd pull it out to show friends what she'd had to endure. But that was only if her mother was around. And since she'd no longer be around, it briefly crossed her mind that she no longer needed to hold on to the photo. Still, she replaced the picture behind all the others, and thought *Emily never had to wear black tie shoes.* She closed her purse.

Her daughter was never at a loss for Emilia's attention. There was an impenetrable bond between the two of them that Mandy recognized almost immediately and came to realize beyond a doubt once her mother moved into their home after her father's death. Mandy never felt threatened by that relationship. In fact, she'd hoped to share in it. Very soon however, it became obvious that there was no room for her. The closeness she observed between Emilia and Emily could only be experienced from a distance, leaving her once again empty and longing.

As she approached her destination, she wondered if the ray of hope she'd sensed with her daughter over the phone was real. It was too late for her to correct the mistakes that were made with her mother, but she wondered, could there be anything salvageable for a better relationship with her estranged child?

The seat belt sign lit up again, that time to prepare for landing as they approached the Harrisburg Airport. As the airplane descended, again it was engulfed in the dark clouds, the storm clouds, and for Mandy Porter, the bumpy ride had begun once again.

Chapter Thirty-Eight

A light mist was falling at 6:15 that evening, when Emily noticed a white, stretch limousine pull up in front of her house. She watched as the driver opened the door for his passenger. She jumped up when she realized that the pretty redhead getting out of the car was her mother. Emily rushed down the steps to greet her.

"Mom, I didn't know it was you. Here, let me help you with your bags."

"Don't bother," Mandy said. "Charles will take them up to the apartment," and nodded to the driver who was already holding the luggage and walking toward the door.

"Charles? I thought you were just taking a taxi from the airport."

"I intended that," Mandy said. Her light blue eyes lit up in a devious smile as she added, "Zach said he was paying for this trip, so…"

Emily let out a laugh, and childishly hugged her mother so hard, she practically lost her balance. "I'm glad you're here," Emily said, and slipped her arm through hers.

Mandy was pleasantly shocked by her daughter's reaction. Her eyes filled with tears, as she responded, "Me, too.

"So, this is the place. I can't say I remember very much about the way it looked."

"A few hours somewhere wouldn't exactly leave a lasting impression," Emily said, chagrined.

Mandy stopped walking when she read the sign in the window. "What happened?"

"Did you know Joel and Mike, the office tenants?" Emily asked.

"Not really. Mrs. Angst took care of all that for us. There was no need for me to know them."

"They're very nice people," Emily said. "Joel just died, from AIDS."

Mandy turned away and remained silent as they continued toward the apartment door.

Emily gave her a quick tour of the rooms. Her mother was quiet but smiled as if pleasantly surprised by the house she'd been denied. She turned to her daughter and said, "It's charming."

"Mom, I have to ask you, do you know why Grams stopped renting this apartment to students?"

Mandy paused, lowered her head and said, "I really don't know. Your grandmother never shared anything about this place with me."

Emily almost told her what she'd learned earlier from Mrs. Angst about Grams saving the property for her, but decided against it. She wasn't sure how her mother would react. She was having a pleasant reunion and so didn't want to say anything that might change it.

Mandy walked over to the mantle and lifted the photograph of Emily and Grams that was turned over. She glanced at the picture and then at her daughter before placing it upright again.

Emily silently waited for her mother's question as to why it was placed down, but it didn't come. She was relieved.

Instead, Mandy asked, "Do you like it here?"

"Oh yes, I do," Emily said, smiling. " I never felt I belonged anywhere until I came here, home."

Mandy's smile quickly faded as she asked, sternly, "What about your life in East Springs? Did you feel so out of place there?"

Emily swallowed hard. She could feel the tension building in her chest, the same feeling that occurred many times before, signaling the beginning of another confrontation.

Mandy then reached over, gently touched Emily's face, and said softly, "I'm sorry I made your life so unbearable."

"Let's not talk about that now," Emily said, feeling reassured that she could approach the, so to speak, "elephant in the room."

"I want to know what's happening with you and Zach."

"What's there to say? Zach has made his choice. He plans on moving all of his things out of our house—I mean *my* house—this week and move in with that Carl.

"I never liked Carl, you know," she said, tightening her lower jaw. "He was always so quiet around me. He ignored me at parties, and if I spoke to him, he answered politely, but never looked me in the eye. They say you should never trust a person who doesn't look you in the eye. I guess I'm just a foolish woman. It had been going on for months before I knew anything about it. Foolish, foolish woman."

"Don't say that, Mother. How could anyone expect something like that?"

"But you knew, didn't you?" she said, turning to face her daughter. "You figured it out before I did."

Emily blushed while answering, "I never figured anything out. I found out about the affair the same way you did. I went to the office to ask him a question, and I found them. You'd think he'd learn to lock the damn door."

"Oh lord," Mandy yelled, and put her arms around her. "That bastard!"

"No! Listen to me," Emily said. "After that, I hated him, too. There's a part of me that will always have incredible anger towards him. But I've been trying to work out a lot of the bad feelings. You must do the same."

Mandy released her grasp, and said, softly, "I don't hate Zach. I love him. You don't stop loving someone just because they hurt and disappoint you.

"I just don't know how to get over the pain. How do you get over the pain of realizing that your life has been a big lie? I trusted Zach implicitly, and he betrayed my trust. He led me to believe our relationship was something it wasn't. He's a total coward for not telling me about Carl, and despite my love for him, I don't think I'll ever forgive him for that." She began to cry.

Emily guided her to the rocking chair and went to answer the phone. When she returned, Mandy appeared calm but was staring into the fireplace.

"That was my friend, Peter. He'll bring us dinner tonight at 8:30. Will you be able to wait that long to eat?"

"I'm not really hungry," Mandy said, barely above a whisper. She added, "Why are there candles inside the firebox?"

"Oh, that's something Gertie; I mean Mrs. Angst showed me. You know how much I love fireplaces. Well, I was very disappointed when I learned this one wasn't functional until she showed me how I could get the same effect of a real fire. Look," she said while bending down to light the lavender scented wax.

Mandy smiled and said, "I always loved the look of candles in the hearth."

"You've done this at home? Why don't I remember that?"

"No Emily, not me. It was my mother who did that."

"I don't remember Grams doing that either."

"Well, never in our house," Mandy replied. She stared at the candles a little longer before speaking from a place deep in her memory.

"It reminds me of when I was a little girl. Late at night, I'd sneak into the living room and hide, just to watch the lit candles. My father was such a funny guy, he would tease Mom when he caught her using the fireplace in that way, and say, 'Five hundred dollars to have a full-wall brick fireplace put in, only to have it used with fifteen cents worth of tallow. Emilia,' he'd say, 'candles belong in church or on the dinner table, not in there.' Mom would then quickly replace them with a piece of oak, set the wood ablaze, and didn't even seem to notice the wonderful fire.

"Late at night though, long after Dad and I went to bed, she'd clean out the burnt timbers and ashes, replace her candles, light them, and rock gently in her chair while staring into the flames. I think she did that almost every night."

"Did she know you were there?" Emily asked.

"No," Mandy said. "I didn't want her to know. It was her time to be alone, and I was just intruding. I'd sit there though, hiding behind a big couch, and watch the flickers of light, sometimes from as many as ten candles reflecting off the brick, sending shadows dancing in every corner of the room. But Emilia never seemed aware of that. She just kept staring into the hearth as if the answers to all her questions were written down there somewhere amidst the flames. I would silently watch and wait."

"Watch and wait for what?" Emily asked.

"For her to notice me and invite me to sit with her. To let me in on all the secrets she kept hidden. But she never did."

"Did that upset you?"

"At first it did," Mandy said. "But then I realized that I didn't mind at all. Despite having to sneak behind the couch, I was happy to do it. I was happy because we were finally doing something together, even if only one of us was aware of it."

Emily sighed and said. "I never knew that, Mother."

After making up the canopy bed in her room for Mandy, Emily thought about how this act would have been totally unnerving only a day ago. She smiled realizing it didn't bother her at all.

"I can't sleep here," Mandy announced, coming into the bedroom. "There's no bed in the other room. Where will you sleep?"

"Oh, don't worry," Emily said while walking back into the parlor. "I usually sleep in this big old rocker."

"A rocking chair?" Mandy asked with concern. "You sleep in a rocking chair?"

"Look," Emily said. "I love reading. And, since I don't have a television here, I've had to pass the time by reading different books and magazines. Did you see all the books in that beautiful bookcase over there?" she pointed. "Well, I often fall asleep with a book in my hand. Besides, it's really very comfortable, really."

She held her breath hoping her lie wasn't too obvious. In spite of the more compatible rapport they appeared to be having, she didn't want to bring up any situations that might be alarming.

Mandy stood quietly for a few seconds staring at the chair, shrugged her shoulders and said, "Okay, as long as I'm not putting you out."

Emily exhaled in relief. *Still walking on eggshells*, she thought.

"What a beautiful cabinet," Mandy noted, while walking toward the bookcase. "It almost looks like a Thomas Cooper."

"What's a Thomas Cooper?" Emily asked, with a slight laugh.

"He was a relatively unknown Long Island furniture maker in the late eighteenth century," Mandy said, while discernibly examining the piece of furniture, opening all of the drawers. "No, I'm mistaken." She went on to describe the signature marks the craftsman would have left, explaining the history behind it all. "But this is still pretty old," she added. "Probably from the early 1800's."

"How do you know all that?" Emily asked, in amazement.

"There's a lot you don't know about me, my dear," Mandy said, grinning. "What's this?" she asked, picking up the diary.

"This book is one of the many remarkable discoveries I've made about our family since arriving here."

Emily began to explain, with great enthusiasm, what the book was all about, and how she'd found it. She described what she'd read about the Civil War, and what the town was like after the battle. Stating also that Mrs. Angst and Peter were aware of the book's existence, and that she'd shared some of what she'd read in there with them, she added, "I also want to share this book with you."

Emily went on to tell her about their ancestors, Jonas and Emilia Wahler, as she flipped through the pages of their personal history, giving little glimpses of what life was like before the two of them existed.

"Whoa!" Mandy said. "Let me read this." She sat down on the rocker and hastily opened to the pages that unlocked the mysteries of the heritage she'd been refused all of her life.

While setting the dinner table, Emily smiled as she watched her mother rocking gently in front of the lit hearth. The evening light began to stream through the window, brightening the short strands of Mandy's hair, while illuminating the pages of the book in which she was engrossed. Emily watched and waited. She was waiting for Mandy to finish, so they could discuss what was just read. For it was there near the light from the candles that the answers to all their questions were written. Emily watched and waited, because it was then she also realized it was one of those rare times in their lives that she and Mandy were doing something together.

Chapter Thirty-Nine

Peter showed up carrying a pizza and a bottle of wine.

"Hi Peter. I'm Mandy, Emily's mom," she said, smiling at the handsome man standing in the doorway.

"How do you do," he said. "Did you have a good trip down?"

"As a matter of fact, I did."

Emily came out of the bedroom to greet him. He looked different. "What happened to your hair?" she asked, in shock. His long waves were reduced to golden ringlets in a very mature, business-like style.

"It seemed time," he said, and grinned.

Emily nodded. "It becomes you."

They spent the next hour at the dinner table getting acquainted and eventually laughing at the fact that the three of them had devoured a large pizza pie.

"I thought you said you weren't hungry," Emily teased her mother.

"I haven't eaten that well in days. I guess I'm getting back my appetite."

All three were engrossed in conversation about nothing, yet to each it was the most pleasurable of times. They reveled in the new relationships before them, oblivious to a thunderstorm roaring outdoors. For Mandy, it was a place she could temporarily forget the problems in her life. Close to her daughter, she was finally where she always wanted to be.

Peter took the large bottle of Chianti and three wine glasses over to the candle-lit fireplace and sat down in front of it. He was amused, watching mother and daughter clear the dinner table, giggling like children as they bumped into one another while carrying plates over to the kitchen sink. To him, they seemed more like sisters than parent and child. When they joined him, he filled each of their glasses to the rim with the potent Italian wine.

"You have to watch him," Emily kidded. "He's very good at inconspicuously filling up wine glasses."

"Well," Mandy said, turning to Peter. "I don't care how much wine you give me. I'm enjoying getting unwound."

Peter smiled and looked sympathetically at Emily. He knew the real reason for Mandy's visit and felt a little ashamed he had knowledge of her secret. Emily stared down into her wine glass, then for a moment they were all silent, and Mandy excused herself from the room.

Peter tapped Emily on the arm and whispered, "Maybe I should go now."

"Why?" she asked. "I thought you said you had the rest of the night off."

"I do," he replied. "I just thought that maybe the two of you should be alone, especially when you read your ancestor's diary. I feel as though I'm intruding on your time. Maybe I don't belong here."

"Don't be silly. Mom and I will have plenty of time to be alone. Besides, I've already shared Emilia Wahler's writing with you. Before you arrived tonight, Mandy read as much as we did, so no one is ahead of anyone else. I really want you to stay. Peter, I want you to belong. You do belong here," she said, wrapping her arms tightly around him until he succumbed in her grasp.

"Yes," a voice called out. "Please stay," Mandy said, smiling at her new friend.

Emily released Peter and said, "It's settled. Shall we begin to read? I invited Mrs. Angst to join us, but she said she rarely stays up late."

"That's strange," Mandy said, looking into the candle flames. "My mother used to stay up late all the time."

"Yes, well, shall we begin?" Peter asked. "I'll be happy to read aloud if you'd like."

"Sure," Emily responded as she handed him the book. "Let's begin here. I think we've all read up to this point. Mother and I already discussed the previous entries."

"Remarkable," Mandy said. "I had no idea who, or even what came before me here."

Peter cleared his throat and began:

Remember...Dear God, please grace your servants. It has been one week since I last entered my witness account. The rain has stopped for two days now, but the pain and despair all around me has not.

Amanda remains at the home of my neighbor, Mrs. Johnson. Though unaware of Sarah's passing, she has not spoken her sister's name in days. I now wonder if she senses her loss.

Today, I went to the place where Sarah lies. I brought her the flowers from our garden as I am certain she'd be very pleased to see the colorful snap dragons and sweet peas she'd helped plant last spring. Standing there alone, I was consumed by the silence all around me. Being the Sabbath, there were no burials in the cemetery or fields, a great reprieve for the hard workers who've spent most of their waking hours in this dreadful place.

My solitude there was enhanced by the fact that the sky above me was absent the usual presence of sparrows and robins, which might be seen and heard singing in the clear, bright sky. Stephen's friend, James, has informed me that they had been frightened away by the noise of the guns and cannons during the siege of our town. I do hope they will return soon, for I miss their songs, which used to bring such good cheer to us all.

I have gratefully been spared the witness of the devil's breed. Both Stephen and James have spoken of the many buzzards that have invaded our town, searching the fields in prey of those unburied souls. Fortunately, their meals are getting few, as Stephen has noted that most of the dead have been attended. However, that has had little effect on the population of our town's flies.

I do so long for the colder days of autumn when both the flies and the terrible stench of death will disappear in the crisp morning air.

Jonas continues to work both day and night. He appears much thinner and considerably weak but has shunned my attempts to encourage more rest. He has not conversed with me in weeks. Last night however, I awoke to the sound of his voice. I peered out of my window to see if he was summoning me. The full moon shone over the barn and lit the opening to his workshop. There, in the silence of the summer night, he called out the name of our Sarah, his wails enhanced by the pounding of the wooden mallet onto the ground. My poor Jonas, such sorrow we witness, yet we each witness it alone as his and now my work has separated us, too.

Dr. Harlow has offered to attend to Jonas, for he seems to be developing a terrible cough, which so reminds me of the onset of Sarah's condition. However, Jonas will not allow anyone near and has held up his hammer in a threatening way to the good doctor and all who attempt to bring him some comfort. Dear mother of Jesus, help my poor husband. I *would attend to him if I could, but alas, I do not have the emotional strength to do so. Please intercede for my human deficiencies.*

Robert—Dr. Harlow, has stated he will not be in our home much longer as most of the injured soldiers have been either sent away or buried after succumbing to illness or injury. I have seen so many of them leave in that manner that I will be grateful when all this will come to an end. I will however miss my doctor friend, as we have assisted each other through so much. I know I will remember him always...E.W.

"One could get very depressed reading this," Peter exclaimed.

"I'm not depressed," Mandy said. "In a strange sort of way, it makes me feel good."

"How is that?" Peter asked.

Before Mandy could respond, Emily interjected, "Just hearing about those horrendous experiences allows one to temporarily forget their own problems. Right?"

Mandy smiled, and said, "I guess so."

Peter nodded as he added, "Here but for a few hours, and you can already feel the power of Gettysburg."

"Still, it is sad to hear about what our ancestors went through during and after the battle," Mandy said. "But I will say this, of all the terrible situations Jonas and Emilia Wahler experienced, the worst had to be the loss of their child." Mandy looked over to Emily. "That indeed is the worst experience a parent could ever have, especially a mother." She added under her breath, "At least most mothers."

Emily understood the point she was making, but did not attempt to pursue it. She turned to Peter and said, "Please read on."

After clearing his throat with a swallow of wine, he continued.

Remember...Dear Jesus, hear our prayers. Although the

conditions all around us are slowly improving, my family's situation is not. Last night, Stephen was arrested. Officers in the Union Army charged him with the murder that night of his friend, James. I cannot understand how he could be accused of such a crime, as I have only known my dear brother to be such a gentle person. He is not even capable of killing any of the annoying flies that have invaded our town since after the end of the battle. The murder of another human being is completely incomprehensible.

I went to the building on Side Street, where the officers have him detained, to inquire whether this accusation might have been a misunderstanding. The officers have told me that there was a terrible disagreement between the two of them, and Stephen had decided to end it with a gun. Since the murdered man was a Lieutenant with the United States Army, Stephen will be charged with both murder and treason.

I was granted several minutes with my brother in the cold, dark cell they had arranged for him. 'This is the appreciation a citizen is granted,' I stated to the authorities there, 'after the Army left our homeland in the situation it is in now?' The Colonel looked coldly into my eyes and said that my comment could be easily mistaken, and had I refused to be silent, not only would I not be allowed a visit with my brother, but I may be charged with treason as well.

Stephen wept in my arms for what seemed a long time and began to recount the tragic events of that night. After arriving at the soldier's camp, as was his usual course for each evening, he was approached by several of the other soldiers. They surrounded him in such a manner that he immediately felt somewhat threatened by the very people who he had once had an amicable alliance.

They questioned why it was necessary for him to return there each night. Stephen, who had volunteered long hours to help them with the burials, said it was out of concern for the greater cause of our nation, and for friendship. As an argument with these men began, James came out of his tent to investigate. With this, one of the other soldiers reached over and took James' gun, and for some inexplicable evil reason, shot him dead with it.

Stephen admits he screamed as he ran to his dying friend, only to realize that he was already dead, and never noticed the soldiers, by that time laughing at their evil deed, placing the gun on the ground beside him. I asked him, 'Why would these terrible men do such a thing to not only a fellow officer, but a civilian who had sacrificed many hours in assisting them as you have done?' Stephen became silent, offering no explanation, looking down into the flame of the single candle that I held tight in my hand. 'Why?' I repeated. 'What secret activity have you been involved in with this Army?' But, once more, my words were met with silence.

I returned to my home shaken and desperate, for there seemed to me to be little recourse. I approached my husband's workshop, seeking his comfort and advice, only to find him once more pounding the senseless hammer onto the senseless wood, repeating the one and only word that still connected us —Sarah.

I retreated into the house in tears where my dear Dr. Harlow found me sobbing near the hearth. He had just ascended from the cellar where he attended the few remaining soldiers who we had nursed back to near health. 'What has happened?' he asked.

I then explained to him in a feeble manner, for the tears had somewhat affected my speech, all that had occurred *that night. Robert reached over and embraced me to calm my shaking body. His arms felt warm and strong, and I was committed to remain there for as long as he was willing. He then kissed my mouth with the passion I'd been denied by my husband for so long. I know I should have turned him away, but I was incapable of doing so. I needed his arms, his lips. I needed him so very much.*

We were locked in this embrace when suddenly touched by a breeze, which seemed to be coming from the back door. We separated to see what it was, and there, standing in the doorway, was Jonas. He quietly stood watching us, his face wiped clear of emotion. Slowly he turned and walked back to the barn where he once again resumed his nightly ritual.

I pray Jonas did not misjudge this one embrace in my moment of weakness. I do believe he was spared as I feel his mind is no longer with us. However, there is little comfort for me in that knowledge. I remain in despair...E.W.

The three of them remained quiet; unable to find words to fit the emotions they were each feeling. Mandy broke the silence. "Jonas must have gone insane. Do you think he realized Emilia's feelings for the doctor early on?"

"No," Emily answered. "I don't think that had anything to do with it." She began to tell Mandy all the details she'd learned from the town's genealogist, Mr. Gelsen, and how Jonas eventually died in the very condition Emilia had been describing in that writing.

Peter said, "The war destroyed his spirit."

Emily walked over to the window, looked out into the night, and added, "He was too weak. They called him the gentle carpenter of Gettysburg with good reason. He should never, never have taken on the challenges that were given to him. His initial reaction was to leave town and take his family to a safer place, but he didn't and then realized that mistake too late. The guilt of his misjudgment consumed him, emphasized by the death of his little girl. That poor soul—poor, lost soul."

"Stephen's situation didn't help either. Was he found guilty of murdering the officer?" Mandy asked.

"We'll see if she writes about it. If not, I'll fill you in on what I've learned from Mr. Gelsen," Emily cautiously stated.

Peter continued to read:

Remember...Thank the Lord in all his mercy. Today, the Army has released my dear brother. Mr. Carroll and Mr. Pugh had been at the campsite the very night of the murder and stated, beyond a doubt, that Stephen was too far away from the Lieutenant to have been the one to pull the trigger on James' gun. However, the darkness that night prevented the real murderer from being detected.

I do believe that my brother's words are true, that another officer was the killer of his friend.

Still, the Army appears to be allowing this case to remain a mystery by refusing to look any further into this dreadful incident. I dare say that inaction appears rather strange to me after they so swiftly arrested my brother. But I will not concern myself with that, as I have Stephen safe at home with me now.

Peter stopped reading when he heard a phone ring. "That's my cell phone," Emily said, and got up to answer it.

"Hello Emily, it's me," Zach hesitantly announced.

She quickly covered the phone with her hand, turned to her mother and said, "It's Zach!" Mandy shook her head and looked away.

"Hello Zach. Mom can't come to the phone right now."

"It's alright, I expected that. I just wanted to make sure she arrived safely. Is everything going well for you down there? Do you need anything?" he asked.

"Everything is going just fine with me. Don't worry, Mandy will be okay."

"Before she left, she asked me to have the separation papers sent down to your address. I'll have them sent Express Mail on Monday." He added softly, "I never wanted our lives to turn out this way, you know. I still love you both very much. You must believe me."

"I know that now, Zach," she whispered into the phone. "I—we —still love you, too."

Emily took a deep breath, returned to the floor near the fireplace, and nodded to Peter to continue. Mandy looked at her inquisitively, but did not ask her anything about the conversation.

Peter read on.

Jonas has remained at work. I continue to bring him his meals and warm blankets, as the nights are getting colder with the onset of a new season.

Dr. Harlow has released the last of the soldiers in our home. The number of wounded men here in town has signifi-cantly decreased, although many will remain in Gettysburg for several months to come. I fear this lesser necessity also means the departure of my dear friend, and love, Robert. What we shared in both heart and soul could no longer keep us apart. He has stood by to comfort me, to embrace me on many more occasions since our first kiss. Still, we have remained true to our vows as we are both committed to others. I know our special friendship must eventually end.

Although our love has not been consummated, I fear that love has somehow caused me to sin. I pray I shall be forgiven this sin, but I cannot fathom how love could ever be considered as such. We have all witnessed so much sin these past few months, the sins of inhumanity. And surely the reasons for fighting this war could never be considered anything less than that. Yet it continues, and all I cherish must depart: First my dear child, now Robert Harlow, and soon I fear my poor Jonas, as his mind I now know is slipping hopelessly away.

I feel grateful to still have Amanda and Stephen. He remains well but is still wrought with despair over the loss of his friend and his imprisonment. I am certain time will heal his wound, my wound, as well as all the others here whose wounds must also be endured. E.W.

"Shall I continue?" Peter asked.

"No," Emily said. "I want a moment to reflect on what Emilia just wrote. She didn't write every night, sometimes not for weeks. And since nothing but the year is dated, it's hard to keep up with the time frame. What month do you think she was up to in that passage?"

"Probably late September," Mandy stated. "She mentioned the new season, fall. Why?"

Emily took another deep breath, and said, "You'll see," and nodded to Peter to continue reading.

Remember. My God, why have you forsaken us? What insurmountable demand is there left for you to bestow on me? Forgive my accusation, but I am too weak to take pardon of your power. Why have you allowed all this to occur? What more is there to be taken from me than what has already been done? I beg your understanding of my anger, and plead to you to end this suffering, this ocean of agony.

When the Armies first invaded our good homeland, you gave us the challenge of compassion and selflessness in dealing with the many needs of our fellow man, and I conceded. When you plucked my poor dear child from the comfort and warmth of her family and sent her to the cold dark place below the earth, I conceded. When you forgot the sweet and gentle man I married and took away his sense of being, I conceded. When you sent me the challenge of denying myself the love I longed for so many months, I conceded. Now, I am left to bury Stephen, another victim of the war you have delivered to us. I can no longer surrender to your will, for I am consumed with my own selfish needs. I beg your forgiveness.

To all who read the writings of this witness, please know my brother to be a good man. He was a fine Christian and always loved his family. Those who had transactions with him in business knew him to be only honest and considerate. A thoughtful and understanding man, no better man could be called a friend. He was indeed a true friend to James Becker, and no matter what contradictory illusion the Army and our town has created toward his character, there is nothing that could alter the minds of those who knew and loved him.

Yesterday, he called me to sit near him by the fire. He seemed absent despair, which was his usual temperament at the very mention of his departed friend. I held his hand as he proceeded to explain to me that his relationship with James, though pure, was not without guilt. I asked if that meant he indeed murdered his friend, perhaps by accident, in which case he would most certainly be forgiven. He assured me that he had not. However, there was in a more compli-cated fashion, a cause to feel guilt.

I implored him to explain the complexity of his statement, for I had no understanding as to why he should feel in any way responsible for what had occurred. 'Was James a trai-tor? Are you a traitor?' I asked. Once more he stared into the hearth. The look was the one I recalled in his cell the night he was arrested. 'Stephen?' I called to him, but he did not respond. He gently kissed my hand and explained I shouldn't worry, as there was too much afoot for us to be concerned with at this time. He then bid me a good night and retired to bed.

Oh, if only I had held him there by the fire a little longer. Perhaps then he would have opened to me what was in his mind, what was in his heart. Being so exhausted from all of the baking I had completed that day I was happy to place our discussion aside for the night. I no longer cared that he may have betrayed our country. The Army found him innocent, and my mind would not dispute it.

Before bed, I checked on Amanda, who was safely tucked in and asleep. Then, I glanced out the window toward Jonas' barn. He continued to diligently pound the nails into the wood to create what is no longer needed, calling out the one name that continues to send a dagger through my wounded heart.

Early this morning, Mr. Carroll came to my door. I thought he'd arrived to pick up the bread I'd baked for his wife as I am now taking that profession to provide in a way Jonas is no longer capable of doing. He implored me to come with him to the Devil's Den, for it was there I would find my beloved brother, dead. I do not recall what then happened, for the room went black in the light of the new day, and when I awoke, Mrs. Carroll and Mrs. Johnson were standing over me, placing a wet cloth atop my head.

They told me Stephen most likely did not feel much pain since his end was most certainly swift. Though laden with grief, I managed a lie. I stated he sometimes went there to just be alone and perhaps he was only cleaning his gun when it accidentally went off. No one was convinced. For they suspected in their hearts what I already knew in mine, which *was that his death was no accident. He was as guilty of ending his life as surely as he was innocent of ending the life of James Becker. Sadly, that is how he will be remembered here despite the many contributions he has made to his town and people.*

Dear Jesus and Mary, protectors of us all, please deliver your poor servant Stephen Klee through the gates of Heaven despite his shunning of your gift of life. He was not responsible for the ending he chose. He was just another helpless soul cast aside by the circumstances from which we could not escape. Please forgive him for all the secrets he takes with him on his new journey. For it is now, with your graces, he will be given the gift of a new life beside our family, Sarah and the many other innocent souls who've been touched by the tribulation that was and remains Gettysburg...E.W.

"There was no end in sight to the misery our people were experiencing," Peter said. "Emilia certainly seemed to have been faced with it from all angles. But you know she was just one of the many who were living a nightmare. Thank God all we do is remember."

"She was ravaged by the war," Emily added. "The battle took away most of her family, her way of life, and even the little glimmer of hope for happiness Dr. Harlow gave her had to end, too. Proper ladies back then stood by their men, even if they were completely insane. You are right, Peter. I'm glad we only read about it and vicariously feel their pain. But, what about Stephen?" she asked. "What do you think was the secret that caused him to commit suicide?"

"Perhaps he was indeed involved in some sort of treasonous activity that led to James' death," Peter said. "I suppose the burden of guilt over the loss of his friend was so great, he could no longer go on." He nodded to Emily while adding, "Guilt is a powerful feeling."

She smiled at him to acknowledge his point.

Peter added, "Maybe the only secret he took to the rocks was the fact that he was too weak to handle the immense burden of loss, all the losses. He might have seen something of himself in Jonas and needed to end it all before burdening his sister with two of the same. But I doubt we'll ever really know."

"I know what it was," Mandy said, as she held the wine glass close to her lips. "I know why he killed himself," she repeated.

Peter and Emily looked at Mandy anxiously awaiting her explanation.

"You are only partially right, Peter." she said. "Yes, I also believe the burden of loss was too much for him to bear, but the loss was not of a friend. You see, when the soldiers shot James Becker dead, they knew in doing that they would also be destroying Stephen. By killing them, they would be killing the two people they perceived in some way as being guilty of treason. They killed James and Stephen because they were lovers."

Peter quickly closed the diary and handed it back to Emily. They were all silent for a few moments, encumbered by the horror of their answered question. How fitting, Emily thought, that her mother would figure out the familiar complex situation, which now seemed so clear.

Mandy stood up and said, "Well, I think I've had enough wine to unwind for tonight. I'll leave the two of you alone and get myself to bed. It was so nice to meet you, Peter. Thanks for dinner, the wine, and of course your good company. Goodnight Emily," she said, and held her daughter tight, kissing her on the cheek.

Peter sat down on the sofa, closed his eyes, and bent back his head in repose. Emily sat beside him, resting her head on his chest.

"Lord," she said. "I thought I'd die when Mom figured out Stephen's ending. Poor Mandy. Don't you think there's such irony in her coming here and then discovering that an ancestor's life was ended because of a situation that tore apart her own?"

"Yes," Peter said. "But more than that, I realize not very much has changed over the years. Intolerance for lifestyles considered outside of the norm still exists."

"But no one would get shot for it now," Emily replied.

"Really?" he said. "I think that's a little naïve. Think about your initial reaction to Joel and Mike. I'm not saying you were loaded for bear, but you weren't very nice."

"I didn't care that they're gay," she said quietly, so her mother wouldn't hear their discussion. "Is that what you thought?" she asked, aghast.

"I did think that," Peter said.

"Oh no," she said, bringing her hands to her face. "No wonder Mike seemed so mad at me. The truth is, beyond the initial shock of the situation, I wasn't that concerned with my stepfather's bisexuality, either. What caused me the most pain was that deep down, I suspected he'd eventually end up choosing Carl over Mandy and me."

"I guess I did some projecting, huh?" she said, looking ashamed. "I'll have to try to make amends with Mike. He's not at all as I initially perceived. Hopefully, eventually he'll feel the same way about me."

"You know, when my mother arrived, she called Zach a coward because he avoided dealing with his feelings for so long. Well, I must agree, but I guess so am I."

"Don't be so hard on yourself," Peter consoled her. "We all make mistakes, but it takes more than a coward to admit them."

"Do you think she'll be alright?" she asked.

"She seems to be."

Emily continued in a whisper, "But Zach just told me he was sending over separation papers on Monday for her to look over. It just seems so soon."

"I'm very confused," Peter said. "A few nights ago, you went out of your way to explain to me how the two of you didn't get along, and how little you cared about that. Now, you seem overly concerned about Mandy's wellbeing."

"It's very different now. I don't want her to fall apart. Not now, when I'm just getting to know her."

"Look, I know she's going through a hard time, but I don't think you give your mother half the credit you should. She just doesn't seem that fragile to me." Peter paused, and cautiously added, "At least less so than her daughter. I suspect you don't know your mother at all."

"You're right. I've learned things about her tonight I never knew."

"Then do yourself a favor. Listen to what she has to say, and maybe she'll listen to you. A lot of disagreements and misunderstandings are worked out that way."

"And a lot of wars, Peter?" Emily added, grinning.

"Especially war," he said with a laugh, kissing the top of her head. "You're not the only one who feels like a coward. I've been living a lie for years. You know, I thought I could put those feelings behind me by ignoring them. Sometimes, it even worked. But they always came back. I would see or hear something that reminded me of Alessa, or that time in my life, and they'd come back. Only then, I felt worse. Guilt and regret are feelings that don't go away. There's no point in denying them. When I met you, I was reminded again. I preached to you about trying to face your fear. What a hypocrite! But you know, I wasn't just preaching to you."

"Why did you bury those feelings inside for so long?"

"I think I kept it hidden to avoid facing responsibility for what happened to Alessa."

"How do you feel about what happened now?"

"Her suicide wasn't my fault. I've always known that. Still, I'm not without blame. I turned away from her at a time when she needed me. That's the guilt I felt, and in a way, I'm still feeling. It was not her death, but my accountability to her as a friend."

"You've been more than a friend to me this past week," she said.

"I don't think you give yourself much credit, either. Somewhere, tucked in behind the emotions of a child, you're a strong woman. You've just convinced yourself that you weren't because you always felt somewhat victimized by life. But as I said before, we're all victims on some level."

"You mentioned yesterday, that when you first met me, you saw a haunting look in my eyes, like Alessa, and that was a little frightening. Is that what drew you to me initially?"

"Yes, but I saw so much more. In your eyes, I saw me, and that's what was really frightening."

"Well, I felt a connection to you from the moment we met," she added. "Somehow, I knew we had a lot more in common than just our history degrees."

"We had our own personal histories in common," he said. "You and me, we were destined to keep repeating our past."

Emily fell quiet for a few moments before noting,"You know, I no longer fear anything from the past. For instance, I now believe that I am really haunted here." She looked around the room and added, "I definitely have a ghost."

"That doesn't bother you?" Peter asked.

"No. Not anymore."

"Do you have any idea who it is?"

"Well, I can't be certain, but I think it's Jonas Wahler. I was thinking maybe he undid the bed that first day to get me to read the diary every night so I could become aware of my ancestors and in that way connect to them."

"I feel that connection, too," Peter said.

"Then the footsteps on the staircase and the pounding noise," Emily continued. "I don't know what that's about except maybe it's meant as a reminder of what he went through while alive."

"I wish I could have heard it. When does it usually start?"

Emily looked at the time, after Midnight. "That's strange, it's not happening tonight. I wonder why?"

"Maybe it's because now with you and Mandy here, his family is together again," Peter said with a smile.

Emily thought about his comment. "I think you could be right," she said as she walked him to the door.

"Would you like to accompany me to Joel Levy's service tomorrow?" she asked.

"Of course. But you know I'd really like to attend Mass," Peter added. "Except for our brief visit the other day, I haven't been to church in years, and I think I really need to go there."

"Feel a sudden surge of spirituality?"

"Yes," he whispered.

"I know what you mean," Emily said. "We have so much to be thankful for. I'm realizing that more and more every day."

"Meet me tomorrow morning at Our Lady of Souls for the eleven thirty Mass. We can go to the cemetery right after that."

They held each other for several minutes before he kissed her goodnight.

Emily gently tiptoed over to the bedroom and placed her ear to the door. She smiled contently, and thought, *No weeping.*

She then glanced out her kitchen window toward the silent barn, listened, and waited. Still no pounding from Jonas' hammer. It was then she sensed the gentle carpenter had completed the work he never intended to begin. For Jonas had taken his family—all his family—to a safer place, a haven, far away from the roar of the lions. He'd taken them home, and perhaps he was now at peace.

Chapter Forty

Witness to Tribulation

Sunday morning returned, marking the one-week anniversary of Emily's arrival to her new home. She was sad to see the light from the sun once again obscured by clouds, but then realized she awoke before sunrise. Walking slowly to the kitchen window, she listened closely for Jonas, but he was as silent as the night before.

As she prepared coffee, Mandy walked into the room. "Good morning," she said, grinning as she stretched her arms over her head.

"Good morning. Did you sleep alright?"

"Yes," she replied. "It was all very peaceful. That is until that racket woke me up this morning."

"Racket?" Emily asked, looking once again toward the barn. "What racket?"

"Come with me and I'll show you."

Mandy escorted her daughter over to the bedroom window and gently pushed aside the curtains. "Look," she said.

Opposite the window was a leafy tree upon whose branch a robin had made her nest.

Completely visible from where they stood, freshly hatched birds were loudly chirping while being fed a morning meal by their dutiful mother.

They watched in silence for several moments as each meal was placed into the delicate, newborn mouths, before Emily broke the quiet. "The simplicity of nature is so beautiful. It would be wonderful to experience just that, without all the complexities people tend to create."

"Nature teaches lessons," Mandy said. "It's when we ignore them that life becomes more complicated."

As Emily watched, she recalled an incident in the past, which had long been etched into her memory.

She was only nine years old, when while playing at a classmate's house, the family cat gave birth to six kittens. Emily watched the pretty black and white angora named Tasha wash away all the products of birth, while gently caring for the many mouths that had begun to nurse the milk from her body. Her heart was pierced by an ache she was not yet able to understand.

Eight weeks later, a few days before Mother's Day, she had an idea. After being granted permission by her friend's parents, she'd decided to give one of the kittens, her favorite one, to her mother.

The Saturday before the holiday, she found a big pink satin bow, donned her gift with it, and proudly carried the fluffy white ball of fur she'd named Samantha to her home. Her grandmother was watering flowers near the front door when she arrived.

"Look Grams," she said, her eyes lit in excitement. "It's a Mother's Day gift for Mom."

Emilia glanced over to the beautiful, white kitten, and immediately seemed annoyed. She turned to Emily, and softly said, "Oh, I'm sorry, but your mother hates cats. You'd better give it back, and later I'll take you out to buy her flowers. By the way, let's not mention this to her, because she might feel bad."

Tears welled in Emily's eyes as she solemnly turned away to return the kitten.

As Emily watched her mother in awe of what was before them, she found it hard to believe that she could hate anything so pure and beautiful.

She asked, "Mom, do you hate cats?"

"No. I like them," Mandy said. "My mother was the one who hated cats. Why do you ask?"

"No reason. I was just thinking of getting one."

They sat down at the edge of the bed and continued to watch the mother and her offspring fulfill the simple act of nature. Mandy placed her arm around her child and lovingly drew her close.

Emily was in the shower when Mrs. Angst came to call. Mandy answered the door. "Hello Mandy, I'm Gertie Angst," she said.

"I know," Mandy replied. "I'm so glad to see you again. How long has it been, twenty, twenty-one years?"

"I think so. But then at my age, time goes by so quickly it's hard to keep track."

"Thank you so much for all you've done for us over the years. I know my mother was grateful to you," Mandy said.

"Emilia and I were such good friends. I was very happy to help her keep her home," she said. "Of course, I thought she would be the one to return here, but that doesn't matter as long as it's still in the same family. Where is Emily?" she asked.

"She just went into the shower. She's getting ready for another meeting with her friend, or boyfriend. I'm not certain of how to address their relationship, but I can tell they really care for each other. I'm happy about that. Peter seems like such a nice guy."

"You're right, Peter is very nice. But then, so is Emily."

Mandy nodded and offered Gertie a cup of coffee, which she brought to her where she was seated in the parlor.

"This is a beautiful room," Mandy said. "The whole apartment is great, but this room is my favorite."

"Yes," Mrs. Angst said, looking around the bright, open space. Her eyes rested upon the painting above the fireplace. "The angel looks just perfect there, doesn't it?" she asked.

"I love that painting," Mandy said. "I miss seeing it. Mom gave it to Emily just after she was born, and it hung across from her bed until she moved here."

Mrs. Angst looked over to the rocker and mumbled under her breath, "Well, that part hasn't changed."

"I especially like the fireplace," Mandy continued. "Emily showed me how you taught her to light the candles in the hearth."

Mrs. Angst smiled as she took another sip of coffee, and said, "But you already knew how to do that, didn't you? Emilia, your mother, used to do that."

Mandy nodded, and hesitated for a moment before asking, "What else did my mother do? I mean, what was she like when she was a young girl?"

"Oh, she was really something else. Most of the kids in town would call on her, especially if they were bored, because she used to make up all kinds of unusual games to play. No one was ever bored when they were around Emilia Stone. She had lots of other friends, but we were the closest.

"The brightest one in the class, she outshone everyone from the third grade on. She helped me study all the time, but I just barely made it out of high school."

"I guess that's where Emily gets her brains from. It certainly wasn't me. I hated school, and couldn't wait to get out. Then my parents insisted I go to college."

"You did go, didn't you?"

"Yes, for a while. Fortunately, my first husband rescued me from that. I dropped out to get married before completing my third year. It was a good thing, too. I still couldn't figure out what to major in."

"But tell me more about her, what else was she like? For instance, what were her favorite songs or places to go?"

Mrs. Angst put down her cup and stared into Mandy's eyes. "How is it that a person can live with their own parent for years, and not know anything like that? Why are you asking someone who's practically a stranger to you about information you should have been privileged to long ago?"

Mandy looked down at the floor, and bit her bottom lip. "I, I guess I never bothered to ask."

Emily came out of the bathroom wrapped in a robe. "Hi Gertie," she called out. "I'm going to get dressed. Please, don't leave yet. I want to talk to you."

Mrs. Angst turned to Mandy, and said, "I bet Emily has all the answers to your questions."

"I know she does. But I don't want to ask her. That's why I'm asking you."

"What's wrong, my dear?" Gertie softly questioned. "Why are you afraid to speak to your daughter about a mother you both shared?"

Mandy was taken aback by the boldness of Mrs. Angst's comments, but the sweetness and sincerity of her face, and tone of voice, quelled any misunderstanding. She said, "It is best Emily, and I do not speak of anything that relates to Emilia. That subject matter has always been a sore one in the past. They were very close, you know."

"I know," Mrs. Angst said. "However, Emilia is no longer here. If the two of you do not talk about her, there will be nothing left of her to be remembered. She hurt you very badly, didn't she?"

"What?" Mandy snapped.

"I told you; your mother and I were best friends and spoke regularly by telephone. I know so much more than both you and your daughter could ever know. But I already spoke to Emily about that yesterday."

"Yesterday?" Mandy asked, raising her brow. "What did you discuss yesterday?" Emily emerged from the bedroom dressed in a plain navy-blue dress.

"Why so dreary?" Mandy asked.

"I'm going to Joel Levy's funeral after church. Do I look okay?" Mandy and Gertie nodded.

"Well, what have you two been talking about?"

"I was just telling your mother about our discussion yesterday," Mrs. Angst said. "Didn't you share any of it with her?"

"No," she sheepishly replied. "Not yet," and looked at her mother, feeling once again deceptive.

Mandy's eyes shifted between the two women. She was about to say something when Emily spoke up. "It seems Grams left Gettysburg all those years ago with as much baggage as I took away from East Springs."

She began to explain all she'd learned the previous day from Mrs. Angst, who in between sips of coffee, nodded in agreement with what Emily was saying. Mandy sat silently staring out the window, showing little emotion to what she was hearing. Emily ended with, "I thought I knew Grams, Mother. But the truth is, I knew as little about her as I know of you."

"My God," Mandy whispered. "I knew there had to be more to it." She turned to them and said, "I always thought that I was the one doing something wrong. I felt like a terrible burden to her. I just didn't know how much of a burden I was."

Mrs. Angst raised her voice, "Mandy! Don't hate your mother for feelings she was too weak to face. I know she loved you and provided for you. You must credit her with at least that."

"Mrs. Angst," Mandy responded, tersely, "I never hated my mother. I loved her."

She turned to Emily, and repeated, "I don't hate people because they hurt and disappoint me." Tears filled Emily's eyes as Mandy turned back to the old woman and continued to speak.

"But it takes more than just providing for someone's physical needs to be a good mother. Emilia forgot the emotional needs a child is dependent upon." Looking back at her daughter, she added, "I did the same."

"It certainly takes more than just physical nurturing to build a healthy individual," Gertie Angst lectured. "A person' s maturity cannot properly develop, and certainly will not thrive, if their emotional needs are not met as well. Oh, I'm so happy you are both here. It is what Emilia wanted in the end."

"In the end?" Mandy asked.

"Yes. She knew she was dying long before you and Emily knew. She knew she'd made mistakes, and she wanted to correct them.

But the only way she knew how to do that was to leave Emily this house.

"Toward the end, Emilia was vulnerable, not only physically but emotionally. She felt so guilty over the way she treated you both. It was only then she realized that her domination over Emily put as wide a wedge between the two of you, as that which existed between herself and her own daughter. But, here in Gettysburg, back in the very place where all the bad feelings started, she'd hoped one day it would all come to an end."

"All those years, all those wasted years," Mandy said. "I tried so many times to get information about this place and my family that was once here, but she just kept refusing me. I asked my father about it, but he was no help. He kept saying it was up to her to share all that with me. I got the feeling he might have been afraid of her, so after a long time, I just stopped asking. I didn't want to be responsible for igniting an argument between them. I think I now know what he was afraid of. He was afraid to rekindle memories he knew she couldn't handle.

"Anyway, after a while I didn't care to learn about her family anymore. I didn't care to learn about anyone else connected to the person I felt cared so little about me."

"But then, why did you allow her to move in with us and take me over the way she did?" Emily angrily demanded.

"From the moment you were born, I could tell she felt very differently about you. After my father died, I seized what I thought was the perfect opportunity to have a better relationship with her. I thought that through you, I could find the mother I longed for all those years. I kept hoping that somewhere in me she'd find the spark of life that had created you, and that would be enough for her to open her heart to me. But it didn't work."

"No, it didn't, "Gertie Angst said. "Yet, you stood idly by and allowed her to take over your child without the compensation you'd initially hoped for."

Emily looked questionably at her mother, and Mandy responded abruptly in defense. "I had no choice. By the time I realized there was no place for me, Emily and Emilia had created a bond. Any action I might have taken to disrupt it at that point would have been criticized and resented by both of them. I couldn't bear the thought of alienating myself any more than I already had from Emily. I didn't want to hurt Emilia, either. For despite the way she rejected me, I still loved her."

"Emily felt rejected, too," Mrs. Angst loudly announced, causing them to face her. "Emily felt rejected by a parent who was appeasing a parent by whom she felt rejected. Unspoken words, unspoken feelings. 'Oh, what a tangled web we weave.' Shakespeare could have been writing about your family."

Emily interrupted, "No one here was intentionally trying to deceive one another."

"Oh, but they were," she corrected. "Anytime you allow a situation such as this to exist and perpetuate on to the next generation is a deception. People must take responsibility for their actions, Emily. Whether it's external relations, or that which exists within the same family. Everyone must be responsible for how they relate to one another."

Emily nodded.

"I'm very happy I know all of this," Mandy said. "I'm happy, and relieved."

"You felt guilty, didn't you?" Mrs Angst asked. "Anger and guilt that is not dealt with early on causes regrets. That's how Emilia felt."

"Grams spoke those very words to me several days before she died," Emily said. "She was referring to my relationship with you, Mom. She said that I shouldn't hate you, because like me, you were just a victim of circumstances. She said the bad relationship that existed between the two of you was all her fault."

"She said that?" Mandy asked, looking surprised. "What else did she say?"

"She said there were other things, but that didn't matter anymore. I guess she was referring to the situation with her mother, and the unresolved feelings she had there—I mean here," Emily noted while looking around the room.

"Did you really hate me, Emily? Is that why you wanted so much to leave?"

"I thought I did. But I now realize that I never hated you. I wanted to be as close to you as I was to Grams, but I thought you didn't want me. Except for the times you disciplined me, set restraints on my life, you just seemed so aloof, so distant.

"I didn't feel close to anyone but her, especially after Dad died. I was so angry with him for leaving me. When I realized Grams was dying, I was angry at her for getting sick, because that meant she would be leaving me, too, as absurd as those feelings were. Then Bill, and Zach. I had to leave, because I couldn't stay where I no longer felt wanted." Mandy gasped and placed her hand over her mouth.

"Don't get upset," Emily reached over, and put her arms around her mother. "It's alright now. I was foolish to let our relationship go on for so long without learning why."

"We were all foolish," Mandy said, wiping her tears. "But I took care of some of my guilt on the day Mom died. Near the end, when Father Vinci came to give her the Last Rites, I realized how little time was left. When she slipped into the coma, I approached her. What a spineless thing to do. I knew I shouldn't have waited so long, but it had to be then or never.

"The doctor said a person's hearing is the last sense to go before death, so when everyone left the room, I spoke to her. I said even though I didn't understand why we ended up the way we did, I still loved her. I told her that I forgave her, and I hoped she forgave me. Somehow, I managed to find the strength to do that, and I'm glad I did."

"Mother!" Emily pleaded. "Why didn't you tell me all this before? Why did you lead me to believe that you didn't care about her?"

"Because, I knew it wouldn't have made a difference in how you felt about me. You were angry with me, Emily, hurt and angry. I was the one you saw as the control freak in your life. Grams was your emotional strength, your freedom. 'We could never have what

Grams and I had.' Didn't you say those very words to me only a few days ago?"

"Yes," Emily feebly managed a whisper.

"Oh Emily, I never wanted to control you," Mandy said. "It just looked that way, because your Dad's death left me so fearful. All I ever really wanted was to get a hold of your love."

Mrs. Angst smiled as she got up from her seat and thanked Mandy for the coffee. Standing in the center of the room, she placed her hands on her hips and said defiantly, "There were some important issues dealt with today, and hopefully some lessons were learned. Remember these lessons! The misjudgment you made was that each of you thought that Emilia was strong, when in fact she was weak. She was the one who was afraid to remember her past and deal with the feelings it stirred up, even if that ignorance meant destroying her whole family. Now, she's gone, and all that is left of her is what's left inside the two of you. She wanted to redeem herself in the end, but even then, was too weak to face you both.

"Now, you must choose to be either strong, or weak, like her. You must decide whether to stir up painful memories from the past, and try to understand them, or push them further into your soul. The choice is yours. But I will tell you this; if you choose the latter you'll be throwing away the one and only chance for Emilia's redemption. You will be throwing away a heritage she never intended to end. And you know she intended it to go on. That's why she held onto her childhood home. This house is full of the sorrow and joy that was, and still is, your family."

Mrs. Angst left the two women sitting pensively on the wide ledge of the parlor window. Mandy turned to her daughter and said, "I think I understand everything now. I'm glad I know about Emilia's pain. Knowing her pain explains my own, and oddly, that makes me feel better about myself. Her behavior had nothing to do with me, or you."

"Was it so bad for you, Mom?"

"Bad? Well, let me say this: I was looking forward to this New Years' Eve, the night of my birthday, when I'd no longer have to hold my breath and wait for a reaction from her. Because this would be the first time in forty-nine years that she'd have a good excuse to not wish me a Happy Birthday."

"Oh no," Emily responded.

"Now, don't feel bad for me," Mandy insisted. " I still had lots of parties, gifts and you know every year there was always a home-baked birthday cake. But, in my heart I always knew that day was nothing for her to be happy about. I just didn't understand why."

They looked out toward the picturesque historic town; the church spires glistened in the bright sun, which had broken through the clouds. Emily said, "All those stories she would tell me about how wonderful and blessed this place is, they're all true. I used to listen and become consumed by her enthusiasm."

"I know," Mandy said. "I used to listen, too. Sometimes, I'd stand outside your bedroom door and listen to all the stories she never told me. I wonder if she knew. I want to believe that she knew I was there, and she was happy. Because that was the only way she was able to share that part of her life with me."

A ray of sunlight lit the window, outlining from below the silhouette of mother and daughter embracing. Gertie Angst looked up and smiled. "Welcome back to Gettysburg, my dear friend. Emilia, welcome home."

Chapter Forty-One

Peter and Emily sat together in the center pew of the church. The sunlight streamed through the stained-glass windows lining opposite ends of the sanctuary, surrealistically casting colorful shadows and halos on the faces and heads of the many who were seated there. Her eyes scanned the space, taking in the beauty she'd admired earlier that week, a week that marked the end to one chapter of her previous life. There, at the beginning of a new week, she felt like she was at the dawn of a new life.

She glanced back at the small window with her family name, Stone, and smiled. The dove, representing peace, had so much more personal meaning. Turning her head to the far left was a large, stained-glass window, which she hadn't noticed during her previous visit. Its proximity to the angle of sunlight made it brighter than all the others. The depiction of an angel was garbed in a blue robe, with long flowing red hair cascaded over its shoulders and wings. The angel's eyes looked directly upon the viewer, and its arms were outstretched in a way suggesting both submission and support. Emily stared for the longest time at the familiar image and saw it once more in a whole new light. It was nearly identical to the painting that Grams had given her.

Below the large window in small italic letters was the name, Wahler. She tapped Peter on the arm and pointed to it. His eyes widened and he slipped his hand into hers. Words were not necessary now. Though they shared one feeling, they did it quietly. The only words needed were those that were leaving the lips of the priest, ordained in their memory, fulfilled in their hearts:

"I believe in all that is seen and unseen..."

Emily knew so much of her life recently was indeed a result of what is seen and unseen. She was sure the unseen forces leading her to a place of enlightenment on her journey in life resided deep within her, and that could be nothing less than divine.

Mandy remained seated on the window ledge inside her daughter's apartment, staring out at Gettysburg, looking beyond all that she could physically see. The sun's rays enveloped her body making her feel warm and relaxed.

The first time alone in her ancestor's home, she imagined the presence of others around her.

It was the feeling of many invisible arms belonging to the fathers and mothers she could not recall, including one loving embrace from the mother she only came to know that day. They all seemed to be beside her then. There, in the place she initially came to in the hope to find the love and support of one, she found that and so much more.

Reflecting on only the day before seemed like a script out of someone else's life. She was suddenly transformed by a missing part of her own life, so her only participation necessary in her past was to remember it. Just the day before, the realization of the end of her marriage to Zach was very frightening. She no longer felt afraid. She had her daughter, as well as the rest of her family near, and she was not alone anymore.

The diary of her great-great-grandmother beckoned from the small table beside Emily's rocking chair, and Mandy reached for it as a child reaches for the hand of a parent. She reread the sections from the night before, mouthing the words as in silent prayer. Then, after taking a deep breath, she opened to the next entry with anticipation and concern, as though uncovering an unknown chapter of her own life.

Remember…May God be with us. The days and nights pass both quickly and slowly as I fulfill my obligations to what remains of my family. Amanda is quiet and tearful no doubt a result of missing Sarah. But alas, she has the naivety and strength the Lord provides for his children. Her pain will one day fade deep into her memory, as hopefully more promising remembrances are made to take its place.

My husband is as he was yesterday and the week and month before. I bless Mr. Pugh and old Mr. Lorhner for they have provided the scraps of wood needed for Jonas to build his useless boxes.

The government has informed me that since a good many of the burials have been completed, his work is no longer necessary, and therefore they will not provide the materials he uses in this manner. I have understood this, as well as all the others here in Gettysburg. Jonas does not understand. He remains trapped in a different world now. To him, the past and the future do not exist, for it is only here in this place that he will ever be, and I have given up hope for any change in the situation. Despite my anger toward his weakness, I have come to accept it.

Today, I visited the field where Stephen was laid to rest. A fortnight ago, I had a very distressing disagreement with an Army official about this matter. On the morning after his death, I requested Stephen to be buried near his friend James, who had already been placed on a hill near the town's cemetery. I was informed that the area was strictly limited to soldiers, and no civilians would be permitted a burial there, especially since a Soldiers National Cemetery was soon to be dedicated on that ground.

I implored him to consider the pain my dear brother and the rest of our family has endured here these past months. I addressed the fact that Stephen had worked with the Army in burying the dead in the weeks after the battle, and that assistance should have been enough to grant him this one last request. Still, I was refused.

I departed the officer's building in such despair when suddenly approached by two young men, soldiers in James' regiment, no doubt taking pity on my desperate need. During this brief meeting they promised a solution to my problem and instructed me to follow their plan.

We buried Stephen that afternoon near our beloved parents, and my darling girl, Sarah. The Irish priest from New York, who was visiting wounded soldiers, was kind enough to lead the prayers over his grave since our own Father Donaldson was taken ill with fever.

The eyes of the few who attended this service seemed torn in judgment of the way he died. But they knew the man that Stephen was, and the Christian way he lived his life. Surely in their hearts they understood he was not responsible for the way he ended it.

That night, just past the midnight hour, I returned alone to Stephen's gravesite as instructed by the two soldiers. They returned, accompanied by an Army chaplain. After I blessed myself with the sign of the cross, they quietly began to dig up the grave. My heart pounded with fear at the horror of this act and began to rethink the situation. But alas, the deed was done and was to be followed through as planned.

Stealthily, they carried the coffin several hundred yards away to where James is laid to rest, looking over their shoulders in fear, making certain their actions were not observed by anyone else. Had they been seen; it most certainly would have resulted in their imprisonment. God bless their brave and honorable hearts.

The chaplain said not a word during this time, as I believe he too had begun to rethink his involvement in this most irreverent act. Once the earth was disturbed revealing James' coffin, Stephen's was placed close beside it, and the ground re-closed. We all said a prayer in haste and departed just as quickly.

The soldiers hurried me away from the scene with but a few words. I was indebted to these nameless men; however, there was little compensation for me to give them save for a few loaves of bread, or some clothing from Stephen's store. The soldiers insisted that my thanks and peace of mind were all they required. 'Why?' I asked, 'Why do you risk your own lives to help a person who you know nothing of?'

'We know of your pain,' said one, 'and that is enough for us to know.' After escorting me to my door, they silently departed into the night, leaving me full of the humanity I'd hungered for in many weeks.

In the blackness of the early morning hours, I sat near the lit hearth, rocking slowly to the pounding of Jonas' hammer, remembering the night when I had sat there with Stephen. Though he was no longer seated beside me, I still felt him near. The request I fulfilled this night was not his own. Nevertheless, I felt in my heart that he would be happier where he now rests, and perhaps he may finally rest in peace...E.W.

Mandy rose from the window ledge and walked over to the rocking chair holding the book close to her chest. Before sitting down, she glanced over to the fireplace, smiled, and lit all the candles in the hearth. The little fires were dwarfed even further in the light from the sunny day, yet she stared into them. For the flames called out to a place deep in her memory. As the light reflected in her eyes, she was returned to that place she longed so much to go.

Remember...May the Lord have mercy on his children. It has been many weeks since I last made my witness entry. I am so very tired. My days are as full now with my occupation of baking, as they were when I spent the long hours with Dr. Harlow nursing the wounded men in my home. Sometimes, only for a short while, I think of him—my dear Dr. Robert Harlow. I pray he remains safe and well and wonder if I am also in his prayers.

Gettysburg this day is as busy as the days before, yet somehow it seems transformed. More military camps have returned, and now many people, strangers, seem to be every- where around me. They come from cities north and west, dressed in their finest linens, the women in hoops, with hats and capes more beautiful than I have seen in many a day. Laden still with many remaining wounded in our hospitals, the arrival of these visitors lends our mournful town an almost carnival appearance. I have been told they are here in anticipation of the dedication of the Soldier's National Cemetery.

Today, as I delivered some loaves of bread, Abigail informed me that the hill upon which these soldiers are buried was hastily being prepared for this occasion. I could not imagine what that preparation required. My only concern was that my secret mission there several weeks ago might somehow be revealed. I had stayed away from Lieutenant Becker—and now Stephen's— resting place, fearing the suspicious eyes that seemed to follow me there on one occasion. Now, after so much time has passed, I felt my presence at the gravesite might be less questionable.

After placing Amanda to bed for an afternoon sleep, I decided to return to the place of my crime and evaluate the situation. The area appeared very different than I had remembered, with so many more freshly dug and planted graves. After a long time, I found what I had come for: a lonely, plain, wooden marker identical to all the others marking James' place:

Lt. James Becker

First Corps. Pennsylvania

But this marker was not like all of the others around it, for this space is no longer lonely. I placed a single, yellow Chrysanthemum on the ground before it and when I looked up, I noticed a soldier standing nearby. He nodded sympathetically, perhaps thinking me a relative. I smiled and returned his gesture—because I am!

I proceeded to walk between rows of markers, glancing down at the names and titles painted on them. So many lost, so far away from home. I searched for a name that I might recognize, one that had spent time under my care, in my home. There were just too many to remember. I could not recall all their names, yet their faces were very clear in my mind, forever etched into my memory. I will pray for them always.

Near where I stood, a woman was anxiously looking at all the markers, reading each in such haste, I could not fathom how she could complete each reading in such a short period of time.

When our eyes met, she stopped and slowly approached me with such a look of despair, I held out my hand to offer support. 'What is it?' I asked.

'Please', she cried. 'Please, my good woman, will you help me to find my husband and son?'

These past months, Gettysburg has seen many a harried and desperate life searching the fields in hope of finding a paper or token that might have been either held or worn by a missing loved one. Wails of anguish could be heard echoing in the long summer days, and nights when their search had finally ended. Each cry pierced my heart, causing it to be momentarily still. So many months, and yet this search continues.

The woman handed me a soiled paper, upon which was written the name and Regiment of her missing family who had served with the 3rd Massachusetts Volunteers.

After several hours of searching to no avail, she turned to me, and said before solemnly departing, 'May the Lord be with you, and remember your kindness to me.'

The Army was certain her men were among those who did not return from the fields at the end of the three-day battle. However, they could not provide with any certainty where they had remained. Oh, what part of Gettysburg's hallowed earth do they call their final home?

Somewhere amidst the dirt, rocks and trees they sleep eternally; safely sheltered within angels' arms...E.W.

The concept of a mother searching for her lost family seemed sadly too familiar, so Mandy paused briefly to wipe the tears, which now flowed freely from her eyes. The sadness robbed her of her initial enthusiasm, but she continued to read on.

Remember...May the Lord and his Heavenly Family grant Jonas the final reward of which he is most worthy.

It has been more than three weeks since I last wrote of my existence here. Though only mid-November, the chill in the air this morning seemed closer to winter than fall. It is fitting. For no matter how cold the morning air may have felt it was no match for the coldness I carried deep in my heart.

Jonas' death came as no surprise to me last evening. His cough these past weeks seemed to be getting worse. Since he had shunned any assistance, I knew his end was near. I dare say I am glad it is done. Each day I was consumed by the fact that it might have been his last, and that anticipation alone had drained me of all the strength I had left.

I am certain Jonas is happy as well. His mind is finally free of the imprisonment, which kept him locked in his workshop all these months. My poor, gentle husband. How did this come to be? How is it that the kindly man I married, whose skilled hand that had created so many beautiful things could be reduced to merely an empty shell? There has been so much pain and suffering. Oh, why did we not heed the warnings and flee from this town as so many others had? Perhaps then we may still be as we once were—together. But it is too late to reconsider our decisions.

As we laid him to rest near Sarah, my eyes were fixed on the empty space upon whose stone is carved the name of my brother. Thankfully, its position is a few yards away, and was not disturbed as the ground was being prepared for Jonas.

The sun disappeared behind the clouds, and after the prayers were done, a light snow began to fall. The snow, and my own frozen tears, melted into the warmer earth, and it was then my emotions could no longer be contained. Abigail and Dr. Wells stood close by my side, and as the wooden box constructed by his own hand was lowered into his space, I fell to my knees in despair.

His madness, though perceived as evil by some, was kindly refuted this day in a pleasant obituary in the newspaper, written by an old friend, Damian Wright. And now, as I put away another piece of my life, the Army has returned to claim merit for it.

Beyond a fence lies the other cemetery, which Stephen had been forbidden to enter. There, a great ceremony began with intention to bestow grace on all those who fought and died here. I have no argument with that. But there were so many others! I wondered why could they not momentarily cease their eloquence if only to hear the cries of pain that were leaving my own lips? I am in pain, a pain no different than what tore apart the flesh of the soldiers on the fields; this pain tore apart my very soul.

I ran to the iron fence and pressed my face against its icy bars. I stared into the faces of all those officers in dress-uniform, petticoat-clad women, and men in tall beaver-fur hats. Though I remained mute, my eyes were full of the words I so wanted them to hear: Look upon this victim's face of the devil you have delivered to us. Here is the work of your war! For war is the damnation of man, and all that is good and holy! Nothing under God can give it honor now, nothing ever will!"

The speaker on the podium continued his lengthy speech, whose content I cannot recall. He, as well as all the others, were fixed on what they had come for, and my presence there appeared to go largely unnoticed—save for one.

One man there looked upon my face with the understanding and sympathy I sought, and his deeply set eyes spoke of a despair that matched my very own. While seated, his shoulders were bent forward, as though the weight of the world were held upon them. It was then I saw who he was, and in fact realized, it is he who holds the weight of this war. Then, all the pity I had felt for myself was given up to him— Mr. Lincoln.

Amanda was seated near the fire upon my return to our home. There, she silently stared into the flames, clutching the cloth dolls I had sewn for her and her sister. She looked over, held out her hand to me and said, 'Mama, why am I all alone?'

The tears blocked my sight as I rushed to her side. I then saw all that was left of importance to my life, as I said, 'You are not alone, dear one. You have me, and more. For all that was bad is gone, and what now remains will be better.'

This evening, before I placed my emotions on the paper before you, I committed myself to go to the workshop. Though the very thought of entering the dreaded place where Jonas had spent nearly five months caused me great distress, I did go. However, I went without any certain understanding as to why I was going there.

The air was cold and very damp. I pulled the quilt closer around my shoulders and looked through pockets of smoke rising up from my mouth as I breathed. Scattered about the space were unfinished coffins made from scraps of broken wood. Then, carefully stacked in one corner, were the remaining government pine boxes waiting to be filled.

Holding the lamp close to his worktable, I swept away with my hand some of the dust that had remained from his last work. It was there I discovered why I was so determined to enter that place. Etched into the top of the wooden table was a perfectly carved heart, whose center was filled with the words he wrote for me on the night of our wedding.

"Be still o mighty wind, rushing past the rain that falls like stones;

Be silent all you restless trees, owl's wings and leaves hath blown;

For my love now slumbers close beside me, never more to sleep apart;

And the only sound I wish for her to hear is the love that beats from within my heart."

The pain of both despair and joy once more tore into my chest, for here I found the piece of my life that had been missing. Here was the man that I knew and loved. Jonas was not found in the ugly pine boxes he made, his being, his spirit is here, etched into the wood. Oh, what sweet remembrances! My God, you have taken away so much from me, and yet I now realize, you have given me so much more. For I will always have Amanda, and memories of Sarah, the reflection of his love. And I will have my own loving memories of him. Those memories will give me the strength to go on.

I do understand though that what has passed here can never be ignored. There is too much at issue for us not to remember it. But alas, I have retrieved what I had lost sight of all this time.

Here, in the very place that took away the one true love of my life, I have reclaimed my beloved husband...E.W.

After caressing with her hand, the pages before her, Mandy quickly closed the book and placed it back on the table. She stood up, wrapped her arms tight around her chest and fought back the painful memories that had snuck up and taken her by surprise.

It had been a long time since she was last reminded so intensely of her first love, Andrew.

She had been witness to a tragedy no different than her great-great-grandmother. Mandy however was never able to write about it. In fact, she could never even remember it without reliving the horror of that dreaded time in her life. So, she did with those memories the only thing she could do, she made them go away. She had rearranged her life in such a way, that she was able to avoid anything or anyone, outside of her immediate family that was connected to those memories. She buried them so deep she almost forgot they were there. But, after reading Emilia's diary, she was reminded again. As she stood alone, far away from where those remembrances originated, she felt safe in allowing them to return once again.

Andrew Tomaso was the first man that Mandy had ever loved. Later, Zach would be the one to fill the empty space in her life. Although she loved him very much, Andrew was the only one she could ever love completely. He was the one to give her the emotional support and encouragement she craved for as long as she could remember. He was the only one who truly understood her life.

She had difficult decisions to make at the beginning of her third year in college. Her parents had paid dearly for her to attend the private woman's university near home, and they were getting very impatient with the fact that her education had little to no direction.

"Where are you going with this?" her father asked, after reviewing her course schedule that September.

"I'm not sure," she replied. "I just can't find anything that I'd really like to do."

"You must have some idea," he insisted. "Maybe you should lean toward a history degree, like your mother. You could eventually teach, something she always wanted to do."

"No!" she emphatically stated. "I don't want to be anything like her."

Allen was shocked by her angry tone; however, he was not

surprised at who the anger was directed. He often stood idle and watched the unspoken sparks fly between his daughter and wife, but passed them off as what he called, "a hormonal thing." The truth was his lucrative real estate sales business kept him out of the house so much that he was mostly just satisfied with keeping the peace and quiet when he returned home after a long, hard day at the office. "They'll settle things eventually," he'd say to convince himself of it. "Mothers and daughters always do."

Emilia never questioned her daughter's actions because that would only lead to arguments she wanted to avoid, and feelings she'd rather not deal with. Mandy wanted her to ask, but she too was afraid of its consequences. So, they each continued to travel silently in different circles within the same house, every so often connecting, giving credence to the unit they called a family.

Andrew Tomaso had just graduated from the Police Academy and was stationed at the college, a safe position for a rookie cop. He and Mandy passed each other daily on campus and were attracted to one another from the moment their eyes met. It would be several more weeks before they'd meet.

Mandy had been studying late one night at the college library, returning to a deserted parking lot, except for the few cars parked close to hers. She didn't see anyone suspicious at first, but while approaching her car, the shadow appeared out of nowhere. The man, whose face was obscured by a knit mask, held a knife to her throat and instructed her to walk quietly to his car.

Her heart pounded wildly, and she whimpered like a trapped animal while following his demands.

Just before she climbed into the dark blue vehicle with out-of-state license plates, there was the sound of a gun firing off into the black sky. The would-be rapist dropped the knife, pushed her away from his car, climbed in, and fled the area with great speed. Mandy lay face down on the blacktop, trying hard to catch her breath, and then looked up.

Standing in the center of the parking lot, replacing his gun was the rookie cop she'd been eyeing for the past few weeks. His long lean body slowly approached, illuminated in the dark by the flash-light he held tight in his hand.

"Are you alright?" he asked while helping her to her feet, his sweaty hands cold and trembling. "I need to make out a report. Please come to the office with me."

In the office, he made her a cup of warm tea, but it was the warmth of his sensitive dark eyes that melted the fear that had consumed her.

After the incident, they dated steadily, and Mandy often brought him home to have dinner with her parents. One evening after dinner, Andrew seemed very quiet and perplexed.

"What's up?' she teased. "Don't you like my parents anymore?"

"Oh, they're very nice to me. But your mother," he added, "she doesn't seem to like you."

Mandy was at first too stunned to respond to his honest observa-tion. She wondered what mannerism had he detected in the short time he'd known her? What inconspicuous clues had Emilia given him that she had missed all those years?

"What do you mean?" she asked, trying to remain shocked by his comment.

"Don't get me wrong," he explained. "I really don't even have the right to say this, but it just seems so odd. I know she loves you and cares about you. I could tell by the look on her face, first of fear, then relief the night I saved you from that creep. But I just don't think that she likes you. I don't think you like her, either."

She opened her mouth to refute his comments, but no words came out. What use was it to deny feelings she knew were true? "Don't be silly," she casually dismissed him and looked away.

After a few quiet moments, Andrew offered, "I never had much of a relationship with my father. He left when I was only nine years old. I used to pray that he would come back to my mother, and me, but he didn't. I always wondered what I did wrong. No one else understood why he stayed away from his only child. Can you imagine a parent doing that to their kid?

"After a long while, he remarried and was settled into a new life when he came looking for me. He wanted a renewed relationship despite all the missing years. All those feelings never spoken, never shared. I just couldn't do it.

"He died last year all alone—well, almost. His second marriage didn't work out either, so there wasn't anyone close left who wanted to attend his funeral, except me. I went because I realized though my life didn't turn out the way I wanted, I couldn't hold him solely responsible for it.

"You see he was reaching out to me, especially toward the end, because I now believe he wanted to redeem himself. But my anger kept me from seeing that and then I realized it too late. Now, I'll never know what really happened to our lives, because I never gave him the opportunity to explain. That's a cross I'll have to bear for the rest of my life."

"Why did you tell me all of this?" Mandy asked.

"I just wanted you to know," he softly replied.

Mandy nodded as she stared deep into his eyes, somehow understanding. Still, she chose not to heed his insight. And so, the silent circles in the Schmidt home prevailed, avoiding collisions and revelations.

The years Mandy spent with Andrew were the sweetest. He was always near to help her through the feelings she did not understand. He supported her decision to have her mother live with them, though it was against his better judgment. He knew how desperate she was for a relationship with Emilia and so he was willing to sacrifice his own comfort for his love. He was her confidant, her pillar of strength. He was the buffer between her and her mother, the antagonists living under his roof. He wasn't always able to prevent their collisions, but he at least seemed to lessen the blow.

Andrew's emotional strength and sensitivity burned so deep into Mandy's soul that it was hard for her to imagine her life before he came into it.

Then, the shots rang out.

The gunfire that had triggered the beginning of her life with him had brought it to a violent end. Her friend, her love and soul mate, was dead.

For years she felt her own life killed with the bullet that had ended his, except for her daughter. She was all she had left of him, and that reminder of his love should have helped her to get through the pain. But Emily's love was already taken, by Emilia.

As Mandy paced the floor of her ancestor's home, she remembered her tragedy as if it had just occurred. It was Emilia Wahler's pain that enabled her to face her own, something she avoided doing for so many years. She released the memories all at once, with sobs that bordered at the edge of hysteria. When it was all over, she felt better.

Chapter Forty-Two

Emily latched onto Peter's arm as they entered the cemetery. Near a recently planted dogwood tree, a gathering of fifty or more people had assembled around a freshly dug grave. Within the earth's hollow rested a plain mahogany casket holding the remains of Joel Levy. Emily scanned the many solemn faces and came to rest on Mike. Once the prayers were completed, the Rabbi nodded to him and stepped back. Mike slowly approached the grave, and while standing directly over it, reached down and picked up a clump of earth. After whispering something into the dirt he held tight in his hand, he threw it on top of the casket. He appeared stoic as he performed this ritual, the final act of his love.

Peter squeezed Emily's hand so tight, it hurt a little. Still, she was glad he did it. For now, she too was struggling to hold back emotions she did not anticipate, no longer feeling distant among the assemblage of strangers.

As each mourner left the area, she noticed Joel's brother Ben and nodded to him as he walked by. Accompanying him was a young woman with long brown hair. Like Ben, she was dressed all in black and seemed to be leaning on his arm for support, dragging her feet, sobbing, as she continuously wiped a tissue over her ruddy cheeks. Someone called out the name, "Sherry," and she turned around. It was Joel's daughter. Emily closed her eyes and took a deep breath.

"We should leave," Peter said, motioning over to the gravesite where Mike was alone, kneeling. "I think Mike needs some private time."

"I can't leave now," Emily said. "I know he needs a few moments alone, but I really must speak to him."

Peter looked at her questionably and said "Now? I don't think it's a good time to do that."

"I know, but I still feel like I have to say something," she said. "I have to do it now."

He shrugged and shook his head. "I'll wait for you here."

After taking a few steps toward him, Emily waited several minutes before approaching Mike. Just before placing her hand on his shoulder, he said in his husky voice, "Hello Emily. Thank you for coming." He stood up and turned around, towering over her.

"It was a very nice, I mean, it was a lovely service," Emily said. "I think he would have loved it."

"Actually, he'd probably think we made too much of a fuss," Mike said. "Joel liked beautiful things, but he was really a very humble man."

"Mike," she hesitated. "I, I need to say something to you. I know this might not be the best time to say this, but I think I might have communicated some feelings to you and Joel that I didn't intend. I'm very ashamed of that. I'm just so sorry."

"Emily," he chastised. "This is neither the time nor the place to unburden yourself." She bowed her head in shame and thought, *What am I doing?*

"You're right," she said. "I shouldn't have bothered you. I'll leave."

Mike's face softened and he said, "No, wait. I accept your apology. I know it's very difficult for some people to understand our relationship. But you know, what people don't seem to realize is all we ever wanted to do was love. That's all, just love. Why is it that we can accept living in a world filled with so much dissension and hate, and yet be so quick to reject love?"

"I understand that and I agree with you,"she said. "But, Joel's in a better place now."

Mike nodded, "I know he is, if there is such a place." He hesitated slightly before asking, "Emily, do you believe in heaven and hell?"

"I think so. Being Catholic that's what I've been taught to believe, and I never cared enough to question it. So, I would have to say, yes. Do you?"

Mike looked up at the sky and said, "I'm Catholic, too. But I question my beliefs all the time. I could believe in some sort of a heaven all right, but I'm not so sure of hell, at least not in the after-life. I think hell exists right here on Earth, as part of the living and dying we do, but mostly the living.

"Just like all the soldiers who met their end out there in those fields, they paid their dues to the devil before they left this world. Certainly, what Joel experienced the last years of his life was nothing short of it. Some may have to return here, to repeat it all over again, and maybe that's the real hell. But what waits for us beyond this life has to be better. It has to be."

"Perhaps you're right," she said. Glancing down at the ground, she added, "So many beautiful flowers. I think whenever I see a Shasta daisy or a pink peony, I'll remember him, and the bouquets he left for me each morning."

Mike snickered, and said, "It wasn't Joel who left you flowers every morning. It was me."

"What?" Emily said, her eyes wide and teary. "Why? I didn't think you liked me."

Mike put his hands on her shoulders, looked directly into her eyes, and said, "That's true. I had you pegged from the moment I saw you. There was Joel, trying so hard to get to know you, and all you wanted to do was get away from him. You wouldn't even let him finish a sentence. For God sakes Emily, you just met him, and already you were judging him. I hated you for that! But then, I real-ized, I was judging you, too. I felt really bad about that. You see, I have my own demon to wrestle. I wanted you to think Joel left you the flowers because I wanted you to be kind to him."

"Mike," she pleaded, "I wasn't judging Joel or you. If I acted that way, I'm sorry, but it had nothing to do with your life together. My stepfather..."

"Stop," he snapped. "There are always reasons why people act the way they do; I don't need to know yours. I knew you had your reasons and so did I. But that can never justify our behavior. We serve our sentence here in hell together. If we don't learn how to get out of it, we never will."

"I don't know what to say," she answered. "I'm just so very sorry."

"Let's not be sorry anymore. Let's just be kind." Mike placed a kiss on her forehead and departed.

Peter watched as Emily solemnly walked toward him, wondering what had been discussed, yet he refrained from asking. The emotional encounter was written all over her face. He said, "While you were with Mike, I made a discovery. Come with me."

He escorted her to the older section of the cemetery, passing broken and tilted headstones partially obscured by overgrown grass. He walked over to one headstone and pushed away a veil of weeds. "Look," he said pointing.

Engraved on top of the stone was the name, "Wahler." Below it was etched a cupid's heart with a cross at its indention. Within this design was written, "Never more to sleep apart." Below the heart were the names, "Sarah" and "Jonas," including the dates of their deaths: July 29, 1863, and November 18, 1863, respectively. Emily knelt, and anxiously began to dig in the dirt, pushing the earth out and away from the stone, so focused she forgot Peter was with her.

"There it is," he said, startling her. Emily exposed the name she was so determined to find, Emilia, Born October 15, 1840, Died June 24, 1930.

Peter said, "Considering all she'd been through, she lived a very long life for her day." Emily stood up and looked around. "I wonder if the rest of my family is here," she said.

She began to search the other stones around the Wahler memorial, uncovering one, two, and three more family graves: Amanda and Harold Jacobs; Stephen Klee, and finally the more recent Sarah and John Stone.

They walked back to the Wahler gravesite, standing near the names of her great-great-great-grandparents when she turned to him, saying astonished, "Today's June 24. It's the anniversary of Emilia's death."

"How about that," Peter said as they smiled wryly, looking down upon the ground where they stood.

Chapter Forty-Three

"How did it go?" Mandy asked, walking toward Emily upon her arrival home. Noticing her swollen eyes, she stopped and said, "Oh, maybe I shouldn't ask. Was it that bad?"

"Yes, but it's what I expected. Those things are never easy, are they Mom?"

Mandy slowly shook her head, and it was only then Emily noticed that her mother's eyes were as red and swollen as hers. "Have you been crying?" she asked.

"No," Mandy said, turning away. "It's just my allergies acting up. Where's Peter?"

"He's working this afternoon, but he'll come by later. Your allergies? Before I left East Springs, you looked the same way. Our relationship is so much better now. Please, don't shut me out of your feelings anymore. What's wrong?"

"What's wrong? Okay, yes, I was crying. No, not crying, it was more like sobbing. But not a thing is wrong," Mandy remarked.

She walked over to the table, picked up the diary and held it up. "This book is the reason why I was sobbing. After reading it, I was able to remember a part of my, I mean *our* lives that had been missing for years. You know, you're right! I don't ever want to shut you out of my feelings anymore. That's why I want you to read the next few entries, now."

"Why now?" she questioned.

"While these feelings are still so intense," Mandy said, "I want to share them with you."

She gently guided her daughter's shoulders until she came to rest upon the sofa opposite the lit hearth. She said, "You sit here and read, and I'll go make some lemonade."

Emily touched the book to her lips and followed her mother with her eyes until she reached the kitchen. She cautiously opened the diary to the next writing with heightened curiosity.

After reading the next entry she called out to her, "Stephen isn't buried near his family?"

"Isn't that an amazing story?" Mandy answered, poking her head around the kitchen archway.

"But I saw his tombstone today," Emily stated.

"You saw it?" Mandy asked, walking toward her, squeezing a lemon into a pitcher.

"Yes, and that's not all. Peter found the old section where all our family is buried. Mom, I found Emilia Wahler's grave. She was nearly 90 years old when she died on this day in 1930. You know, it's so strange, all this time they just seemed like people from another place in history with little connection to us. But the truth is, it wasn't all that long ago, and we are all still very connected."

"Reading about our family through Emilia's writing has given us more than just a physical connection to her," Mandy said. "Now we're also emotionally tied."

Emily nodded and continued reading, gasping and smiling at the incredible story. After completing another entry, she said, "The entry about Jonas' death has to be the saddest writing thus far."

"It's not sad, Emily. It would only be sad if Emilia remained bitter. In the end she was able to retrieve the sweetest memories of him, and that is joyful!"

Mandy stared blankly as her face softened with a look of contentment. "Mom, what is it?" Emily asked, smiling curiously.

Mandy turned to her daughter and said, "Emilia Wahler and I

share more than just a bloodline, we share an experience no one should ever have to go through—the untimely death of a spouse. When your father was murdered, I thought my life had come to an end. I loved him so much. I still love him. What we shared went beyond the physical and emotional aspect of a relationship. You see we weren't just husband and wife. We really were soul mates.

"If not for you, I don't think I could have gone on with my life. My mother was there to help with you, the house, and I'm grateful to her for that. But I got nothing else from her, or you."

"Mother," Emily interjected. "I know that, and I'm sorry for it. But why bring all this up now after we've settled so much?"

"Don't get me wrong," Mandy corrected. "I'm not blaming you or your grandmother. I just want you to understand why I acted so insensitive. I was alone! Andrew was so strong, strong enough for both of us. I was so weak, and weaker still after he was gone. My life was just falling apart.

"After a while, I realized I had to do something to change the way I was living. So, I forced the memories of him to go away. It wasn't easy, but I was determined for my life to be better for us. I don't think I could have possibly opened myself up to another relationship, no less a second marriage, if I hadn't done that.

"Today though, after I read Emilia's story, I was reminded of what I had hidden. Suddenly, I felt as if I was standing at the edge of a shore being pulled further into the water. A rush of those memories came crashing back.

"I relived that horrible night, and the lonely months after it. The pain tore through me the same way it did then. But, after that was over, I was able to recall sweeter nights I had spent with your father. I remembered the day he asked me to marry him, our wedding night, and the best day ever, when you were born. Reliving those memories felt just as good as it did then. Don't you see what I'm saying? Today, I got back my Andrew."

"Mom, I knew you loved Dad, but I never really understood how much pain you were in. I'm so glad you shared this with me."

"He was, as Emilia described her relationship with Jonas, my one true love. There may be many loves in a person's lifetime, but there can only be that special one love. I forgot that, but I know I'll never forget it again. Do you understand that feeling at all yet?"

Emily grasped her mother's hands, and said, "I thought Bill would make me feel that way, but he didn't. It's different with Peter. I know it seems strange, with it only being a week and all, but I have something very special with him, and I know he feels the same way about me. I don't mean that we're rushing into anything, that's not going to happen now. But it's really nice having him in my life."

"I'm happy for you," Mandy said, smiling. "But, don't let the one-week timeframe fool you. Weeks, months, years, what does it matter? A week is just another cycle in our lives, boundaries we set up to count the time as it quickly passes. Our relationship is totally different after just one week. Imagine a lifetime of questions answered within seven days. If you feel that way about Peter, time is irrelevant."

"How do you feel about Zach now?" Emily, cautiously asked. "I mean, I know you're still very upset about that."

"Well, I still love him, so I can't say I'm happy about it. Zach will always be very special to me. I just wish he had told me about Carl sooner. But you know, I always sensed that I was not his one love. Now, I realize Carl is the one who has always filled that space in his heart. But then, I suppose he also knew that he wasn't mine."

"I have to warn you; last night Zach told me he was sending over separation papers for you to look over as early as tomorrow," Emily said.

"I think it's wise to get it over with as soon as possible. Don't worry about me," Mandy consoled her, "I'm fine."

Emily reached over and gently touched her mother's face, caressing with her fingers the smooth skin around her moist eyes. "Mom, I don't think you're weak at all. You're stronger than I could have ever imagined you to be."

"The end of my marriage is different this time, because now I'm no longer alone. Wait here, I have something to show you."

Mandy got up from the sofa and swiftly walked into the bedroom, reemerging seconds later with a suitcase. She placed it on top of the kitchen table and opened it. "Come here and look at this," she said.

Emily walked toward the table, uncertain of what was being uncovered. Inside the suitcase were many photographs of people she didn't recognize. There were old snapshots, some portraits and a few others, older tintypes from the 19th century. She picked up the one of two little girls with long curls that were held by ribbon bows. Underneath the picture was engraved, "Amanda and Sarah, 1862."

After glancing quickly at her mother, she anxiously began shuffling her fingers through all that was there. Another tintype revealed an attractive blond bearded young man, impeccably dressed in a dark suit with waistcoat and tall top-hat, typical of mid-nineteenth century style.

Below, was engraved the initials, S.K., Stephen Klee. He posed with his right hand inside his long overcoat and looked directly into the camera with his chin pointed upward, suggesting defiance and dignity. "Where did all of this come from?" Emily asked.

"Do you remember at the reading of Emilia's will a trunk was mentioned as part of my inheritance? Well, despite all the valuable things she left me, that trunk was the most important. I was only a young girl when I found it in the attic of my parent's house. I uncovered the memories she had hidden away, and when I confronted her with it, she threw a fit.

"After you left last week, I opened it again. I went through all these pictures, getting angrier all the while, because I didn't know who these people were. Now with her gone, there was no one left to explain them all to me. This is our family, Emily. These are the people we have been reading about, and more. Look..."

Mandy removed a picture, a wedding portrait of a young Grams and the grandpa who died when Emily was too young to remember him. She also held up another tintype, whose inscription was, "Emilia and Jonas, 1856." Emily took it and held it to her heart. The couple in the portrait faced each other away from the camera, gazing dreamily. Jonas, the groom, appeared very tall, and had a large build, and a full beard. The bride's hair was parted in the middle and pulled taut, with the rest covered up by a long, lace veil.

Her profile was clearly defined, accentuated by high cheekbones and a square jaw line.

"Emilia Wahler," Emily said softly. "She looks very strong."

Buried under many other pictures was another wedding portrait, and Emily carefully dug it up. Once she got a good look at the picture though, she gasped. "Who is this? She looks just like me."

Mandy smiled, and said, "No Emily, you look just like her. This is your great-grandmother, Sarah Stone. This portrait fascinated me when I first discovered it all those years ago. I was determined to know everything about my grandmother, but my mother was even more determined to keep that information from me. When I redis-covered it last week, I felt as though I already knew her. The resem-blance is uncanny."

"I can see that. Grams used to say that she and I had the same color and shape eyes, but that was it. So, this is Sarah. In a way, she looks sad, doesn't she?"

"Initially I felt that way, but she doesn't seem sad to me anymore. Based on what Gertie Angst told us, Sarah has now gotten back what she never wanted to lose in the first place: her family and her family home. In fact, so have we all."

"What do you mean?"

"We have a better understanding of my mother now, and that must mean as much to you as it does to me. More importantly, we have each other".

Mandy sat down beside Emily and her voice took on a more serious tone. "I know this may sound a little bizarre, but in a way, I feel my mother and Sarah Stone's presence here. And not only them, but everyone else we've been reading about, too. I don't know if it's because of the diary readings or all the remarkable things that's happened between us, but I just don't feel that we're alone in this house. Am I frightening you?"

"Not at all," Emily said. "Well, I have to admit; the past week has been a little unnerving at times, because I had that same feeling. There were other reasons though. Some strange things have happened here."

"What sort of things?" Mandy asked.

"Let's just say I'm convinced there's a spiritual presence here, but I now realize it's nothing to be afraid of. Somewhere inside us, we hold the spirits of our family, and it's being here, in the very place they once were, that completes our connection to them. You see, none of us was ever meant to leave this town or this house.

"Emilia Wahler's legacy goes way beyond this little book. She exhibited incredible courage while facing the worst experience a person could ever endure. Both during and after that ordeal of the war, she was able to leave this reminder of the evil we all carry deep within us. Her account wasn't meant just as another way to document history. It's here to warn us of what people are capable of doing to one another, not just in war, but also in everyday relationships. We know about that probably even better than she did.

"Gertie told me that people like us, who are descended from the survivors of that terrible three-day battle, and the months afterward here, carry the emotional scars of our ancestors. With those scars comes a great responsibility."

"What responsibility?" Mandy asked.

"Look at it this way: The tourists who visit Gettysburg experience an emotional transformation after walking through the battlefields," Emily said. "They feel a connection to all the pain and suffering that was once here. But they only get a sampling of the understanding you and I already have.

"We are also the survivors of Emilia's war, for we hold within us the wisdom born out of her survival. It's our responsibility to live our lives in a better way that will set an example for others. We are Emilia's legacy! Sarah Stone knew and accepted that, but Grams rejected it. Since we've been reacquainted with our heritage, we must make certain it's never forgotten again. Do you have any idea of what I'm saying?"

"Yeah, I think so," Mandy replied. "We must remember and learn from our past, because if not, we may have to repeat what we don't remember, and then all our forefathers' suffering would have been in vain?"

Emily nodded.

"I understand all that," Mandy said. "But you know, some

lessons in history are never learned. The town of Gettysburg isn't the only place that's experienced the horrors of war. Certainly, the horror of slavery that led to the Civil War was immoral and devastating to those who were trapped in it. There's still so much suffering and tribulation in the world, and we're all witness to it on some level."

"That's right, Mom. We are all witnesses to tribulation, and we are all responsible for it."

They sat on the floor of the parlor for several more hours, sorting through the collection of family pictures and letters that were tucked away for nearly two generations. They laughed and wept while working, happy to be sharing the chore of fixing their broken family chain, a chain now repaired with its own missing links. When most of the unknown faces were somewhat identified and labeled, they relaxed and once more opened to Emilia's diary, prepared to share the last writing she had entered.

As Emily read, the light from the setting summer sun brightened the hearth, accentuating the flames from the candles and filling the room with an amber glow, just as it did, they imagined, nearly a century and a half ago.

Mandy sat on the sofa, gently took hold of her daughter's hand, kissed it, and wondered if Emilia had also held Amanda's hand in that room the same way. Both mothers and daughters were set to face the world alone, with tribulation behind them, and an uncertain future ahead. So much has changed, yet so much more remains the same.

But Mandy and Emily knew they were not alone. For they had all their family seated there beside them, and just as sure as the warm amber sun and the candles in the hearth illuminated their lives, they had each other.

Chapter Forty-Four

When Peter arrived later that evening, he was surprised to see the many family pictures, carefully separated into neat piles, some of which had a slip of paper on top, marked with the name, birth date and date of death of the person or persons in that photo. He turned to Mandy and asked, "Did you find all this here?"

"No. Let Emily tell you about it. I'm going on a mission to get acquainted with my town tonight."

"Your town?" Peter asked. "Does this mean you plan on staying?"

"Not really. This is Emily's house now. Besides, I have a lot of unfinished business to take care of back in New York. But I'll be visiting frequently."

"You'd better," Emily called out as she entered the room.

"Don't worry, you can count on it," Mandy said before descending the stairs. "Have a nice night, and maybe I'll see you later, Peter."

"Who are all these people?" he asked while randomly lifting the photographs.

"Mom found these pictures in an old trunk my grandmother

had hidden away. Aren't they great? Look, Emilia and Jonas Wahler," she said while holding up the tintype for him to see.

His reaction was like hers. The diary readings connected him emotionally, as well. Emily went on to show him the tintypes of Emilia's daughters, Stephen Klee, and pictures of her Grams and her grandfather. Finally, she held up the picture of Sarah Stone.

"Unbelievable," he said, and sat down. Staring at the image, he softly added, "She's almost as beautiful as you."

Emily bent over and kissed him. He pulled her onto his lap, locking her in a passionate embrace for several minutes, before he said, "I'm glad everything is working out between you and your mother. But I hope that doesn't mean you'll eventually return to New York."

"I don't ever plan on leaving Gettysburg. This is my home."

"Good, because I don't ever plan on letting you go. Let me take you out to dinner."

"Okay, but after that I'd love to go for a ride," Emily said.

"Sure. Any place in particular?"

"Actually, I'd like to return to Little Round Top."

Peter glanced at his wristwatch, and said, "By the time we finish dinner, it might be too late. The park will be closed."

"There are no gates to close us out. Right?"

After dinner, they drove through the streets of their town, passing the many restaurants, a museum, and the quaint little brick houses with electric memorial candles in all the windows. They stopped at a streetlight in front of the Wick N' Wax Shoppe that supplied Mrs. Angst with the significant gift that only she, and now Mandy, could truly appreciate.

After turning a corner, the college campus came into view. Emily looked up at Peter's building, Old Dorm, to the cupola in which she'd once felt very cold, and smiled. For she was warm, as warm as she ever wanted to be. The imposing structure no longer seemed threatening to her.

The gates of the Soldiers National Cemetery disappeared into the blackness of the night, accentuating the white marble statue at its entrance. Emily said a little prayer under her breath as they passed. Her prayers meant more than just a patriotic gesture of respect. She knew that Stephen, one of her ancestors, was buried there, too.

As the road grew darker with the absence of streetlights, the battlefield seemed vast and still. Their path once more began to curve up and around the tall silent trees, except for a gentle hum from the rustling of leaves in the slight wind. Emily recalled hearing that sound before and still wondered what it was. Perhaps the trees whispered a warning to all who pass there. In the slit between two worlds, they whisper, "remember." She did remember. For as they entered the very place she was so frightened by only a few days before, Emily realized she no longer felt unwelcome.

Peter turned into the same spot they had occupied earlier that week and parked his car.

"Thanks so much for bringing me back here," she said, looking out over the battlefield. "I'm glad we went to church today, but you know, this place is also our sanctuary."

He raised his brow before nodding in agreement. "It is indeed," he said.

They were each quiet, meditating on what was before them, when Peter sat up straight in his seat and asked, "I thought you'd never want to come back here. I'm very happy you do, but what's changed?"

"Everything," she said. "I told you last night that I understand what you were trying to tell me here. Being in the very place where there had been so much suffering, and where so many sacrifices were made, we're forcibly reminded of the spiritual aspect of our humanity. How beautiful life would be if only everyone realized that.

"You know, I feel so stupid! I call myself a history teacher, and yet I forgot the most important lesson that history teaches us. Unless we learn how to value one another, all the suffering that has resulted from war, all wars, whether they're fought on the battlefield or in our own homes, would have meant nothing. Now, I too can feel our forefather's scars. I guess now I'm truly a Gettysburg townie."

"You always were."

After a few moments of silence, Emily reached into her purse and took something out. "What's that?" Peter asked.

She held up the little blue book, opened the glove compartment of the car, which contained a small light, and rested the book on the inside panel. Upon realizing what it was, Peter settled back in his seat waiting to hear the next entry with as much anticipation as ever.

After Emily read the entries she'd read earlier with her mother, Peter was even more excited to hear the final message from Emilia Whaler.

Emily cleared her throat before beginning the passage.

Remember...May the Lord and his mother grant this mother the strength to go on. It has been one week since my last entry. The ceremony for the new cemetery here has ended, and now most of the people who had stayed on from that occasion have left our town as it was. It is so very strange that I should think that, for our town will never be as it once was. The friends and strangers who remain here, buried beneath the earth, have hallowed our ordinary ground, and my family has done the same.

To all who read the document of this witness, please heed all that is intended with this writing. For so much has passed here from which to learn, and yet so much that passed may still be forgotten.

The suffering that was endured, though desperate at times, could not be avoided. Though many of the sufferers, such as my family, were considered the innocents of this terrible war, we remain no different than those who fought in it. We are all a part of the spirit that is God, and there too we are a part of his adversary.

War is the work of the devil, no doubt, yet we must all be responsible for it. For no matter how differently, we see our fellow man, we are each of a similar soul. No one should have the right to judge that soul, any more than they have the right to own it. It is the fact that we are so similar, and yet different—that is the absolute beauty of mankind.

Today, as I delivered my loaves of bread, I passed a woman whose head was covered by a cotton shawl. She was bent in a way so I could not see who she was, but when she turned around, I realized her to be the Negro woman, who was living with her family at the edge of our town with many others. Some had traveled here with the Rebel Army to assist in the battle, breaking free with the help of our citizens, once the battle was done. They joined others that ran away from plantations, and settled here to live and farm quietly, away from the oppression they had escaped. Though most in Gettysburg knew of their existence, few seemed to notice any of the people living here, and fewer still, including myself, had offered them any assistance.

This woman approached, looking directly into my eyes, and I feared for myself solely by the difference in the way she looked. I covered my bread and drew the basket close to my body, uncertain of what she was after. She then held out to me her own basket, which was full of turnips, cabbage and potatoes, gifts from her garden. Her hands were more worn and calloused than my own, her eyes weary and traced with blood from lack of sleep. My heart was struck by the kindness and generosity she showed, and I wept first at the sweetness of it all, then in shame for my initial reaction to her. I offered her several loaves of my bread, which she accepted respectfully, and quietly departed.

As we struggle to survive the work of the demon, our

travail is made easier by the work of the Lord. During my difficult months, I questioned the reasons for the conflict that was fought here, but the answer to its purpose was obscured by my own desperate needs. Yet, my desperation was naught compared to that which I had just witnessed on the hands and in the eyes of the woman from the edge of our town.

The days and nights are growing colder as we approach the lonely winter months, but my soul is warm with the understanding of the abundant goodness that rests within, and what wonderful things can come from it. This ugly war has released a beauty here in Gettysburg that will last for generations, and hopefully beyond that as well. Do not forsake the understanding that has been given to us. For it was through tribulation that our triumph was born, and perhaps now we may live together in peace. May God be with you, and in you, and may you all be witness to a better world as a result of it...E.W.

Emily closed the book, carefully put it back into her purse and moved closer to Peter. He put his arm around her shoulder as they looked out on the field of tribulation and triumph.

After several quiet moments, Emily sat up very quickly, leaned forward and placed her face close to the windshield of the car, blinking and rubbing her eyes.

"What is it?" Peter asked.

"Do you remember telling me about all the strange things that sometimes happen here? Like, on nights close to the anniversary of the battle, you can see small lights on the fields, ghosts of soldiers wandering in search of their dead comrades?"

"I remember, but I don't want you to be frightened by that now. Emilia's last entry was so beautiful, let's just relax and reflect on it for a while."

"Don't worry, I won't want to leave. I'm now very fascinated by what once terrified me. In fact, look..." She pointed to an area in the distance below where they parked, immortalized in history as the Wheatfield.

"Do you see that, too?" Peter asked, excitedly, stretching his neck to get a better look.

"Yes," she replied. "I can't tell if it's flashlights, fires or maybe lanterns?"

Peter adamantly replied, "They're definitely not flashlights or a fire, that's for sure."

They watched the pale, bluish-colored phantom lights as they moved swiftly from one side of the field to the next. Emily rubbed her eyes and wondered if what she was seeing was real. Like Peter, she realized sometimes our desire to see or hear something is so strong we tend to unconsciously create it. She was no longer afraid to see something she couldn't logically explain. So much of what she experienced there the past week was just a feeling, and she knew that sometimes there really was no way to logically explain that. So, she couldn't tell if the lights— perhaps ghosts—she was seeing were really there, or were only there because now she wanted them to be.

The End

Author's Note

Being married to a historian has many advantages, and perhaps the most profound advantage for me has been a heightened interest and thus knowledge of American history. My husband Robert has been a guiding force in my quest to gain as much information as possible on this subject.

He introduced me to the Gettysburg National Military Park in 1985 when our eldest son Bryan was barely two years old. Before that time, the town's role in the Civil War lingered only as a distant memory left over from a few chapters in a textbook that I had to memorize for an exam along with the Gettysburg Address by our 16th President. But as we drove to all the battle sites, which were mapped out by the National Park Service, and listened to the accompanying audiotape, I began to feel further drawn into that historic place.

The Battle of Gettysburg in July 1863 is said to have been the turning point for the Civil War. The gruesome episodes of death spread out over three days, and beyond are very well documented in the park's Visitor's Center. Those stories are told daily by seasoned park historians at each of the battle locations, and the various monuments.

However, aside from a plethora of Civil War monuments to visit there—Gettysburg has the largest number of them anywhere—and the many history lessons to be learned in the park, there's nearly as many noteworthy stories to hear about the town.

Today, many sections of Gettysburg seem frozen in 1863, both architecturally and aesthetically, which only adds to its enchantment. Scores of merchants there have certainly bought into that attraction and sell mostly items of historical interest. Some other lucrative businesses in town sell ghost stories, which are dramatically recounted in local theater, and on various nightly ghost tours. Gettysburg is said to be one of the most haunted places in the United States. I've no doubt that is true.

Despite my initial reaction to the place though, we did not return there until Bryan was nine, and our youngest, Timothy, was five. After that, we began our nearly annual visits to Gettysburg, appeasing the children with a trip to nearby Hershey Park beforehand. Years later, we returned with my brother and sister-in-law, with our friends, and even later, we returned several times with Bryan and his family.

During each visit, I learned something new about the famous battle. I was fascinated by all the stories, from attack strategies dictated by generals to personal accounts left by those citizens who had lived through that tribulation. My fascination with the town did not wane after many visits. And I've been repeatedly amazed by how many people I'd met there who felt the same way; that after just one visit, there's a need to return to Gettysburg to experience it all over again in a way that can only be likened to a pilgrimage.

So, what is the otherworldly draw that seems to exist in that town?

I've concluded that aside from the historical significance, Gettysburg is also a spiritual Mecca, a place to reconsider the soul. For it is while standing on hallowed ground in the space where so many deaths were brutally realized that visitors experience a mutual sorrow, and humanity is reappraised.

If Gettysburg could have that effect on visitors today, I wondered what impact it might have had on those who experienced the battle firsthand. Could the result of their experience be ingrained in successive generations? And were that true, wouldn't their descendants work to foster a place where all of life's conflicts could be reexamined and peacefully resolved?

I began writing this book on that theory in 1995. Although I have always found Gettysburg's citizens to be friendly, I've had no definitive reason to believe that my theory is in any way rooted in fact. Still, that possibility intrigued me.

The book was completed before editing in 1997 but then was put aside and forgotten as I began a new career in journalism. Another trip to Gettysburg reignited my interest to finish it for publishing. However, a promotion to editor of two newspapers, pushed that goal back many more years.

This story could have taken place in any of the other towns that had firsthand experience with the American Civil War. I chose Gettysburg as the setting to highlight what I believe is the most important location in our nation's history. And in doing that, I hope due homage is given to those witnesses of the battle, both military and civilian, so they will be remembered for the ultimate sacrifice they paid for our nation, and humanity as well.

For more information on the Battle of Gettysburg and the town's struggle during the months that followed, visit the following websites: Gettysburg National Military Park (www.nps.gov/gettys burg); The Gettysburg Foundation (www.gettysburg foundation.org) and The American Battlefield Trust (www.battlefields.org).

About the Author

This is Liz Finnegan's first novel.

She started her work career as a registered nurse but always had a desire to write. Liz turned that desire into a new career when she began working as a newspaper reporter and then editor. After spending over two decades as an award winning journalist, she retired in 2019.

Liz has been married to her husband, Robert, for 45 years and they have two grown sons and grandchildren. She and her husband currently reside in Long Island, New York.